W9-BUE-378

THE DEVIL WEARS KILTS

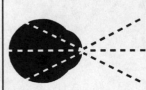

THE DEVIL WEARS KILTS

SUZANNE ENOCH

THORNDIKE PRESS

A part of Gale, Cengage Learning

GALE
CENGAGE Learning®

Farmington Hills, Mich • San Francisco • New York • Waterville, Maine
Meriden, Conn • Mason, Ohio • Chicago

Copyright © 2013 by Suzanne Enoch.
Thorndike Press, a part of Gale, Cengage Learning.

Thorndike Press® Large Print Romance.
The text of this Large Print edition is unabridged.
Other aspects of the book may vary from the original edition.
Set in 16 pt. Plantin.

LIBRARY OF CONGRESS CATALOGING-IN-PUBLICATION DATA

Enoch, Suzanne.
    The devil wears kilts / by Suzanne Enoch. — Large Print edition.
        pages cm. — (Thorndike Press Large Print Romance)
        ISBN 978-1-4104-6772-0 (hardcover) — ISBN 1-4104-6772-4 (hardcover)
        1. Large type books. I. Title.
    PS3555.N655D48 2014
    813'.54—dc23   2013049885

Published in 2014 by arrangement with St. Martin's Press, LLC

Printed in the United States of America
1 2 3 4 5 6 7 18 17 16 15 14

THE DEVIL WEARS KILTS

PROLOGUE

"Why would ye do that, Bear?" Rowena MacLawry looked at the scattering of white and red rose petals all over the morning room floor.

Her brother Munro looked up from running a cloth along the edge of his two-handed greatsword. "How else was I to show how sharp the blade is, Winnie?"

"But ye took the tops off *all* the roses!" Rowena shook the vase with its bare stems at her brother. "Wouldn't one have done ye?"

"Nae. Not nearly as impressive. And they came off with one cut."

"They were my birthday flowers, Bear, ye stupid lunk. From Uncle Myles." She glared from him to her oldest brother, who was reading a newspaper and pretending not to notice any of the chaos going on in front of him. "Ranulf, do something."

"The flowers are gone, lass," Ranulf Mac-

7

Lawry, the Marquis of Glengask, commented, glancing up from the paper. "Should I have Munro glue the petals back on?"

"You can stop him from swinging a sword in the morning room. All the way from London, they were," she said, sighing.

"Who wants posies for a birthday, anyway?" the third male in the room, Lachlan MacTier, Viscount Gray, asked, taking the claymore from Munro and experimentally slashing it through the air. "Now this is a gift. Did Roderick forge it for ye, Bear?"

"Aye," Munro answered. "Cost me a keg and four bottles."

"I'd pay twice that."

"If ye're tryin' to say ye bought me a claymore for my birthday, Lach," Rowena broke in, clearly displeased at being ignored in favor of a broadsword, "ye can turn around and take it right back home."

Lachlan eyed her, light green eyes narrowing. "A lass has no business with a sword, Winnie."

"Hence me not wanting one. So what did ye get for me?"

With a half grin, Lachlan produced a paper-wrapped lump from behind a chair. "I reckon ye'll get more use from this than ye would a broadsword. Happy birthday,

Winnie."

From his seat in the deep windowsill, Ranulf finally lowered the newspaper he was reading. The information it carried was a week old, at best, but he didn't like what it said. In fact, he would have enjoyed giving the damned thing a few whacks with his brother's sword.

He couldn't actually remember when he had last liked any news from London, in fact. More rules and regulations that did him no good, but cost him in ever-rising taxes. If the Sasannach couldn't breed the Highlanders away or kill them all, they'd surely found the way to defeat them once and for all — by bankrupting them. As he shifted, the two Scottish deerhounds at his feet uncoiled and sat up, likely already wondering why they hadn't yet left for their morning run.

The delay was entirely due to the young lady standing beside her morning room chair. Any time Rowena's birthday came around the clan turned itself inside out to celebrate, but this one was special. So his ride, and the dogs' run, could wait until his sister opened her gifts.

An excited grin on her face, Rowena tore the paper from the misshapen gift Lachlan handed over. With the same swiftness, though, her expression dropped again. "Boots," she said aloud, looking up at their nearest neighbor. "Ye bought me boots."

Lachlan nodded, a strand of brown hair falling across one eye. "Ridin' boots. Because ye ruined yers in the mud last month." His own smile faded at her glare. "What? I know they fit; I had Mitchell give me yer shoe size."

"I'm a lady now, Lachlan. Ye might have brought me flowers, or a fine bonnet. Or at least shoes fit for dancing."

He snorted. "I've known ye since ye were born, Winnie. The boots'll do ye better."

Ranulf set the newspaper aside entirely, motioning the two pipers standing in the hallway, out of sight of the occupants of the morning room, to withdraw. His sister and youngest sibling was a fine, good-humored lass, but he'd seen this storm lurking on the horizon for days. And bagpipes weren't likely to improve anyone's mood.

"But I'm nae a girl who rides hell-bent across the countryside any longer, Lachlan," Rowena said, her expression a mix of annoyance and sorrow. "Dunnae ye see that?"

Lord Gray laughed. "That was yesterday, then? Today ye cannae ride any longer? Dunnae be daft, Winnie."

Wordlessly Rowena turned to face Ranulf.

"Ye're my last hope then, big brother," she said, her voice faltering a little. "What's my gift?"

For a moment her eldest brother eyed her, the unsettled feeling of approaching thunderstorms flitting again along his skin. "Ye said ye wanted a new gown," he finally returned. "A green one. Mitchell has it laid out for ye upstairs, so ye can wear it for dinner. Unlike the boots, it's fit for dancing."

As he watched, a large tear formed and ran down one of Rowena's fair cheeks. *Bloody Saint Andrew.* He'd erred, then. How, he wasn't entirely certain, but clearly something had gone awry.

"Winnie, why are ye weeping?" another male voice asked from the sitting room doorway, as Arran MacLawry, the fourth sibling and the one closest in age to Ranulf, strolled into the room. "Do Lach's boots pinch ye, then?"

"She didnae start weeping till Ran told her aboot the dress," Munro returned. "I reckon she wanted a blue one, after all."

"Well, this should cheer ye up." Arran walked up and handed their sister a small, cloth-wrapped parcel.

"Let me guess," Rowena commented, wiping at her cheek. "It's a compass, so I willnae get lost when I go riding on the new

11

saddle from Bear, in the new boots from Lachlan."

Arran frowned. "No. It's a wee clock, on a pin. Very clever, it is. I had it shipped all the way from Geneva after I saw an advertisement in *Ackermann's Repository.*"

"That's very nice, then. Thank ye, Arran."

Munro took back his claymore from Lachlan and jabbed it none too gently into the scarred wooden floor. It wasn't the first weapon to rest there, and likely wouldn't be the last. The pipers and half a dozen of his servants were crowded back into the hallway again, and Ranulf gave them a sterner look and a dismissing wave. Clearly his sister wasn't in the mood for a damned parade — even one of well-wishers.

"So Arran gets thanks, and all the rest of us have is tears and being called idiots?" Munro retorted.

Instead of answering, Rowena set down her pin clock and slowly walked up to Ranulf. The dogs shoved their heads against her palms as she approached, but she ignored the obvious request for scratches. That didn't bode well. She hadn't called *him* an idiot, but it did seem to be implied. And Ranulf didn't much care for that. His sister had asked for an emerald-green gown, after all, and he'd seen to it that she had

12

one. A very pretty, and very expensive one. From Paris, damn it all.

When she pulled him to his feet, he didn't resist. But when Rowena kept both of his hands in her small, delicate fingers, he frowned. "Ye wanted something else, then," he rumbled, wishing, and not for the first time, that he'd brought another female into the house. Then someone, at least, would have a chance of understanding the youngest MacLawry. It had been a simple matter when she was a bairn, but lately she more and more often seemed an entirely foreign creature. "What is it? Ye know if it's in my power, I'll get it for ye, Rowena."

"Ye — you — know what I want, Ranulf. I'm eighteen years old today. I want my Season. In London. That's w—"

"Nae," he cut in, scowling as much at the way she altered her speech as at the notion itself. "We've set on Friday to celebrate yer birthday. The whole clan is coming. All the bonny lads'll be here, fighting to dance with ye. That's finer than any London soiree."

With a poorly hidden sigh she glanced over her shoulder toward the other three men in the room. "Would ye fight for a waltz with me, Lachlan MacTier?"

"And get my feet flattened for my trouble?" The viscount laughed again. "I see ye all the time. Let the other bonny lads fight for a dance."

"No bonny lads will brawl for a dance with me, because they're all afraid of my brothers," Rowena retorted.

"Well, so am I, then."

"Ye are not."

Ranulf stirred, unwilling to listen to why a man should or should not fear him. A man should. And that was that. "Ye'll nae want for a partner, Rowena. It'll be a grand party."

Finally she faced him again. "I don't want a stupid party with people I've known all my life, and who all think a dance is an excuse for a fight. I want my Season. In London. Mama had one."

"Mama was English," he snapped, snarling over the word. "Ye know who lives in London, Winnie. Fops and dandies and weak-hearted Sasannach. Ye have a fine party here to look forward to. And if a man cannae abide the notion of standing toe-to-toe with the chief of his clan, he doesnae deserve to dance with ye."

She put her hands on her hips and lifted her chin. "Ye want me to prefer Glengask to everywhere else in the world, Ran, but ye won't let me see anywhere else. I've nothing to compare it to except my own imagination, and in my mind, London is very wondrous, indeed."

"For the last damned time, London is full of useless bootlickers who couldn't lift their own saddles. Go upstairs and try on yer dress. This discussion is finished."

"Ranulf, y—"

"Finished," he repeated, and crossed his arms over his chest. Rowena was a wee, delicate thing, far more resembling their mother than made him comfortable. To her credit she didn't back away from him, but even so she knew as well as he did that he'd won the argument. She was not going to London. Ever.

With a last damp glare she turned and fled through the door. A moment later he heard her door upstairs slam closed. The other three men in the room looked at him, but none of them said a word. They wouldn't, though; his brothers, at least, knew the rest of the argument he hadn't bothered to level at Rowena — that London was also full of aristocrats who claimed Scottish land while they denied Scottish blood and ancestry, men who lived as far from the Highlands as they could manage while driving their own tenants from their homes in order to turn their lands over to sheep. That London was also full of traitors. Traitors and killers.

15

"I'm going for a ride. Fergus, Una," he said, and left the room without a backward glance, the dogs on his heels.

Debny, the head groom, must have seen him coming, because by the time he reached the stable yard Stirling was waiting for him. Swinging into the saddle, he kneed the big, rangy bay and set off down the pathway that wound to the east, crossing a portion of the windswept hillside and then twisting down into a tree-lined gorge, the dogs flanking him on either side. The river Dee roared down the center of the canyon, descending into the valley and then the lowlands far beyond over a series of granite cliffs that looked liked the stairs of a giant.

Every time he rode this trail the beauty of it struck him all over again, but today he barely took a moment to notice that one of the old trees had come down in the last storm. Rowena only *thought* she wanted to go to London, and that was only because she'd taken to reading their mother's journals and the damned Society pages from the newspaper. For the last month he'd had Cooper burn them the moment they arrived, but clearly it hadn't made a bit of difference.

Slowing to a walk to round the deadfall, he continued upstream. Down below where

16

the river spilled out into the valley lay the village of An Soadh — his village, full of his cotters and herdsmen and pottery makers and shopkeepers. This morning he didn't care to hear any of them praise his graces or bless his dear family or thank him for the invitation to Glengask Hall for the party on Friday.

A light mist hung in the tops of the trees this morning, the wan sunlight falling in visible streams to the mossy, sharp-edged rocks and low, weather-beaten shrubs tucked in between them. How in God's name anyone could prefer soft, spoiled London to this, he had no idea. A deer darted out from behind a cluster of boulders and sprang up one of the narrow ravines toward the heather-blanketed moors above. The deerhounds roared and sprinted after her, and Ranulf reached for his rifle — then realized belatedly that he hadn't brought it along. With a curse he whistled Fergus and Una back to his side.

Forgetting his rifle had been foolish. As solitary as the Highlands felt, as empty of people as most of the nooks and crannies were becoming, there were always places a fellow who meant no good could hide. For a moment he considered turning around and heading back to Glengask for a weapon,

17

but today he was more likely to be ambushed by his sister at home than he was by any ill-wishers out in the wilderness.

Or so he thought. At the faint, moss-muffled sound of hoofbeats behind him, Ranulf edged Stirling into the trees. An attack in broad daylight in the middle of his own lands would be bold indeed, but he was the one who'd neglected to arm himself against such a thing. Bending, he pulled the long, narrow blade from the sheath in his boot. The damned turncoats would find that he wasn't helpless. If they meant to spill his blood, he would see to it that they lost a quantity of theirs, as well. "Fergus, Una, guard," he murmured, and the big deerhounds' hackles rose.

"Ran! Ranulf!"

At the sound of his brother's voice Ranulf lowered his shoulders. "Fergus, off. Una, off." He kneed Stirling back onto the narrow trail. "Do ye not know the meaning of the word 'alone'?" he asked.

"Ye didnae say 'alone.' " It wasn't just Munro, but Arran and Lachlan as well, trotting alongside the river in his direction. Munro, the youngest of them but for Rowena, tossed a rifle in his direction. "And ye know better than to go off unarmed," he continued, frowning.

Ranulf caught the weapon in his free hand, and with the other twirled the blade he still held in his fingers before shoving it back into his boot. "I wasnae unarmed. And I'd wager Fergus or Una could run down a horse, if they wished it."

"They couldnae outrun a musket ball." Arran gestured at the knife hilt. "And that'll do ye up close, but cowards rarely strike from close by."

"It takes three of ye to deliver a gun, now?" True or not, he wasn't going to let any of them chastise him. He was the damned eldest, and by four years. Arran wouldn't see thirty for another three years — or at all, if he didn't mind himself.

"I'm here because it's safer than stayin' in the house," his heir apparent drawled back at him, unconcerned. He patted the sack strapped to the back of his saddle. "And I brought fishing tackle."

"I came because I didnae want a saddle thrown at my head," Munro, Bear to his family and friends, seconded with a grin. "She's locked herself in her room, but who knows how long that'll last?"

"And I wasn't aboot to be left there alone with Winnie," Lachlan put in.

"I dunnae know why not," Arran countered. "Ye're the one who said ye wouldnae dance with her, ye coward."

"She's a wee bairn. I've known her since her hair was too short fer pigtails. I dunnae know why she's been acting so odd lately, but I want no part of it."

"She's acting odd because she fancies you, Lachlan," Arran countered. "Though I dunnae know how Ranulf feels about that."

"Neither do I," Ranulf said, though that wasn't entirely true.

Lachlan eyed him. "I feel like we should go fishing. And she only thinks she fancies me because I'm the only man close to her age you allow about her."

That was likely true, but as Ranulf had several years ago decided that Lachlan would be a good match for Rowena, he hadn't seen any reason to go parading her about. Instead of commenting on Lachlan's statement, he gestured toward the waterfall and rise ahead. "Up to the loch, then, while she cools her temper."

A full day of bringing in trout and perch, and especially of watching Munro slide backside first into Loch Shinaig, certainly improved Ranulf's mood. He could only hope that a day spent with Mitchell, Rowena's commiserating maid, would lighten his sister's mood, as well. If she would only stop with her fanciful daydreams for a moment, she was bound to realize that she'd received some fine gifts from brothers and friends who doted on her, and that Friday would be the grandest party the Highlands had seen in decades.

It was nearly sunset by the time the lot of them handed their strings of fish over to Cooper as the butler pulled open the front door. "Lady Rowena?" Ranulf asked, shedding his caped greatcoat and stomping mud off his boots.

"Nary a sign of my lady," Cooper returned, signaling for a footman to come and collect the makings of their supper. "Stewart Terney came to call on ye, m'laird, but said to never mind as ye're to meet tomorrow down by the mill, and it could wait till then."

Ranulf nodded. "My thanks."

"Aye," Bear put in. "If ye'd sent him up to the loch after us, that man's dour face would've turned all the fish belly side up."

"Enough of that, Munro." Ranulf favored his brother with a brief frown. "Ye'd be sour-faced too, with only Glengask sending ye grain. In his grandfather's time he had business from the Campbells and the Gerdenses and the Wallaces, in addition to us." Hopefully he would be able to increase the quantity of wheat he sent to the mill, at

21

least, depending on the fee agreement he could make with Terney and on the summer weather.

"Wait till Winnie catches the scent of baked trout," Munro drawled, heading upstairs. "That'll entice her." He paused, glancing over his shoulder. "A game of darts, Lach?"

Once the other two men had gone, Arran turned and angled his chin at the butler. With a quick nod Cooper and two accompanying footmen disappeared into the bowels of the great house. Ranulf leaned back against the foyer wall and crossed his arms over his chest. "What?"

"Just that ye and I and Bear 'ave all been to England and returned undamaged."

" 'Tis nae the same," Ranulf countered. "I, at the least, wasnae wide-eyed and expecting a fairy tale. And as I recall, ye had something of a run-in with a war."

"I served, just as I was supposed to. Don't evade the point, Ran."

"What point was that?"

"Winnie's got a bee in her bonnet, and telling her no isnae going to stop her wanting to go."

"I'll nae have it, Arran. If the Sasannach had their way, there'd be naught but sheep in all the Highlands, and our entire clan tossed into the wind with all the rest. All the English want is money. And control. I'm not giving my only sister over to them. She's Scottish, and she'll stay in Scotland. She has a husband waiting for her, once Lachlan comes to realize she's nae a bairn any longer."

"Unless Lach has a different lass in mind. But that's beside the point, now. Rowena's also half English," Arran said quietly. "As are ye and Munro and I."

"Not the half that matters," he retorted, then took a breath. "I'm nae having this argument with her, or with ye, or with anyone else. She stays at Glengask. She's safer here."

Arran opened his mouth, then closed it again. "Ye might at least explain your reasoning to her, then."

He'd done so, until he was out of breath, voice, and patience. "If she doesnae know why by now, she'll simply have to accept my decision for what it is. She stays, and she'll have a grand party she can sulk through if she wishes to."

"Ah. Sounds grand, that."

Ranulf sent his brother a sideways glance that had Arran taking a half step back. "She knows better than to push me," he said. "I willnae discuss it with her again, and I'm nae wasting any more breath on it arguing with ye."

"Aye, we all know better than to fight ye." Arran turned for the door. "Think I'll join Munro and go throw some wee pointy things at the wall."

For a moment Ranulf considered joining his brothers and Lachlan, but odds were that the three of them were discussing whether a Season in London would be so bad for Rowena. They would be reminiscing about the handful of years they'd spent at Oxford, and their own infrequent trips down to Town. Arran, especially, would reflect that his four years spent in His Majesty's Army hadn't made him any less a Scot. They were all correct, and they were all wrong.

Rowena didn't want a holiday in a faraway place. She'd read their mother's journals, and she'd become enamored of a soft life of parties and lace gowns and men who spent as much time on their dress as any woman. She thought she wanted to be English.

She would grow out of it, of course, realize that a life of dull, idle distractions and snobbery wasn't much of a life at all, but until then she would damned well stay at Glengask. Under his watchful eye. Under his protection. Whether she appreciated his efforts, or not. It was a simple equation, really. He was the Marquis of Glengask, the chief of Clan MacLawry and all its dependents, and whatever rules they might try to make in England, here his word was law.

He still should go down to one of the villages, as he did nearly every day, but he had little desire to do so. Instead he sent Cooper to have Mrs. Forrest, the cook, make an extra pan of baked fish for the morning. Father Dyce would make good use of the bounty for the poorest of the cotters below. All of which left him with an unexpected bit of the most rare of things: time. He'd seen most of his tasks done yesterday, so that he could devote the day to Rowena's celebration. Scowling, Ranulf glanced in the direction of the stairs. Perhaps he'd spoiled her, but what was an older brother to do but see that his only sister and youngest sibling had everything she could ever desire?

"M'laird?"

Ranulf turned. "What is it, Cooper?"

The old Scot shuffled his feet. That in itself was odd; Cooper generally had a fierce pride about his station, and he'd been known to box the ears of footmen for the offense of slouching. "There's . . . a bit of confusion over someaught."

"What confusion?" Narrowing his eyes,

Ranulf resisted the urge to order the butler to hurry it up. That would only rattle the fellow, and he'd never get out a sensible word.

"The . . . ah, Debny mentioned to Mrs. Forrest that they'd borrowed the phaeton, but since it was early she didn't see fit to mention it to me, but now . . . well, it's past sunset and there's no . . . that is to say, the —"

"Who borrowed the phaeton?" Ranulf interrupted, realizing that if he didn't direct a question they would never get to the end of the tale.

"Mitchell, m'laird. I presume fer Lady Winnie. A'course they do go out, but like I said, it's getting late, and they've nae taken the dogs or any riders with them, and —"

Ranulf missed the last bit of the butler's speech, as he was already halfway up the stairs, ice piercing his chest. "Arran!" he bellowed as he ran. "Munro!"

Rowena's bedchamber looked as though a stiff north wind had blown through it. Clothes and bedding were strewn everywhere, bits of burned paper spilled out of the generous hearth, and the wide-open windows let the Highlands evening chill flow into the room. But at the same time . . .

"Ran! What th'devil is —"

"Christ. Did someone take her?" Arran stumbled in just behind Munro, Lachlan on their heels. "Damned Gerdenses. They'll bleed for this!"

"Wait, Arran," Ranulf ordered, squatting down to run his hand through the burned papers and shoving away the dogs when they crowded in, yipping nervously. He'd seen true chaos before, and this looked a mite too orderly. Old clothes thrown about, but nothing that she truly liked to wear. Bed unmade, but she hadn't been in it for hours and hours. He lifted up one of the larger pieces. The words "lue shoes" were just visible, with something directly below that looked like "hairbrush."

"What've you got, Ran?" Munro asked, crouching beside him. His brother's jaw was tight, his fists clenched. There was a reason they'd nicknamed Munro the Bear, and it wasn't because he enjoyed logical discussion. "We're wasting time."

"It's a list," Ranulf returned, straightening. "Or part of one. No one took her anywhere. She took herself, her and Mitchell. To London."

"In the phaeton?" Cooper broke in.

"No doubt we'll find it at the nearest coaching inn. That's how they'll travel."

"To L— By herself?" Arran slammed a

27

fist into a bedpost. "She's daft."

"What she is," Ranulf returned slowly, digging out another piece of paper with a singed bit of address on it, "is in a great deal of trouble."

Lachlan stirred. "Ye three get packed. I'll have Debny saddle the horses."

"Nae, Lachlan. Have Debny ready the heavy coach." He looked up to see Cooper lurking in the doorway. "Cooper, have Peter and Owen pack their things. And send Mr. Cameron up here."

"The coach?" Arran repeated as the butler hurried downstairs. "Ye'll never catch up with a mail coach in that beast."

"They have nearly ten hours head start, and a plan which no doubt includes a false identity," Ranulf said, the deepening fury in his chest mixing with a fair amount of worry. "At least it had better."

"What are ye talking aboot, Ran?"

"What I'm talking aboot, Bear, is that she'd best know by now that she has more to avoid than just us. And I'll nae be seen by the Gerdenses and their lot screeching like a banshee as I race across the countryside. I'll follow close enough to make certain no one stops her, and I'll catch her up in London." He glanced down at the half-burned scrap again. "At Hanover House, evidently. And then I'll drag her arse back home."

"And us? Ye expect us to sit on our hands?"

Ranulf looked over at Arran. "I do, indeed. Ye know that we need to have a MacLawry here at Glengask. And two sets of eyes'll do ye both better. Word will get oot that I've gone. I dunnae want anyone to see that as an invitation to come and make trouble. Or that I've abandoned our people."

"The Gerdenses and Campbells'll more likely see it as a chance to waylay ye on the highway," Munro growled. "Ye can't go with naught but two footmen for protection, Ran."

"I'll go," Lachlan put in.

"No, ye willnae. I'll nae have Rowena doing something even more foolish to try t'make ye jealous or someaught."

"But she's . . . she's like my sister, Ran. I would never —"

Ranulf lowered his brow. "Even more reason for ye to stay behind." Whatever it was Rowena thought she was up to, he wasn't about to muddle the stew any further. Not even with the man for whom she'd set her cap. "I'll have the dogs with me. And both of those footmen, as ye call 'em, fought on the Peninsula with Wellington just as ye did, Arran. They'll do fer me."

"Aye, but —"

"No more arguments. Any of ye. I'm leaving for London in an hour. Stay here and make certain Rowena and I have a home to come back to. Ye'll see us within a fortnight, even if I have to tie her up and throw her over a horse."

London. *Damnation.* Rowena would be lucky if his throwing her over a horse was the worst that happened to her. To both of them.

CHAPTER ONE

"There's no need to worry on that account; Jane welcomes any excuse to shop." With a grin, Lady Charlotte Hanover kissed her sister on the nose, then stood.

"I've no wish to upend your schedule," Lady Rowena MacLawry returned in her soft, lilting accent. "It's poor enough of me to arrive on your doorstep with nary a warning."

"Nonsense." Lady Jane Hanover gripped her friend's hand. "I've been inviting you to visit for what seems like years. Your mother and my mother were practically sisters. Weren't you, Mama?"

"Yes, we were." Elizabeth Hanover, the Countess of Hest, nodded. "And I'm so pleased you began corresponding with Jane. You do look so like Eleanor, you know." She sighed, offering a soft smile. "You're welcome here, my dear, for as long as you care to stay. And of course I'll sponsor your

Season. It's only fitting that you and Jane debut together."

Jane clapped her hands together. "You see? You should have come down ages ago, Winnie."

"Oh, I wanted to, believe you me. It's only Ran who dug in his heels about it. He thinks every Englishman is . . ." She trailed off, clearing her throat. "Well, he's very narrow-minded when it comes to London."

She flipped a hand, laughing, but to Charlotte's gaze young Lady Rowena didn't look entirely at ease. Of course she was fairly certain she wouldn't be, either, if she'd traveled alone with no one but her maid through half of Scotland and nearly the entire length of England. Clearly Winnie had badly wanted a London Season.

For an overprotective brother, this Ranulf MacLawry had failed in rather spectacular fashion. A young lady who'd never left her own shire had no business navigating England alone. Or of traveling in a mail coach. Charlotte had half a mind to write Lord Glengask and tell him precisely that. Surely no one could be so ignorant as to think it unnecessary even to send a letter to precede his sister to ensure that someone would be home to greet her and to take her in for the Season. It was . . . it was unconscionable, even for someone ignorant of English custom. Surely he could read a newspaper, after all. And he must have a modicum of common sense.

She exchanged a glance with her father, who lifted an eyebrow before returning to the conversation. Jonathan Hanover, the Earl of Hest, was not a fan of chaos or upheaval of any kind, but he did dote on Jane and her to excess. Of course Lady Rowena would be welcomed into the house, and she would never see so much as a hint from him or anyone else that he would rather the family didn't have live-in company for the Season.

Longfellow, the butler, and two footmen arrived with cold sandwiches and tea for them; it was far past dinner, and evidently Mrs. Broomly had gone from the kitchen to spend the night with her very pregnant daughter near Tottenham Court. As the servants set out plates, the knocker at the front door rapped.

"I'll see to it, Longfellow," Charlotte said, since she was already standing and nearest the hallway door.

"Thank you, milady."

By the time she'd made her way the short distance from the sitting room to the foyer, the rapping had turned to pounding. "For heaven's sake," she muttered, and pulled open the door. "What is so ur . . ." Charlotte began, then nearly swallowed her tongue.

A wall stood on the front portico. Well, perhaps he wasn't as wide as a wall, though his shoulders were certainly broad. But he towered over her by a good ten inches, and most of her fellows considered her tall. As all of that rattled nonsensically through her brain, though, what she most noticed were the blue, blue eyes currently glaring icily down his straight, perfectly carved nose at her.

"I'm here for Rowena MacLawry," he said without preamble, rich Highland Scot in his voice.

Charlotte blinked. Winnie, as Rowena had asked them to call her, had arrived less than an hour ago; taking a hack from the coaching inn. As far as she knew, no one else was aware of their visitor's presence in London. No one but Rowena's family, that was. They, however, remained in Scotland — so far as she knew.

"I didnae come all this way to be gaped at," the mountain stated into the short silence. "Rowena MacLawry. Now."

"I was not gaping at you, sir," Charlotte retorted, though she was quite aware that

34

she didn't seem to be able to look away from that fierce, stunning countenance. It was if a black-haired god of war had simply . . . appeared on her doorstep. "Most visitors come to the door with a calling card, or at least with a word or two of polite greeting and introduction before they expect to be allowed past the foyer."

His eyes narrowed. It wasn't ice she saw in that deep blue, Charlotte realized, but something much more heated and angry. "I'm nae a visitor," he said, steel beneath the soft lilt. "And if the English think a wee lass barring the door is enough to keep me from what's mine, they're madder than I recall."

His? This was becoming very strange, indeed. And there was no blasted need to be insulting. "I am not a wee anyth—"

He stepped forward. Putting his large hands around her waist, he lifted her off her feet only to set her down behind him on the portico — all before she could do anything more than take a gasping breath. By then he was well inside Hanover House.

"Rowena!" he bellowed, striding down the hallway.

Charlotte settled her skirts and charged after him. "Stop that yelling at once!" she ordered.

For all the attention he paid her stalking behind him, she might as well have been an insect. "Rowena! I'll see yer arse here before me, or I'll knock this house down around yer blasted ears!"

Longfellow and a trio of footmen dashed out of the sitting room. The big Scot pushed them aside as if they were no more than bowling pins. He shoved into the room they'd exited, Charlotte on his booted heels. Given the physical . . . presence he radiated, she expected to see Lady Rowena cowering behind a chair. Instead, however, the petite young lady stood in the middle of the room, her color high and her hands on her hips.

"What the devil are ye doing here, Ranulf?" she demanded.

"The coach is outside. Ye have one minute to be inside it."

"Ran, y—"

"Fifty-five seconds."

Rowena seemed to deflate. As she lowered her head, a tear ran down one cheek. "My things?" she quavered.

"What . . . what is the meaning of this, and who the devil are you, sir?" Lord Hest demanded.

The dark-haired head swiveled to pin the earl with a glare. The devil, indeed. "Glengask." He returned his attention to Rowena. "Go get Mitchell and yer things. If ye run in the meantime, we'll return to Glengask by way of St. Mary's, where I'll leave ye off. A decade or so with nuns should cool yer heels."

Another tear joined the first. "Ye're a beast, Ranulf MacLawry," Winnie whispered, and fled past him and Charlotte out of the room.

"Glengask. Lady Rowena's brother?" her sister, Jane, said in a thready voice. "The marquis?"

"Aye," he returned, his tone still clipped and angry.

"It was our understanding that you sent Lady Rowena to us for her Season," Charlotte's father stated. From his tight expression he was furious, and that didn't surprise her at all. People — much less bellowing blue-eyed devil Scotsmen — did not barge into proper households such as theirs unannounced. Ever.

"Because ye wouldnae think twice over sending a young lass into a foreign land with no advance word. Or is it only a Scotsman ye'd believe would do such a mad thing?"

"She told us you'd sent her here," Charlotte put in.

The Marquis of Glengask turned around

to face her. "She told an idiot lie and ye believed it. Now get out of m'way, lass, and we'll be gone from this damned place."

Rowena had called her brother a beast, and Charlotte saw nothing to contradict that assessment. And she did not like men who thought with their fists and large muscles. Not any more than she liked being called a lass and dismissed — twice now — as something no more significant than a flea. She squared her shoulders. "I am Lady Charlotte Hanover, and you will address me properly, sir. Furthermore, until we are assured that your sister is safe in your company, she isn't going anywhere."

"Charlotte!" her mother hissed.

Yes, her family would more than likely simply be relieved to have this disruption gone from the house. But this was not the way anyone remotely civilized conducted business, or anything else. She refused to look away from his gaze, though he was clearly expecting her to do so.

"Well then, Lady Charlotte," he said succinctly, exaggerating the roll of the *r* in her name, "I don't suppose MacLawry family business is any of yers. I ordered my sister to remain at home, and she didnae. I am therefore here to bring her back where she belongs. As I've clearly offended ye, I'll be waiting outside. Happily."

He took a step closer, lifting an artfully curved eyebrow as he did so. Obviously he was giving her the choice between stepping aside or being bodily lifted out of the way yet again. She elevated her chin to keep her gaze squarely on his. "Your sister traveled a very great distance on her own and against your wishes, then, Lord Glengask. It seems to me that she wants very badly either to be in London, or to be away from you. I do not take you for someone who is crossed lightly."

The eyebrow dove with its twin into a scowl. "It seems to me that this is still none of yer affair." He sent a glance at her father, who still stood in front of his chair and looked as though he'd rather be in the House of Lords discussing taxes. "Do ye allow yer women to speak for ye, then?"

Lord Hest cleared his throat. "My daughter is correct, Glengask. You've stormed, clearly enraged, into a proper household and continue to behave like a bedlamite and a devil. It would be irresponsible of me to release Lady Rowena into your care without knowing her feelings and without some assurance of her well-being."

" 'Her well-being'?" Glengask repeated darkly. "How would ye respond, then, if

39

Lady Charlotte here fled without a word and then when ye ran her down some foreign stranger refused to return her to ye?"

"Firstly, I would hope I never gave my daughter — either of my daughters — cause to flee her own home. And secondly, we are hardly foreign here. Nor are we precisely strangers, as your mother and my wife were the dearest of friends."

"You somehow knew to come here to find Winnie," Charlotte added, before the marquis could begin an argument over the degree of their acquaintance. The man seemed to have an argument for everything, after all. "Clearly we are not unknown to you. Nor you to us."

"Ye'll have to keep me locked away forever and ever." Rowena's unsteady voice came from directly behind Charlotte. A moment later shaking fingers gripped hers. "I only want to see London."

"And so now ye've seen it." Glengask looked from his sister to Charlotte to where their hands clutched together. "Let my sister go," he said after a moment.

Charlotte tightened her grip. "No. You are already in London. What possible harm could there be in allowing her to remain for a time?"

" 'What possible . . .' " He trailed off. "I

will not stand here and argue with a female over what's best for my own family," he finally growled.

She refused to flinch at his tone, though beside her, his sister did. "Then as I am not giving in, I assume you mean to let Winnie remain here," she countered. Just when this young lady's cause had become hers, she had no idea. But this mountain of a man was not going to call her a wee lass and discount her. Not even if he'd lifted her as if she weighed no more than a feather, and not even if he looked to be made of solid sinew and iron.

He opened his mouth, then snapped it shut again. Charlotte allowed herself a moment of satisfaction. So the English kitten had spat at the great Scottish bear, and he didn't know how to react. Good. And good for her.

"So this is what ye aspire to, *piuthar*?" he asked his sister a moment later, though his gaze remained disconcertingly steady on Charlotte. "To surround yerself with Sasannach who keep ye from yer own family? To hide behind mouthy lasses who decide yer battles and fight them fer ye?"

"You're the one who's making this a battle, Lord Glengask," Charlotte retorted, straightening her shoulders. "And I am only

41

'mouthy,' as you call it, in the face of an overbearing bully."

"Oh, my," Winnie whispered almost soundlessly, her fingers tightening.

A muscle in his lean, hard jaw jumped. "A bully, am I?"

"That is certainly the impression you give. Your own sister is hiding behind a stranger rather than approach you."

The intense blue gaze shifted immediately to his sister. "Rowena, ye know I . . ." He trailed off, then said a single word in Gaelic that didn't sound at all pleasant and that made his sister draw in a stiff breath through her nose. Finally he gave a slight nod, as if to himself. "I'm nae a bully," he finally said. "One fortnight, Rowena. Ye want to see London, then see it. I'll take a house here, and ye'll have yer damned debut." He held out one hand. "Let's go from here, then."

"I don't believe ye, Ranulf."

"I give ye my word. Two weeks."

Charlotte bit the inside of her cheek. He'd just given far more ground than she expected, and she'd likely pushed him far past where she should have, already. In addition, her parents wouldn't thank her for what she meant to say next — but Rowena likely would. And this was for her new friend's sake rather than for her own. "If you truly mean for your sister to have a proper Season — or a fortnight's worth of one — then she should remain here. You'd be a bachelor household with no one to sponsor Lady Rowena or provide her with introductions. Unless you have a female relation here who's acquainted with London Society, that is."

"I have no female relations," Winnie said, her fingers tightening around Charlotte's hand again. "And everything you do will be to show me how it's no good here. I only want to see it with my own eyes, Ran. Please."

He blew out his breath. "By all rights I should take ye over my knee and have ye back on the road north within the hour."

"But ye won't."

"But I won't," he repeated after a moment, his glance finding Charlotte again. "Stay here, then, if they'll have ye. But ye'll inform me where ye mean t'be at all times, and I'll go about with ye when I choose."

With a squeak Rowena released Charlotte's hand and flung herself at her brother. He enveloped her in his muscular arms. "I agree, Ran," she said fiercely. "Thank ye. Thank you."

For a moment he closed his eyes, something close to relief — or sadness — briefly crossing his expression. "I'll call on ye here in the morning. At eleven." Setting her down, he bent to kiss her on one cheek. "Ye had me worried, *piuthar,*" he murmured, then straightened again. "Is there some nonsense ceremony aboot exiting, or may I take my leave?" he asked, pinning Charlotte again with his gaze.

She stepped aside. "Good evening, Lord Glengask."

"Lady Charlotte."

Only when Longfellow had shut the front door rather firmly behind him did Charlotte let out the breath she'd been holding. From the way her family swept up to her and the fast beating of her own heart, anyone would think she had just faced down the devil himself. But then she just had, really.

And he would be back in the morning.

"I do hope this is acceptable, Lord Glengask."

Ignoring the thin man dogging his heels, Ranulf continued his tour of the hallways and rooms of the small house on Adams Row. The building was old, but well made, with twelve rooms and half a dozen windows looking out over the quiet avenue. It stood three stories tall, which he imagined was the origin of its name — Tall House. "It'll do," he finally said, realizing that the bony fellow wouldn't stop nagging at him until he gave an answer. "Though I'd like it better if it had more than two doors to the outside."

"I'm glad you approve, my lord. You gave me such little notice — only an hour, if you'll recall — but I believe Tall House is the finest establishment currently available to let. With the Season beginning in earnest, you know, simply everyone flocks to London."

Everyone plus one damned stubborn younger sister. "You'll have yer fee by the end of the day," Ranulf returned, wondering if it was permissible to call Tall House by a different name while he stayed there. Frivolous House with Nae Enough Escape Routes, perhaps.

"Oh, I didn't mean to press — of course you're not well known here, but your uncle is, and I've no worry that you would keep me waiting."

Ranulf angled his chin toward the front door. Immediately Owen, who'd spent the previous twenty minutes shadowing the solicitor, stepped forward. "Let's get ye on yer way, Mr. Black," he said, blocking the fellow when he would have followed Ranulf into yet another room.

"Certainly, certainly. With you being new to London, Lord Glengask, if you require the services of a solicitor I would be honored to —"

"The laird has yer wee card, Mr. Black, as ye nearly shoved it into 'is pocket. The door is this way."

Mr. Black blinked. "I say, that's quite forward of you. Lord Glengask, your servants need more schooling in proper behavior."

Drawing in a breath, Ranulf faced the red-cheeked solicitor. "I think it's ye who needs schooling, if it takes a man three tries to get ye to leave when ye're no longer needed. Good mornin', and if that's not clear enough fer ye, good-bye."

The solicitor opened his mouth. Ranulf continued to gaze at him levelly, and then Una began a low, rumbling growl from where she stood at the window. A heartbeat later, still wordlessly, Mr. Black turned around and left the hallway, Owen grinning behind him.

"*Amadan,*" Ranulf muttered, though Mr. Black seemed more a bootlicker than a fool. Or, more likely, *he* was the fool in all this.

After all, he'd agreed to allow Rowena to remain in London, in an English household, of all damned things, for a fortnight. Where he couldn't hear what nonsense she was being told. And worse, where he couldn't be assured of her safety.

"M'laird, the Sasannach has departed," Owen said, returning to the doorway. "I doubt he'll darken these halls again, at least while we're in residence."

"Good. Thank ye, Owen."

The footman nodded. Shifting, he scowled. "I need t'say someaught to ye, Laird Glengask."

"Then do so."

"Peter and I are pleased and proud to be here with ye. Very proud. And so is Debny. But . . . we are nae enough. With ye staying on in London, ye'll have need of a cook and a valet, and more eyes ye can trust t'keep ye and Lady Winnie safe."

Ranulf nodded. He'd intended to retrieve Rowena, spend the night at an inn, and be on the way north by sunrise. Nothing his sister said would have changed his mind or his plans. No, for that he could thank *that woman.* Lady Charlotte Hanover. She hadn't so much as raised her voice, and yet now he'd rented a house in Mayfair and given his sister over to an English aristocrat's family.

"My uncle's in Town," he said slowly,

wondering what Myles Wilkie would have to say about all this — and not liking the answer he came up with. "I'll send Peter over with a note, asking if he knows of any likely lads we can trust."

"But Lord Swansley's English," Owen said, making the word a curse.

"Aye, but he's also family. And he spent ten years at Glengask, raising the likes of my brothers and sister. He'll know what we require, whatever he is."

"As ye say, m'laird."

After he scrawled out the note and sent Peter off to deliver it, Ranulf made his way back to the bedchamber he'd chosen for himself. It looked over the street on the north, and the stable yard on the east, and gave him a good view over a fair part of the lane. He'd left for London with almost no luggage and no wardrobe at all fit for so-called proper Society. At least the bed looked more comfortable than the one at the inn where he and the lads and the hounds had spent the night.

He'd worn buckskin trousers, riding boots, and an old coat to call on Hanover House. He supposed he could do the same today, and then find a tailor's shop to see him in something better suited to Mayfair. While he didn't give a damn about what the

English thought of him or his attire, Rowena would. Embarrassing her would not be the way to convince her that Scotland and Glengask held more promise for her than did London. A damp nose pushed at his hand, and he absently scratched Fergus behind his rough gray ears. "What in God's name are we doing here, boy?" he murmured, answered only by a tail wag.

Owen rapped at his door and leaned in. "Shall I valet ye then, m'laird?"

"I can put on my own boots, but thank ye, Owen. And valet isnae someaught ye do; it's what ye are. See that Debny saddles Stirling, will ye?"

"A 'course."

When he arrived back downstairs ten minutes later, the dogs on his heels, the silence of the place finally struck him. Back home the grand house was occupied not only by his siblings and himself, but by myriad servants, friends, and on numerous occasions, various clan subchiefs and their families, in addition to the pair of pipers who sounded off every morning and evening from the rooftop. If it was anything, it wasn't quiet or solitary. This was, and while at the moment it felt peaceful, he was fairly certain that wouldn't last. Trouble had a way of finding the MacLawrys.

Touching a hand to the pistol in his left coat pocket, he opened the front door himself, stepping to one side of the wide entry as he did so. No sense in making himself an easy target. Three horses waited in the drive, with Debny and Owen already mounted. "Are ye ready for this?" he asked, taking Stirling's reins from the head groom and swinging up into the bay's saddle.

"I'd rather face all of Bonaparte's army in naught but a kilt," the footman answered, "but ye cannae go aboot London alone."

"One day in London and 'e's already uppity," Debny drawled. "Don't ye worry, m'laird. We'll see ye and Lady Rowena safe, or die in the tryin'."

Ranulf nodded, appreciating the sentiment. "Let's be off, then. And keep that blunderbuss 'neath yer coat, Owen, or ye'll panic the Sasannach."

The dogs padding behind them, they clattered down the street toward Hanover House. His rented home might be quiet, but compared to the Highlands, London seemed far too close and too crowded, and amazingly, chaotically loud. Practically elbow to elbow, the residents were, all of them talking at the top of their lungs to be heard over their fellows. He hadn't noticed it so much last evening, but then he'd had only one concern — finding Rowena. Today the cacophony didn't so much rattle his nerves as it ground his short patience into gravel.

What the devil had he been thinking, to let Rowena have her way and remain here? She'd fled from home without even leaving a note, damn it all, and deserved nothing so much as a switch across her backside and a long ride home. In fact, this was ridiculous. He would see to it that she returned with him to the house he'd rented so he could keep an eye on her, and then they would head north on the morrow. She could hate him for a year if she chose, but at least she would be safe and where she belonged. And that did *not* make him a bully. It made him a responsible brother and head of his family.

At Hanover House he tossed his reins to Debny before one of the earl's grooms could appear, told the dogs to stay, and then strode for the front door. It opened before he reached it, depriving him of the satisfaction of pounding on the solid oak again.

"Good morning, Lord Glengask," the fat butler intoned, bowing. "You're expected. I'll show you to the morning room."

As the morning room turned out to be four feet from the foyer, the taking of him there seemed ridiculous, but he would tolerate the nonsense until he had Rowena back in hand.

"Lady Charlotte, Lady Jane, Lady Rowena, Lord Glengask," the butler announced, bowing as though he'd just met the king.

As if they weren't all acquainted since last evening. The three women rose, curtsying. Since Rowena had never curtsied to him — or to anyone — in her life, she'd clearly already taken to modeling herself after the other two. That did not bode well.

That woman stood there, as well, gazing at him as if she hadn't a fear or worry in the world, which annoyed him further. She was everything he disliked in a female, tall and skinny and blond, like some delicate porcelain doll likely to shatter if anyone attempted so much as an embrace. Even worse, she interfered in matters that had nothing to do with her, and spoke when he would have much preferred a moment or two to think.

"I'm so glad you've permitted Winnie to remain in London," she was saying now, her mouth curved in a rather attractive smile that didn't touch her eyes. "And we could certainly use your escort today."

"And where am I to escort ye to, lasses?"

he asked warily, watching for another trick or trap like the one that now had him residing in London for a fortnight.

"Mama wishes to present Winnie at Almack's on Wednesday. She'll be presenting Janie as well, and —"

"Nae."

Lady Charlotte blinked her pretty hazel eyes, as if no one had ever naysayed her before. Likely no one had, considering the weak-headed, weakhearted Englishmen that surrounded her and that sharp tongue between her teeth. "Beg pardon?" she said faintly.

"Nae. No," he repeated, exaggerating the sound to make certain she understood.

"If she doesn't come out at Almack's and receive her voucher to the Assembly, traditionally she won't be able to waltz anywhere else. She won't even be considered as 'out,' by more traditional households."

"I'll nae have my sister paraded before a herd of spoiled, fatheaded Sasannach lordlings like a prize cow."

Rowena stepped forward and took hold of his sleeve, as she'd done when she wanted his attention since she was two years old. "It won't be just me there, Ran," she said softly. "Jane will be there, too. Every young lady who wants to have her Season goes to

53

Almack's first. And I do so want to dance."

Damnation. He'd never been able to refuse her a thing she truly wished for. Except for London, but then she'd managed that on her own. "Ye'll be there as well," he asked, turning to eye Jane, smaller and lighter haired than her mouthy sister. "Right there, beside her?" he asked, hating both that he didn't know how the damned process went and that he had to ask an English chit for confirmation.

"Yes. And a dozen or so other young ladies, too," the younger Hanover sister said, her voice unsteady. In fact she looked at him as if she expected him to leap on her, claws and teeth bared.

Beside her, the older sister looked much more composed as she nodded her agreement. The golden curls hanging from the knot at the back of her head swayed silkily from side to side. "This is the first Assembly of the Season. She won't be standing there alone."

"And who is it gives them permission to waltz? Who are these patronesses the bloody Society page is always wagging on about?"

"Well, it's a group of very influential, aristocratic women. Lady Jersey, for one, and Lady Cowper, and Lady Est—"

"Jersey. She's Prince George's old mistress."

Lady Charlotte's fair cheeks darkened. "No, that was her mother-in-law," she said crisply. "But proper young ladies do not discuss such things, regardless."

Ranulf cocked his head. "Ye lot have an odd idea aboot what's acceptable, then. Why give any o'them the leave to pass judgment on every lass who walks into the Assembly rooms? That's daft."

From Charlotte's expression she didn't appreciate having to explain her peers to a barbarian such as himself, but he'd be damned if he'd let Rowena walk into something where he didn't know all the facts. It would be bad enough if some elderly woman of unblemished reputation were to give the nod, but foreign princesses and daughters of royal castoffs? Ridiculous.

"Aren't there people in your . . . village or town or —"

"Clan," Rowena supplied.

"Clan," Charlotte took up, nodding her thanks, "who have to acknowledge when a girl becomes a lady, or a boy becomes a man, or when two people may marry? All the social minutiae a society requires?"

"Aye," he returned, not seeing any similarity in the two situations at all. "That would be me."

Her eyes widened, hazel darkened almost to brown by the yellow sprigged muslin she wore. "You?"

"Ran's the chief of Clan MacLawry," Rowena explained, a touch of pride entering her tone. Good; at least she wasn't embarrassed to be a MacLawry. Not yet, anyway. "It's the largest clan still with its main seat in the Highlands."

"With its *only* seat in the Highlands," he amended with a slight frown.

"I'm not quite certain what all that means, I'm afraid," Lady Charlotte said, continuing to eye him. It wasn't the same apprehensive look he had from her sister, though. Mostly, she seemed curious.

"I've nae the time nor the inclination t'explain it to ye at this moment." She wouldn't understand, and he didn't like being ogled like some two-headed lamb. Ranulf gestured at his sister. "If she's to be presented at Almack's, what's required?"

Rowena threw her arms around him. "Thank ye so much, Ran! This means the world to me!"

He put a finger beneath her chin, tilting her face up to look at him, admitting to himself that he'd lost yet another argument before he'd even begun it. At least this time he could blame himself rather than the blond-haired witch. "I know it does, my dear one. Just ye keep in mind that ye're the world to me. I do mean to keep ye safe, Rowena."

"I know ye will, *bràthair.*"

"Oh, it's perfectly safe on Bond Street," Jane said emphatically. "We need to get Winnie fitted for a gown. I've had mine for ages."

Clearly he was missing something again, but rather than beginning another conversation over what was wrong with the gowns she'd brought with her — the gowns he'd bought for her — he nodded. "It'll be safer still with me aboot. Let's be off then, shall we?"

As they left the foyer the two eighteen-year-olds linked arms and practically skipped down the front steps. Ranulf gestured at his two men, and both of them dismounted, handing the reins over to the affronted-looking Hanover stable boys.

"We're off to Bond Street," he said in a low voice, as they reached him. "Owen, ye stay to the left, and ye get the right, Debny."

"On foot?" Debny returned, scowling.

"Aye. On foot."

"I'm a groom. Nae a . . . man who walks."

"Today ye're a man who walks," he returned, hiding a smile. Turning, he caught sight of the Hanover sisters eyeing Fergus and Una, who seemed to be viewing them with equal interest.

"What are those?" Jane asked with an obvious shiver. "They're big as ponies."

Ranulf flashed a grin and whistled the dogs to his side. "These are my hellhounds," he drawled.

"Oh, stop it, Ran." Rowena walked over and knelt between the hounds, who then nearly turned themselves inside out with licks and tail-wagging. "The big one is Fergus, and the wee lass is Una. They're Scottish deerhounds."

" 'Wee' one?" Lady Charlotte repeated, lifting an eyebrow. "Good heavens."

"They'll keep an eye on us," Rowena said, standing again. "Let's be off, Janie."

That left Ranulf gazing at Lady Charlotte. "Do the dogs frighten ye, my lady?" he asked.

"No. They are very . . . wild looking, though."

"Aye. They're a touch bristly. But they'll outrun a greyhound on uneven ground." For a moment he continued looking at her, but beginning to feel rather . . . odd, he gestured toward the vanishing debutantes.

"After ye, my lady."

With the other two giggling and whispering, he fell in with Lady Charlotte several yards behind them. This afternoon he would find a map of this damned place so he would know where he was going. At the moment he felt far too vulnerable, following two bairns thirteen years his junior.

"Guards truly aren't necessary on Bond Street," Lady Charlotte commented, glancing over her shoulder at the dour Debny and then at the hounds on Ranulf's heels.

"It may be safe and civilized for ye, my lady," he returned, "but I'm a stranger here, and I'll keep watch over those under my protection."

Her lips curved again in a smile. To himself he could admit that she had a pretty smile; if he'd favored tall, skinny English women who spoke when they shouldn't, he would even say she had skin that looked as smooth as fine cream, and that up close her hair shone like silken sunshine.

"Are Janie and I under your protection, then?" she asked, amusement in her voice.

"Laugh if ye want, but aye. Ye've taken in a member of my family. That makes ye clan to me."

"But we're not Scottish."

He tilted his head. "Nobody's perfect."

Ranulf moved a breath closer to her. Her hair smelled of roses, he noted, ignoring the responding tug in his gut. "And I'd thank ye to keep in mind that what's safe for Mayfair ladies might not be so fer a Highland lass."

This time she looked full at him, spears of green lit by sunlight deep in her eyes. "It speaks well of you that you're so protective of your sister," she said after a moment, "but have you considered that she might not have tried to escape if your grip hadn't been so tight?"

So this skinny, fair-haired woman thought she had him dissected and analyzed and stuck on a pin. "I'll nae have a Sasannach woman telling me the right or wrong of what I'm doing," he snapped. "Ye dunnae know me, or mine, or anything aboot me. And ye'll nae advise me how to raise my own sister."

CHAPTER TWO

Charlotte stared at the Marquis of Glengask. *Good heavens.* She'd seen his lack of manners last night at being delayed in seeing his sister, but she had the sudden realization that she wouldn't want to be there when he was truly enraged. His blue eyes practically crackled as he met her gaze, daring her to argue with him further.

Taking a breath, she inclined her head. "You're absolutely correct, my lord. I don't know you, and I have no right to criticize or advise you. What I *do* know is how I felt when I was Winnie's age. She's not a girl you can raise any longer. She's a young lady with her own goals and dreams."

"And still ye argue," he muttered.

"You don't mean to tell me that women in Scotland are mute, do you? You've had conversations with females before, surely."

For a moment he walked beside her in silence, his massive wild-haired gray hounds

61

keeping pace with him. Hellhounds, indeed. Undoubtedly he'd been called the devil, before. And this devil was an impressive specimen, indeed.

"Aye," he said after a moment. "I've had conversations with females before. None who cared to risk a brawl, though. Lasses who know their place," he finally said, something warmer touching his voice.

As if she would ever attempt to brawl with anyone. "Their place being in total agreement with everything you utter, I suppose? And for your information, an argument does not equate a wish to brawl," she said stiffly, picking up her pace.

"Where I come from, it does. If ye question a man's judgment in caring for his own, ye're like to meet his fist. If ye're a man to begin with, that is. I'd nae strike a woman."

"What a relief," she returned sarcastically. "A fight is the resort of those who can't sensibly and logically defend their position with words. It's for prideful braggarts and bullies who think only of themselves."

"Words dunnae win battles, lass."

Evidently he enjoyed an argument as well, whether he'd admit to it or not, since he persisted in countering everything she said. Goodness, he had no manners at all. "No, Lord Glengask. Words prevent battles — or brawls, or duels — from beginning in the first place."

"Hm."

She glanced up at him again. He could disagree with her, of course, even though his philosophy of battle before compromise was clearly wrong. But dismissing her — her argument — as insignificant, was not acceptable. "That's your response?" she said aloud.

"My response is that I cannae argue the reasons I'm willing to fight. Nae to someone who's never met a cause worth fighting for, lass. Ye're English; I cannae expect ye to understand."

That rather made her want to yell and stomp her feet, but luckily they arrived at the dress shop before she could conjure an appropriate retort. No wonder the Scots had such a reputation for savagery and barbarism. The men, at the least, were clearly lunatics.

Winnie went directly to the skeins of rich, jewel-colored fabric, which would never do for Almack's. "A debutante must wear white," Charlotte said, turning her back to the hot-blooded mountain and nodding as the dressmaker herself appeared from the back of the shop. "Mrs. Arven, we require an Almack's gown for Lady Rowena here.

Would you show her some appropriate material?"

"Oh, certainly, my lady. This way, Lady Rowena, Lady Jane," Mrs. Arven replied, somehow managing to clap her hands together, curtsy, and walk all at the same time.

The massive dogs stood in the corner where the marquis had ordered them to go, their muzzles wrinkled as if they couldn't puzzle out the scent of perfume and freshly laundered cloth. The two guards or grooms or whatever they were looked nearly as out of place in the small, feminine shop, and even more so when a chattering quartet of young ladies and a glowering mama crowded inside, as well. The Marquis of Glengask, barely dressed for polite company, wasn't much better suited, and he was even more difficult to overlook.

"Lady Charlotte Hanover, isn't it?" the mama said, pushing past her brood to walk closer and offer her hand.

Charlotte looked at her more closely, not easy to do considering the woman's enormous green hat. "Lady Breckett," she returned, putting on a smile. "And this must be Miss Florence."

The round brunette with the freckled nose tore her gaze from Glengask and giggled. "I am. And these are my cousins, Elizabeth, Victoria, and Lucille Hunsacker."

"Ladies."

"Is Lady Jane selecting a gown for Almack's?" Lady Breckett asked, joining her daughter in glancing past Charlotte at the hard, shadowed mountain in the corner. She should likely introduce him, but abruptly she didn't want to.

She told herself that her reluctance was entirely logical. All she needed was to begin tongues wagging that she traveled in the company of Scottish brutes and devils. Heaven forfend if he began a brawl with the faint-hearted Lady Breckett. Or even an argument.

"Jane has hers already," Charlotte said aloud. "My mother is also sponsoring a dear family friend. Are you attending the assembly this Wednesday, Miss Florence?"

"Oh, yes." Florence bounced on her toes. "I've been practicing every dance, and most especially the waltz. It will be so very exciting."

The trio of Hunsacker girls were now all openly staring at Glengask behind her, muttering and giggling and batting their lashes behind their hands. She supposed if she didn't say something now, it would cause more of a stir than if she simply introduced him. *Damnation.* With a tight smile, hoping he wouldn't discuss walloping in front of four impressionable young women, she gestured at him.

"My apologies. Lady Breckett, Miss Florence, Miss Elizabeth, Miss Victoria, Miss Lucille, may I present Lord Glengask? It's his sister, Lady Rowena, making her debut."

They curtsied in a ragged wave. "I don't recall seeing you in London before, my lord," Viscountess Breckett commented.

"I've nae been here," he returned in his low, rumbling brogue.

"Oh, you're Scottish," one of the Hunsackers exclaimed, in the same tone she might have noted that he'd jumped down from the moon.

"Aye. I am."

"We've been to Edinburgh," the Hunsacker girl went on, while the other two blushed and nodded. "With our papa and mama. Papa has a baronetcy there. He's Lord Terrill. He says his side of the family started out Scottish, but saw . . ." She trailed off, her pink cheeks paling.

Charlotte couldn't see Glengask's expression from where he stood at her shoulder, but she could almost feel it. *Oh, dear.* Under cover of shifting her reticule she elbowed him in the ribs. She might as well have been shoving at Gibraltar, but then he stirred.

"Is it only Miss Florence here being presented at Almack's?" he asked in a surprisingly mild tone.

"Oh, yes. I debuted last year, Lucille's nearly twenty, and Elizabeth won't be able to attend until next year," the shortest of the trio — Victoria, by process of elimination — explained. "Lucille and I will be there to dance, though." She lowered her head, eyeing the marquis through her lashes.

Glengask nodded, then turned his attention to the stiff statues by the door. "Keep an eye on Rowena," he ordered, then offered his arm to Charlotte. "Will ye show me where that boot shop is now, Lady Charlotte?" he drawled.

Half by reflex she put her hand on his sleeve. His arm beneath felt like iron. "Certainly," she heard herself say.

"Ladies," he continued with a very slight nod, and walked past them to pull open the shop's door. "Fergus, Una, come along."

Outside he began walking with a long, ground-eating stride that had the deerhounds trotting. Charlotte kept up for a block or so, then tightened her grip on his sleeve and pulled. For a heartbeat she thought he might simply drag her off her feet, but then he came to an abrupt stop.

"Where are we going?" she asked, keeping hold of him so he couldn't walk off and leave her standing there, mouth agape.

He faced her, six feet four inches of annoyed Highlander. "So in this polite Society of yers," he murmured, his voice a low growl, "the polished, schooled lass is permitted to insult nae just me, but all of Scotland — and I'm the one asked to pretend all's right with the world?"

"She didn't insult you. Well, she very nearly did, but then she stopped herself. And the reason you have to be polite about it is because your sister knows no one in London but Jane, my mother, and me. If you begin walloping people, verbally or otherwise, you'll only make things difficult for her."

His gaze became more speculative. "Ye're to be my conscience then, are ye?"

Charlotte offered him a smile, though she was fairly certain she wasn't at all capable of assuming that tremendous responsibility. "A guide, perhaps. When you wish one."

"Or when ye feel I need one. You were certain I was aboot to blast that lass, or ye wouldnae have knocked me in the ribs."

Other shoppers were beginning to eye them — or rather, him — curiously, but no one complained about having to move

68

around the two of them as they blocked the way. She couldn't imagine, though, that many of them would dare challenge such a formidable-looking man. Not directly, anyway.

"I think you know what's polite and acceptable, whether you choose to behave in that manner or not — which is why you left the shop when you did." She grimaced. "The Hunsacker girls know better as well, silly things. What I didn't know was whether you would take your sister's situation into account."

She half expected that to spark another argument, but when his gaze met hers again she saw a fair degree of amusement in them. The sight made her forget for a moment what they'd been discussing. Charlotte had seen paintings of some of the Scottish lakes, and his eyes were precisely the color she imagined one of the those deep, still lochs would be under a Scottish summer sun.

After a moment he gestured down the street with his free hand, and they set off at a much more sedate pace. "I've a question for ye," he asked conversationally.

"I'm listening."

"Ye're what, three-and-twenty?"

"Twenty-five. I had my birthday this spring." And she knew what was coming next. Why was she still unmarried? What foolish thing had she done to make herself unmarriageable? She'd heard them all by now, after all. The only real question was how she wished to answer. And how she felt having this large, volatile Scotsman asking her such an intimate thing.

"Were ye in London, then, the year Donald Campbell came down and made all that ruckus?"

"The . . ." Charlotte stifled a frown. It took her a moment to even recall what he was talking about, it was so far removed from the conversation she'd thought they were about to have. "That was actually the year before my debut," she said slowly, remembering, "but we were in London for the Season. Mr. Campbell was pursuing some woman, as I recall. He wouldn't leave her alone, and her brother shot him."

"So that's the story."

By now they'd reached the end of Bond Street, and he turned them right along Picadilly and then south on Queen's Walk, heading away from Mayfair. Green Park lay to their right, but once they passed that, she would have very little idea where they were. And of course he was likely lost already. But the conversation was quite interesting. "That's not the true story, then?"

70

"Nae. Campbell came down after Jenny Baxter. The Campbells and the MacMillans — that's the Baxter clan — have had a feud going on fer a hundred years or more, now. Her brother Thomas caught wind of the courtship and shot Donald dead on 'is own front step. Then he hauled his sister back to Scotland and married her off to a cattle drover afore the end of the month. A year later someone shot Thomas Baxter in the head while he was out fishing. Rumor has it, it was Donald Campbell's uncle."

"That's terrible!" she exclaimed.

"That's the Highlands. The order of faith there is clan, country, and God."

Charlotte looked up at him again. "You're the chief of your clan."

"Aye."

"How many people are in Clan Mac-Lawry, then?"

He shrugged. "All the MacLawrys, the Laurences, MacTiers, Lenoxes, Tyrells, and all the families under them. These days it's more aboot land and coin, but when we measure it by true strength, near three thousand fighting men."

"That's . . . that's an army."

"Aye." The smile on his sensuous mouth was grim and cynical. "Nae someaught the other clans can manage any longer, with the lairds clearing out their cotters to make room for grazing sheep. And nae someaught the Crown likes, with us sitting on their shoulder, as we do."

They stopped beneath an oak tree at the far end of Green Park, and the dogs flopped to the ground, tongues lolling. Just how far had they wandered from Mrs. Arven's dress shop? "Why are you telling me this?"

"Because I've given Rowena into yer household," he returned quietly, his gaze studying hers. There was more to him than arrogance and brute strength, she realized abruptly, wondering why she hadn't noticed it before. Behind his brogue and his bold words she glimpsed a keen, measured intelligence, a thoughtfulness she would never have expected on first — or second — meeting.

"Yes?" she prompted, even more curious now about the point he was obviously attempting to make.

"I want ye to understand why I have guards watching over her, and why ye and yer family need t'keep a careful eye on her. She's accustomed to feeling safe, and doesnae consider that she's *been* safe because she has three brothers and a great part of her clan keeping her that way."

"Is it truly that dangerous for her to be

here?" And for him to be here, for that matter, but she didn't ask that aloud. With every ounce of her being she wanted to look around the quiet edge of the park for danger, though she had no idea what to look for.

"It could be. I ken ye didnae expect this trouble. If ye no longer wish the responsibility of having her in yer household, I'll collect her today. I doubt an English family wants to be this close to clan troubles. And with yer distaste of punching, ye especially."

That was an insult, of course, but she thought she understood the reason for it. This man standing before her, gazing at her, close enough to touch, was the nearest thing to a king that could be found in Scotland these days. He had enemies. Scottish — Highland — enemies who shot each other on the front steps of their own houses. Stupid, avoidable, prideful violence, more than likely over something no one remembered any longer.

"I should discuss this with my father," she said evenly, "but I imagine he'll only say what I'm about to."

"And what might that be?"

"None of this . . . mess would seem to be Winnie's doing. She wants only to enjoy a fortnight in Mayfair. I believe we can manage that for her."

After a long moment he nodded. "Good. Though I'll still be keeping a close eye on ye."

Charlotte lifted an eyebrow, attempting to ignore the way her heartbeat accelerated at his words. "On me, or on Winnie?"

Glengask leaned in, his gaze on her face intent and unreadable. "Aye."

Her heart fluttered again, a low shiver beneath her skin both warm and unexpected. Why, she had no idea; she couldn't fall for his charms, because he had none. Or none that she cared to recall. And he was *not* the sort of man who interested her in the first place.

Before she could tell herself that she hoped he wouldn't . . . kiss her or something, he straightened again. A glint of humor warmed the blue of his eyes as he held out his arm. "I think we'd best make our way back to the dress shop, before anything uncivilized happens."

With a sigh she couldn't quite hide, Charlotte took his sleeve again. He still seemed determined to antagonize her, but somewhere this morning she'd stopped finding it quite as annoying as she had at the beginning of their conversation. Of course she'd known him for less than a day. At least she

74

could be assured that he hadn't gone out of his way to be other than what he was. She doubted he could dissemble if he wished to, and that, at least, was . . . refreshing.

"What are ye smiling at?" he asked, his glance taking her in before he shifted his attention back to their surroundings.

"Honesty," she replied.

Almack's.

Ranulf had read about the supremely proper Assembly, of course, mostly with a degree of disbelief that anyone would actually tolerate attending such a place. He'd half decided that the stories must be an exaggeration, tales that grew in spectacular fashion with each retelling.

As he stood, stiffly dressed in a new black jacket and gray trousers, with a plaid black-and-gray waistcoat — a poor tartan lacking the red threading of the MacLawry banner, but the only bit of Scotland the strict dress code would allow — he could see with his own eyes that the stories were all true. Damnably, horrifyingly true.

"What do you think?" Lady Charlotte asked from beside him.

He chewed at the inside of his cheek. If he said what he truly thought, he would be asked to leave. While that notion actually cheered him a bit, a glance at his pink-cheeked, white-draped sister clutching her new friend Jane's hand was all he needed to tell him he should curb his tongue.

"It's an odd mix," he finally commented. "Old frumps and fresh-faced lasses."

She nodded, her wavy golden hair pulled into a tight knot from which not a strand would dare escape. "The older *ton* like it because it's so . . . conservative. The young ones are only here because, well, everyone must come at least once."

"And it's amusing to attend when there aren't any other parties going on," Jane put in. "Or so I've been told." She pointed at a small group of mature ladies seated to one side of the room. "Those must be the patronesses," she breathed.

"Yes, they are." Lady Charlotte stepped between the younger lasses and the objects of their interest. "Don't stare."

"Oh, they don't look so fierce," Rowena commented. "I expected a gaggle of warty-faced witches and harpies."

"Don't be fooled," Charlotte said quietly. "They are the arbiters of fashion. If you wish to be able to waltz, you need the voucher they can give you."

"Then they'd best nod," Ranulf murmured, studying the half-dozen women.

76

"Harpies" was likely an apt description.

"And being banned from Almack's means being banned from many of the older, more conservative households . . . and their soirees."

He turned his head, catching her gaze and hearing the note of warning in her smooth voice. "So they mean to judge me as well, do they?"

"You walked through their front door, my lord. So yes, they feel they have the right to judge you."

For a moment he wished he'd allowed Arran and Bear to journey down with him to London. Together the three of them would give those stiff-necked geese something about which to disapprove. That, though, would only leave Rowena heartbroken and once again blaming him for a life unexperienced.

"I'll stand here," he said aloud. "I'll smile when they look at me. But if they give Rowena anything other than a damned nod, I'll show 'em precisely what I think of their strutting little peahen ways."

Lady Charlotte cleared her throat, the hint of a smile in her expression as she looked away. Tonight she'd worn a simple, high-necked silk gown of a light meadow green. If he'd been the sort of man who preferred

English ladies, as his father had, he would have been hard-pressed to keep his hands off her. As it was, the idea that he desired her only served to annoy him. A great deal.

"Ran, thank ye again for allowing this," Rowena whispered as she walked up to him, her teeth chattering. "I know ye don't like it here. Ye do look very fine, though."

He reached out to grip her shoulder. "Not as fine as ye do, my heart. Dunnae ye fret aboot anything." He caught himself nearly telling her how much she resembled their mother, but that was the last thing he wanted in her head. Even if it was true. She was Scottish, and this was only a holiday. She would enjoy herself as much as he could possibly arrange for her, and then they were going home.

A dozen lasses wore white this evening, each one more pristine and virginal-looking than the last. With Lady Charlotte whispering in his ear to tell him what was afoot, one by one they were introduced to the ladies who'd now arranged themselves along the far wall like bead-sprinkled, glittering gargoyles.

"Ranulf."

Only because of long practice did he avoid jumping at the low rumble of his name coming from behind him. "Uncle Myles," he returned in the same tone, not moving from his vantage point.

"How's our Winnie doing?"

"I dunnae know yet." Belatedly he noted that his right hand had curled into a fist, and slowly he straightened out his fingers. *Not here. Not now.* "I ken why ye're here, Myles, but I dunnae think it requires us t'have a conversation."

From the way Lady Charlotte's shoulders stiffened, she didn't approve of his brusque retort. What she didn't realize was that she should be grateful for it, and that the only reason no one's nose had been immediately bloodied was because he was apparently being judged along with Rowena.

The line of debutantes moved forward slowly, until Lady Hest stood with Jane to her left, and Rowena to her right. The two lasses looked nothing alike; one was tall and yellow haired, the other petite with hair black as pitch. Even more tellingly, one was English aristocrat through and through, and the other a well-born lass fresh from the Highlands. Could they approve one and deny the other? Would they dare?

"It's going well," Lady Charlotte murmured below the sound of her mother reciting the two young ladies' pedigrees as if they were horses at auction.

"How can ye tell?"

"They're looking at our girls rather than whispering to each other."

"Does having two debutantes there diminish the odds of both being accepted, or increase them?"

She glanced sideways at him. "They won't care that Winnie is Scottish. It's all about her bearing and her breeding."

Was he that transparent? After fifteen years as the Marquis of Glengask he was well aware how most English lairds regarded one of their fellows who chose to remain in the Highlands. He knew how the Sasannach in general viewed Scotsmen — scrappers and drunks and ultimately the losers, with hundreds of years of war and disputes finally settled in favor of the English. They weren't finished yet with asserting their authority, either. "*I* care that Rowena is Scottish," he said under his breath.

Whether by accident or not, her fingers brushed his. It made his gut tingle as if lightning had struck nearby. By the time he'd sorted out that it must have been the luncheon he'd forgotten to eat making him light-headed, one of the patronesses stood and nodded. "Welcome to Almack's, ladies. And to London, Lady Rowena."

Beside Ranulf, and despite her statement

that everything was going well, Charlotte looked relieved. Perhaps it was a good thing that he remained ignorant of the minute machinations involved, or he might have been tempted to intercede, after all. When Rowena came bouncing up to him, he smiled. "Now ye can have yer waltzes, my heart."

"Aye. So dance the first one w—" Her eyes widened as she looked beyond his shoulder. "Uncle Myles!"

She released her brother to give their uncle a sound hug. Unsurprising, as she was a warm, kindly, naïve lass — which was, he was beginning to realize, to a great degree his fault. He felt a much cooler wind blowing where their mother's brother was concerned, but tonight was for his sister. And so he clenched his jaw and kept silent.

"You've grown up in three years," Myles Wilkie, Viscount Swansley, said, taking her hands in his. "You look so much like Eleanor it almost brings me to tears."

"Do I look like Mother?" she asked, swishing her skirt almost shyly. "My brothers have never said so."

Because it wasn't allowed. Myles had the good grace to clear his throat. "You do look very like her, Winnie. Will you dance your first waltz with an old man who adores you?"

Now *that* was interfering where he wasn't wanted. Ranulf took a step forward — and felt slender fingers wrap around his arm, slight and gentle and burning through the heavy cloth of his sleeve like a brand.

"That certainly saves your brother from a dilemma," Lady Charlotte said with her sunlight smile. "I don't think he realized there would be no dancing until after the presentations, because he asked me to dance the first waltz with him."

"Oh, splendid!" Rowena towed her chuckling uncle toward the dance floor as the orchestra on the balcony began to play the traditional first waltz. "Ye're my second dance, Ran. Don't give it away."

"I willnae."

In a moment he found himself standing at one side of the dance floor while his sister took her first official steps into English Society. If he'd been able to overcome his instinct to keep a watchful eye on her, he would have turned away from the sight. How the bloody hell had he allowed any of this to happen? It certainly wasn't like him; Rowena herself could attest to that.

"Shall we, Lord Glengask?" Brown-green eyes beneath long, curved lashes gazed up at his face. "Don't make me into a liar, if you please."

He glanced from her to his sister. "Ye *are* a liar, Lady Charlotte."

She nodded. "So I am. No one else needs to know that, though, do they?" When he still didn't move, she tugged on his sleeve. "You're not worried you'll make a poor showing and embarrass Scotland before the English tyrants, are you?"

Ah, just the incentive he needed. Keeping his expression still even though he would rather have been shoveling shit in a stable than prancing before the English tyrants, as she named them, in one of their assembly halls, Ranulf took her fingers in his, slid his other hand around her slender waist, and stepped with her into the dance.

If he hadn't had a younger sister he likely wouldn't have bothered to learn the waltz, but abruptly he was grateful that she'd nagged him into it. Half the clan's better-born men and woman all knew the waltz because of Rowena, in fact.

"You dance quite well, my lord," Lady Charlotte commented in a merry voice. Her pale cheeks had taken on a rosy glow in the warm room. He found it rather attractive, though he would deny it if asked. Nor could he explain why he enjoyed just looking at her, when firstly she was English, and secondly she saw fit to argue with nearly every statement he made.

"Ye may as well call me Ranulf," he returned, "as ye've already stripped me of every bit of dignity and authority I possess."

She gave him an unexpected smile. "I doubt that's possible."

"Well," he murmured, deciding he felt somewhat mollified. "I'll take that as a compliment, then."

Charlotte cleared her throat. "I'm merely attempting to see that tonight goes smoothly for your sister. And for mine." Hazel eyes studied his, in a direct way most people didn't dare. "We do have the same goal, I think."

"I'd rather she fell on her face and returned to Glengask determined never t'leave again." Ranulf forced a smile at his companion's shocked look, as if she couldn't understand why anyone wouldn't wish to be Society's darling. "I couldnae bear t'see her slighted or embarrassed, though, so I suppose I'll tolerate the shenanigans."

"For a fortnight."

"Aye. Fer a fortnight." And not a damned moment longer. All around the floor young ladies in white twirled about in ecstatic happiness — after all, they were now part of

London's elite. They were women, and had just embarked on their one task in life, that of finding wealthy, titled husbands. English husbands with English estates, the same men who wished him gone from the Highlands so they could continue the task of turning Scotland into nothing more than grazing grounds for their fat Cheviot sheep.

The irony was they didn't wish him in England, either. Not until he'd lost his brogue and put away his tartan except for quaint holidays when everyone could pretend to be barbarian Scots in order to ridicule the culture. And that was when they weren't talking behind their hands to accuse every Highlander of being a damned Jacobite.

"You're holding my hand rather tightly, my lord."

He shook himself, immediately loosening his grip. "I apologize," he said stiffly. "My mind was elsewhere."

"Then I'm clearly not holding up my end as your dance partner."

That made him smile. The bonny lass had spleen, that was damned certain. The shift of her body beneath his hand, her quick, sure steps that matched his — now she had him thinking back to the last time he'd bedded a woman. And thoughts like that would do him no good here. At all.

"I was thinking of Glengask, my lady," he improvised by way of explanation. It was partly true, anyway.

"You truly love it there, don't you?"

She didn't sound cynical or skeptical, so Ranulf nodded. "Glengask is a wild, lovely land as like to bludgeon ye as to cradle ye."

"I think you'll find that London Society is much the same."

"Ye know," he said slowly, feeling her muscles tense beneath his hands as he drew her a breath closer, "fer a lass willing to lie to keep two men from coming to blows, ye don't shy away from an argument, do ye?"

Just when Charlotte had decided she knew how Lord Glengask would react to a given comment, he surprised her. Much the way she kept surprising herself by edging the conversation into what she knew to be dangerous territory. But in her defense, it was all rather confusing. He was rather confusing. Glengask had told her to refrain from giving advice where it wasn't wanted, then he'd given her leave to use his Christian name. And as much as he seemed to . . . look forward to walloping people, he danced quite well.

"I enjoy a good debate," she said aloud. Abrasive and defensive or not, he did seem to appreciate honesty. As far as she was concerned, that spoke in his favor. As did the way he protected and indulged and clearly adored his sister. "I detest when men decide an argument needs to be decided with their fists or with weapons, especially when it's over something as idiotic and utterly useless as their own pride."

In a heartbeat he'd pulled her still closer to his large, hard body. "And ye think a man can engage in a good debate without risking a physical confrontation?"

"I do."

Stating that to him might be overconfident of her; until three days ago she hadn't known of his existence. And one of the few things she did know about him was that he seemed to regard physical violence with the same nonchalance her peers granted to hailing a hack.

If her family hadn't agreed to sponsor Lady Rowena, Charlotte would have taken pains to stay well away from him, though she wasn't certain she would have been able to refrain from looking. She'd had more than enough experience with men who thought themselves immortal, only to fall prey to their own stupidity. More than enough to last her a lifetime.

"Ye look quite sad, lass," Lord Glengask

murmured. "If I've caused ye distress, I apologize again. Ye've been nothing but kind to Rowena."

Charlotte swallowed, meeting his direct gaze once more. "It's nothing you've done, Lord Glen—"

"Ranulf," he interrupted, his fingers shifting a little on her waist and making her aware all over again of the intimacy of their contact.

"Ranulf," she repeated, liking the taste of his name on her lips. She wanted to say it again, to savor it. Just not here, and not now.

"Better," he drawled in his deep brogue. "If it wasnae me who's hurt ye, tell me who it is."

"So you can do violence to the offender?" she returned, though it was far too late for such a thing, even if she'd been so inclined. "As I believe I've stated how little regard I have for walloping, I hope you realize I would never want such a thing."

"Aye, but *I* might."

He had a very sensuous mouth, she decided, and not just because of the soft, rolling *r*'s of his brogue. The serious downturn, the slight upward curve when he glanced over to see his sister twirling about the floor. It was devilishly attractive, really. "That's gallant of you then, I suppose," she said when she realized he expected a response, "but as I just condemned men who fight for something as stupid as their own pride, I'm not about to approve a man brawling on behalf of someone else's. I decline your offer."

Lord Glengask — Ranulf — looked as though he meant to disagree, but before he could say anything further, the music stopped. Charlotte, torn between gratitude and an unexpected . . . disappointment at the interruption, led the way to the edge of the dance floor where her parents waited. Winnie was already there with Viscount Swansley, both of them out of breath and laughing.

"Did you see me, Ran?" she asked, catching both of his sleeves in her fingers. "I'm a debutante now."

"I did see ye," her brother returned with a warm grin of his own. "Ye were practically glowing. Put the other lasses t'shame, ye did."

A hand touched Charlotte's shoulder, and she was so focused on the conversation going on in front of her that she jumped. "Yes?"

She turned quickly to see the top of a balding head bowing at her. The head straightened to reveal the round face and kind, hopeful eyes of Mr. Francis Henning, and she relaxed — as much as anyone could at Almack's, anyway.

"Mr. Henning. So grand to see you."

"Lady Charlotte. I wondered if you would do me the honor of the next dance." His brows dove down in a brief frown. "It's a quadrille, I think. Though it might be a country dance."

She felt rather than saw the Marquis of Glengask move up behind her, large and formidable as a mountain. If he thought she needed protection from Francis Henning, of all people, he must consider her entirely helpless. Charlotte smiled and nodded. "Whatever the next dance may be, it is yours, Mr. Henning."

"That's sterling. I'll just be . . ." He glanced past her, his ruddy cheeks paling a little. "I'll be by the punch bowl," he finished. "With my grandmama."

"Very good."

Almost before she'd finished speaking, though, he'd retreated. *Oh, this was unacceptable.* "What did you do?" she demanded, facing Glengask. He stood closer than she expected, and she had to lift her chin quite high to look up at his face. "Did you scowl at him?"

"Who was that?" he returned, rather than

answering her question.

"An old friend. Francis Henning. Should I have introduced you?"

Glengask cocked his head, making him look an attractive mix of endearing and lethal. "I dunnae. Should ye have?"

"Certainly not, if you only meant to glower at him."

He met her gaze levelly. "Ye're under my protection, lass."

From the way he said it, that statement was clearly meant to explain everything. And she likely should have let it be, because he was the chief of a clan, accustomed to his words being accepted as law and obeyed without question. But they weren't in Scotland, and he simply could not go about bullying and intimidating people. "Then with whom did Jane dance?" she asked. "And with whom is she about to dance the quadrille?"

The marquis swung his head around to glance at her sister. From his quickly hidden expression of confusion, he'd completely forgotten about Jane. So it seemed to be something about her in particular that he felt required his protection. The very idea should have annoyed her to no end. It did, of course, though annoyance didn't quite describe the thrill of heat running beneath her skin.

"I'll find that oot."

He took two long steps before Charlotte caught up to him and blocked his path. "I know who they are, for heaven's sake."

"Then why did ye ask me, woman?" he shot back. The guests nearest them turned to look, abruptly interested in their conversation. Of course, a number of the young ladies had been eyeing him from the moment he'd entered the assembly rooms.

But he wasn't the only one to feel flummoxed. "I was making a point." The orchestra sounded a note, then began playing a quadrille. "Now go dance with your sister, as you promised."

For a long moment he gazed at her. Then wordlessly he went to collect Winnie. Only then did Charlotte go find Mr. Henning. Tomorrow she needed to do some searching into the background of the Marquis of Glengask. Luckily for her, the best person to ask happened to be residing three bedchambers away from her own.

CHAPTER THREE

"M'laird, Uncle Myles is awaiting yer pleasure in the front room."

Ranulf looked up from the newspaper he'd been reading over his breakfast. It felt odd to have hold of news that wasn't a week old. And unsettling to read that the Marquis of Glengask was in Town and residing precisely where he was. "He isnae yer uncle, Owen. To ye, he's Laird Swansley."

"Aye, m'laird. It's just that he was at Glengask fer so long —"

"I know. Bring 'im in here." He'd long ago learned the advantage of claiming a room and a seat, and had no intention of allowing Myles Wilkie the opportunity to do so. London might be Myles's domain, but the MacLawrys claimed Tall House for themselves. For a fortnight, anyway.

A moment later Myles Wilkie stood in the breakfast room doorway, kind brown eyes taking in the setting and finally resting on

Ranulf at the far end of the table. Ranulf watched him in return. Sympathetic gaze or not, the man had the wits of a fox and the stubbornness of a badger. He wasn't about to forget that. Not for an instant. Not even when Una trotted forward, tail wagging furiously, to greet the viscount. Fergus remained under the table at Ranulf's feet and huffed his disapproval. If he'd needed any further proof that most lasses didn't have any sense, that provided it.

"You sent me a request to find you some likely servants," the viscount finally said, and produced a folded paper from one gray pocket. "Keeping in mind your . . . particular requirements, I thought I'd best bring it by in person. I've located half a dozen men and three maids who should suffice."

Ranulf nodded, flicking a finger at Peter. The footman went to retrieve the paper and unfolded it himself. "I cannae read these hen scratches, m'laird," he proclaimed after a moment spent squinting at the page.

From the opposite side of the room Owen blew out his breath and walked past Myles to snatch the paper from Peter's fingers. "Ye cannae read *any* scratches, and ye've nae fooled a one of us aboot that." After a moment he looked up from the page, frowning. "These ain't Scots names, Laird Swans-ley."

"No, they're English. Born and bred." Myles squared his shoulders. "May I sit, Ranulf?"

"Aye. Give 'im back the paper, Owen, and go have Stirling saddled. We're off in twenty minutes. Take Peter with ye."

"But —"

"Now."

The gray that had once sprinkled across Myles Wilkie's temples had lightened and spread, turning his brown hair almost blond. That had all happened sometime in the past three years. His edges all seemed a bit worn, Ranulf realized, though it remained to be seen whether it was more than skin-deep. Nor did he judge anything based on the fact that Myles took the chair directly to his left rather than the opposite one at the far end of the table.

"I missed you, boy," the viscount finally said. "You and your brothers. And Rowena, of course. You're all that's left of my family." He took a breath. "And Rowena, for God's sake — she was just a child when last I saw her. And now . . . She's a lovely young woman."

"Why only Englishmen on yer list?" Ranulf broke in, attempting to put a halt to the reminiscing. He hadn't caused the split between them, after all.

"So it's to be nothing but business, then?"

Ranulf picked up his slice of toasted bread. Slowly and deliberately he spread a thick layer of peach marmalade across it. "I believe I told ye that we're no longer family, so we've naught to discuss but business."

Myles sat forward, jabbing his forefinger into the polished tabletop. "If you still don't trust me, why was it me you asked for help in finding servants?"

"Better the devil ye know. Isn't that the saying?"

The viscount glared at him, then slapped the paper down beside Ranulf's elbow. "Here in London, *you're* the devil."

"Aye. That I am."

"I chose Englishmen because they're less likely to know who you are, and less likely to have been approached by anyone who might wish you harm, especially now that everyone knows you're in London." He took a breath. "None are from my household, because I knew you wouldn't allow that, but I have met and spoken to each one of them personally. And discreetly. They all come from fine households and with high recommendations. For that reason they'll also cost you a fair penny."

With a nod, Ranulf continued eating. "I'll keep that in mind."

"Oh, for God's sake!" his uncle burst out. "I've apologized a hundred times. I was trying to help!"

Help. The word punched into Ranulf's chest, dark and heavy. "Yer so-called help nearly got Munro — Bear — killed."

"You're all alone up there, Ranulf! You need allies outside your own clan, even if you won't acknowledge that fact. The Donnellys made overtures. They seemed genuinely interested in the education system you've put in place for your cotters."

"Aye, because they genuinely wanted to burn every one of my schoolhouses to the ground. The Donnellys and the Gerdenses are two of a kind, Myles. They allied their clans decades ago. And ye gave 'em a bloody map."

"To show them how you've divided your land into districts, sharing the work and the income, allowing all the youngsters a chance at an education. I was bragging about all you've managed to accomplish, even with the Crown breathing down your neck."

Ranulf took a hard breath. "Whatever yer intentions, because of ye I lost three schools. And if Bear had been two minutes earlier, he would have been right in the middle of the third blaze. He took a ball to the shoulder, as it was."

"You think I don't know that? It still keeps me awake nights."

"Good." Finally Ranulf sat forward. For a time he'd thought three years' distance might blunt his anger and his fear over what had nearly happened, but every time Rowena or anyone else mentioned Myles's name, it all flooded back. "Ye may have spent ten years in the Highlands, Myles, but ye're nae Scottish. Ye dunnae understand how deep old wounds go. Ye never will. And I'll never trust ye again, because ye still think ye were right in trying to step in."

"I helped raise ye."

"Nae. I was eighteen when ye came north. I'll give that ye helped raise the others. And I'll give that when Eleanor swallowed poison and orphaned Rowena and us lads, ye did come north. I know that wasnae an easy thing for ye."

Myles swallowed. "She shouldn't have done that. My sister — your mother — we all knew she didn't belong up there. But she loved your father."

"She loved being a marchioness. When I took the title, she wanted us all to move down to London. From the beginning she wanted us raised English. We'd be English aristocrats, with a seat up in Scotland. Just like all the others. Father wouldnae have it, and neither would I." He'd been fifteen when they'd all lost Seann Monadh — the Old Mountain — as the clansfolk referred to Robert MacLawry. And from the first day he'd taken his father's title, he'd had to fight.

"I know. She . . . didn't do well by you. But if I might ask, why have you permitted Rowena a Season, now?"

"That's her tale to tell, if she so chooses."

The sad, hopeful look returned to Myles's expression. "Then you'll let me see her?"

"She's nae here."

"Oh."

Damnation. "She's staying at Hanover House, so Lady Hest can sponsor her. Go see her there, if ye will. But ye'll nae take her from the house unless Debny or Owen or Peter is with ye."

"Understood." The viscount pushed to his feet. "Thank you for that, Ranulf."

"If she's hurt in yer company, ye'd best nae let me find ye. And I'll come looking. I swear it."

Myles nodded. "If anything happens to her, I'll already be dead."

That almost sounded Scottish. "Ye can

call on her tomorrow, then."

For several minutes after Myles left the house, Ranulf sat where he was, gazing sightlessly at the remains of his breakfast. The last time they'd crossed paths Myles had found himself with a bloodied nose and bruised ribs. Arran had had to pull Ranulf off their uncle, in fact. Any Scotsman of his clan would have known better than to trust the Donnellys. That betrayal had been bad enough. But when Bear had stumbled, wounded and bloody, through the front door — *that* made Myles's mistake unforgivable. This time seeing him, though, Ranulf had felt more . . . constrained than he had three years ago.

And he knew precisely why. That tall, blond lass. Charlotte Hanover. She didn't like violence. Which wouldn't have swayed him an ounce, because a Sasannach female knew nothing about how to survive in his world — except that he'd caught that look on her face when they'd danced. That look said things. That look said that she did know of what she spoke.

It had made him curious. And that was why he thought of her as he rose to collect Stirling and his pair of outriders, as he trotted past finely manicured gardens and tall, white houses, and as he turned up the

Hanover House drive. Curiosity. Naught else. Because there couldn't be an attraction. Not when she was English. No, however mad his rivals might think him, he was not so mad that he would voluntarily bring an Englishwoman to the Highlands. Not after he'd seen one — a woman with a five-year-old daughter and three sons under twenty — poison herself to escape it.

Ranulf shook himself as he dismounted in the shade of Hanover House. The places his mind went at times surprised him. His imaginings had led him to build schools and to go against the trend of clearing his land of cotters in order to graze sheep. They'd taken some of his father's ideas and made them reality — at great cost both to his purse and to his safety.

And in all that, in all his adult years, he'd never so much as thought of bringing an Englishwoman to the Highlands. So he could only consider the unbidden thought of showing the Highlands to Charlotte Hanover an aberration. Either that, or the lass was a witch — though if she meant to entangle him, she would likely have spent less time arguing the philosophy of violence with him.

The front door opened as he reached the bottom step. "You've arrived just in time,"

Lady Charlotte said with a warm smile. "We've decided to show Winnie the sights, beginning with Hyde Park."

His first thought was that though he'd never seen it himself, Hyde Park would be too open, and far too crowded for anything less than an army to provide Rowena adequate protection. Or rather, that was his second thought. His first thought was more primal, and had a great deal to do with the form-fitting peach riding habit Charlotte wore. More precisely, with the slender curves beneath it.

"Good morning, Ran," Rowena called, prancing up to kiss his cheek. "Look, I'm wearing those idiotic riding boots I had from Lach, after all." She lifted the straight skirt of her dark green riding habit to show him her ankles.

"That's enough of that," he grumbled, swatting her hand away so the skirt fell back to its proper place. "Ye'll have the Sasannach calling us savages and devils."

"Oh, pish," his sister returned, then giggled. "That's a grand word, isn't it? 'Pish.'"

Ranulf narrowed his eyes. "Ye know what else is grand? Keeping to yer own k—"

"May I have a private word with you

before we leave, Ranulf?" Charlotte interrupted.

If she hadn't used his given name, saying it in that prim, musical way she had, he likely would have ignored her. Instead, clenching his jaw, he turned and walked over to where she stood beside her horse. "Aye?"

"I wanted you to know," she said in a low voice, her direct hazel gaze meeting his again, "that I spoke with both my parents last night about your concern for Winnie's safety. My father has asked Longfellow to assign two additional footmen to patrol the house all through the night, and the grooms have begun a twenty-four-hour watch of the grounds." She smiled again. "Nothing to make her feel caged, but enough for us all to be aware before anything untoward can happen."

It wasn't enough, but it was more than he'd expected. And considering that Rowena had managed to slip away from Glengask even with all the men he had there, he wasn't precisely in a position to complain.

"I appreciate that," he said, inclining his head. "I'll tell Peter he can stay in at Tall House tonight. But I'll be leaving Una here."

Her brow furrowed. "You've had someone

watching Hanover House?"

"From dusk till dawn, aye."

For a moment she cast her gaze about as though she expected the stout footman to leap out of the shrubbery. "I had no idea."

"Ye were nae meant to."

"And the dog?" she went on, glancing down at the smaller-framed Una.

As dogs went she was still at least a head above most, and any foxhound had best have three or four siblings if they thought to have half a chance against her. "She's a mild-hearted lass, but she'll give her life to protect Rowena. Ye've naught to fear from her, my lady. And ye've naught to fear from me." He wasn't certain what prompted him to say that last bit, but it seemed . . . necessary. Because of the MacLawrys she and her family were likely to find themselves in circumstances they could never even have dreamed of, after all.

She reached up, straightening a fold of his simply tied cravat. "Well, then," Lady Charlotte said, then abruptly patted his chest and lowered her hand again. Clearing her throat, she turned away. "Benjamin, hand me up, will you?" she asked, looking at the groom who held her horse.

"I'll do it," Ranulf grumbled, warning the servant away with a glance.

Unsteady inside and not entirely certain why, Ranulf slid his hands around her waist and lifted her. He'd had his hands on her before when he'd moved her out of his way and again last night for the waltz, but this felt more . . . intimate.

Charlotte placed her hands on his shoulders. "The saddle?" she said breathlessly.

Christ. Attempting not to dump her over backward, he set her onto the sidesaddle. The way he felt abruptly singed — the way his gut reacted to touching her — it did feel almost like witchcraft. He stepped back, wiping his hands on his thighs. "There. All proper now, I hope?" he grumbled, and turned his back to swing onto Stirling. Beside him Rowena was grinning excitedly, up in the saddle of a pretty gray mare and no doubt pleased to be having her way once more. "And who put ye into the saddle?" he asked.

"I did, m'laird," Debny said, before she could respond. "One o' them Hanover grooms near tried it, but I knocked 'im back."

"Oh, dear," Charlotte muttered from Ranulf's left, but he pretended not to hear. No one was bloodied, so as far as he was concerned it had all been handled amicably.

The sedate walk they settled into hardly

seemed worthy to be called a ride. Admittedly the mid-morning crowd of vendors, carts, hacks, shoppers, and other people meandering about aimlessly as they were, made anything above a trot near lethal, but that hardly made it more tolerable. By the time they turned up Park Lane and the grand park came into view on the left, even the dogs had their tails tucked.

Another breath of uneasiness ran through him. They'd never manage more than a walk there, either. Just in his limited view through the trees an endless sea of carriages and horses and parasols and hats spread before them. Somewhere behind him he caught Owen's muffled curse, and he silently agreed. Not only would it be nearly impossible to make an escape, but they'd likely never see any trouble coming until it was far too late.

He cocked his head. Much as he hated to admit it, any attackers would have precisely the same difficulty. And a hundred witnesses on top of it. The Campbells might risk it anyway, but luckily they were more likely to call him out to his face than stab at his kin behind his back. Clan Gerdens concerned him more, but mainly because he had nothing more than suspicions and third-hand rumors about what they might have been up to.

"It's fairly well ordered once you join the throng," Charlotte commented on the tail end of his thoughts. He seemed to have drawn even with her sometime during the ride to the park, though he couldn't consciously remember doing so.

"Dunnae any of ye have anything better to do?"

Well, that seemed unfair, Charlotte thought, though she had to admit that Hyde Park was quite crowded for this early in the day. Unusually so. Generally, visiting didn't begin in earnest until after luncheon. "There's no Parliament today," she said, remembering her father packing up his fishing gear this morning. "And I believe there are to be races on the Thames this afternoon."

They bypassed Rotten Row, as the morning was quite warm and none of the ladies — or she, at least — wanted to bother with the canter. Charlotte did point the riding trail out to Glengask, as he looked like a man who required exercise. In fact, as she sent another sideways glance at the marquis, she decided he was quite fit. He must have spent a great deal of his time in the Highlands out of doors.

As they joined the line of riders and carriages along the path, she realized she wasn't the only one noticing Lord Glengask, either. From the fluttering eyelashes and batting fans, half the female populace was either flirting, or fighting off a horde of midges.

Ranulf kept up the slow pace, ostensibly more interested in seeking out likely shrubbery-shrouded hiding places than in all the pretty eyes cast in his direction. Was this single-minded enemy-hunting of his why he remained unmarried? By her calculations he was somewhere in his late twenties or early thirties, he had wealth, land, and a great deal of power — and yet there was no Lady Glengask. Not that she cared about that, of course; she was merely curious.

Jane and Winnie had somehow managed to put a barouche and a phaeton between them. Ranulf gave a subtle wave of his fingers, and his two outriders pressed ahead to join them. The dogs evidently knew their duty as well, because they kept pace on either side of his big bay as if they'd all done it a hundred times before. An elderly woman, Lady Gavenly, she thought, passed by in a barouche, a small yapping dog struggling in her arms. The bigger deerhound,

Fergus, swiveled his head around to look at the little thing, then returned to his walk. Evidently small yapping dogs were below notice in the Highlands. Either that, or the hounds had already eaten their daily meal, and weren't hungry.

"Speaking theoretically," she said, wondering if she was about to begin another disagreement, "aren't you, as the chief of your clan, the one who should be the most protected?" What she wanted to ask was whether all of this was truly necessary. Especially in the middle of Mayfair, in the middle of the morning, in the middle of the Season.

"I know aboot trouble," he returned in a thoughtful tone. "Rowena, for the most part, doesnae. At home it didnae so much matter, because she always had clan around her. Here, I'm beginning to wish I'd encouraged her to take it all a wee bit more seriously."

"How do you know about trouble? I'm not questioning that you do; just about what's happened to make you so cautious."

He glanced sideways at her. "That's very carefully worded, lass. Am I so fierce?"

Charlotte couldn't help her smile, though it was a fairly apt description. "I'm attempting to be diplomatic."

"Ah." To her surprise, he chuckled. "The clansmen called my father Seann Monadh — Old Mountain. That man was tough as winter and strong as a draft horse." Obvious affection in his voice, he smiled a little, then briefly lowered his head. "They say he drooned."

It took her a moment to decipher what he'd said, partly because it was so unexpected. "He drowned?" she repeated, to be certain. "I'm so sorry."

"Aye. Drowned," he said, this time exaggerating the vowel sounds. "Though I imagine having his hands bound and his head held under the water makes it closer to murder."

Good heavens. Charlotte put a hand over her chest, though she wasn't certain why. His words, the ill-hidden pain and anger in them, had already dug into her heart. "I take it not everyone agreed with your assessment?" she asked after a moment.

Blue eyes met hers. "Nae, they didnae. I was fifteen when it happened, but I think that's old enough to ken what rope burns around a man's wrists look like whether or not they were bound when we found him, and to realize what torn sleeves and scratched arms mean." He took a slow breath. "None o' that signifies, I suppose, except to answer ye when ye ask why I'm so cautious."

She couldn't even imagine what he must have felt, to *know* something even more foul had been done on top of what was already a tragedy. Just the image in her mind of someone binding and drowning her own mild, jovial father made her fight back tears. "I have no words," she whispered.

Ranulf shrugged. " 'Twas sixteen years ago."

"Do you know who did it?"

This time his grim smile chilled her to her bones. "That's a tale for another time — when ye and I are better acquainted."

"You mean, when you've decided you can trust me."

The expression on his face eased a little. "Ye've a way of cutting to the heart of a matter, lass."

That made her smile, though she wasn't entirely certain it was a compliment. "I've found there are fewer misunderstandings that way."

Ahead of her, Janie turned in the saddle. "Char, the Lester twins are over there," she said, half mouthing the words behind her hand. "Please don't come over."

With a sigh, Charlotte nodded and reined in her gray mare, Sixpence. Ranulf drew up beside her. "What was that all aboot?"

"Jane's in love with either Phillip or Gregory Lester, and she has some silly notion that I find them . . . ridiculous."

" 'Either'?" he repeated, lifting an eyebrow. "I take that to mean she doesnae know which one?"

"They're entirely interchangeable."

He continued to look at her, bafflement in his expression. "Then why doesnae yer father tell Jane to keep her distance from them? Or tell them to keep themselves well away from her?"

As he likely wouldn't appreciate it, Charlotte stifled her laugh. "That would only convince her that she was Juliet and one or other of the Lesters was Romeo. Being a star-crossed lover doomed to pain and longing seems terribly romantic to a young lady, you know."

"Hm. Doom and pain does explain some of the looks I've been getting from various lasses, anyway," he returned with another glance around them. "I suppose there is something . . . intriguing about wanting someone ye cannae — and shouldnae — have."

His gaze when it returned to her sent something unsettled and shivering through her. Were his words a message meant for her? Or was he merely speaking hypothetically and attempting to ruffle her feathers? He did seem quite proficient at that, after all. "Anyway," she resumed, "the more time Janie spends conversing with the Lesters, the more likely she is to realize all on her own that they're both complete nodcocks."

With that she turned Sixpence toward the bridge leading across the Serpentine and to the less crowded half of the park. It took more willpower than she expected not to turn and see if the marquis followed her. A moment later, though, he and his monstrous bay clattered across the bridge and joined up with her again. And of course it did not give her a moment of satisfaction that he'd chosen to continue his ride with her rather than shadow his sister. It was only that he'd clearly decided that two large Scotsmen were sufficient protection for Winnie — at least for the moment.

"A false river in a false wilderness," he commented, eyeing the Serpentine as though looking for a plug and a drain.

"The Serpentine is an actual river," she returned, trying not to sound indignant at the insult to her favorite London park. "And Hyde Park was originally wilderness. They've both merely been . . . enhanced, so

113

the citizens might make the most use of them."

" 'Enhanced,' " he repeated. "Glengask overlooks the river Dee. Rapids, waterfalls, sheer cliffs — a thing that's an Eden to yer eyes but'll snatch yer life in a heartbeat if ye dunnae respect her. Nae 'enhancement' necessary. In fact, a man would be daft to attempt such a thing."

A river, the Bray, ran by the edge of her family's estate in north Devon. Like the majority of rivers in southern England it was for the most part placid and slow, as if it had given up the fight to be wild long ago. That didn't make the Bray better or worse than the Dee; a river was simply what it was, after all.

Knowing her companion as she was beginning to, he likely expected her to argue his point, anyway. Well, she didn't always like to do the expected. "That sounds breathtaking," she said, following now as he guided his horse over for a closer look at the shore and the overhanging willows, their long, sad branches dipping into the slow-moving water. "Is Glengask forested, or pastureland?"

"Both. We're high up in the mountains, so the trees grow mostly in the gorges and valleys where there's more shelter from the weather. And our idea of pasture and yers are two different things, but we make do."

"And you graze sheep, I presume?" From what she knew of other families with seats in the Highlands, they *all* grazed Cheviot sheep.

"Nae." His voice was sharper than he expected. "We raise cattle at Glengask. A few Highlands sheep fer our own use, but a MacLawry will nae burn our own people out t'make more grazing land fer those bloody Cheviot beasts. Never."

"The Highland Clearances," she said, not certain she'd spoken aloud until he nodded.

That explained his caution over his sister's safety, and a great deal more. The reason his clan was the largest still in the Highlands, and perhaps even the reason he suspected his father had been murdered. The MacLawrys were evidently resisting the clearances, despite the lure of income from the Cheviot sheep and the "urging" of the Crown to thin out the peasants and comply. There was nothing England feared more, she knew, than an organized band of free Highlanders.

As she considered all that he stopped in the shade of a cluster of willows and dismounted. "The clearances do tend to color every bit of business north of Hadrian's

115

Wall," he said, walking up to her and lifting his arms.

"How have you resisted?" Looking down at his upturned face, the question abruptly seemed to apply as much to her as it did to him. Willing her fingers not to shake, because she was far from being some schoolgirl miss, she gripped his shoulders.

Warm hands slid around her waist and then she was in the air again, as if she weighed no more than a feather. Her insides felt just as fluttery — which was utterly ridiculous. Perhaps she wasn't immune to his physical charms, but just from their handful of conversations she knew their temperaments couldn't be more different. Their philosophies were as far apart as the two ends of the Earth.

Her feet touched the ground, but he didn't release his hold on her. Instead he tugged her closer, so she had to put her hands on his hard, broad chest to keep her balance. "Shouldnae," he murmured, the blue of his gaze sinking into her like warm summer. And then he leaned in and kissed her.

Charlotte closed her eyes. She didn't know how a man could taste of the Highlands — or even what the Highlands would taste like — but Ranulf MacLawry did. Windswept cliffs, fierce storms, the welcome warmth of a hearth fire on a chill day. That was what the Marquis of Glengask tasted like. Utterly intoxicating.

"Charlotte! You didn't put Lord Glengask into the river, did you?"

The sound of Jane's voice made her start. Gasping, she uncurled her fingers from Ranulf's lapels and shoved. For a heartbeat he held where he was, one arm around her hips and the other cupping the nape of her neck. Then he let her go and stepped back almost awkwardly.

Perhaps he felt as startled as she did. Resisting the urge to look him in the eye and see precisely what he might be thinking and feeling, Charlotte wiped a hand across her mouth and scurried out from beneath the willow branches. "No one's fallen in," she said a bit too loudly, nearly tripping over one of the hounds in her haste to retreat. "Though if Lord Glengask continues insisting that the Serpentine isn't a real river I shall be sorely tempted to push him in and see if he gets wet."

Winnie looked startled. "Ye'd do that? To Ran?"

"That might convince him, don't you think? It was only a jest though, my dear," Charlotte returned, forcing a smile when

117

what she really wanted to do was put her hand to her lips and see if they were as warm and swollen as they felt.

The marquis's sister leaned down in the saddle, craning her neck to see into the bower. "Ran? Charlotte didnae kick ye in the man bits, did she?"

Charlotte's face heated. "I did no such thing!"

Janie was giggling behind one hand. "Ladies don't talk about man bits, Winnie."

"Truly? My brothers hardly talk aboot anything else, it seems."

Leaves rustled behind Charlotte. "True enough," Ranulf said dryly. "I hate t'admit it, Rowena, but perhaps ye could stand to learn some London refinement."

And with that, the other two utterly forgot about what she and Ranulf might have been up to beneath the willows. Whatever his faults, and they seemed numerous, the man was masterful at turning a conversation — and about not answering questions posed to him.

Winnie squealed, flailing her arms until one of Glengask's men helped her to the ground. As soon as she had her feet beneath her she strode up to her brother, her skirts bunched in her hands. "Does that mean ye're giving me longer than a fortnight here?"

He grimaced. "It means we'll see."

His sister threw her arms around him. "Oh, thank ye, Ran. Thank ye, thank ye."

Blue eyes met Charlotte's over his sister's head. "It still means we'll see. I make ye no promises."

"I know, I know," Winnie returned, releasing him and pirouetting back to Honey, the mare Charlotte's father had given over for her use. "Because once ye give yer word, it's as good as carved into stone."

"Aye." He watched as his man lifted Winnie back into her saddle, then offered his arm to Charlotte. "What shall we do now?" he drawled.

If it hadn't been for her riding gloves and his sleeve, she thought touching him might have caused her to burst into flame. "The . . . um . . ."

"We should get ices," Janie thankfully put in. "And I want to show Winnie the Kensington Palace gardens. They're so lovely, and there's a pond with fish."

Charlotte cleared her throat. "I believe Janie's planned out the rest of our morning quite well," she managed, then lost her composure again when Ranulf put his large hands on her and lifted her back into the saddle. Good heavens, what was wrong with her?

He swung onto his own brute and nudged it up beside Sixpence. "Was that yer first kiss, sweet lass?" he murmured, a soft, self-satisfied grin touching that very capable mouth of his.

For heaven's sake. This time, at least, she was glad for his arrogance. It quite dumped her out of whatever silly stupor she'd fallen into. "You surprised me, Ranulf," she returned in the same tone, willing her voice into steadiness. "But no, that was not my first kiss."

She caught sight of his smile dropping just before she turned Sixpence around and took the lead. Urging the mare into a trot while they had a moment's space to do so, she headed them back across the bridge in the direction of the closest ice vendor's cart.

She wasn't entirely certain why she rushed, or why she felt so . . . unsettled both by the kiss and by the man. Had she flirted with him? Certainly she'd enjoyed some of their discussions, even if his appreciation of violence didn't sit at all well with her. And perhaps there had been some satisfaction in the way the other ladies had looked at him at Almack's when it had been her dancing the waltz in his arms, and again today in the park when he'd been riding beside her. But that didn't mean . . .

Out of the corner of her eye she caught sight of the bay's nose drawing alongside her again. Frowning, she nudged Sixpence in the ribs, and the mare smoothly accelerated into a canter. She was not some simpleminded little thing to be kissed and dazzled by a rude Scotsman. She knew better than that.

The head drew up even with her knee again. The bay was still at a trot, damn it all. She gathered the reins in her hands and clucked. In an instant they were galloping. Somewhere behind her Jane called her name, but for once she ignored her sister. And she ignored the startled, annoyed looks of the pedestrians and other riders hurrying out of her way.

She risked a glance over her right shoulder, but the bay's nose — and his rider's — were nowhere in sight. Good. She needed two blasted moments to think.

A hand reached over from her left and grabbed Sixpence's bridle. "Whoa there, lass," Ranulf said in his deep brogue, and he reined in his big bay with one hand while holding her mare with the other. *Blast it all.* He likely juggled bears for fun and amusement, as well.

He pulled them easily to a halt. "Lord Glengask, is she unhurt?" Jane's rather high-pitched voice came. "Charlotte?"

"She's fine," he said, before she could answer. "Dropped a rein, is all."

"I did no such —"

"Ye want to explain to these sheep why ye were stampeding them, then?" he interrupted in a terse voice.

He made a good point, damn it all. "No," she muttered back. "I'm fine," she called in a louder voice, twisting to glance back at her sister before she straightened again.

"If ye dunnae like me kissing ye, lass, just say so," he continued in the same tight voice. "Nae need to flee from me."

"It's not — I wasn't —"

"Ah," he broke in again, his voice warming. "Good, then." She heard him take a breath. "What were ye thinking, galloping off like that?"

"I was thinking about James Appleton, if you must know," she burst out, turning Sixpence away from him and setting off again at a much more sedate pace.

"And who is James Appleton?" he demanded.

She kept her gaze between Sixpence's ears. "My fiancé."

CHAPTER FOUR

Fiancé.

Ranulf stared at Charlotte's deliberate profile. It made no sense. Neither did the angry, sick feeling in his gut, as if he'd just missed the last boat leaving a sinking ship, but he preferred to consider her statement itself rather than how . . . surprised it left him feeling. Because it must be surprise roiling through him. Nothing else made sense.

"So where is this bonny James Appleton, then?" he forced himself to ask.

Her hazel eyes flicked in his direction, then away again. "I beg your pardon?" she asked faintly, an unexpected affront in her tone.

He had no idea what had raised *her* hackles; he was the one who'd just had a fiancé flung at him. Not that it affected anything but his curiosity, of course. Even if he might for a moment consider her attractive, even if he might for a moment have imagined her naked in his arms, she remained the one thing that could never be a part of his Highland life — an Englishwoman.

"Ye heard me," he pressed anyway. "Who is this fine fellow who couldnae be bothered to join ye at Almack's, or fer a pleasant ride on a fair morning in Hyde Park?" He shifted in the saddle, wanted to grab her arm, to make her look at him, but restrained himself. It was still merely curiosity, after all. "Ye ken what I think?" he continued when she didn't respond.

"I'm certain I haven't the slightest interest in what you think, my lord."

Somehow he'd gone back to being "my lord" again, a sure sign that he'd stumbled across something that made her uncomfortable. A true gentleman would likely stop pursuit of the topic, but everyone in London knew he was no true gentleman. Instead he edged Stirling closer. "Well, I'll tell ye, anyway," he pushed, keeping his tone low enough that the throng around them couldn't overhear. "I think there's nae such man as James Appleton."

This time she turned her head to face him fully. Her fair cheeks went white. *"What?"*

"That's it then, aye?" he went on, his gaze

lowering to her soft mouth almost in spite of himself. "Ye cannae abide a devil like me giving ye a kiss, so ye conjure an imaginary beau fer yerself instead of telling me to my face that ye want naught to do with a Highlander. It's a cowardly English lie, Lady Charlotte, and I'm sorry t'admit that I thought better of ye."

For a long moment she stared at him, her entire body shaking. If she meant to faint he would have to ·catch her, he supposed, but that would be the end of it. No more touching her, no more thinking about her. He was the damned chief of Clan Mac-Lawry. And he had better things to do than waste a moment daydreaming about a lass who wanted naught to do with him. For Christ's and Saint Andrew's sake, women fought among themselves for a night in his bed. This was ridiculous.

Her hands clenched around the reins, and for a heartbeat or two he thought she meant to slap him. *Ha.* That would put a nail into her coffin of abhorring physical confrontation — though that had all likely been a lie, as well, something meant to keep him at a distance.

Then she reached up and with trembling fingers unfastened the small oval locket from around her neck. She held her arm out, the locket dangling from her fingers. "Take it," she bit out.

Kneeing Stirling closer, he took it from her fingers. "I didnae give it to ye, lass."

"I know that. Open it. The little fastening on the side."

Reining in the bay, he did as she ordered. The thing was old and absurdly delicate, but with a bit of effort he managed to get it open without breaking it. On the inside of the lid he made out the inscription "Forever in My Heart." The opposite side held a wee portrait, a young man with light hair and rosy cheeks, a high cravat covering what looked like a soft chin, and soulful green eyes that gazed out at nothing.

"That, Lord Glengask, is James Appleton." She'd stopped close beside him, he realized, her voice quiet and controlled. "The reason he didn't join us at Almack's, and the reason he isn't here riding with us today, is because three years ago he tripped on a dance floor and fell into a potted plant. And then he decided to challenge the first man who laughed at him — and there were several — to a duel. He was killed the next morning. Because of a waxed floor and a potted plant, and because he was embarrassed." She held her hand out to him again, palm up. "Now return him to me, if you please."

"The . . ." Trailing off, he handed her locket back to her. This time he'd put his foot in it, all the way up to his thigh. No wonder she loathed prideful violence. "Lass, I —"

"No. You kissed me, and I thought of James. He reminds me not to fall for the charms of hotheaded, thin-skinned brawlers ever again. I did not lie to you, sir, and I am not a coward. You, however, are a savage and a devil. And I am finished talking to you." With that she clucked to her horse, and the chestnut mare trotted over to where her sister and Rowena giggled about something or other.

A savage and a devil. Well, he'd been called worse, and with less cause — which was likely why Charlotte Hanover's words stung. He deserved them. However much an idiot her fiancé might have been, Ranulf had jumped to a damned conclusion — a wrong one — and she'd called him on it. Almost no one had ever done that to him before. The lass owned a bloody ocean of courage to stand up to him, and that was damned certain. And those things she'd been saying about how words could bite as deeply as a sword felt abruptly and painfully true. She'd cut him deeply, no doubt about that.

Now he needed to apologize. It wasn't something he did often or well, but by God he was man enough to own up to a mistake when he made one. He turned Stirling — and Fergus gave a low growl to his left.

At the same time the hair on the back of Ranulf's neck pricked. That wasn't a growl for showing off. One hand sliding toward the pistol in his pocket, he shifted a little to look in the direction both dogs were now staring, bodies low and tails stiff and parallel to the ground — awaiting his order to charge.

A trio of riders stood to one side of the path, all three of them gazing at him. None of them had weapons aimed at Rowena or him. Good. Then he might not have to kill any of them today.

Out of the corner of his eye he noted Owen and Debny cutting a path through annoyed park visitors, closing in on where Rowena and the two Hanover lasses were now enjoying a lemon ice. They knew their duty. Above all else they — Rowena — needed to be protected. Likewise a lass with sunshine hair who'd lost her love to his own pride was not to be put in danger because of another man's. The strength of that particular thought surprised him, but just as swiftly he put it aside for later contemplation.

Turning his attention back to the motionless trio twenty feet away across the path, he deliberately took a moment to assess each of them in turn. The man to the right possessed so many overly large muscles he likely didn't have much space left for thinking. He would be the enforcer, then. By contrast, the man seated to the left was sleek as an otter, garbed all in black and his eyes shadowed by the black beaver hat on his head. The adviser, who would try for a knife to the back rather than a punch to the face. By far the more dangerous of the two. Which left the man in the middle.

"Good morning, Lord Glengask," that rider said, inclining his head and smiling too widely. Pale blue eyes flicked from him to the three lasses and back again.

Ranulf wondered if the man realized how precariously his life was balanced, and how swiftly it would end if he moved so much as an inch toward them. "Berling."

"How pleasant to see you out of the Highlands," Donald Gerdens, the Earl of Berling, continued coolly. "The last time we spoke, I believe you said something about it taking the devil and a dozen horses to remove you from Scotland."

The precise speech, the way Berling carefully quashed any trace of brogue in favor of the most polished of Oxford-educated accents, had seemed pitiable in Scotland. Here, it felt almost criminal. But Ranulf was well aware that the residents of Mayfair thought otherwise. Here, *he* was the ruffian, and Berling was the civilized English gentleman with a country seat in the Highlands. "I recall that conversation," he said aloud. "Ye ended with a broken nose and a warning to stay well off my land."

The muscled man gathered in his reins and sat forward, as eager to charge into battle as the hounds were, all of them only waiting for a word from their respective masters. Berling, though, kept the smile on his face, as if some lass had told him he looked less like a donkey when he grinned. She'd been wrong, whoever she was.

"Yes," the earl returned. "There I was, visiting my small holding just north of Glengask, and offering —"

"Sholbray," Ranulf interrupted for clarification, since they were evidently reciting their history for any onlookers. "Yer small holding is called Sholbray. A hundred years ago it was the Gerdens family seat, until ye burned out yer cotters and handed it over

130

to a thousand sheep."

"My family's seat is Berling Court in Sussex," Berling said stiffly, his smile as chill as an icy northerly wind. "And when I offered you a very reasonable sum for grazing rights on your ill-used pastureland, you pulled me from my horse and broke my nose."

"I was trying fer yer jaw, to stop its flapping. I see ye still have the problem of speaking when ye shouldn't." He tilted his head. "Shall I give it another go, then?"

"Brave talk for a man with three servants and two dogs for a clan." Pale eyes darted again in Rowena's direction, but evidently the earl knew what would happen if he as much as mentioned her.

"I suppose we'll find that oot."

Berling laughed loudly. "Yes, I suppose we will find that 'oot,' Glengask. But not today. Don't you have some cows or cabers that need to be tossed?" With that he turned his black gelding, and the three men vanished into the crowd back the way they'd come.

"Dogs, off." Only then did Ranulf notice how large the circle of onlookers had become. "Be off with ye," he growled, and guided Stirling back to where the three white-faced lasses waited. On one side of them Debny faced into the sea of English gadabouts, while on the other Owen had one hand inside his coat, likely resting on the butt of his pistol.

"Ranulf?" Rowena said tightly.

"All's well," he returned, forcing the anger that had been pushing to escape back into his chest. "Finish yer ices, and we'll —"

"We'll be returning home now," Charlotte interrupted. "And you will go . . . elsewhere, my lord. Your sister does not need this tiff attached to her reputation."

" 'This tiff'?" he repeated, wheeling his bay to fall in with her.

"You were an inch away from brawling with Lord Berling, sir," she stated. "Don't pretend otherwise."

"I wasnae pretending anything. I was merely questioning why ye'd call it a tiff. It wasn't as wee as all that."

"And don't attempt your quaint colloquialisms on me. I don't find them amusing."

He narrowed one eye. "And to think, I was looking fer a way to apologize to ye fer insulting yer Mr. Appleton."

"Stop that. I am furious with you. We do not threaten each other on the streets here. And certainly not over clan rivalries or some such thing."

For a moment he thought he might suffer an apoplexy, right there in the middle of

Hyde Park. "Some such thing," he repeated. Hadn't he just told her that clan was everything to a Highlander? "It was a warning I gave Berling; not a threat."

"Semantics," she retorted.

"Aye, perhaps," Ranulf conceded, admitting to himself that as . . . frustrated as he was with this woman at the moment, he was still allowing her to take him to task in a way that no one had ever been permitted before. Ever. "Three years ago he or one of his men put a musket ball through my brother Munro's shoulder. And then last year he tried to buy my land for his bloody Cheviots. I'll threaten him every time I set eyes on him. And if he ever takes another step toward me or mine, he's done."

She glanced sideways at him then quickly away, as if she didn't even care to acknowledge that he was there. And he still wanted to kiss her again, damn it all. "Have him arrested, then," she said.

"I've no proof yer Sasannach courts would listen to. And as the coward likely won't set foot back in the Highlands, there's naught I can do. Legally." If she wanted to hear him say that English courts favored men who'd taken English titles and lived on English estates, he would do so, but she likely already knew it. Not that she'd agree with him; that wouldn't be ladylike, or some such thing.

"Perhaps you should stop trying so hard not to fit in, then, Ranulf."

The moment she spoke Charlotte wished she hadn't. Yes, he troubled her ears and her thoughts no end, but she already knew that making him angry was not a wise thing to do. Glengask's sensuous lips flattened, his deep blue eyes flashing. Then he whistled, a short, shrill sound that made her jump and brought the dogs and the pair of servants instantly to his side.

"Una. Guard Rowena," he said, his tone clipped and precise. "Lads, see 'em safely home, then back to Tall House with ye."

"And ye, m'laird?" the older, grizzled servant asked.

"I'll have Fergus with me."

His sister reached a hand out toward him. "Ranulf, the Evanstone soiree is tonight. Are ye —"

"I'll be there," he interrupted, sparing Charlotte a glance that both chilled her and started a spark of flame deep in her chest.

With that he and the big bay and the big gray deerhound moved off through the crowd, traveling at far too fast a pace to be civilized. But then, Ranulf MacLawry wasn't at all civilized.

For a moment she worried that she'd also offended Winnie, but the marquis's sister drew even with her on one side, while Janie came up on the other. "Are you acquainted with Lord Berling?" Charlotte asked their houseguest.

"Nae — no. I mean, I've seen him from a distance once or twice, but no one's ever introduced us. I wouldn't want to be introduced to the likes of him."

Out of her brother's presence Winnie had been attempting to "improve" her speech, as she termed it. Charlotte liked the brogue, herself, especially when spoken by a deep-voiced, mountainous male, but she understood Rowena's reasoning. If she spoke like a Highlander no one would ever see her as a proper Englishwoman, and that — more than anything else — seemed to be what she wanted for her short Season. To not be Scottish.

"Is it true that he shot your brother Munro?" Jane asked, her color still wan. Public displays of male aggression were not something with which either of the Hanover sisters had much experience, thank heavens.

Winnie nodded. "Someone began burning down the schoolhouses Ran had been building. Bear went to look in on one and rode up to see it on fire. He came back with his shoulder covered in blood and said he tried to go in and make certain everyone was safe, and then some bloody coward shot him from behind."

"Winnie," Jane gasped, putting a hand over her own mouth. "Ladies don't say that word."

"Which word? 'Bloody'?"

"Winn— yes, that word."

"Oh. It's Bear's favorite word, though, and that's what he said."

"If they shot him from behind, how does he know it was Lord Berling?" Charlotte pressed, more interested in the facts than the language used to present it.

"Because Berling is allies with the Campbells and the Donnellys, and Uncle Myles gave the Donnellys the map and told them about the schoolhouses."

Well, that explained the tension between Ranulf and his uncle, even if the logic of it all was abysmal. Charlotte wondered briefly if the marquis had broken Lord Swansley's nose, as well. "That makes it possible, then, but it doesn't make it proof."

Rowena sent her a bemused look. "That's what Uncle Myles said. And then Ranulf said that a Highlander knows in his gut when a man's violated his trust, and that only someone who'd turned his back on his own people like Berling did would fear a schoolhouse."

That might have passed for facts in Scotland, but Charlotte could see why Ranulf hadn't bothered to take his grievances before a court of law. Supposition, superstition, and hate — that's what it had been. No wonder Scotsmen were no longer permitted to govern themselves.

It was only after she returned home and settled into the library with the latest *Ackermann's Repository* that the rest of the conversation sank into her. Ranulf had been building schoolhouses — several of them, apparently — on his land. For his cotters.

While there was certainly a line of thought that educating peasants only served to enlighten them as to how miserable their own conditions were and to encourage them to rise up against their so-called betters, she didn't agree with that. Giving anyone an opportunity for an improved life had to be a good thing. And part of her had to admire a man who offered that to those dependent on him, especially when it meant going against the wishes of his own peers. It took courage and conviction, both of which Ranulf MacLawry seemed to possess in great quantity.

It was quite aggravating of him, really. He

gave the appearance of being the exact opposite of enlightened. He even seemed to perversely enjoy being seen as a devil Highlander and nothing more. His contempt for the English — or the Sasannach, as he called her kind — couldn't be more obvious. And yet he'd kissed her, and that had felt anything but contemptuous. Molten and savage, perhaps, but she had no complaints about it. At all.

Shaking herself, Charlotte set aside the *Ackermann's* and stood. Her father was a great reader, and he had quite an extensive collection of biographies, plays, and novels. She perused the library shelves until she found the collection of titles that most interested her. Slowly she pulled the first one from the shelf. *Waverley,* written by an anonymous author everyone now knew to be Walter Scott, the Scottish poet.

She'd read the account of young Edward Waverley and how he was seduced by the fiery Highlander Flora MacIvor with her Jacobite leanings, but that reading had been about the romance of it all, and how she'd hoped Edward would return to the mild, steadfast Lowlander Rose Bradwardine — which he had. This time as she sat down and opened the book, she wanted to read about the Highlands. And the Highlanders.

After an hour or so of trying to sink into the story, however, Charlotte had to set the book aside in favor of standing and walking about the large room. Why had Ranulf been so angry and skeptical when she'd mentioned James? All she'd said was that when Ran had kissed her it had made her think of . . . Oh. *Oh.*

But she hadn't meant it that way at all. She'd only meant that no one had kissed her since James had done so, the evening before he'd gone off to get himself shot in the heart. And so naturally when Ran had given her that rather spectacular kiss, she'd then thought back to both the kiss and the rest of the nonsense and pain her hotheaded betrothed had caused. She certainly hadn't been thinking of James at the moment Ranulf kissed her, because her mind had stopped working altogether.

Well, if he'd misinterpreted what she'd said, what did it matter, anyway? She'd explained it, perhaps inadvertently, but he had to have realized what she meant. And he'd seemed far more interested in looking for an excuse to beat Lord Berling than in defending his own bloodthirsty ways, anyway.

How odd, that she hadn't even known that Donald Gerdens was Scottish. She'd danced with the earl, and on several occasions. They'd chatted about the weather, and the latest plays being performed at Drury Lane Theater, and even if now she remembered that he'd several times flattened his *a*'s, she hadn't noticed it then. Ranulf had said she didn't understand what it was to be Scottish, and evidently he was correct. None of this hate and conflict and hiding accents made any sense to her at all.

Nor did it make any sense that a man so different from her in outlook and temperament could be so . . . intriguing. Now Charlotte slowly reached up and ran a finger across her lips. The taste of him had faded with ices and luncheon and arguments, but she remembered it. That kiss had positively curled her toes and weakened her knees, and sent a keen excitement over . . . something, crashing through her entire being.

Not that that mattered, either, since her parting words to him had been a suggestion that he stop trying so hard to be Scottish, or some such thing. She likely could have conjured a worse insult, but it would take some time and effort. "Fribble," she muttered.

"Charlotte?"

At the sound of her father's voice she stopped pacing and left the library. "Up here, Papa," she called, leaning over the banister and thankful for the distraction, whatever it was.

He looked up from the foyer. "Meet me in my office, will you, darling?"

"Certainly."

She arrived before he did, and wandered to the window overlooking the carriage drive. The sky had gone gray with the afternoon; they would be lucky if it didn't begin raining before they arrived at the Evanstone ball. There was nothing worse than trying to walk through mud and horse excrement in dancing slippers.

"Where are the girls?" Lord Hest asked, walking into the small office and closing the door behind him. His nose and ears were red from being out in the wind; even if she hadn't seen the string of fish in his hand earlier, she would have known what he'd been up to.

"Trying on gowns for tonight. The excitement is positively making my teeth ache."

He chuckled. "Ah, you were insufferable once, too. I remember it well."

"Perhaps, but there are two of them."

"Too true." Sobering, he gestured her to take one of the pair of seats facing his desk. "I heard about a row today, in Hyde Park."

Oh, dear. "It wasn't a row, precisely. Lord

Glengask and Lord Berling caught sight of each other and had words. Nothing came of it."

"That's something, anyway," he returned, looking relieved. "From the way Kenney explained it, I thought they'd been at it with broadswords."

"No. I do recommend that we never invite the two of them to the same dinner party, however."

Her father looked at her for a moment. "What was it about? Do you know?"

"Well, evidently Lord Glengask has refused to graze sheep on his lands, and is instead building schoolhouses. And Lord Berling didn't like that. According to rumor Berling or one of his men shot one of Winnie's brothers in the shoulder, and then the last time they encountered each other in Scotland, Glengask broke Berling's nose." She frowned at that. It was all so stupid, and so senseless. Why couldn't men simply sit down and discuss things?

"So Glengask doesn't like Englishmen *or* his fellow Scots, eh?"

She sighed. "Apparently not. I told him that he needed to make a better attempt to behave, but he didn't take that well."

The earl's lips twitched. "You told him what?"

"Yes, it was stupid, but after two hours of blasted England this and damned English that, I'd had enough." And that was as much of the story as she would ever tell him. Because no one at all was ever allowed to know that Ranulf had kissed her. Or that she'd kissed him back.

"Yes, I'm already taking a ribbing from some of the fellows at the Society Club over having a Highlander lurking about. I have to admit, I'll be somewhat relieved when this fortnight is over."

Charlotte frowned. Ranulf hadn't precisely said he would allow Winnie to remain longer, but he had hinted at it. Of course that had been before she and he had argued. "Don't plan a farewell dinner yet, Papa," she said anyway. Lord Hest should know what was afoot in his own household.

"What?" His frown likely matched hers. "What happened?"

She shrugged. "He adores his sister, and she wants to stay."

"Well." Slowly the earl blew out his breath. "Then I suppose we'll make do. I have to admit, your mother couldn't be more pleased. Having two young things to introduce about is her idea of paradise. I just wish they were both English."

That was precisely the sort of thing Ranulf

likely thought people said behind his back at every opportunity, so she refrained from agreeing, instead offering her father another smile. "Don't forget to save a dance for me tonight, Papa," she said, standing and giving a twirl.

"Oh, good God. It's the Evanstone to-do, isn't it? Is Glengask attending?"

"He said he was. Why?"

"Just that Evanstone's grandfather helped put down the Jacobite uprising at Culloden."

"Oh. That should go over well. I'll inform Lord Glengask at the first opportunity not to mention Bonnie Prince Charlie." She scowled again, only half jesting. "Or perhaps I simply won't mention it at all."

"That might be best."

Chapter Five

The tailor didn't much like him, Ranulf decided, but then given the way the man kept trying to add padding to his shoulders, the feeling was mutual.

"But it's the very height of fashion, Lord Glengask," the thin fellow pleaded, wringing his hands.

"I dunnae care," Ranulf returned. He already stood a good head above most other men; padding his shoulders would look absurd.

"Yes, clearly, given . . . that," Mr. Smythe countered, gesturing at the half-finished coat Ranulf had commissioned.

"Just make it fit, Smythe. Withoot padding. I'll send my man by at six o'clock."

"Yes, very well. Just please don't tell anyone you came to me."

"Oh, I willnae. You neednae worry over that."

He and Fergus left the tailor's shop, and

with a swift glance up and down the street, Ranulf swung up on Stirling and headed at a trot for Tall House. Charlotte said he should try to fit in. The lass might have more sense than most, and if she'd taken a moment she would have realized that he would never fit in. Not in Mayfair. And so he might as well be what he was.

Once she'd entered his thoughts again, she refused to leave. It was very like having her there in person, actually, stubborn and lovely and commanding his attention whatever he might prefer. If she'd mentioned at the beginning that she had a fiancé, he would have taken pains never to think of her as . . . well, as a woman, as a bonny lass to be kissed and stripped naked and bedded well and thoroughly. And often. But he did think of her that way — which was why he'd felt like someone had cut off his balls when suddenly she *did* have a fiancé. And now she didn't again.

All of which meant he'd likely never have another decent night's sleep. Because his wee, stubborn brain knew that taken by another man or not, Charlotte Hanover was not for him. He knew that four days of acquaintance shouldn't have left him feeling this way.

A few Scottish lairds remained scattered

across the Highlands, and of those, a number had unmarried daughters. He would wed one of them, because that was what the Marquis of Glengask should do. A Highland lass for a Highland life.

In fact, when he and Rowena returned to Glengask, he would make marriage his next task. Taking a breath, Ranulf climbed the stairs to his rented bedchamber. A single kiss, and his mind turned all to stew. Thank Saint Andrew the younger lasses had interrupted them when they had. Especially now that he'd foolishly agreed to let Rowena extend her stay.

He'd done it for his sister's sake, of course, because she looked so very happy. But if he'd been thinking of himself, of how he might welcome more time to become acquainted with Charlotte Hanover, for example, well, what a fool that would have made him.

Ranulf shoved open his bedchamber door so hard it rattled the windows. In response a figure by his dressing table squeaked and whipped around like a startled mouse. So now Gerdens was sending vermin after him.

Christ. It served him right for being distracted. "Who the devil are ye?" Ranulf spat, pulling the knife from his boot and striding forward. With a feral growl Fergus crouched, circling in from the other side.

"Ginger! Ginger, my lord," the wee man rasped, picking up a hairbrush and holding it before him like a shield as he backed into the corner.

"What damned sort of name is that fer a man?"

"What? Oh! Edward, my lord. Edward Ginger. I'm your valet! Don't murder me, for God's sake!"

Someone thundered up the hallway behind him. Moving swiftly, Ranulf put the tall wardrobe between himself and the doorway, while Fergus kept the Ginger fellow at bay. The end of a blunderbuss sped into the room, followed by a winded Peter Gilling. "M'laird, where be ye?"

"Here, Peter. Don't bloody shoot me."

The footman immediately lowered the skittish weapon and removed the flint. "God split me in two and throw me into the pit before I'd ever do such a thing, m'laird."

That was a colorful image. Ranulf flicked the end of his dagger toward the corner. "Ye let him in here?"

"Aye, m'laird. I would've told ye, but I were in the privy when ye came in."

Given the footman's flapping breeches and untucked shirt he was telling the truth — or he was already at one of the new maids Ranulf had also approved for hiring. "All right, then. Fergus, off. Go put that thing away, Peter. Both things. And take Ginger with ye. He looks like he could use a whisky."

"My lord," the valet put in, his voice still quavering, "I do prefer to be called . . ."

Ranulf looked at him. The servant's lifted forefinger curled slowly back into his palm again. "What's that, Ginger?"

"Nothing, my lord."

"Good. And next time ye surprise a body in this house, don't move except t'show yer empty hands or ye might get skewered on principle."

"Yes, my lord. I shall remember that, I'm certain."

"See that ye do."

Once Ranulf changed out of his riding coat and boots, he returned downstairs to his office. Now he had English servants running through Tall House, but there was little he could do about that. Myles's assessment of his situation was correct, and hiring people who knew nothing at all about Highland troubles made sense.

He sank into the flimsy chair behind the too ornate mahogany desk and pulled out pen and paper to write a letter to Arran. His brothers needed to know that the fortnight had now become an open-ended excursion, and he needed a few more of his things sent down to London.

For a moment he considered asking for one or both of them to join him here, but with Donald Gerdens making his presence known, they were likely safer where they were. Especially Bear; if he and any Gerdens ever ended up in the same room, only one of them would leave it on his own two feet. And he didn't want Munro put into an English prison. Not for anything.

Yes, he was accustomed to a loud, full house of family and friends, but that was at home. This, whatever else it was, was not home. It never would be. He sat back for a moment. What he could most use here was someone who knew the lay of the land, someone who knew which other "reformed" Scots were in London and in what numbers.

That made his thoughts turn to his uncle. Yes, Myles Wilkie would have been perfect, except Ranulf remained unsure whether he could trust the viscount's judgment. The fact that Myles had been trying to help and caused such a near disaster almost made it worse.

On the other hand, when a man had limited resources, there were no perfect options. He could always ask Charlotte, he supposed, except for the fact that firstly, she wanted him to be less Scottish; secondly, he wasn't certain they were speaking; and thirdly, that would mean a quiet, protracted conversation where he could very likely do something idiotic like kiss her again.

Perhaps Myles was the wiser choice, after all.

"M'laird?"

He looked up from the half-finished letter to see Owen standing in the doorway. "Everyone is safe back at Hanover House?"

"Aye. And I think Lady Winnie's pleased to have Una there with her. A touch of home, I ken."

Ranulf nodded. "I feel a mite better with Una there, as well. Anything else?"

"Well, I'm nae entirely certain. Peter says footmen and such've been coming by all morning, saying 'by yer leave' or 'with respect,' and handing over these." The former soldier held up a tray piled high with cards and notes, and one ribbon-wrapped box.

Hm. "Let's see 'em."

He'd attended Oxford, because it was the law that the firstborn son of every Scottish laird receive an English education. He'd then insisted that his brothers go as well, because he'd wanted them to know who and what they were all up against. And so he knew what sat on his salver: the most dangerous and insidious of all things English. The calling card.

Dismissing Owen, he went through all of them. A few were from men and women to whom he'd been introduced at Almack's by Charlotte. Most were from people he'd never heard of, inviting him to breakfast, luncheon, and soirees. Evidently the Sasannach were excited to have a devil in their midst. Perhaps they thought he'd dance a jig and play the pipes for them.

It was tempting to toss all of them into the wastebasket, but he resisted the impulse. The Hanovers, and thereby his sister, might well be attending some of these events, so an invitation for him would come in handy — like the one he'd received yesterday for the Evanstone soiree. Still, though, it felt like looking at pieces of some silver-embossed puzzle when he didn't know what picture they all formed.

He saved the box for last. No note or card accompanied it, and he shook it a little before he untied the ribbon. It felt heavy for such a small thing, and caution made him set it flat and push back in his chair before he flipped off the lid with one finger. Nothing moved inside, no scent emerged, and he slowly stood to look down into it. A small ball of wool had been stuffed inside, leaving no open space at all. Wool to him meant Cheviot sheep, which meant some sort of message from another laird with a seat in the Highlands who didn't like his so-called anarchic plans to keep his people close and see that they were educated and fed and employed.

Wool, though, wasn't that heavy. Frowning, he picked up the box and tipped it over. The wool fell with a dull thud. Taking a breath, he pulled the thing apart with his fingers. A moment later a solid lead musket ball dropped onto the polished surface of the desk. Now that was a better threat than a handful of dirty wool.

"Well, now," he murmured, not surprised to see that someone had scratched the word "MacLawry" onto the surface of the ball. He picked it up, letting it roll about in his palm. After Almack's, everyone would know he was in London. But not everyone would wish him to know that he was in danger. "Peter!" he called, seating himself again.

The footman reappeared in the doorway. "Aye, m'laird?" His gaze dropped to the desktop, and he stepped forward. "That was in that wee box?"

"Aye. A ball with my name on it. Poetical,

don't ye think?"

Peter picked it up, clenching it in one fist as though he wanted to grind it into dust. "The man who brought the box wasnae in livery," he said after a moment, his lined face grim. "Tall lad, light hair, but I doubt I'd recognize him again. Damnation."

Shaking his head, Ranulf held out his hand for the ball. "Dunnae worry yerself. We knew trouble waited here. Kind of it to make itself known, really." He pushed to his feet. "Have someone go by Mr. Smythe's tailor shop in the next hour or so, will ye? He's prettying up a coat fer me."

"Aye. And where're ye off to, then?"

"A stroll. I ken we'd be better off if I knew the streets around here better."

The footman scowled. "Ye can't think to go out now, m'laird!"

"Why not, because someone wants me dead? Since when has someone not wanted me put under the ground? I find it more helpful at the moment to know who might be in London fer the Season and living on my doorstep."

"Well, Owen and I are goin' with ye."

"No, ye aren't. Fergus is. Ye're going to watch the door. Owen!"

The second footman arrived quickly enough that he must have been listening by the door. "M'laird?"

"Owen, ye are going to show Ginger how to dress a man in a kilt."

"Ginger? Who's Ginger?"

Charlotte picked up the hand mirror and twisted around to view the back of her ornately piled hair in the large dressing mirror. "It's lovely, Simms. I would never have thought of weaving a pearl necklace through my hair."

The maid dimpled. "Lady Newsome's maid showed me the trick of it. But I thought of using the matching earbobs."

Shining pearls peeking through her blond curls and then matching ones dangling from her ears — added to the dark green silk and lace of her gown and the pearl buttons on the dark green elbow-length gloves, the effect really was quite dramatic. More so than she generally cared for, but tonight was special. The first grand ball for both Jane and Rowena.

It was fortunate that she felt put together on the outside, because her insides were something else entirely. And she knew precisely who to blame for that. Glengask had stomped off quite regally this afternoon, but it still left the question of how he meant to behave tonight. Would he dance? Would he ask her to dance? If he did, what would she say? After all, she was angry with him. More than likely, he was just as angry with her, too.

Oh, he was like a great bear growling his way through London and upsetting people's equilibrium. Everyone knew everyone in Mayfair. That was simply a given. Having Lord Glengask stride onto the stage with his unruly black hair and fierce blue eyes therefore turned everything on its head. Every other man who went riding with her in the park, for instance, knew that she'd lost James three years ago. They knew that she danced and chatted, but that she didn't flirt, that she wasn't looking to make another match in the foreseeable future, and that she didn't kiss. Ranulf MacLawry clearly knew none of these things — and she wasn't certain it would make a difference if he *did* know.

Her bedchamber door opened, and Jane waltzed into the room with Winnie, the waist-tall deerhound padding behind them. "Oh, Char, you look stunning!" her sister exclaimed, parting from her friend with a flourish. "Has a gentleman finally caught your eye again?"

Charlotte felt her cheeks warm. "Why in the world would you say that? Do I generally look so shabby?"

"No! Of course not. It's just . . . Well, you look exceptionally nice."

"That, I will accept. And thank you." With a grin, Charlotte took in the two excited young ladies. "Blue is definitely your color, Winnie," she said after a moment. "It lights up your eyes. And I'm jealous of all that hair you have."

Winnie swept an elaborate curtsy. "Thank ye, Charlotte. Mitchell nearly had to tie me to my chair, I was so nervous about how high she was piling my hair." The marquis's sister gave the black, lustrous mass a careful pat. "We've been practicing London styles for weeks, but this time it's not just for fun."

Janie bounced on her toes. "Say something flattering about my gown too, Charlotte," she urged, chuckling.

"You are a vision in violet, Janie," Charlotte offered obediently. The girls' enthusiasm must have swept her up, as well, because otherwise she couldn't explain the tingling in her fingers and all the way down her spine. "I wouldn't be at all surprised if some gentleman asked for your hand in marriage tonight."

"He can ask," her sister returned with a laugh, "but I'm not marrying anyone yet. There are far too many parties yet to come this Season."

With a loud sigh, Winnie plunked herself down onto the floor to scratch Una. The portrait of young despondence almost made Charlotte smile, but she refrained from doing so. "What's amiss, Winnie?"

"It's only the talk of marrying," Rowena said, sighing again.

"You did mention something about a beau back at Glengask. Do you miss him?"

"Aye. Lachlan MacTier. I miss him dreadfully. But I've been here for nearly five days and been gone from home for nearly twice that, and he still hasn't sent me a single letter."

"Have you written him? Perhaps he doesn't know your address here."

"I've written him every day."

Charlotte hid her grin behind her hand. Had she ever been that young? "Perhaps that's the difficulty, then," she said aloud, sinking to the carpet and joining in on scratching the wiry-haired hound.

"What do you mean?"

"Just that a man can't miss you if you're always about."

"But I'm not about. I'm hundreds and hundreds of miles away."

"Your letters aren't. They're there to greet him, every day. And if he isn't writing to you, then it's because you've answered all of his questions."

Gray eyes much less fierce than her brother's blue ones gazed at her for a long moment. "You're absolutely brilliant!" Winnie chirped, hugging her. "I'm not going to write him another letter." She frowned. "Unless . . . Should I write to say that I'm not writing him? I don't want him to think I'm angry with him — though I am, a bit."

"No," Janie chimed in. "Let him wonder. Perhaps he'll think you've found a beau here in London. And you might, because you do look very pretty tonight."

With Simms's assistance Charlotte climbed once more to her feet. "You two will only find beaux if we actually attend the soiree." Taking a last glance at her hair to make certain it would stay in place, she urged them out her door. With some difficulty they closed Una in Winnie's bedchamber and then hurried down the stairs.

Her parents were already waiting in the foyer, and had to take a moment to admire each of them in turn. Evidently she generally didn't dress so fancily, because both of them commented on her attire and her hair, as well. How odd that they and Jane all thought some man must have caught her eye; in the past two years none of them had

159

ever mentioned such a thing when she dressed for a party.

Longfellow helped her with her wrap, and then she took Winnie's to assist the marquis's sister. "May I ask you a question?" she murmured, beneath the sound of the chattering around her.

"Of course."

Charlotte took a breath. It was just curiosity. Nothing more. "I don't know Highland or clan tradition, but your brother is one-and-thirty, yes? Is there a reason he hasn't yet married?"

"I think he's been too busy," Rowena replied, her expression becoming more thoughtful. "And I think he worried before that I would feel pushed aside if he brought another lass into the house. But I'm eighteen now, so that'll likely change." She grimaced briefly. "I just hope he doesn't decide to marry Bridget Landry. Her family lives the closest, and she's pretty and all, but when she laughs it sounds like crows are dying."

Charlotte snorted. "Oh, Winnie."

"No, it's true. And she takes all the best bits at dinner for herself. Ran would let her, because he wants everyone to be happy, but sometimes I'm happiest to see him with the last strawberry of the season. I don't know that Bridget would ever think of that." Winnie shrugged. "Though worrying over who gets a wee strawberry is a mite silly, isn't it?"

"I don't think so," Charlotte replied, trying to reconcile her image of Ranulf MacLawry with that of a man who enjoyed strawberries and who liked to see everyone around him happy. "I think it's lovely."

"Come along, ladies," her father said abruptly, making her jump. "If we're late you'll only have me to dance with."

"I wouldn't mind that, Papa," Jane said stoutly.

He kissed her on the cheek. "Perhaps not, but I would."

The Evanstone soiree was the first grand ball of the Season. As such, it would likely see guests packed nearly to the high, vaulted ceiling of its two adjoining ballrooms. Luckily the rain held off, and they had only a chill wind with which to contend as they made their way past the crush of carriages to the large house's main entrance.

Even Winnie had stopped chittering, instead taking in the sights with wide, round eyes. Charlotte couldn't even imagine how it must all look to someone whose idea of town was a tiny village in the middle of nowhere. "Is this very different from dances at Glengask?" she whispered.

Winnie nodded, barely blinking. "We have two grand parties a year, one down at An Soadh and the other at Mahldoen, but they're not dances, precisely. More like fairs, I suppose. All the clan comes together, and we set up tents. There's all sorts of food and drink, and singing and dancing and pipes, caber tossing, shooting, swords. Not nearly as grand as this."

Shooting and swords? Hopefully at targets and not at each other. Charlotte kept that to herself, though. Tonight was for Rowena and Jane. For a moment she tried to imagine some of the carefully coiffed guests here tossing cabers and drinking ale from mugs and dancing to bagpipes. If not for the accompanying violence, it would likely be . . . exhilarating.

Once the butler introduced Lord Hest and party in a ringing voice, they made their way to the nearest of the two interconnected ballrooms. They'd opened the folding walls in between them, making one breathtakingly huge space with chairs lining the walls, huge fireplaces at either end, and a dozen floor-length windows leading outside to a balcony with steps down to the garden and pond below. The outside was lit with torches, the inside with eight chandeliers, and everything glittered.

"Oh, glory," Winnie murmured. Charlotte turned to agree with her, but then realized that the debutante wasn't looking at the decorations. She was gazing at her brother.

"Oh, glory," Charlotte echoed, following her gaze.

The Marquis of Glengask stood close by one wall, his gaze moving from man to man as though searching for enemies. But for once it wasn't his deep blue eyes that caught Charlotte's attention. Every other male present wore proper coats, waistcoats, and trousers or breeches with either boots or shoes. Like them, Ranulf had donned a coat — his a dark gray with large black buttons edged in silver, and a trio of identical buttons bright on each sleeve. His waistcoat was black with the same black and silver buttons, while his snow white-cravat was pierced by a silver and onyx pin.

From the waist down, however, he was clearly not an Englishman. Instead of trousers he wore a kilt of black and gray, with red thread cutting through the darker squares like blood. In front of his . . . manhood a silver and black pouch hung from a silver chain that looked like it went around his waist. His knees were bare, while black wool stockings covered his calves. On his feet he wore black leather-looking shoes bound halfway up his calves with more strips of leather.

The effect was . . . Charlotte swallowed. He looked wild and mad and dangerous and simply mesmerizing. On occasion some of the older statesmen wore kilts to soirees, but no one paid much attention to their quaint ways. This was very different. All around her she could hear the whispers, too, mostly from women. Piercing blue eyes met hers, and then he was walking across the floor, the crowd parting to make room for him as he approached. She felt abrupt heat between her thighs.

"Rowena, ye look very fine," he said in his low brogue, smiling at his sister.

That smile was dangerous, too, because it made Charlotte's heart flutter, and made her remember his capable mouth and that extraordinary kiss. Rowena, though, wasn't smiling back at him. "What are you doing?" she whispered.

"I'm standing here," he returned coolly.

"Ye're wearing clan colors. Are you looking for a fight?"

"Nae. I'm Scottish. I'm a Highlander. And this is how a Highlander dresses. Or have ye already forgotten?"

His sister looked at him closely. "No

trouble?"

He shook his head. "Nae trouble. Not from me."

Charlotte didn't know how he could say that, when every inch of him practically radiated trouble and very male heat. When he turned his gaze to her, she refused to look away, or to lower her eyes to take in his attire. She tried not to blush, but given the warmth of her cheeks she hadn't managed that feat. "I see that you heard my advice," she finally said.

Ranulf tilted his head. "What advice was that? Oh, the bit where ye told me t'fit in." He held his arms out from his sides. "I decided against it."

"Yes, I can see that."

He took a half step closer. "Will ye give me that wee dance card of yers, then, or do ye reckon I'm too Scottish fer yer taste?"

She'd expected him to ask whether she was too cowardly to dance with him or not, and she had an answer for that — she preferred not to make a public stir. But he hadn't worded it that way, and now she couldn't refuse him without looking like the aristocratic English snob he so obviously disdained. And she wasn't prepared to be disdained. Not by him. And aside from that, part of her did want to dance with him.

Silently she pulled the small dance card and pencil from her reticule and handed it over. Their fingers brushed, and even through her emerald-colored gloves she felt the heat of him. Out of the corner of her eye she noted that the rest of her family was chatting with several other late arrivals and introducing Winnie around. Or they were pretending to, anyway. *Wonderful.* Did they think that a man had indeed caught her eye, and that Ranulf MacLawry was that man?

"So this is you simply being you, is it?" she ventured in a low voice. "You're not making a statement or showing your contempt for my fellows?"

His grin deepened. "It's just clothes, lass." He patted himself on the chest, his silver buttons glittering. "All proper up top, and fun down below."

"Oh, good heavens." Because of that, now she couldn't help recalling every bawdy song and poem she'd ever heard about a Scotsman and what he wore beneath his kilt. Which, if the stories were true, was precisely nothing. "Write your name down, and return my dance card."

"Call me Ranulf again."

She took a deep breath, feigning annoyance. What was it about him that roiled up her insides? Everything logical said she

166

should want nothing to do with him, or his kilt, or his beastly manners. "Write your name down, Ranulf, and return my card. Better?"

His lifted his eyes, shadowed beneath dark lashes. "Most people dunnae speak t'me the way ye do, Charlotte," he said softly, scrawling something on the card and handing it back to her.

She didn't quite know how to take that. "Our sisters have become dear friends. There should be a certain honesty between us, don't you think?"

"Is that what we're calling it?" He studied her face, the scrutiny making her not uneasy, but unsettled. "Honestly then, Charlotte, I dunnae know what to make of ye. But I'm inclined to stay close by until I figure ye out."

"I'm not that complicated."

"I beg to differ."

Because she didn't want to meet his gaze any longer, and because people were beginning to notice her as well as him, Charlotte looked down at her dance card. And frowned. "You can't take both waltzes."

"I just did."

"It's not done, Glen— Ranulf."

"Then if any other man cares to claim ye fer one or the other of them, he can come and try to take ye." His smile dove into something devilish and delicious. "Though that would likely mean a brawl."

So now he meant to use her own antipathy to violence to make her give in to something scandalous. Well. He could have the first waltz, then, but she would claim an aching head before the second one. That would eliminate both the scandal of waltzing with him twice, and the need for anyone to brawl to prevent it. Not that anyone was likely to fight for her favor; ladies without beaux seldom had champions. Especially when they'd reached her age.

"You should go claim a dance from Winnie while she still has one," Charlotte suggested when he seemed inclined to remain standing there in front of her.

He lifted his head to glance over toward where his sister and Jane both stood surrounded by young men. Briefly his expression became alarmed, then settled back into one of slightly amused arrogance. Ranulf took a step past her, then paused to lean down. "I think ye may be a witch, Charlotte Hanover," he murmured in her ear, "because only if I were bewitched would I forget my own duties."

Before she could conjure a response to that, he strode over to take his sister's card right out of Lord William Duberry's hand. And Lord William, not known for his patience or his even temper, simply allowed it. Likewise, now that he'd left her side, other men came crowding in to claim dances from her. Most of them she refused, of course, with a smile and a verbal nudge toward the other, younger ladies, but it was . . . pleasant to be asked.

"You glitter like emeralds tonight, Lady Charlotte."

The cool, careful tone caught her attention at once. Inwardly cursing, Charlotte turned around to face the man who'd spoken. "Lord Berling. What a pleasant surprise."

He lifted an eyebrow. "A surprise that I would attend an event that everyone else in Mayfair wouldn't miss?" The earl sent a glance over his shoulder. "Ah. A surprise that I would appear after being growled at by the barbarian Highlander. Between you and me, my lady, he growls at everyone." He shook his head, clucking his tongue at the same time. "It must be wearying, to be so defiant about everything. I almost feel sorry for him. I *do* feel sorry for his sister, trying to have a pleasant time while he strides about flinging men away from her."

"Did you grow up in the Highlands, my lord?"

"Heavens, no," Berling responded, his brow dropping again as he scowled. "Why do you ask?"

Charlotte shrugged, surprised to realize on whose side she stood — and that it wasn't that of the reasonable-sounding earl. "You seem to be very well acquainted with Lord Glengask."

"The Gerdens side of the family has land up there," he explained with a smile. He wasn't at all ill-looking, even if there was something she didn't quite like about his eyes. "We spent the autumn there on occasion," he continued, "and I do like to look in on my holdings from time to time." He lifted her dance card from her hand. "I hadn't realized that *your* family was acquainted with the MacLawrys."

So now it was her turn to attempt to minimize the Hanovers' connection to the MacLawrys. It would likely be wise to do so, if even half of what Ranulf had told her was true. There were times, though, that she prided herself on being true rather than wise. "My mother was dear friends with Eleanor MacLawry," she said, "and Janie and Rowena have corresponded over the years. We were delighted she was able to

170

come down to London for her Season."

"I see. Lady Rowena's civilized enough, I suppose. But you'd be wise to keep your distance from the brothers."

A chill crept up Charlotte's spine. "And why is that?"

Slowly he handed her card back. "Because they're outspoken and stubborn and refuse to keep up with the changes in the world. It's a dangerous combination, my lady, and people around them tend to get hurt."

Oh, dear. She glanced down at her card as he vanished back into the crowd. He'd written his name by the evening's second quadrille — the one immediately after the first waltz. Which meant that Ranulf would have to hand her over to Berling.

If she wanted to keep the peace, evidently she was going to have to work a miracle to do so. The easiest solution would be simply to leave — immediately. Charlotte looked over at Ranulf, who was currently writing his name on Jane's card. Half the women present at the soiree seemed to have found urgent business on that side of the room, as well.

They all wanted to dance with him, and she could hardly blame them. He could say she'd bewitched him or some such nonsense, but there did seem to be . . . something drawing them together. Because otherwise she couldn't explain why she'd already decided to remain and dance at least one waltz with him.

CHAPTER SIX

If Ranulf had been of a mind to share his — or someone else's — bed after the soiree, it would have been a simple thing to manage. As he walked over to the refreshment table one young lady even blocked his path to give him her name, her address, and to tell him which upstairs window she would leave open later that night. It was all done behind the cover of her ivory fan, but she said it, nonetheless.

Fortunately for all the English lasses, and likely for him, he had no intention of entangling himself in their pretty ribbons and well-manicured nails. He took a swallow of the whisky he'd liberated from a footman's tray, eyeing the dance floor over the rim on his glass. Well, perhaps there was an English lass he wanted in his bed, but that wouldn't be happening tonight.

He didn't think he'd ever seen anything as exquisite as Charlotte looked this evening.

The emerald of her gown chased all the brown from her hazel eyes, and the pearls and gold chain in her golden hair glinted like starlight. She'd piqued his curiosity and his interest almost from the moment he'd set eyes on her. But now, tonight, his thoughts were more physical and more difficult to ignore.

He couldn't be the only one to notice her, but in the evening's first four dances she'd partnered with her father, that Henning fellow, a bent-shouldered lad who looked enough like her mother that he had to be a relative, and now an older man whose jolly wife used a cane and currently sat in a chair against the wall, cheering every time the couple rounded to her side of the room.

Finishing off the glass, he set it on a passing tray and signaled for another. The country dance had already been going on for ten minutes. One silver-haired woman had fainted, and two other couples had left the dance floor and sought chairs. It was still tamer than a clan gathering; until someone had gotten bloody, it wasn't a party.

When his uncle walked past for the third time since the dance had begun, Ranulf relented. The problem with spending so little time out of the Highlands was that he wasn't as well acquainted with the extended clan members of those families who'd relocated themselves southerly. And his uncle would be, however questionable his judgment. "Myles," he said, as his uncle crossed the ballroom yet again.

The viscount stopped. "I'm not here to intrude, Ranulf. I was invited. I merely didn't want my presence to surprise you."

"I'm nae asking ye to leave." He backed closer to one side of the room, and his uncle followed. "I know the redheaded lout, the one in the brown coat, is Berling's younger brother." With his chin he indicated the burly fellow from the earlier encounter at the park.

"Yes. Dermid Gerdens. He's not the most brilliant of men, and he has a short temper on top of that. Not a pleasant combination."

"And the thin fellow by the fire has the chin of Campbell." The otter from the park still wore black, and still looked just as oily.

His uncle moved closer. "You have a good eye, lad. That's Charles Calder, old William Campbell's grandson. I saw two of his cousins off in the gaming room earlier." He accepted a glass of wine from one of the wandering footmen and took a generous swallow. "In other words, Ranulf, you are badly outnumbered here tonight."

175

"I promised Rowena that I wouldnae make trouble."

"Ah. You've an interesting way of going about that, then." Myles flicked a finger at one of the buttons on Ranulf's sleeve. "Not that you exactly blend in with London Society, anyway."

Why the hell did everyone keep seeing the need to point that out? "This is formal attire for any fancy Highland party. Ye know that. And the lot of ye here must've seen a piper before, at least. I've nae idea what's so bloody shocking." He had meant to be as much himself as he could possibly manage, but he'd actually expected to be shunned, not mobbed by females.

"Mm-hm. Since you're speaking to me I won't argue that you know precisely what's so bloody shocking."

"Aye. If the Bruce had known the Sasannach could be so easily overset by a bare-arsed Scotsman, we might have marched down through York naked and saved all the bloodshed."

Myles snorted, then recovered himself enough to frown again. "You're generally more cautious than this, Ranulf."

Myles moved against the wall beside him, so they were both facing the crowded ballroom. And as much as Ranulf hated to admit that London Society had him in over his head, it was pleasant to have another set of eyes to watch for trouble.

"So why don clan colors with enemies all around?" Ranulf finished, then scowled. "I blame the lass."

Myles frowned as well. "What lass?"

"The emerald one."

"The . . ." His uncle searched the dance floor. "Lady Charlotte Hanover?"

"Aye. She said if I didnae't like being looked at sideways, I shouldnae try so hard nae to be English." He finished off the second whisky. "Acted like a poor-mannered schoolboy, I did." And the why of it all continued to elude him. God above, she aggravated him.

Beside him, his uncle stood very still. Likely he worried that a cross word would have him drummed from the family permanently. How odd that Myles chose his words so carefully, when the lass with the sunshine hair didn't seem to feel the need to curb her tongue at all. Of course he would never strike a woman regardless of what insult she handed him, but it was more than that. It was something about *her,* in particular, that sent him spinning off balance.

"Are you dancing this evening?" Myles asked.

"Aye, with Rowena and the Hanover lasses."

"Ah."

Ranulf glanced at his uncle. " 'Ah,' what?" Yes, he was the chief of Clan MacLawry and a marquis, but it would be . . . pleasant on occasion not to have to pull words out of people like teeth.

"It's only that if you dance with a select few ladies, you may start the wags thinking you've a particular . . . affection for one of them."

"Well, I do! Rowena's my blasted sister."

"I mean the other two. And you may also give the impression that you have a certain disdain for this Society."

"Which I d—"

"Which could affect which other young ladies are willing to or are permitted to befriend Winnie."

That nonsense again. With a brief curse in Gaelic that would have had the ponsy blue bloods around him blushing if they'd understood it, Ranulf left the refuge by the wall. A few delicate lasses tried to catch his eye, but their eagerness made him shudder. Finally he spied the round girl from the dress shop, standing close by her worried-looking mother.

"Miss Florence?" he intoned.

She turned scarlet as she faced him. "Yes, my lord."

"Would ye care to finish off this dance with me, lass?"

"I . . . Yes. That would be splendid."

Ranulf held out his hand, and she placed her fingers in his. They shook a mite, but hopefully she was sturdy enough to make it through the remainder of the boisterous country dance. He moved them smoothly into the loose line, let her go, bowed and turned, and caught her up again.

"This is splendid of you, Lord Glengask," she said as they stepped through the middle of the dance and down to the end again.

"Why is that?"

"I . . . I don't seem to be a favored dance partner, is all," she returned, ducking her head. "Mama says it's my freckles. I scrub them with lemon juice every night, but it doesn't seem to make any difference."

"In the Highlands we say a lass with freckles is sun-kissed. It's a blessing, and naught to be ashamed of."

Light green eyes gazed up at him hopefully. "Truly?"

"Aye." He nodded, hoping he hadn't somehow gotten himself betrothed by being kind to her. "Truly."

"That's so nice. Lord Stephen Hammond

said I had the shape and skin of an orange."

Well, that was a dastardly thing to say to any woman. "I'd wager this Hammond has the brains of an orange," he retorted, and she chuckled.

Thankfully the dance ended before she could begin telling him that she would enjoy seeing the Highlands and would he show her about. Ranulf joined in the applause and returned her to her mother, then escaped as swiftly as he was able.

Charles Calder, the Campbell's grandson, still stood by the fire, as if he couldn't catch enough heat to warm his bony frame. Berling had been dancing, but luckily for the earl it had been in the other line of dancers. If the man had so much as touched Rowena's hand, he would lose his own.

"That was a very nice thing you did," Charlotte's voice came, and she wrapped a hand around his sleeve.

Ranulf looked down at her, ignoring the skitter in his chest. "I beg yer pardon?"

"Dancing with Florence Breckett. It was very nice of you." She angled her chin back to where he'd parted from the stout lass. When he followed her gaze, a half-dozen young ladies, including two of her yammering cousins, surrounded her, all of them talking excitedly and sending glances in his direction.

"That. Oh. Aye. I'm a nice man."

She snorted, covering the sound with a polite cough. "We've a few minutes before the waltz, and I am desperately in need of some fresh air. Will you accompany me out to the balcony?"

"I cannae leave Rowena with no one to watch over her," he returned, the sharp pang of regret he felt at having to say the words startling him a little.

"She's talking to your uncle. And I happen to know that the man who'll be claiming her for the waltz is Robert Jenner, a very nice young man whose uncle is in the prime minister's cabinet."

"Ye have it all figured oot, then," Ranulf commented, sending a last glance in Rowena's direction before he allowed Charlotte to guide him toward the tall windows on the far side of the room. He'd have been easier standing directly beside — or in front of — his sister and demanding the credentials of every man who approached her, but she would never forgive that. Given Myles's familiarity with his fellows, she was likely better off in her uncle's company, anyway.

Either that, or he was grasping for reasons he could go walking thirty feet away with Charlotte Hanover. He would have either of his brother's heads if they went off and left Rowena as he was doing, but he kept walking. The lass could lead him over a cliff and he'd likely follow. Given what he was and what she was, the fall over the cliff seemed highly probable, anyway. Ranulf lowered his gaze to her swaying hips and remained on her heels.

A handful of people stood out on the wide balcony, while another dozen or so wandered the gardens below. The air smelled like rain and horseshit, which was still more pleasant than the heavy, hanging aroma of dozens of French perfumes mingling inside.

"I am not trying to bewitch you," Charlotte said into the relative quiet.

He grinned at the annoyed, matter-of-fact tone. "I ken that. If ye were, ye'd be nicer to me."

Her hazel eyes, darker now in the torchlight, narrowed. "Why is it that when I'm trying to be pleasant and helpful you argue with me, and when I'm telling you not to be ridiculous, you're amused?"

"I'm a conundrum."

She scowled. "Oh, never mind, then."

Ranulf put a hand on her shoulder before she could turn her back on him. "Ye're a puzzle to me as well, ye know," he said, keeping his voice low.

"Am I?" she returned, her smile a bit forced and brittle to his eyes. "It isn't intentional."

He moved in closer to her, taking his hand from her shoulder only to run a finger down her gloved arm to her wrist. Beneath his touch he felt her shiver, and he hoped it was from him rather than the cool evening. "And why is that?" he asked. "Why do ye dance only with old family friends and fools?"

She held very still, her gaze set on the stone railing by her elbow. "I don't know what you're talking about, or what you're implying. I'm not doing anything improper. And I've danced with you."

"Aye, I'm the exception, likely because I bullied ye into it," he conceded. "And of course ye've nae done a damned improper thing. Nor have ye ever, most likely. So why aren't all the young bucks chasing after ye with their tongues hanging oot?"

"Well, that's a fine image." Her shoulders lowered a fraction. "They don't chase after me because I'm five-and-twenty. Because I had a Season and found a beau, and then I spent a year in mourning."

"Ye're dead then, are ye?" Over her head he noted the last of the guests leaving the balcony as the orchestra inside began playing a few sour notes in preparation for the waltz.

Charlotte faced him straight on, what might have been a rueful smile briefly touching her mouth. She didn't feel sorry for herself; he had to grant her that. "No, I'm not dead, sir, but I am firmly on the shelf. This is my sister's Season. I am not going to compete with her for the attention of some young man looking to be struck by Cupid's ar—"

Ranulf kissed her. *Firmly on the shelf, my arse,* he thought, the heat of her sinking into him. He nibbled at her lower lip, tasting Madeira and desire. When her arms swept around his shoulders, he placed his hands around her waist and lifted, sitting her on the wide stone railing.

Once their mouths met, his mind stopped yelling at him to leave her be, to walk away. He knew what entangling himself with a proper English lass could mean, but his body refused to go beyond knowing that he wanted her. Badly.

Her soft moan that made him hard; perhaps wearing a kilt hadn't been the wisest decision tonight, though not for any reason of fashion. His grip on her waist firmed, but then her mouth stilled. Abruptly she shoved against his chest. Covering his annoyance at being denied, Ranulf lifted his head a fraction, their lips parting.

"Stop that," she ordered, her voice breathless and unsteady.

"I already did." With slow regret he shifted to set her feet back on the ground again. "Seems t'me ye have the wrong of it," he drawled, wanting another glass of whisky to wash the intoxicating taste of her from his mouth.

"The wrong of what?" Charlotte demanded, brushing a hand down her skirt even though her insides felt far more disheveled than her outside must have looked. *Good heavens.*

"Ye're nae dead, or put away on a shelf. Not even nearly so." He took her chin in his fingers, lifting her face up so she had to meet his gaze. "I think ye want me, lass," he continued in a soft murmur.

She frowned, attempting an air of defiance when what she truly wanted was for him to kiss her again. "Yes, I believe I've mentioned that I have a penchant for mannerless, forward barbarian devils. I gave you no leave to kiss me."

His smile nearly turned her insides molten. "Next time ye will."

"You overestimate your charms, Ranulf MacLawry."

185

He leaned a breath closer. "Do I?" he countered in his soft brogue. "Then why do ye still have a hold of me, Charlotte Hanover?"

She blinked, uncoiling her fingers from his lapel. "I . . ."

"Conjure up yer lie later. They've begun the waltz, and I want my hands on ye again. With everyone watching."

Charlotte tried to find both her breath and her scattered wits again. When she nudged at his shoulders, the lean mountain gave way, letting her move past him toward the ballroom door. "It's just a dance, my lord."

"All of life's a dance, my bonny lass."

That seemed a very poetical thing for him to say, but if she stopped to argue that it was out of character they would miss the waltz. And whatever she might pretend, she wanted his hands on her, as well.

Perhaps she had a fever and was delirious, because none of what she felt made the least bit of sense. Lord Glengask was exactly the sort of hotheaded man she'd had her fill of with James Appleton. When James courted her she'd felt . . . pleased, that so earnest a man had set himself after her. And then she realized that earnest had very little to do with good-humored, and what a flaw that had been. Now, though, whatever lesson she knew she'd learned, a single kiss — or rather two kisses now — from Ranulf sent her spinning, not certain where her feet were or if she wanted to find the ground again.

Inside the grand ballroom half a hundred couples had begun the waltz. In one smooth move Ranulf had her around the waist, took her hand in his, and swept her into the dance. The idea that the well-muscled Scotsman was nearly naked from the waist down but for a knee-length scrap of black and gray and red wool and a single pin to keep it from flapping open felt nearly as intoxicating as did the dance itself. And the way the other women looked at him with such . . . open lust, and the way they eyed her with only slightly better concealed envy — it baffled and aroused her all at the same time.

"What are your intentions, Ranulf?" she asked after a moment, keeping her voice pitched low.

He lifted an eyebrow. " 'Intentions'?" he repeated, a slow smile once more on his sensuous mouth.

"Yes. You've kissed me twice now and said that you want me."

"Those are my intentions. To kiss ye, and to have ye."

A blush warmed her cheeks. Had she ever

had a similar conversation with James? If so, she couldn't recall it — and it seemed the sort of thing a body would remember. "And after that?" she pursued. "You know I am the daughter of an earl, and a female without an interest in causing a scandal."

"So ye've said." His amused expression faded as he no doubt sensed another argument approaching.

"So I have," she agreed, taking a breath and trying to push away the very pleasant sensation of being in his arms. "And if you say you've come to Mayfair looking for a bride, I shall call you a liar to your face. You've made your . . . contempt for the Sasansack very clear over the past few days."

"Sasannach," he corrected, his brogue making the word sound prettier than she knew it must be. "Nae, I've seen what the Highlands does to a proper and delicate English lady. I willnae make the same mistake my own father did."

Her first thought was to inform him that while she had her sensibilities and her belief in right and wrong, she wasn't particularly delicate. But in the next moment it occurred to her that in comparison to him, perhaps she *was* delicate. After all, he spoke of murders and fistfights as if they were done over breakfast. And that was something she would not — could not — tolerate. She knew firsthand what pain and heartache such things wrought, and to willingly place herself in the middle of a barbarians' feud — it was simply unthinkable.

Given that, wondering what his father's mistake had been where his mother was concerned, wondering what had killed the "delicate" daughter of a baron, seemed a waste of her time. Ranulf's reasoning aside, they simply wouldn't suit.

"Ye've nothing else to say, then?"

"What should I say? You've just told me you want to bed me while having no intention of marrying me. I decline your . . . offer, sir."

Blue eyes flashed. "Do ye, now?"

"You've offered me nothing but ruination and an exile from a life I find quite enjoyable," she retorted, affronted that her refusing such a base offer — pleasurable and unforgettable though it likely would have been — would offend *him.* What about her, for heaven's sake?

"So ye like being yer sister's nanny and stepping out to dance only when an even number of couples is required?"

Ha. "Excuse me, but what are you doing here in London but serving as your sister's nanny?"

189

He glared at her for a long moment, his grip on her so firm that she didn't think she would be able to pull free of him if she'd wanted to. Even so, she wasn't afraid of him. Perhaps she should have been, but she knew with a certainty that Ranulf MacLawry would never injure her — except, perhaps, with a few choice words.

"Faic tùsan," he finally muttered.

"And what does that mean?" she demanded.

"It means that I find ye maddening."

"Likewise, Lord Glengask. And as I've heard what you want of me and I've refused you, you will henceforth stop flirting with me and attempting to kiss me."

A muscle in his jaw jumped. "In response to that, I say that a lass willnae order *me* to do anything. I also further say that ye've not convinced me that ye find my touch distasteful. In fact, I think ye enjoy having me aboot to argue with. I think ye were bored before Rowena and I arrived on yer doorstep."

For a man so caught up in his own rivalries and troubles, he'd done a fair job of assessing the last year of her life. Because she *did* feel that she'd become not Janie's nanny, but her chaperone. And without plans for her own future to occupy her thoughts, she *had* felt . . . bored. Listless, finished. Dead, as he'd said. And she hadn't felt that way over the past few days. Frustrated, annoyed, aroused, amused, flustered — but not bored.

"Whatever state I might have been in," she returned, "I've not lost hold of my sanity."

To her surprise, his lips curved upward, reminding her all over again of his very splendid kiss. Kisses. "I dunnae think we'll settle this impasse here, lass. It requires more . . . private conversation."

"I am not —"

"If ye tell me now, honestly and to my face, that ye wish not to exchange a single further word or touch or glance with me, I'll honor that and make myself scarce from ye. If not, I'll call on ye tomorrow at noon, and ye can attempt to improve my view of London. Or to dissuade me from wishing to spend time in yer company fer the purpose of getting beneath yer skirts. Whichever ye choose."

Charlotte took a deep breath. She wasn't certain that honesty played into it, but logically she should open her mouth to say that she wished him gone from her life. Of course if she did so then he would likely conjure up an excuse to go back on his word to Rowena and immediately remove the two of them back to Glengask. And that would be terribly unfair to Winnie, quite aside from the state of her own skirts.

"There now," he murmured after a moment. "That's the first time I've been pleased not to hear yer voice, Charlotte."

"It doesn't mean anything but that I don't wish to see an injustice done to Winnie because I naysayed you."

He nodded almost imperceptibly. "That's what we'll call it, then."

It hardly seemed like him to concede just when he'd won, but Charlotte was relieved enough at having a moment to think that she decided not to question his motives. Or her own, for that matter.

When they'd first met — heavens, had it only been four days ago? — she'd thought him boorish and arrogant and abrupt. What she hadn't realized then and that she saw now was his cleverness, or his humor and a surprising amount of charm. That deep brogue of his certainly didn't hurt, either. None of that, though, explained why she hadn't simply slapped him and stalked off the dance floor when he'd proposed ruining her because it would be pleasurable.

Except that she was fairly certain she *did* know why she still swayed in his arms. As she'd said, she was five-and-twenty. Even with James's death, if she'd truly wanted to marry she could have — would have — done so before now. There were times, especially when Jane had begun planning her wardrobe and her Season and all her romantic conquests, that she'd felt passed by.

"If ye keep wearing that thoughtful look, I'm likely to kiss ye again," Ranulf murmured.

"In front of everyone?" she countered, more amused than truly alarmed.

"Aye. That's how we do it in Scotland," he returned with a grin. "Sweep a fine lass off her feet and give her a kiss so everyone else knows ye've claimed her."

" 'Claimed her'?" she repeated faintly, as three things happened at once: she remembered who'd claimed the next dance with her; the waltz ended; and she caught sight of Donald Gerdens walking toward her — them — from the other end of the dance floor. *Damnation.* "Ranulf, I need t—"

"I believe this dance is mine, Lady Charlotte," the earl said smoothly, stopping in front of them.

Ranulf looked at him. Silently, steadily, like a great lion coolly sizing up a gazelle. "Ye gave him a dance, lass?" he asked, not shifting his gaze an inch.

"It's just a quadrille," she said, not certain

why she felt the need to minimize the thing. A dance was a dance, and it was no more significant than the handful of minutes it last —

A fist shot out before she could finish her thought. Catching Berling squarely on the chin, it sent the earl reeling. Before he could regain his balance, and in a queer way that seemed so slow it couldn't be real, Ranulf hit him again with the other fist on the other side of his face.

Charlotte shook herself out of her stupor. "Stop it!" she screamed, grabbing Ranulf's forearm. It felt like solid, inflexible iron beneath her grip. "Stop punching him at once!"

Lord Evanstone and three of his footmen raced over. At the same moment several male guests stepped in, lifting the stumbling Berling to his feet and shoving at Glengask. A few feet away Miss Florence Breckett fainted into the arms of her dance partner, and they both fell to the highly polished floor.

Berling shrugged off his helpers, and with a red half smile unsteadily straightened his coat. "You are a devil, Glengask," he drawled.

"Aye. And ye're a bloody poacher."

"Ha." Abruptly the earl lunged forward.

Striking out with his coiled fist, he caught Ranulf in the left eye.

"Och, now it's a party!" Glengask threw off the men hanging on to his arms and stepped forward again.

"No!" So angry she could scarcely force the word out, Charlotte stepped between the two men. "I don't care what your private quarrels may be," she snapped. "This is not the time or the place to settle them. Nor is it the means by which gentlemen conduct their affairs." It was all about their stupid, useless pride, and she refused to see men battle over who was more infatuated with themselves.

"Hear, hear," Lord Evanstone grunted. "I'm asking both of you to leave my home. If I have to ask twice, I will see you thrown out."

For a breathless moment Charlotte thought Ranulf would ignore the threat. Or worse, that he would consider it a challenge. His gaze ignored everything else in the room in favor of her. Finally and wordlessly, not bothering to wipe the trickle of blood from his face where Berling's ring had cut his cheek, he inclined his head, turned on his heel, and left the room. The other guests parted before him like the Red Sea before Moses.

Looking less splendid and holding a palm to his bloody lip, Lord Berling followed a moment later, several of his friends exiting with him. That left her alone, standing in the middle of the room with everyone staring at her. The edges of her vision began to dim, and she drew in a ragged breath.

"Charlotte," her father's welcome voice came, and his strong hand cupped her elbow. "Let's find you a chair, my brave girl."

She sagged against him. "I don't feel brave. I feel ill."

"You stepped into the middle of a feud and stopped two men from pummeling each other," he countered in a louder voice than seemed necessary, considering that he was close enough to wrap an arm around her shoulder.

Then she realized what he was doing — making that brawl about something other than her. "They nearly came to blows this morning in Hyde Park," she returned. "Over sheep or grazing land or some such thing."

A moment later the music began again for the quadrille, and some people thankfully decided to take the floor rather than continue staring at her. Slowly she sat in one of the chairs by the wall, her father on one side of her, and her mother abruptly on the other.

"Are you well, Charlotte?" her mother asked, taking both her hands and squeezing them. "Do you wish to leave?"

"Heavens no," she forced out. "Though I do think I'm finished with dancing for the evening."

"Quite understandable. That man is a brute."

Of course the countess meant Glengask; he'd struck the first blow. But she'd already had more than a sneaking suspicion that Berling had known it would happen — had wanted it to happen, and that was precisely why he'd asked her to dance that particular quadrille with him.

Yes, perhaps she'd thought the two men would have words. And she couldn't quite bring herself to believe that Lord Berling had intended to be punched. It was more likely that he'd anticipated an argument, which he figured to win.

As for Ranulf, he'd almost seemed to enjoy the fisticuffs. He'd certainly failed to impress her, however, and he'd done even worse at keeping an eye on his sister. Belatedly she lifted her head to look for Winnie, only to find her out on the dance floor with her uncle. Rowena didn't look happy, but she *was* dancing. And that was good; if she continued to represent herself as the "civilized" MacLawry sibling, she might escape censure for her brother's actions.

Some kind soul brought Charlotte a glass of wine, and she sipped it gratefully. Stupid man. Whatever despicable things had happened in the Highlands, this was London. And one did not brawl in the proper homes in London. If he hadn't kissed her earlier, she was fairly certain she would be hating him at this moment. Instead, she mostly felt angry. And a little sad, for reasons she refused to consider. Not now.

After the quadrille Jane, along with Winnie and Lord Swansley, joined them at the side of the room. "You were a lioness, Char," her sister said. " 'Stop that punching,' and they did."

Rowena seemed even more surprised. "He backed down," she half whispered, her brogue stronger than it had been for better than a day. "Ye put a hand out, and he backed down. I'd never have dared."

Myles Wilkie nodded. "He's a crafty man, your brother," he commented.

"Crafty?" Charlotte retorted. "How clever is it to begin a brawl? That's precisely the opposite of crafty, I would think."

"It's very clever, if you're outnumbered

by your enemies and you want them to know you're not at all troubled by that fact. When Berling left, he took his allies with him. How could he plot his revenge, otherwise? But when Ran left, he took all his rivals with him, leaving Rowena safe under our protection and with nary an enemy in sight."

Charlotte looked at him. Had Ranulf seen Berling write his name on her dance card? Had he predicted the earl would try to force a confrontation? If so, why hadn't he said anything? Why had he simply allowed her to be put in the middle as the apparent bone of contention?

Even as she wondered that, though, she knew the answer. He hadn't said anything to her in advance because she wouldn't have tolerated it. She would never have agreed to dance with either of them, and she certainly — well, more than likely — would never have gone out to the balcony with him and kissed him. Even if going out there had been her idea, and even if she hadn't been looking for an excuse to kiss him on the chance that he wouldn't kiss her first. Oh, but he had.

"I don't care what he was doing," his sister said, tears in her eyes. "It was terrible and loud and oh . . ." Winnie stomped her foot.

"I shan't forgive him. And I am not going back to Scotland. Ever. He might well have ruined everything, just because he has to control everything but the sun's rise."

"I'm mad at him too, Winnie," Charlotte agreed, though "mad" wasn't nearly a descriptive enough word. "And I have a few choice words to say to him, when next we meet." If he still dared to call on her tomorrow, she intended to tell him precisely what she thought of him and his . . . method of solving problems at her expense.

And seeing him tomorrow would only be so she could yell at him. It had nothing to do with that look in his eyes when he'd ignored the rest of the world to gaze solely at her. And it had less still to do with the way her feet had literally and figuratively left the ground when he'd kissed her. Nothing to do with that, at all.

Chapter Seven

"Just leave it be, Ginger."

"But my lord, I have — there are ways to conceal blemishes."

Ranulf pulled the cravat from his valet's hands and finished knotting it himself. "It's nae a blemish; it's a black eye." He viewed the thin fellow in his dressing mirror. "Do ye think there's one body in Mayfair who doesnae know I have this?"

The valet lowered his head, flushing. "Well, I —"

"Then there's no point in hiding it, is there? Now fetch me that new coat and we'll see how bloody English I look in it."

The dark brown coat did fit quite well, and it gave his gray one a rest. In fact, with a dark green waistcoat and buckskin breeches and finished off with a pair of Hessian boots, he felt fairly well put together. And that was a good thing, because he needed every advantage he could get today.

Charlotte was likely to rip his head off after last night, anyway, and she wouldn't care about his reasons for any of it.

The fact that he looked forward to being chastised by a delicate English lass was in itself a surprise. With the exception of his brother Arran arguing over whether a new plan was likely to cause more trouble than it was worth, people didn't chastise him.

As he left his bedchamber with Fergus at his side, Owen met him at the top of the stairs. "Ye have letters from Lord Arran and Bear, both, m'laird," he said, holding them out. "I hope all's well at Glengask."

"As do I," Ranulf returned, taking both missives. "How are we for calling cards today?"

"Nary a one." The footman narrowed his eyes as he gestured at Ranulf's cheek. "I'm thinking yer sudden unpopularity has t'do with that."

"Aye, I reckon it does. Let me see to my correspondence, and have that phaeton brought 'round before noon." He paused halfway to his rented office. "And if ye catch scent of anything interesting, let me know."

"Could ye define 'interesting,' m'laird?"

"Men storming the house with muskets and torches would be interesting."

"Oh, aye, I'll keep an eye out fer that, then."

With a half grin Ranulf settled into his chair and opened Bear's letter first. In Munro's usual straightforward, good-humored words he read that half the clan had been wandering by Glengask, asking if anything was amiss and offering one and all to ride — or walk — down to London to help him fetch Rowena back. And Lachlan had offered again to make the journey, which might or might not be significant, but was at least interesting.

Arran's letter was, as he expected, more detailed, with the latest information about the weather and the growing herds of Highland cattle they'd been breeding, and a summary of the last month's expenses from the schools matched up against the profits of the new pottery manufacture. So far his experiment to prove that a clan working together could not only sustain itself but profit seemed to be showing itself sound. And the fact that the Colonies were filled with outcast Highlanders who hated Cheviot sheep and all they represented but longed for good Highland cattle and Highland tartans and pipes and plates and bowls could only continue to aid them.

Both of his brothers also offered again to

come south, as they had with every letter they sent. He set them both aside to answer later; he wasn't nearly foolish enough to arrive late to call on Charlotte. He'd said noon, and by God he would be there by noon.

"No torches or muskets," Owen reported from his post by the front door as Ranulf strolled into the foyer.

"That's something, then."

"And don't ye worry, m'laird. I'll put the boot to any Gerdens or Campbell as dares to show his face at yer doorstep."

Ranulf smiled. "I expect no less."

"Aye. And do give Lady Winnie our love, m'laird." Owen sighed. "I miss hearing her bonny laugh."

So did he. Settling for a nod, Ranulf walked out to the drive. Together he and Debny lifted Fergus onto the back perch of the phaeton where the liveried tiger was generally supposed to sit, and then he climbed into the high seat and sent the fine pair of bays into a trot. With both Debny and Peter riding alongside and his great horse of a hound perched behind him, he wasn't a sight easily missed. It was likely too early for Berling to come back at him with anything, but he meant to keep an eye out, regardless. His father would be the last

MacLawry who was ever caught unaware.

Charlotte stood on the shallow granite steps of Hanover House when he turned up the short, semicircular drive. He didn't know if her being out there boded good or ill, but he couldn't deny the . . . satisfaction he felt deep in his chest at seeing her. All wrong for him she might be, but his heart sped at the mere sight of her, regardless. No, she wasn't fit for the Highlands. But he wasn't in the Highlands at the moment, and he was a damned red-blooded man who enjoyed women. And she looked very fine.

"I wasn't certain ye'd let me near the house," he said, waiting for Debny to take charge of the horses before he hopped down from the seat, "much less wait out of doors fer me."

"It was a close decision," she returned. "And I'm not going trotting about London with you in a high-perch phaeton so that everyone thinks either that last night was about me, or that what you did is in any way acceptable behavior."

Now that was closer to the reaction he'd expected. "What makes ye think last night's tussle wasnae about ye?" As he spoke, he closed the distance between them, his body reminding him that a kiss would stop her mouth.

"I did, at the beginning. And then your uncle pointed out how effectively you'd cleared the room of your enemies."

Uncle Myles, helping again. Ranulf stashed that bit of information away for later contemplation. "That's only because cowards cling together." He stopped on the bottommost step so that they were eye-to-eye. "Shall I point out some things to ye, then?"

She shook her head. "No. Now it's my turn to point out some things to you, Ranulf."

Folding his arms across his chest, he nodded. "Enlighten me aboot my spurious Scottish ways, then."

"Aha!" Charlotte jabbed a finger into his chest. "*That* is your problem."

He cocked his head. "What, that I'm Scottish? Ye and yer Sasannach friends are the ones named us devils. I am —"

"Stop it," she cut in, the fact that she'd interrupted at all surprising him into silence.

Banter was one thing. But now she thought to stop him from talking? "What, then?"

"I looked some things up. The Battle of Culloden was seventy-three years ago. I daresay that most — if not every — man who fought there, English or Scottish, is long dead."

She kept tapping her finger into his chest as she spoke, though he wasn't certain whether it was because she was making a point or because she wanted to touch him. He preferred the latter explanation, and kept silent for that reason.

"I know what you're going to say," she continued. "That Culloden was only the beginning of the most recent troubles, that the English tried to rob you of the right to wear kilts, to play the bagpipes, even to arm yourselves."

"Very well," he said, the list of wrongs beginning to make him lose his sense of humor. "Let's say I did mention all that. I suppose ye have a point t'make aboot it?"

"Yes. You've gotten those rights back. And I know that most of the other clans have fallen, that for a great many of your peers bringing in the sheep was the only way to earn an income. And that they chose the sheep and the grazing land and their immediate families over the welfare and survival of their own clans."

"That's a very nice history lesson ye've provided me, lass, but I can tell ye it wasnae necessary. Ye read aboot it in yer books. I lived it. I still am living it."

"I know that," she snapped back, then blew out her breath. "I wanted you to know that I'm aware of the recent history of the Highlands."

"Shall I give ye a prize, then?"

"Oh, be quiet." Scowling, she lifted her finger away from him. "I need to pace. Come into the garden with me."

"O'course. What sane man would refuse the offer to be privately yelled at in more detail?" With a grimace he turned to whistle for Fergus. "Peter, go discover what Rowena's up to today, and keep an eye on 'er."

"Aye, m'laird."

Following Charlotte, his gaze drawn once more to her swaying hips beneath soft green and yellow sprigged muslin, Ranulf decided the mild English weather and the not-so-mild English beauty before him must have pushed him completely into madness. He simply couldn't explain it, otherwise.

When she stopped, he nearly ran into her from behind. It wasn't like him to be so unaware of his surroundings, but even mad enough to spit — unless she also considered that to be doing physical violence — she continued to distract him. "Sit down," she said, pointing at the stone bench beneath a towering elm tree.

"I thought we were pacing."

"*I'm* pacing. You're listening."

This was coming very close to being

beyond his ability to tolerate, but he took a slow breath and dropped onto the bench. "Go on, then."

True to her word, she walked to the row of roses and then back past him to a chest-high hedge. "Very well." Finally she faced him again. "*You* are the problem, my lord. Since you've come to London, have you actually run across any Englishman — any at all — who haven't been kind and helpful to you?"

"I —"

"I'm not finished. Not everyone in Mayfair is my friend. I find some of these people . . . despicable and hateful and petty and small. My point being, they're just people. So when you ride in and start calling everyone Sasannach" — and this time she pronounced it very carefully and correctly — "you're doing them — and yourself — a disservice."

"So if I'm hearing ye correctly," he said slowly, using every ounce of self-control he possessed to keep his seat, "where we lay our heads doesnae matter to ye or to anyone else? A man's a saint or a devil depending on his own preference, and I've made myself a devil?"

"No. Well, yes and no. Of course some people hate others for . . . where they lay their heads, as you said. But if you don't stop being so suspicious and so angry at . . . everyone, you will be the cause of your own downfall."

"Hm. Fascinating." Slowly he stood. "Ye willnae mind, I assume, that while I consider yer wisdom I go collect my sister and remove her from this Sasannach household?"

She clenched her hands together. "Maddening," she muttered. "Your sister doesn't wish to speak to you. And last night she stated that she intends never to return to Scotland again."

Ranulf blinked. "What?" he growled, ice piercing his heart.

"I won't keep you from her, of course, but I suggest that you give her a day or two to remember how much she loves you and to forget what a spectacle you created last night." She curtsied. "Good day, my lord."

Ranulf turned on his heel and strode for the carriage drive. In his entire life, even when his father had been killed, even when Bear had been shot, he couldn't remember feeling such . . . intolerable frustration. He wanted to shout at the sky, he wanted to grab Charlotte and shake her, he wanted to kiss her senseless and bury himself deep inside her until she cried out in pleasure.

210

At the edge of the garden he stopped and turned around. "Does this mean ye've done with me, lass?"

He watched as her shoulders rose and fell. "I suppose that's up to you," she said slowly, and went around the back of the house.

When he reached the drive he hoisted Fergus up onto the main seat of the phaeton himself. "Debny, stay aboot here for a time and make certain Rowena's seen to. Have Peter inform Lord Hest that he'll be staying on here. I doubt Hest will object."

The groom looked puzzled. "Did someaught happen, m'laird?"

"Aye, someaught happened. But nothing to concern ye."

By concentrating on breathing and nothing else, Ranulf made it back to Tall House without exploding. With Debny still out he unharnessed the team and went to saddle Stirling himself. Standing about and waiting would have been intolerable, anyway. Evidently sensing his mood, Fergus stayed by the stable door and watched in silence.

At Glengask, as full as the house generally was, finding a moment of solitude was as simple as walking down the path to the river. Here he could be alone in an office or bedchamber, but it wasn't solitude. Servants lurked, and just beyond the wood and plaster walls a city seethed, all ears and tongues and spite.

Ranulf swung up on Stirling, ducked through the stable doors, and set off north at as fast a pace as he could manage. It seemed to take forever for the houses and then farms to thin, for the trees and glades to appear. Only then did he cut off the road, kneeing the gelding into a hard gallop.

On and on they went, until nothing lay around them for miles but scattered trees, streams, and meadows. He and the horse and the dog stopped, winded. And only then did he begin swearing, bellowing, ranting at the empty, overcast sky.

From the day he'd been born he'd carried the title of Earl of Dombray. From his earliest memories he'd known that he would one day be the Marquis of Glengask — and more significantly, the chief of Clan MacLawry. He hadn't expected to inherit it all at the age of fifteen, but he'd managed. He'd led his family, and his clan, and brought his cotters employment and the security of knowing they could remain on the land where they and their fathers and their father's fathers had been born.

In all that time, in all of his thirty-one years and in all the battles both literal and figurative he'd fought to protect his people, no one — *no one* — had ever spoken to him the way Charlotte Hanover just had. She'd put him on the rack, cracked his bones, and flayed him till he bled. And she'd done it with a smile and an apology, as if it were for his own good.

The rain that had been threatening since last evening finally let loose. Ranulf lifted his face to the sky, willing the chill wet to cool his raging temper. What damned nerve she had, to tell him *he* was the unreasonable one, to say he created trouble where there was none, to insist that no one alive had done the harms he railed against and that that thereby made his anger unfitting and dangerous to those he loved.

And then at the end, when she'd so coolly informed him that Rowena wanted nothing more to do with him or with Scotland . . . she'd pierced him to the heart. He'd spent his damned *life* protecting his family and his people, in exchange for what? Failure? Being called a fool?

For a long moment he closed his eyes, letting the rain run down his face and seep into his skin. As his temper eased, one thing became clear; either he was wrong, or Charlotte was wrong.

In truth, he *had* spent very little time in England, and this was already the longest he'd ever stayed in London. He didn't so much know the English aristocracy as he knew *of* them. His mother had constantly flung them up as examples of what she wished her boys were — proper, mild, and above all, English. Of course he'd hated even the idea of the Sasannach nobles.

When Eleanor killed herself and her brother Myles came to look after her orphaned children, Ranulf had detested the man for the way he spoke, the way he dressed, the way he'd insisted that Bear and Arran and Rowena learn the latest English dances and English literature and English rules and laws. Eventually he'd joined in as well, but only because he wanted to know his enemy as well as he possibly could.

His enemy. Aye, the English had done terrible things to the Highlanders, taking away bits and pieces of culture and pride every time the Scots pushed against the harness. His own grandfather, Angus MacLawry, had been killed at Culloden. Why, then, had his father seen fit to marry the most English of Englishwomen? Had it been to try to convince her to love the Highlands, or so that his children would have a sense of what it was to be English?

Finally he shook water from his eyes and turned Stirling south again, back toward

London. Damn Charlotte Hanover for making him question every point of his life, for making him wonder if he'd turned left when he'd been meant to turn right.

He needed to think, and he needed to plan. He could force his sister to return to Glengask, but he couldn't make her wish to be there. Ordering Charlotte to keep her opinions about him to herself wouldn't cause her to change them — if he could order her to do anything. A bit of persuasion would seem to be in order, but first he would have to see about persuading himself.

Evidently he needed to make the acquaintance of London and the *haute ton* before he could decide whether they were actually worth knowing or not. And he needed to decide if he was willing to risk becoming better acquainted with Charlotte, given that in five days she'd already managed to upend his life. In a fortnight she could well kill him — unless she were correct in all this, and meant to save him from himself.

When he returned to Tall House, Owen and Debny were standing on the front portico, ignoring the rain and arguing over whether they needed to go out searching for him or not.

"M'laird," the footman said, relief showing in every muscle of his stocky body. "Ye had us near frighted to death. Debny should never have left ye to go oot on yer own."

"I didnae —"

Ranulf silenced them both with a look. "Debny did as I asked him to. End of discussion."

"Fine, fine. But ye and Fergus are wetter than the ocean."

"Dry off Fergus," Ranulf returned, heading for the stairs so he could change his clothes. "And then go find that solicitor — what was his name? — and bring him here."

"Mr. Black?" Owen offered stiffly. "The soft fellow with the damp hands?"

"Aye. And don't insult him when ye've fetched him."

He couldn't see the look the two servants exchanged, but he could feel it. They could think him mad if they wished; for all he knew, he might be.

"Why am I fetching him, m'laird, if I might ask?"

"Ye may not."

Arran MacLawry took the letter Cooper, the butler, handed him and opened it as he reached the breakfast room. Ranulf generally wrote short, pointed letters, instructions about what needed doing and when, without much other flourish or description.

As he opened this missive, though, a second page fell to the floor, both pieces filled to the very edges with ink in their oldest brother's spare hand. At the first sentence he stopped in his tracks. "Munro!" he yelled. "Bear!"

A moment later his younger brother, half dressed and dark hair sticking out from one side of his head like a crazed weed, stumbled into the breakfast room. "What the devil's got into yer bonnet?" he demanded, dropping into a chair, thunking his head onto the table, and gesturing for coffee.

Arran cleared his throat. " 'Arran,' " he read aloud, " 'In future correspondence you'll find me at Gilden House, 12 Market Street, the residence I've purchased in London.' "

Munro's head shot up from the tabletop. "What? That's from Ranulf? He's bought a house? In London?"

"Aye. That's what he says."

"Why, in God's name?"

"Let me go on, will ye? To continue, 'Rowena has declared that she means never to return to Scotland. I may therefore be here for longer than we'd anticipated, until such time as I can persuade her otherwise.' "

" 'Persuade'?" Bear echoed, scowling. "Put her arse into a coach and drive her home, is more like."

"Evidently not."

"I wonder what Lach'll have to say about that. Yesterday he complained that Winnie didnae send him a letter."

That was interesting, Arran decided. "Wasnae he complaining that she wrote him every day?"

"Aye. He said she was too full of girlish glee, and now he wants to know what she's up to that keeps her from writing."

"She's up to refusing to come home. Tell him that, and see what he does."

"I'm nae certain I want to know." Bear grunted. "Ran wants a love match, but poor Lach's caught between his chief and a lass who's been chasing after him since she could walk." He shook his dark, disheveled head. "If Ranulf's nae dragging her home, then what's he up to?"

Arran perused the rest of the letter, three sides of closely written instruction, then sat down heavily at his brother's side. "He's gone mad."

"What else does he say?"

"That Berling's in London, along with the Campbells' grandson, that we should remain here, and that some lass named Charlotte is full of herself and needs a lesson or two as to why she shouldnae scold a

MacLawry."

Munro's brow furrowed. "Charlotte. Isn't she the other Hanover lass? Jane's sister or someaught?"

"I dunnae know. I didnae pay that much attention to it all." Now Arran was beginning to think he should have paid quite a bit more attention to what was happening in London. "Does any of this make sense to ye?"

"Nae. Let me see it."

Arran handed Munro the letter, watching as his younger brother read through it with much the same expression of confusion that he'd likely worn himself. "Did ye notice how many times he names this Charlotte?" he asked

"Aye," his brother returned. "More than he mentions Rowena." Bear pushed to his feet and handed the letter back. "Well, that settles it."

"Settles what?"

"I'm going to London."

Bloody hell. "Ye are not. Ran says we're to stay here."

"Someaught's afoot down there, and half the bastards we're looking out fer here are doon there. Ye can stay behind."

Arran took a breath. "Bear, ye need to stay here. I'll go."

"And why should ye be the one to —"

"He says Rowena's embarrassed by us. Who's more 'us' than anyone?"

Bear frowned. "I can behave."

"Ye gave her a saddle for her eighteenth birthday. And I'd wager the reason ye were still to bed at nearly noon is that ye're sharing a pillow with Flora Peterkin. Or is it Bethia Peterkin? If ye cannae keep yer own affairs straight, ye cannae expect to be of help to someone else. Especially not Ranulf."

"Fine, then." Bear slumped back into his chair. "Ye'd best see this straightened oot, Arran, or ye'll find me riding down on yer heels. Or I'll put a wee whisper in Lachlan's ear and turn him loose."

"I'll see to it." And he would also see who this Charlotte lass was, and discover why Ranulf couldn't seem to stop talking about her even when he clearly had more trouble than he could wish for on his hands.

Jane tugged Charlotte into the morning room and gestured at the floor. "Help," she said with a laugh.

She and Winnie had laid out every invitation they'd received, for breakfasts, luncheons, recitals, picnics, dinners, the theater, soirees, and even a proposed excursion in rowboats up the Thames. Seeing them all arranged by date and time like that, the sheer volume was stunning.

"What do you need help with?" she asked, reaching down to pet Una as the hound sat on her foot.

Winnie, on the far side of the stacks, pointed. "For the seventeenth we have one breakfast invitation, two for morning excursions, four luncheon invitations, three more for afternoon visits or shopping, and a soiree and an evening at the theater. What do we do?"

Charlotte looked from one of them to the other. Not for the first time she felt old, or at the least, jaded. Each year seeing the same people, some of them pairing off in marriage, but others — like her — simply growing older and smiling the same forced smiles and talking about how very young and silly the new crop of debutantes seemed to be, felt as heavy as lead in that moment. And she'd driven off the only man who'd showed any interest in her, even if his aim had been for the bed rather than the altar.

"Char?"

She shook herself. "Firstly, you need to ask Mama and Papa if there's an evening event they particularly want to attend — or to avoid. And then look to see if you're attending other events that same day or week with the same people, and choose which one you prefer." Bending down, she picked up a luncheon invitation. "This is a picnic with Lord Harold Onless," she said, stifling her scowl.

"Yes. He's very handsome," her sister said, fanning her face with one hand.

"And his second cousin is Donald Gerdens."

"What does that signify?" Winnie returned, her cheeks reddening. "There's Parliament that day, so Berling won't be at the picnic."

"Rowena, your brother wouldn't like it." Evidently she'd become a nanny after all, and to both young ladies.

"I don't care what my brother thinks," Winnie said, too shrilly. "I haven't even seen him for a week."

Charlotte hadn't, either, but she'd been listening. And she'd heard rumors, rumblings that didn't make much sense. "You said you didn't want to see him. He's honoring your wishes. That doesn't mean you should disregard his, does it? This is a matter of your safety."

"Well, he won't know, and I'll be fine, so that doesn't signify."

"Winnie."

A tear ran down Rowena's fair cheek. "How am I supposed to ignore him and be mad at him if he won't even show himself?" she managed, sinking onto the couch. "No one cares that I'm here all alone in London!"

Oh, dear. Charlotte had no idea how to answer that, especially when she'd been the last one from the household to speak with Ranulf. Or to speak *at* him, rather.

"You're not alone in London, Winnie," Jane said briskly. "And that Lachlan Mac-Tier doesn't deserve your affection if he can't even be bothered to send you a note. As for Lord Glengask, you know he adores you. It's as Charlotte says; he's honoring your wishes."

Actually, Charlotte had more than a suspicion that *she* was the reason Ranulf had made himself scarce. But he'd made her so angry, and even jested about the brawl at the Evanstone party — a brawl the wags were still gossiping about, for heaven's sake. And the kiss, then suggesting they simply . . . become lovers, because of course they were all wrong for each other otherwise — *not* giving him a piece of her mind would have been wrong of her. She'd actually said more than she'd intended, but once she'd begun she hadn't been able to make herself

223

stop. Oh, he aggravated her.

And then he'd vanished from public view for a week. Not completely; evidently he'd gone riding in the early mornings and had taken several meetings with various people, but he hadn't attended any parties at all. Of course she wasn't certain he'd been invited to any, after what had happened last week.

But as for this picnic, if she allowed something to happen in his absence that endangered his sister, then all her talk about how he was the one making trouble and how Rowena was safe among the English aristocracy would become a lie. And if that caused him to discount her words, then she would have ruined the most interesting . . . friendship she'd ever had, and for no good reason. "Yes, he does adore you. So you can be mad at him and not risk your safety at the same time, can't you?" she persisted. "You have two other overlapping invitations for that same day."

"Two so far," Longfellow intoned from the doorway. The butler produced a silver salver laden with still more invitations and correspondence.

All the doldrums forgotten, the girls dove into them, laughing and squealing as they recognized a name here or an address there. Charlotte supposed she couldn't begrudge them their excitement; she'd had a splendid debut Season, herself, culminating with her betrothal to very pretty James Appleton.

"This one's for you, Char," Janie said, handing over a folded missive.

She didn't recognize the address, but broke the plain wax seal and unfolded the note, anyway. As she read the brief paragraph her heart skittered to a stop and then unsteadily resumed again. Taking a breath, she read it again, to make certain she hadn't missed anything. Then she cleared her throat. "Winnie, you should read this," she said, holding it out with shaking fingers.

Rowena took it from her and read it, then looked up again. "He . . . he bought a house?" she whispered, tears glistening in her eyes again. "He *bought* a *house*? In London?"

"I only know as much as you do, Winnie. It does lend some sense to a few odd rumors I've been hearing."

"Well, what does it say, for heaven's sake?" Janie asked.

Winnie didn't look capable of answering, so Charlotte did so. "Ranulf — Lord Glengask — purchased Gilden House on Market Street. He's invited our family to dinner there tomorrow evening, if we are available."

"My goodness," her sister exclaimed. "I

225

thought he hated London."

"He does," Rowena finally put in, wiping her eyes. "I don't understand."

Charlotte thought perhaps she did, but she had no intention of telling either of the young ladies that she'd taken the marquis to task about his unfounded prejudices. Not ever. "Do you want us to accept the invitation?" she asked, rather surprised at how desperately she wanted Rowena to say yes. Had her arguments had an effect on him? Had he listened to what she'd said? It seemed that he had, but she wanted to know for certain. And she wanted to know what that meant.

"I suppose we should," Ranulf's sister said slowly. "It would be rude to ignore a direct invitation after all, wouldn't it?"

"Yes, I think it would. And we don't wish to be rude." Not when she'd already exceeded her quota for that particular behavior to that particular man.

She should barely have noticed that he'd been absent for a week, a mere seven days. The Season was in full swing, and she attended dinners and soirees and recitals nearly every night. But she *had* noticed. And she didn't want the last words they'd exchanged to be the last words they ever exchanged. No, she didn't seem to be finished with the Marquis of Glengask just yet. Whether that was a good thing or not, though, she had no idea.

CHAPTER EIGHT

Ranulf paused at the top landing of the main staircase — his staircase, now — and took a deep breath. In the foyer, below, Owen and Peter seemed to be having the same trouble accepting the move to Gilden House as he was.

". . . more Sasannach servants traipsing aboot," Peter was saying in his hoarse whisper. "I might as well have stayed on at Hanover House."

"Ye are staying on at Hanover House," Owen returned. "Ye're here tonight to help us look civilized. So stop bellowing about Sasannach and move those posies into the drawing room."

"But why'd the laird go and buy this place? Do ye think he means to abandon Glengask?"

"Nae. Never. There'll always be a Mac-Lawry at Glengask."

This was the gossip Ranulf had been hoping to avoid. Pushing upright from the railing, he descended the staircase. "Everything ready for tonight, lads?"

"Aye," Owen returned, sending his partner a sharp look. "We've nae done much in the way o' formal dinners, but I've been reading them etiquette books. We'll do ye proud."

"I know ye will." Deliberately he clapped Peter on the shoulder. "The English look at us as barbarians and devils because they don't know us or our ways. I've caught myself making some broad assumptions about them, through the same ignorance." He gave a brief grin. "I'm knowing my enemy." And if some of them proved to be other than enemies, well, all the better for him, he supposed.

As Peter hurried upstairs with the flowers, Owen peered around the edge of the narrow foyer window's curtain. "Coach coming up. Ye should be in the drawing room, m'laird. Sas— Englishmen — dunnae greet their guests in the doorway."

With a nod, Ranulf retreated back up the stairs. When he'd begun this, he'd been angry and resentful — mostly at Charlotte Hanover. Now that he'd moved past the point of no return he remained half convinced that the evening would be a disaster.

At least, though, it was likely to be an interesting one.

In the drawing room, he poured himself a glass of whisky and took a generous swallow. He'd been drinking the stuff practically since he was five, and a glass or two would leave him more sober than a preacher, but he did hope it would settle his nerves some. He wasn't accustomed to being nervous, and he didn't like the sensation.

Owen stomped into the doorway and stopped, standing ramrod straight. "M'laird," he intoned, "Laird Swansley." With that he ducked a step backward. A moment later an amused-looking Myles walked past him and into the drawing room.

"Ranulf," he said, continuing forward and offering his hand. "Thank you for inviting me. It was . . . unexpected. And exceedingly welcome."

Ranulf shook his uncle's hand, then released him again. "Ye're family," he said slowly, full knowing he was reversing the decree he'd made three years ago. "And Rowena will expect to see ye here."

Visibly swallowing, Myles nodded. "This is a fine house. Should I say I'm surprised you've brought a property in Mayfair, or are we avoiding those discussions?"

"I'm walking a mile in English boots,"

Ranulf returned. "They're wee and they pinch, but I'm still doin' it. Let's leave it at that, shall w—"

"M'laird, I'm pleased to present Laird Hest, Lady Hest, Lady Rowena MacLawry, Lady Charlotte Hanover, and Lady Jane Hanover."

"Thank ye, Owen."

The footman did his backward step and gestured. He'd donned white gloves, Ranulf noticed; Owen *had* been reading etiquette books. As Hest stepped into the room, though, Ranulf set aside his . . . wariness over what Owen might have in store for them next.

He walked forward to shake the earl's hand and bow over the countess's. All his attention, though, remained on the doorway. Yes, he'd missed his sister, missed seeing with his own eyes that she was safe despite the twice-daily reports from Peter Gilling, but Rowena wasn't the lass about whom he'd dreamed for the past seven nights. No, a golden-haired, hazel-eyed beauty contin- ued to torment his thoughts as much as she'd tormented him in person a week ago. He remained uncertain how he felt, and even less so about how *she* felt, except that he knew he wanted — needed — to see her.

Rowena walked into the room, an uncertain smile on her face that widened as she caught sight of Uncle Myles. True to her bold self, she continued directly up to Ranulf. "Is it true ye've bought this house?"

"Aye."

"Why?"

He shrugged. "I can't very well judge London from the outside looking in, now can I?"

She looked up at him searchingly for a moment, then closed the distance between them to fling her arms around his chest. "Whatever's gotten into ye, Ranulf, thank you."

Ranulf hugged her back tightly. "What are ye thanking me fer, lass? I know ye havenae forgotten the brawl at the Evanstone soiree."

"I don't know," she returned with a short laugh, straightening again to wipe at her eyes. "I suppose because you're still here, at all. And because I'm still here."

"I gave ye my word, *piuthar*." He refrained from reminding her that she'd sworn never to leave damned London; one thing at a time.

A figure in a yellow gown entered the room, but he let out the breath that had caught in his throat. Jane was pleasant enough, but she wasn't the Hanover sister he wanted to see. And then there she was, in a simple green silk with a gray pelisse over it, her hazel eyes taking in the tasteful décor of the tasteful room. And he knew it was tasteful, because he'd bought it fully furnished.

Resolutely he returned his gaze to the younger sister. It wouldn't do to be rude, after all. "Lady Jane," he said, taking her hand and bowing over it.

"Lord Glengask. You have a . . . very nice home."

"My thanks, lass. I'm still awaiting a heavy rain to see if the roof leaks, but I believe it to be sound."

Only then did he face Charlotte. "Well, my lady, what do ye think?" he asked, putting his hands behind his back. It seemed the best way to keep from grabbing her for a kiss — especially when he was just as likely to be greeted with a slap.

She kept her gaze on his face. "I think I'm surprised."

"Ye shouldnae be," he returned in a lower voice, as the rest of her family went to greet Myles. "Ye're the cause of it."

Her brow lowered. "I didn't suggest you purchase a house."

"Nae. Ye told me to stop judging where I have nae knowledge. I'm gaining knowledge."

Twisting her fingers together, she glanced away. "That's good, then."

"Aye. I think so. I've also bought one o' those barouches. Not very practical fer the Highlands, but I wondered if ye'd care to go fer a drive with me tomorrow. I've been wanting to take a look inside the British Museum."

She took a step closer. "I don't understand. You —"

"I handed ye an insult to yer sensibilities, and ye pierced me to the bone with yer response," he interrupted. She'd done it in a way that no one else he'd ever met would even have attempted, but that had only made it more forceful. "So might it suffice to say this is a new day? A new beginning, perhaps?"

After a moment she shook her head. "No new beginnings."

A muscle in his jaw clenched. He hadn't expected sunshine and roses, to be sure, but to be denied a chance when he'd done all this . . . A thought struck him. Had he decided to make a better acquaintance with the English for himself, because it was a wise thing to do? Or had he done it to erase the look of disgust from a pair of kind, wise hazel eyes? And what the devil did that mean? "Well, then," he forced out. "I thank

234

ye for being honest with me."

"Then you may collect me at ten o'clock tomorrow," she said.

"Wh-what?"

"I'm not going to ignore what I know of you any more than you'll set aside what you know of me," she commented, reaching out to fluff his very proper cravat. "And I will admit that I feel . . . drawn to you, Ranulf. Despite my better judgment. And despite what you've stated you want of me."

"Ye've kept me awake nights, Charlotte," he returned. "Because of what I want of ye. Ye'd be wise to run the other way."

"And yet here I stand."

"Aye. There ye stand." His gaze lowered to her mouth, to the soft, warm curve of her lips. God, he wanted a taste of her. It had been a damned week of pushing away impatience and frustration and old hatreds. All because of something he couldn't even put a name to, but felt the desperate need to pursue.

"Ranulf!"

He jumped. From Charlotte's expression she'd been startled, too. Hoping what he'd been thinking didn't show through his trousers, he adjusted his coat and faced his sister. "Aye?"

"Do you have time to show us the house

now, or should we wait until after dinner?" Her gray gaze flicked from him to Charlotte and back again.

"Let's go now," he heard himself say. Without daring to look back at Charlotte he strolled over to join the main group. "Before I took it, this house was the London residence of Matthew, Viscount Danvers. It came to him from his grandmother, Lucille Gilden, Marchioness of Huntly. Did ye know either of them, Lord Hest?"

Charlotte's father nodded. "I was fairly well acquainted with Danvers, though in his later years he became sickly and quite reclusive. This is the first time I've set foot in Gilden House, though."

"Let's begin with the rooms on this floor, then. Across from here is the library, though Danvers seemed mostly to collect old newspapers here."

Charlotte stayed where she was as the rest of the dinner party crossed the hallway to the library. A week ago she'd been beside herself with fury at Ranulf MacLawry. And this evening she'd very nearly kissed him, and in front of her family.

For heaven's sake, she'd never even kissed James until they were engaged, because to do otherwise . . . Well, it simply wasn't done. But in two years of knowing Mr. Appleton, as . . . adamant as he had been, she couldn't ever remember feeling such a rush of heat and need as she felt when Ranulf looked at her.

Jane had called him fearsome and manly, and Charlotte had laughed at her sister. But she couldn't argue that there was a certain aliveness to him that most other men with whom she was acquainted seemed to lack. He'd insulted her, suggested she become his mistress — just for the time he was in London, of course — and then begun a brawl.

Why, then, did she currently have her hands clenched in front of her, and why was she wondering what would happen to her life if she *did* fall into bed with him?

She would never be able to marry, of course, without her prospective husband knowing she wasn't chaste. But then, she'd given up on marriage several years ago, and each year her prospects dimmed further. If they were indiscreet then she would find herself the subject of gossip, of being ostracized from most of polite Society. But that was only if someone else realized what they were up to. If they were up to anything. If she decided that the lure of being in his arms outweighed her wish for propriety.

"Charlotte?"

She blinked herself back to the present as Rowena glided into the room. "I'm sorry," she said, smiling. "I was lost in thought." Moving forward, she wrapped her arm around Winnie's. "What did I miss?"

"I think perhaps *I* missed something," Rowena returned, not moving despite Charlotte's gentle urging. "Are you after my brother?"

Oh, heavens. "Why in the world would you think such a thing?" she said, sounding a bit more shrill than she wished. "Lord Glengask and I agree about nothing!" Oh dear, oh dear. If Rowena had noticed, then had her sister? Her parents?

"Nobody stands toe-to-toe with Ranulf. But you do. I think that means you enjoy it."

Charlotte grimaced a little. "I do enjoy a good argument," she conceded.

The marquis's sister tilted her head. "Are you ashamed that you like him? Because he's Scottish?"

"Heavens no, Winnie." This was not going at all well, and the last thing she wanted Rowena or her brother to think was that she was just another blue-blooded snob. I . . ." She blew out her breath. "There is an attraction," she admitted, speaking slowly and sounding out the words before she said them aloud. "He asked me to go with him to the museum tomorrow, and I agreed. As for being after him, I think we both know that your brother has no intention of taking an English bride."

Gray eyes opened wider. "Marriage? Good Saint Andrew, ye want to *marry* him?"

Charlotte coughed. "I never said any such thing!" she managed. "I just meant that none of this could be very serious."

"My goodness. Ye nearly stopped my heart," Winnie said, chuckling as she hugged Charlotte's arm.

"And you nearly stopped mine!" Charlotte kissed her on the cheek, taking that moment to hide the hurt that Winnie's matter-of-fact assumption had caused. Was it such an outlandish idea? Because she was twenty-five? Because she was English? A roll in the blankets was perfectly acceptable, but nothing serious, nothing permanent. "We'd best catch up, or your brother will think we don't like his house."

Rowena seemed satisfied, but Charlotte's heart and head continued spinning. If she'd had any silly thoughts that a fairy-tale ending awaited her, Winnie had just dashed them. But that was likely a good thing. She and Ranulf weren't precisely kindred kind, after all. And she did prefer to know where the path led. Ranulf MacLawry waited by the gatepost — they would merely be playing about in the stable yard rather than going into the house. The proverbial house. Because the one through which she walked at the moment was his, and it was quite nice.

Gilden House stood on a stately street lined with towering old elm trees that had likely looked down on pedestrians since the great fire. He'd set himself in the middle of Mayfair both literally and figuratively. If he'd done so because of her . . . A warm shiver ran up her spine despite the dourness of her thoughts. He was a very intriguing man, after all, and he seemed to find her intriguing, in return.

A moment later the hair on her arms lifted, and a warm hand cupped her elbow. "I can very nearly see yer house from here," Ranulf murmured, joining her at the master bedchamber's front window.

She wanted to sag back against him, feel his arms wrap around her waist, forget all the silliness trying to complicate the simple . . . lust running beneath her skin. "I honestly thought you and I would not be speaking again," she said in the same low tone.

"Likewise. I'm nae accustomed to being bellowed at. By anyone." He leaned in as if smelling her hair. "It took me a good day or two to admit ye'd made a fair point." Ranulf glanced behind him. "This might be a conversation for another time," he drawled, his soft brogue sending excitement swirling just beneath her skin.

Whatever had happened over a week spent thinking about little but the Marquis of Glengask, it had overwhelmed her dismay at seeing him beginning a fistfight because someone he disliked had wished to dance with her. Perhaps he'd been provoked, perhaps he'd done the provoking, but regardless the violence made her sick to her stomach. The male thirst for honor or power or superiority — it was nearly all James Appleton had thought about, and then it had killed him. Whatever the old saying about pride going before a fall, history books were full of stories about men whose sense of honor or pride sent them tripping to their deaths. And Ranulf faced all manner of blows to his pride straight on and beckoned all comers.

They were back in the drawing room when a gong sounded, reverberating through the large house like the rumble of thunder. The double doors connecting the drawing room to the small dining room beyond swung open, and Owen the footman stood there in black livery and white gloves. "Dinner is served, lairds and ladies."

"Thank ye, Owen." Ranulf rose and gestured his guests toward the door.

"Nae, m'laird," the footman whispered loudly. "Ye must go first, and take the highest-ranking lass with ye. Lady Hest, that is."

Rowena stifled a laugh behind her hand and walked over to take Lord Hest's arm. Lord Swansley offered an arm each to Charlotte and Janie — which wasn't strictly proper, but she knew Jane appreciated not having to walk in alone.

"I hope ye dunnae mind," Ranulf said, as they all took their seats, "but we'll be dining on Scottish venison with rose hips and beetroot. It's generally served for Hogmanay, but I thought we'd make an exception."

"What's Hogmanay?" Janie asked.

"Ah. The end of the year. New Year's Eve." He smiled. "And ye must at least try some haggis, prepared in the style of the Highlands."

"What's the style of the Highlands?" Jane whispered, leaning over to tug on Rowena's arm.

Rowena grinned. "Boiled lungs of a sheep or cow or deer, diced and minced and served with oatmeal and other vegetables and spices."

Her uncle, Myles, took a sip of wine. "You might consider filling up on the venison," he said, sotto voce. "I've learned to tolerate haggis, but I wouldn't say I like it."

"Bear used to say it would put hair on my chest," Winnie continued, chuckling. "Then I would cry when they made me eat it, until Uncle Myles boxed his ears." She sat forward to look toward the head of the table. "Do you have a proper Highlands cook then, Ran?"

"Nae. Mrs. Flost is definitely nae Scottish. But Peter and Owen and I've been showing her how to make the venison and haggis."

"Oh, dear," Jane whispered.

The venison actually turned out to be delicious, and the group surprisingly merry. Ranulf explained how the celebration of Hogmanay involved the entire community, with farmers bringing in the choicest of their stores, and the laird of the clan hosting a night — or two nights, more likely — of dancing and singing and drinking and eating.

The way he spoke of it, with helpful interruptions from both Winnie and Lord Swansley, painted such a vivid portrait that she could almost see the dancers in the firelight, and see the young ones running about and trying to empty out the mugs of ale before their parents could spy them out.

"M'laird," Owen announced as two footmen appeared carrying platters, "we have brought the haggis." He frowned. "If ye'd allowed me to hire a piper, I could've announced it more properly."

"I think ye did fine, Owen," Winnie said, her accent deepening as she worked her way through a third glass of wine. "Finer than any piper."

"I thank ye, Lady Winnie," the footman said, blushing.

Charlotte studied the dish placed in front of her. It did look grainy, with bits of onion and liver, and what must have been the diced organs. The smell was quite pleasant, anyway.

"Take a bite, lass," Ranulf urged with a grin. "It willnae kill ye."

She giggled, a clear indication that she'd also had too much to drink this evening. That seemed to be part of the Scottish tradition, though, so she supposed she was only being friendly. Taking a breath, she scooped a large portion onto her fork and slid it into her mouth.

The taste wasn't bad, but the texture

reminded her of the worst parts of blood pudding. She kept chewing, forcing a smile. "Interesting," she managed, lifting her napkin to cover her mouth as she spoke.

Ranulf laughed. She'd never heard him laugh before, she realized. The deep, rich sound delighted her to her toes. It warmed her everywhere, including places ladies weren't supposed to talk about. Tomorrow, next week, next month — what did they truly signify? He, and tonight, were both supremely interesting.

"I don't think I could eat another bite," Jane exclaimed with a chuckle, eyeing her full plate as if it were a snake.

Swallowing, Charlotte shook her head. "Oh no, you don't. Everyone has to take one bite, at least."

Both Ranulf and Winnie were halfway through their servings of haggis, Ranulf especially eating with great gusto. "It's nae perfect," he said between mouthfuls, "but it'll do."

As the rest of the family tentatively scooped up choice forkfuls, Charlotte met Ranulf's gaze across the table. His amused smile deepened, and he lifted his glass of whisky, tilting it in her direction before he took a swallow. Perhaps it was the generous amount of wine she'd been imbibing, but abruptly she wished the rest of her family — and his — were elsewhere, that it was just the two of them and the candlelight and the warm fire in the hearth opposite the windows.

The way the firelight behind her reflected itself in the window was quite remarkable, actually. She wondered if the architect had slightly altered the angle of the windows with that very thing in mind.

Except that the light from the windows kept glowing brighter. Her heart gave an odd thump. Charlotte stood, the fork forgotten in her hand. "Ranulf. The —"

The side door burst open in the same moment. Peter Gilling, the footman who'd been lodging at Hanover House, lurched into the room. "Fire, m'laird! The stable!"

Ranulf was already halfway to his feet. "Ladies, stay here. Dogs, guard!"

The two hounds who'd been lazing by the fire behind her came to attention, their tails outstretched and their noses in the air. "What can we do?" she asked, as he and Myles and her father hurried from the room, the two Scottish footmen and then the pair of English ones behind them.

His fierce gaze caught hers. "Stay safe," he said, and vanished out the door.

"Oh, dear," Winnie said, hurrying to the

window. "This is like when the schoolhouses burned and Bear got shot."

"Nonsense," Charlotte forced herself to stay. "This is an old house with a new owner and a new group of servants. Someone likely kicked over a lantern."

"I hope so. Oh, I hope so. Stirling's in the stable. Ranulf's owned him for years and years. If he burns . . ."

Both young ladies were now in tears, and even her mother looked close to it. Frowning, Charlotte went forward and pulled them away from the window. "When they come back in they'll likely be wet and cold and covered in soot. Let's find some blankets and some cloths and bowls of clean water, shall we? Bring what you find to the drawing room."

"Yes," Lady Hest put in, sending her a grateful look. "Come along, girls. We must do our part."

They left the room in the direction of the kitchen, Una on their heels. When Charlotte looked down, Fergus stood directly beside her, his hackles raised and his muzzle wrinkled as the scent of smoke drifted into the small dining room.

She didn't want to gather blankets. She wanted to go outside and do something to help. Gathering her skirts, Charlotte ran for the front door. It stood open, smoke curling into the foyer as the breeze carried it eastward. Once she stopped outside she closed it behind her; otherwise even after they extinguished the fire Ranulf would have to replace all his curtains.

It seemed an odd thing to worry over, given the circumstances, but as she rounded the corner of the house she stopped dead, all thoughts of curtains fleeing. Fire lapped orange and angry out of the hayloft window, and the entire back of the building was nothing but smoke and flames. And she knew immediately that no tipped-over lantern had sparked this blaze.

She shivered, then ran forward again at the sound of Ranulf's shout. Men and horses darted in front of the flames. And as she drew closer she made out the ragged line of men hauling buckets from the well behind the house.

A very worried-looking young man cranked the handle at the well to bring the bucket up and down while others used the water to fill still more buckets and hand them down the line. Charlotte took a breath, coughing. She might not be able to haul a quantity of heavy buckets about, but she could certainly help turn a crank.

"Let me help," she said, moving to the

opposite side of the rig and joining her hands with his.

"Thank you, miss," he said feelingly, panting.

Working together, they dropped the bucket and pulled it up at nearly twice the speed it had been going before. Servants from the neighboring houses began to appear, and she instructed them to drop more ropes with buckets into the well to speed the flow of water to the fire.

Her arms began to feel like lead, but she clenched her jaw and kept turning the crank. However exhausted she was, the men hauling the full buckets of water must be even more so. She closed her mind off from the numbness and the sharp ache, and concentrated on nothing but making her arms move.

A hand closed over hers, and with a creak the crank stopped turning. "Well done, Ginger," Ranulf's low brogue came. "Well done, lass. The fire's out."

She couldn't uncurl her fingers. After a moment he seemed to realize that, because with a surprisingly gentle touch he pulled her hands free. "Did we save Stirling?" she heard herself ask, even as her legs sagged. How long had she been standing there? It felt like both years and seconds all at the same time.

"Stirling's well. All the horses are oot. The stable's lost, but the fire didnae spread to the house, thank Saint Andrew and all the angels."

She took a look at him, tall and formidable even with a missing coat and rolled-up shirtsleeves, singe marks and soot covering nearly every inch of him. And then before she could protest that she just needed a moment or two for feeling to return to her arms and legs, he swept her up into his arms and carried her back to the house.

"Oh, thank goodness, Charlotte!" she heard her mother say. "We've been looking everywhere for you!"

"I was helping pull water from the well," she said. Abruptly she realized that Ranulf still carried her, and she elbowed him in his hard chest. "I'm not an invalid," she stated. "You may put me down now, if you please."

His grip tightened momentarily, and then he set her down lengthwise on one of his lush couches. "I'll fetch ye some whisky," he said gruffly, and moved off.

Immediately Jane sank down on the floor beside her and reached for her hand. "Oh, you have blisters," she said, and began rubbing Charlotte's fingers.

"I feel like one large blister," she returned,

wincing as pins and needles began dancing up her arms.

"As ye should," Ranulf said, squatting down beside Jane and holding a glass to Charlotte's lips. "Ye stood there fer near three hours, to hear my valet tell it. He says ye organized the neighbors and their wells, too."

Three hours? No wonder she felt so prickly. "I wanted to help."

"And so ye did. Nearly worked poor Ginger's arms off. He won't be able to knot a cravat for a week. Drink."

With the rest of her family looking on anxiously, she did as he bid her and choked down several swallows of strong whisky. Her muscles began to relax, and she closed her eyes. The last thing she remembered was Ranulf rubbing her fingers and calling her a bonny, brave lass. Well, that was nice to hear.

Ranulf carried the sleeping Charlotte out to her family's coach and set her carefully down on the seat, moving back as the rest of the Hanovers and Rowena climbed in after her. This evening he sent both Peter and Debny back with them and Una; just because mischief had been done didn't mean it was finished with.

As he stepped back from the coach, Rowena reached out the window and grabbed his wrist. "Charlotte said someone knocked over a lantern. Do you think that's what happened?"

And even tired and worried, she still made an effort to stifle her brogue. It reminded him of Berling and his cohorts. "I dunnae, lass. We'll take a look in the morning, when the light's better."

She nodded. "Be safe, Ran. And please don't do anything mad."

"I willnae. Keep Una in yer room with ye tonight, just to ease my mind. Good night, *piuthar.*"

"Good night, *bràthair.*"

The moment the coach left the drive, he stalked back to the smoldering stable. The grooms would have to keep watch all night, to be certain flames didn't erupt again. The five horses he'd kept inside the building were safe and likely still jittery at the Duke of Greaves's house on the next street over.

"You're not going to attempt anything mad are you, Ranulf?" his uncle asked from several feet behind him.

"I happen to know a man with a reputation fer setting fires, Myles," he said, his shoulders aching from keeping such a tight leash on his temper.

He wanted to hurt someone — Berling —

for this. The man had put his household, his family, in danger. He might well have burned a dozen more houses along the street if the wind had been wilder, or their response slower. And beneath all that, buried beneath a ton of smoldering embers, lay the thing that troubled him the most — the idea that Charlotte had been out in the middle of the chaos and that she might have been hurt.

When he'd found her at the well she'd been white-faced and clearly exhausted, her hands clenching the crank so hard she'd needed his help to let go. Seeing her there standing firm amid the chaos had been . . . It had been a revelation. She was proper, aye, and she had no stomach for bloodshed, but she was not timid and she was not weak.

And with all his prejudice against the English, it was English servants and their masters who'd helped him put out the fire. It was an English duke who'd offered to stable his horses. And unless he was greatly mistaken, it had been a Scotsman masquerading as an Englishman who'd set this fire.

"Ranulf, we don't know for certain that Berling is to blame," Myles said, as if reading his thoughts. "We don't even know if it was he who burned the schools or shot Bear. It was the Donnellys I told, after all."

Ranulf rounded on his uncle. "*I* know," he hissed. "I should have seen to him when I had the chance. Breaking his nose clearly wasnae enough."

"Perhaps you should have. In the Highlands you would have had a fair chance of getting away with it. But this is London, and he has more friends and allies here than you do."

"Then they can be allies to a dead man." With a last look at the smoking rubble, he turned back for the house.

Myles grabbed his shoulder. "At least wait until morning," he said tightly.

When Ranulf looked from him to his hand, his uncle released him again. "He'll be waiting for me tonight. Tomorrow's soon enough."

"Thank God. Come stay at Wilkie House tonight."

"Nae. I'll help keep watch over the stable till the smoke stops rising." In addition he had some thinking to do, and this setting fit his mood far better than a comfortable bed at his uncle's residence.

"Well, get some sleep. I may only barely be a part of the family, but I do worry about you, lad."

With a grimace, Ranulf stopped and turned around. "I was wrong," he said evenly. "Ye're my uncle. Ye're part of my clan, and I do love ye. I give ye my word I willnae go after Berling tonight."

Myles looked away for a moment, then wiped a hand across his face as he turned back again. "I must have smoke in my eyes," he grumbled, his voice not quite steady as he blinked and rubbed at his eyes again. "Thank you, Ranulf. Going up to Glengask gave me a family, you know. Losing you . . ."

Ranulf clapped a hand on his uncle's shoulder. "Ye willnae lose us again. I cannae guarantee peace, but family stays together."

That, at least, he could see to. Berling would be more complicated. He wanted nothing more than to remove from this life a man he knew to be a threat before anything else could happen. But Myles was correct; this wasn't the Highlands. Little as he liked it, he would have to tread carefully. But he would see to Donald Gerdens. That, he swore.

CHAPTER NINE

Ranulf woke to the sound of raised male voices and a loudly barking dog. Every muscle felt stiff, which made sense once he realized he'd fallen asleep sitting at his desk. A page of the English law book he'd been reading was stuck to his cheek, and he scratched at his scraggle of beard as he lifted his head. Groaning, he pushed to his feet.

"Damnation," a familiar brogue came from the doorway. "Ye look like hell spat ye out into a fireplace."

Sharp relief hit him at the sight of the tall, black-haired man standing there. "I told ye to stay at Glengask, Arran," he returned, rounding a chair and walking up to his brother. Abruptly he didn't feel quite so outnumbered — by enemies, by English, or by females.

"Aye. I decided against it."

Ranulf pulled him into a hard embrace. "I'm glad to see ye."

"Certainly ye are. Ye need someone to help ye clean up that mess ootside." Arran patted him on the back, then stepped out of the embrace. "Owen said ye got the horses oot, and no one was more than singed. He also tried to wager me ten quid that it was Donald Gerdens who did it."

"Dunnae take that bet. Ye'd lose."

Together they walked down the hallway to the breakfast room, where the sideboard had been set with a simple breakfast of rewarmed haggis, toasted bread, and hard-boiled eggs. Fergus danced around them, alternating between shoving his head beneath Arran's hand and Ranulf's.

"Una's with Winnie, I assume?" Arran asked, selecting a huge breakfast and hooking his boot around a chair leg to pull out the seat.

"Aye. Peter and Debny are at Hanover House, too."

"Good. Let me put someaught in my stomach, and then we can go kill Berling."

Gathering a much more spare breakfast for himself, Ranulf took a seat opposite his brother. Arran was the most levelheaded of the MacLawry brothers, the best educated, and arguably the most clever. If what little he'd heard about the fire had convinced him that Berling was involved, then it was so.

"Well?" Arran prompted after a moment. "Do ye have someaught else in mind?"

Ranulf sat back as the overly attentive Owen poured him a brimming cup of hot coffee. "Myles reminded me last night that this isnae the Highlands. I've nae difficulty with separating Berling's head from his shoulders, but I dunnae think England appreciates revenge the way we do."

"Not anymore, anyway," Arran agreed. "The Sasannach are very nearly civilized." He wolfed down a mouthful of haggis. "Ye've a different idea, then?"

"Not as of this moment." He took a swallow of coffee, closing his eyes as the warmth of it spread all the way to his toes. "Now that ye're here we can keep a better eye on him, though."

Arran glanced at him, light blue gaze curious, before he returned his attention to his breakfast. "An eye. That's different."

"What do ye mean?"

"I mean it's different. I may only have been eleven when *athair* died, but I knew what it meant when ye went oot 'hunting' with a musket and a shovel and came back two days later covered in dirt and not bringing any game with ye."

Ranulf took a breath, pushing away the abrupt memory of the cold and the fear and the deep, bottomless anger that had driven him out when the men of his clan had been torn between advising caution and calling for a full-out war. It had been sixteen years ago, and he still remembered the crunch of leaves beneath his feet as he crept forward in the dark toward Sholbray Manor. He shifted in his chair. "And yer point is?"

"I know ye didnae chase down Berling before because we had to tend to Bear. Even if we'd had any doubts then, I dunnae see what's stopping ye now, the Highlands or London or Boston, Massachusctts." His gaze lowered again. "Unless it's some lass named Charlotte Hanover."

Bloody hell. He didn't even know his own thoughts; explaining her to his astute brother would only have him sounding like a lunatic. "What does Lady Charlotte have to do with anything?" he asked, deciding on an attempt at ignorance.

Arran sipped at his tea. "You tell me," he said succinctly.

"There's naught to tell." He looked at his brother. Looked at the mound of food on his plate, the shadows beneath his eyes. "When did ye leave Glengask?"

"Four days ago. And aye, I ken I should-nae have traveled alone, but I doubt anyone could have kept up with me fer long even if

259

they had been trying to follow me."

"Well, then," Ranulf responded, suspicion creeping through him. "Since the fire was last night, what, exactly, prompted ye to fly down here like a damned bat?"

"If ye've nothing to say on a particular topic, neither do I."

Generally Ranulf appreciated their middle brother's cleverness, but this morning he would have preferred Munro and his more straightforward manner. "Ye mean to say ye hurried down to London because I mentioned a lass in a letter? Do ye think I'm a monk, then?"

"Nae. But I do think when Ranulf Mac-Lawry mentions a Sasannach lass five times in one letter, together with adjectives like 'bossy' and 'headstrong' and 'unfathomable,' then someaught's afoot." Arran rubbed at his forehead. "And since ye also said ye were outnumbered *and* Winnie said she's nae coming home *and* ye went and bought a house, I thought ye might be able to use another MacLawry in London." He cocked his head. "Am I wrong?"

Ranulf shook his head. "I'm glad to have ye here, as I said. But keep yer damned opinions to yerself."

"I can do that."

After they finished a quick breakfast, the

two of them went out to the stable. There was little left but part of one wall and a pile of broken, blackened rubble. All of the stableboys swore they'd done nothing to cause the fire, and that in fact they'd all been in the side room eating when the fire started at the back of the stable.

Walking the rear perimeter, Ranulf's foot crunched on broken glass. When he squatted down and dug through the burned grass and ashes he found the half-melted collar and burner of a lantern. After he called Arran over, they found a few more pieces of shattered glass. Whatever this had hit, it had done so with some force.

"It could have come down from inside the wall," his brother said absently, marking a spot four feet from where the wall had stood — the place where they'd found the most distant piece of glass. "But it's more likely it was thrown against the wall from the outside."

Ranulf had already come to that conclusion, himself. When Berling had burned down the schools around Glengask and An Soadh — and he *knew* it had been Berling and his men, with or without definitive proof — he'd flung oil and then lanterns at the walls. Not identical to the way the stable fire had likely begun, but close.

"Arran, ye make a decent sketch. Draw the back of the yard here, and mark where we found the pieces of lantern. I'll fetch a box fer all the bits of it."

"We're gathering evidence, then?" his brother asked skeptically.

"Aye, we are. Shut up and find some paper and a pencil."

"As ye order, m'laird."

Debny rode up as Ranulf was putting the last piece of lantern safely in a box. Immediately he straightened to approach the head groom. "How are Rowena and the Hanovers?" he asked, stopping himself from asking specifically about Charlotte.

"All well. Lady Charlotte said she feels like she has cannonballs strapped to her arms, but she's well otherwise." The servant dug into his pocket and pulled out a folded note. "She sent this for ye, m'laird."

Ranulf wiped his sooty hands on his trousers to give himself a moment to steady his racing thoughts before he took the missive and unfolded it.

" 'Ranulf,' " he read, " 'Thank you for an unforgettable evening. If you need to cancel our visit to the museum, I completely understand, but please let me know. Affectionately, C.H.' "

He grinned. "Remarkable lass."

According to his pocket watch it was nearly half ten, and he badly needed a bath and a shave. Because not only did he plan to visit the museum with Charlotte, but he meant to look his most civilized while doing it. Why that was suddenly more pressing than proving who'd set fire to his stable, he would debate later.

Arran leaned in the doorway of the master bedchamber as Ginger was struggling with the knots in Ranulf's cravat. "Do ye mind if I take the room at the other end of the hallway?"

"That's fine."

His brother hesitated. "Ye look very bonny."

"Shut up. I'm off to Hanover House. I can leave ye off there if ye want to see Rowena."

To his credit, whatever additional observations or questions Arran had, he kept them to himself. Instead he retrieved his satchel and wandered toward the back of the house. He'd arrived with even less luggage than Ranulf had; if he meant to stay for a time, they'd be making another visit to the prissy, padding-obsessed tailor.

Arran's presence gave Ranulf an additional body to watch over, but he couldn't pretend it wasn't a relief to have an ally. Even a nosy one who noticed things he

263

shouldn't. The most immediate question was whether Berling would see the arrival of another MacLawry in London as a threat or as an invitation to make more trouble.

And figuring that out would have to wait until he'd set eyes on Charlotte again, devil take the rest.

"Two letters and a poem, Winnie, and that's just today!" Jane said, taking the perfumed paper from Rowena's hand and smoothing it over her knee. "I don't know that 'N'er a copper penny as bright as the smile of Winnie' is terribly romantic, but it does rhyme."

When Charlotte looked over at their houseguest, Winnie seemed more interested in studying the clouds passing by outside the drawing room window than in giggling over her latest conquest's attempt at poetry. "Winnie, your brother would send word if anything further happened. You know that."

With a sigh Rowena sank back onto the couch. "Aye, I know." She scooted over and took Charlotte's hand, careful not to press at the blisters. "Thank you for keeping me away from the picnic. I sometimes forget there's a difference between being independent and being responsible."

Charlotte nodded, smiling. "That's a very

wise thing to say."

"I've been thinking about it for a time, now. My brothers, and especially Ran, have spent so much of their time making certain I'm happy and well protected that they've stopped considering themselves. Perhaps it's my turn to look after them, for once."

"But two of the three of them are in Scotland," Jane put in. "And Lord Glengask seems supremely capable of looking after himself."

Rowena looked up at Charlotte's face. "You'd think so, wouldn't you?"

Charlotte wanted to ask if she was referring to something in particular, but before she could do so Jane resumed looking through their morning correspondence. "What I want to know is, does looking after your brother mean we can't go looking for hair ribbons today?"

"Oh, I think we can do both, Jane."

"That's a relief."

Whether Rowena's sudden sense of responsibility was due to the fire last night or not, Charlotte was relieved to hear it, and so likely would Ranulf be when she told him. Even if perhaps she'd thought he might be exaggerating the quality and quantity of the danger that lurked around the MacLawrys, she'd certainly become a believer last night.

A shiver ran through her. She'd half hoped he would send back word that he needed to cancel their outing today — not because her arms ached, which they did, or because she didn't wish to see him, which she did — but because he would be spending the museum visit angry and plotting revenge. She would, and already did, feel the need to counsel him about how he planned to retaliate, and then they would argue again. Not the interesting type of argument, either. She couldn't quite pin any of this to pride, but she wouldn't be surprised if it came down to that in the end.

The morning room door opened at two minutes past noon, and she and the other two girls rose as Longfellow came to attention in the doorway. "My ladies, Lord Glengask and Lord Arran MacLawry," he intoned, and moved out of the way.

Winnie was already halfway to the door. "Arran!" she exclaimed, throwing herself into the arms of a dark-haired man who looked like a leaner, less chiseled version of his older brother.

"There ye are, my sweet Winnie," he drawled, and kissed his sister on both cheeks.

"How did you get here so quickly?" she

demanded.

"I try to anticipate trouble."

They continued gabbing excitedly and introduced a blushing Jane into the mix, but Charlotte ceased paying attention as Ranulf moved around them and approached her. Something had happened last night; she couldn't define what it was, but when the Marquis of Glengask walked into the room, everything else seemed to fade away. It was ridiculous that after a pair of kisses and a pair of waltzes and a handful of fascinating, aggravating conversations she felt so . . . drawn to a man who was so wrong for her, especially when he only meant more trouble.

And yet she had to stop herself from meeting him halfway across the room, from throwing her arms around his shoulders and kissing him. She swallowed. Clearly she'd become overtired last night, and had lost her bearings. *Be logical,* she ordered herself. Facts could never lead her astray.

However impressive he'd been in his kilt, he seemed to have done away with it entirely; today, if she didn't think he would consider it an insult, she would say that he looked very English, from his brown coat to his buckskin trousers to his highly polished Hessian boots.

"How're yer hands, lass?" he asked, taking them both in his larger, broader ones and turning them palms up.

Not so English after all, once he spoke. A tremor ran down her spine, settling into a low excitement between her thighs. "They sting a bit," she said in as even a voice as she could manage, "but I think with a pair of gloves and some caution I'll manage quite well. How are you?"

Deep blue eyes raised to meet hers. "The fire's stayed out and the worst injury seems to be a pair of blistered palms. I'm relieved. And furious."

The way he said it so matter-of-factly made the words somehow even more deadly sounding. She could understand his anger, but he was not a man who would settle for exchanging words. "I am not going on a drive with you if you mean to jump out and bash people along the way."

"So I expect. I'll do nae bashing or jumping whilst I'm in yer company."

And he agreed so easily she couldn't help being suspicious. "The fire was an accident, then?"

"Nae, I reckon it was done deliberately."

Charlotte frowned. "Then why —"

"Why do I mean to be a proper gentleman today? Because of these hands," he said quietly, stroking his thumbs gently across her palms. "Because of what ye did fer me last night, *leannan.*"

"I'm not the only one who helped. For heaven's sake, all I did was turn a crank."

A slow smile curved his mouth. "What say we forgo the museum and I'll find somewhere quiet just for us?" he murmured, moving a breath closer to her. "I'll explain my gratitude to ye."

Somehow, the way he said it made it sound even naughtier than it already was. And there she stood, five-and-twenty, past the age of making a good marriage, looking at a man who couldn't possibly want her for a bride. And a man far too dangerous for her to want as a husband. Perfect, in its imperfection.

"If you can manage that without ruining the life I have," she whispered back, "I might well be amenable."

Brief surprise lit his gaze. "What changed yer mind, lass?"

Men. Charlotte favored him with an exasperated grin. "Do you really want me to explain it to you?"

"Nae. Not if there's a risk of ye deciding against it again. Let's be off then, shall we?"

"It might not be as simple as all that, you know."

He nodded, his slight smile sending butterflies through her chest. "Leave that to me, *leannan*. Where are yer gloves?"

"Simms has them. Simms?"

Her lady's maid came forward, and together they managed to get the soft white kid gloves over her blisters without overmuch teeth-gritting on her part. She had to fight a wince every time she flexed a hand, but a few blasted blisters were not going to keep her home today. No matter what.

When she looked up again Ranulf's brother Arran stood gazing at her, his lighter blue eyes curious. No wonder; she'd completely forgotten he was in the room. "So you're Arran," she said, offering her hand. "Winnie talks about you and Munro all the time."

He grinned. "I'll give ye a bow, and I hope ye don't take my refusing to shake yer hand as an insult, Lady Charlotte."

She grinned back at him, sensing in him an easier temperament than his older brother possessed. Equally handsome, perhaps, in a different way, but not nearly as compelling. "I'm quite relieved, actually. Thank you."

With almost absurd caution Ranulf took her outstretched hand and wrapped it over his sleeve. "Arran, I leave ye to do Winnie's bidding. Don't cause too much of a ruckus, either of ye."

Charlotte chuckled as he led her through the foyer and out the front door to his waiting barouche. "Your poor brother. You've just sentenced him to go hair ribbon shopping."

Ranulf shrugged as he helped her into the open carriage. "Arran's accustomed to it. According to Rowena, he's the only brother with taste other than in his mouth."

"I don't know about that. You look very fine this afternoon."

"I'll tell bloo— black-hearted Smith the tailor ye said that. He accused me of shaming his entire profession because I wouldnae let him put padding in my shoulders."

If there was one man in London who didn't need the cut of his shoulders enhanced, it was Ranulf MacLawry. "I'm glad you didn't give in."

"As am I. Th—" He started to climb into the barouche beside her, then stopped when he noted Simms standing directly behind him. "And what do *ye* want?"

"I'm going with you, my lord," the maid said, putting every ounce of affronted dignity she possessed into the sentence.

"The hell ye say."

Charlotte stifled a laugh. "She's our chaperone. I can't accompany you without her or another appropriate female present."

With a low breath that sounded like a bear growling, Ranulf moved back and handed the lady's maid into the carriage. Simms started to sit beside Charlotte, but he shook his head. "Nae. Ye can sit there," he said, pointing at the backward-facing seat.

"Ranulf."

"I'll be sitting beside ye, Charlotte. From over there she can better see if I try to ravish ye — which clearly I willnae be doing now."

Warmth crept up Charlotte's cheeks all over again. "I told you it wouldn't be a simple matter," she murmured as he leaned in to sit next to her, warm and solid and compelling.

"Ye might have warned me of the details," he returned, settling in close enough that their thighs brushed. "She didnae come along with us before."

"Because Jane and Winnie were along. We all guard what we and Society say is precious."

"Bloody Puritans," he grumbled.

Well, she wasn't a Puritan, of course, but she understood his meaning. Evidently the Marquis of Glengask intended to be only as much of a gentleman as circumstance demanded he be. And as she rather wished Simms elsewhere, herself, she could only nod.

"Is your other brother here as well?" she asked, to distract herself from thoughts of being ravished.

"Ye want to talk aboot my family, now?"

"I think a different topic might be helpful, yes."

He sighed. "Nae, then. Bear's still in Scotland. For the last four hundred years there's always been a MacLawry at Glengask. It's even on the family crest, *i gcónaí MacLawry ag Glengask* — 'always a Mac-Lawry at Glengask,' literally. And these days, well, I'd never allow that oath to be broken."

Charlotte nodded. "So your clan will know you mean never to abandon them."

"Aye."

It and the meaning behind it were quite possibly the most noble family motto she'd ever heard. And the fact that it was in Gaelic rather than Latin seemed . . . brave, and proud, rather than quaint. "Say it again, will you? In Gaelic, I mean."

"With pleasure. *I gcónaí MacLawry ag Glengask.*"

She found herself watching his mouth as he spoke, savoring the elongated vowels and the musical roll of his words. "Do you speak Gaelic at home? At Glengask?"

"Here and there. Mostly we speak English. We all had to learn it in school, and for a while during my father's time we werenae allowed to speak Gaelic at all." He hesitated. "As satisfying as it might have been not to know any English, it wouldnae have served any of us well."

"And your mother was English."

The look in his eyes cooled again. "Aye. That she was."

From what Winnie had said, Eleanor Mac-Lawry, nee Wilkie, had taken her own life three years after her husband's death. Even if he'd wished to discuss it, which he clearly didn't, today didn't seem the appropriate time. Instead she nodded, searching for anything to take her mind away from how very close he sat to her, and how very warm he seemed even through two sets of clothes.

"So tell me — was there something in particular you wanted to see at the British Museum?"

Silence.

When she glanced sideways at him, he sat with his jaw set, his gaze squarely on Simms. And her maid didn't look terribly comfortable with the scrutiny. No, he hadn't expected or wanted a chaperone, but that was hardly the servant's fault.

"Ranulf."

"Ye know I wasnae going to take ye to the damned museum."

"Well, we're going there now, so what would you like to see?"

His gaze slid over her, slow and lingering. "What would I like to see, Charlotte?" he repeated. "Shall I begin at the top, or the bottom?"

Good heavens. "Even if you don't wish to review the history of England because of the fighting with Scotland," she said hurriedly, heating from the inside out, "there are some lovely Greek and Egyptian items on display." The breeze blew a lock of his long, curling black hair across one of his sapphire eyes, and she nearly brushed it off his face before she caught herself and stilled her hand again.

"Aye. I'm certain there are." He sat back for a moment, the restless tap of his fingers against his thigh hypnotic. Then he muttered several words in Gaelic that she was certain, if translated, would sound much worse in English. "I cannae," he muttered.

"You can't what?"

"Do this all day without touching ye." He abruptly sat forward to pin the lady's maid with his fierce gaze. "Simms, aye?"

"Yes, my lord," the servant responded, her cheeks becoming a blotchy red.

Charlotte tensed. If he meant to order Simms out of the barouche, she would have to step in — both for the maid's sake and for her own. Whatever she might want privately, they were on the street in the middle of London. Some measure of propriety would be observed.

"If ye knew yer mistress was misbehaving, but that no harm would come of it, what would ye do?"

Simms looked from him to Charlotte. "My lady's reputation will always be safe with me," she said after a moment, a fierce pride in her voice that Charlotte couldn't recall ever hearing before. "I would never speak of her private affairs unless the silence endangered her safety."

"Hm," he mused, settling back again. "Debny. Take us to Gilden House. I want to show Lady Charlotte the stable damage by daylight."

"Aye, m'laird."

"And this is your idea of discreet?" Charlotte whispered, fleetingly wondering if she'd stepped out of Mayfair and into some wild Gypsy romance.

"It is precisely my idea of discreet," he returned in that rumbling, low-pitched

276

whisper that started heat between her thighs. "If I had t'stand beside ye all afternoon looking at damned statues, everyone would know how much I want ye, *leannan*. And that wouldnae be discreet."

"But driving directly to your house and walking inside?"

"With Simms to chaperone ye." He cocked his head. "Ye drive me to madness, lass. If ye dunnae want me, ye'd best say so now. I'm nae a man ye tease, Charlotte Hanover."

Her heart skittered. The idea of parting from him today without . . . touching him, made her ache. He'd made it clear from the beginning that his pursuit was solely about satisfying a physical desire, but he wasn't the only one who wanted something. "Whether this is a mistake or not, I can't think of a better moment to make one," she finally said.

Ranulf grimaced. "I've heard better praise, but that'll do."

For the next fifteen minutes she tried not to let the bouncing of the carriage press her against his side. She attempted a bit more casual conversation, something at which she generally excelled, but nothing worked. London had never seemed so big, or the distances so great.

By the time they turned up Market Street and the barouche stopped before the main steps of Gilden House, her jaw hurt from being clenched so tightly. Before Owen could even emerge from the house Ranulf had the carriage door open and cupped her elbow to help her to the ground.

"M'laird," the footman said, "we didnae expect ye to re—"

"Take Simms here down to the kitchen for someaught to eat," he interrupted, keeping Charlotte close by his side. "I want everyone else on the ground floor till I say otherwise."

"Aye, m'laird."

"Ye and Fergus included."

"I'll fetch him at once, m'laird."

Charlotte walked through the front door, though she had the feeling that if she'd hesitated he would have picked her up and slung her over his shoulder like a sack of beets.

"That way," he muttered from directly behind her, indicating the staircase.

She remembered where his master bed-chamber lay. He'd shown it off just last evening, after all. "Don't rush me," she ordered, pushing a shoulder back against him and stopping on the landing. "I am not a cow being herded to slaughter."

"My lady?"

Charlotte looked down to see Simms standing at the bottom of the stairs, Owen glaring at her and seeming ready to drag her down to the kitchen by force. "What is it, Simms?"

"I shall be discreet — if this is what *you* wish me to be."

Clearly Simms didn't approve of any of this, but it warmed Charlotte's heart that she'd asked the question despite being outnumbered by large Highland men, and at the way the maid had worded it.

Feeling as though she were about to take a step into purgatory — which she was, according to most proper ladies — she smiled. "Thank you, Simms. Have some luncheon. I'm where I wish to be."

At the top of the stairs she turned right and stepped into Ranulf's generous master bedchamber. A moment later the door clicked shut behind her, and she heard the key turn to lock them in.

"A good thing the Simms lass cooperated," Ranulf drawled, not moving from the door. "I might have had to set her loose in the wilds and hope she couldnae find her way back."

"Like a dog?" Charlotte turned around to look at him. She'd actually expected he

279

would begin mauling her the moment they crossed the threshold. But there he stood, one shoulder against the door frame and his arms folded across his chest.

"It might've worked. It might still, if need be."

As he spoke she moved to the front window, standing out of sight of the street as she pulled the curtains closed. The other window looked out over the empty space where the stable had been, so she left it alone. This felt clandestine enough without extinguishing all the light in the room.

"Are you just going to stand there?" she finally asked, eyeing him as he watched her wander about the room.

"Ye told me not to rush ye. I'm here where I want to be with ye, so I figured ye can come over here and kiss me in yer own time."

Taking a deep breath, trying to quell the flutter in her chest, she walked up to him. "I want to be clear about one thing," she said, putting a gloved forefinger against his chest.

"Ye have my attention."

"This is because we have a mutual . . . desire," she said slowly, curling her finger into his cravat. "I'm not some weak-kneed miss, and you are not a heartless cad. It's simply a matter of attraction." There. For her own . . . pride she needed it made clear that she understood the circumstances, and that she didn't want what he wasn't offering.

"A simple matter," he repeated, reaching up to twirl the blond curl hanging from her temple about his finger. "I think ye should kiss me now, Charlotte."

CHAPTER TEN

She fluttered, inches from giving him the moment about which he'd been dreaming for the past week. It would have been such a simple matter, to lean a little forward and touch her sweet mouth with his own.

But Ranulf held himself precisely where he was, every muscle aching with tension. This had been his suggestion, in his house, and according to his timing. He was accustomed to leading, to ordering that something be done and then seeing it accomplished. Allowing Charlotte to decide the next moments was both maddening and supremely arousing.

Gloved fingers toyed with his cravat, the gentle tug and pull quite possibly the most erotic sensation he'd ever experienced. His breath came slow and deep, his heart keeping time as he waited.

Finally she slid her palms up his chest, lifted on her toes, and featherlight pressed her lips against his. *Thank God.*

Allowing himself to move again, Ranulf cupped her face in his hands, kissing her back until her lips softened and she opened a little to his seeking teeth and tongue. When she moaned the pressure in his groin tripled, and he shifted to grip her hips, pulling her closer against him.

She called it a mutual attraction. He called it an obsession with a stubborn, maddening woman who with a few words had made him reconsider decades of resentment and prejudice. His eyes felt opened. If she had decided she didn't enjoy his company, or that his views made him unacceptable even as a temporary lover, he remained uncertain what he would have done.

Still kissing her, he shed his English-tailored coat. Next he unbuttoned his waistcoat and dropped it to the floor, as well. "Yer turn, lass," he murmured, turning his attention to the trio of buttons that held her pretty, dark green pelisse on over her green and yellow sprigged muslin gown.

His hands brushed her breasts as he worked, and she jumped a little. "I feel very wicked," she breathed unsteadily, breaking from his mouth to watch his hands travel down her front.

He opened the pelisse and pushed it down

her shoulders. Ripping every stitch of clothing off her would have been more satisfying, but he'd promised a measure of discretion, and she already thought him a violent devil. Returning her home with all her buttons and seams torn away would be neither discreet nor wise.

Lowering his gaze from her face, he cupped her breasts through the thin muslin. Just the size to fit in his hands, they were, as if she'd been made with him in mind. He firmed his grip and she gasped, pressing against his palms. "Ye're wearing too many damned clothes," he noted, trying not to jump as her hip brushed against his cock.

"I think I'd like to sit down," she commented faintly, leaning up for his mouth again.

"I'll do ye one better." Bending, he scooped her up into his arms and carried her over to his big, soft bed.

As he set her down in the center of the plump mattress she tangled her fingers into his hair, pulling him down over her. Ranulf sank down onto his hip beside her, keeping her lithe body wrapped in his arms. He fought the sensation that he wasn't close enough to her, that he had to be inside her immediately, to satisfy his own need, to claim her for his own. He would. He would, but for both their sakes he would go slow. The last thing he wanted was to frighten or hurt her.

But then she grinned up at him and tugged at his cravat. "Who in the world tied this?" she asked with a chuckle, pushing his chin sideways as she worked the knots loose with her gloved fingers.

Both actions served to remind him that she wasn't as delicate as he'd previously thought. "Poor Ginger," he returned. "My valet. He said he nearly lost both his arms because of yer stubbornness."

"My stubbornness?" she repeated, finally pulling the cravat free and tossing it off the bed.

"Aye. He said he would have let go of that bucket crank after twenty minutes last night, but he couldnae let ye best him."

She chuckled. "Poor man."

Taking advantage of the momentary conversation, he rolled onto his backside and sat up to yank off his English boots and drop them to the floor. "I know what my valet was thinking, then, but what about ye, *leannan*? And give me yer feet."

"I don't remember thinking much of anything," she mused, lifting one foot to put her ankle into his waiting hand.

He pulled off her low-heeled walking shoe

and set it beside his boots. "I doubt ye've ever thought nothing. Were ye worried aboot me, lass?"

She handed over her other foot. "I hadn't seen you in a week. I thought that after you went to all the trouble of acquiring a house and hosting a dinner and being so . . ."

"Gentlemanly?" he suggested, though he didn't feel at all gentlemanly at the moment.

"I was going to say open-minded," she countered, sitting up to help him pull his shirttail from his trousers. "It was wrong that someone else's poor behavior might convince you to leave London. I didn't want you to go."

"That's very nice to hear," he murmured, and captured her gloved fingers in his. "I want to feel yer hands on me, Charlotte."

She nodded. "So do I."

"Yer blisters?"

"I'll manage."

That made him grin. "I certainly hope so." Bending over her hand, he opened the wee pearl buttons and carefully pulled off the glove. "Good?" he asked, lifting his gaze to find her studying his face.

"Good. The other one, now."

He helped her remove it. The moment he did so, she pushed up the front of his shirt and brushed her palms lightly across his

286

chest. The tickling featheriness of it made him shudder. When she ran curious fingers across his nipples, he drew in a hard breath, took the ends of his shirt, and pulled the thing off over his head.

"You look like a Greek carving," she mused, her fingers warm and unsteady against his skin.

"Nae. A Scottish one."

Charlotte laughed, the arousing sound nearly causing him to burst the seam of his trousers. *Sweet Saint Andrew.* Twisting to face her again, he drew her muslin sleeve down her arm. Slowly Ranulf leaned in to kiss her bared shoulder.

She tasted faintly of lemons. Did she have freckles she was trying to fade? He hoped she wouldn't do such a thing; in fact, he would enjoy finding and kissing every freckle on her fair skin. As she curved her neck to him, he ran his lips across her ear and the pulse at the base of her jaw, then down her shoulder again, pulling down the front of her gown as he went. The top of her breast, the soft, perfect curve, the stiff pebble of her nipple.

"Ranulf," she gasped, wrapping her hands around his forearms.

Still toying with her breast, he looked up at her. "Do ye wish me to stop?"

"No. Definitely not. But you don't look terribly comfortable down . . . there."

"Oh, I'm nae. Strangled, more like."

"Then let's do something about that," she suggested unevenly, sliding her hands down his ribs to his waist.

Ranulf grinned, kissing her exposed breast. "I'd be a fool to argue with that. But dunnae hurt yer hands. I'll do it."

Sliding off the bed, he stood and swiftly unfastened the buttons of his trousers. Then, figuring now was good as later, he shirked the buckskins down his hips and kicked out of them. He watched her face, waiting for a maidenly exclamation, or . . . something. Though if she'd seen Greek statues she would have some idea of male anatomy.

Her lowered gaze lingered. Finally, hazel eyes lifted to meet his. "So that's what you have under your kilt, Ranulf MacLawry."

He laughed. "Now who's being wicked?" he taunted, and returned to the bed. "Kneel, and lift up a bit."

When she did so, he took the bottom of her gown and pulled it up, past her knees, up her thighs, above the tangle of soft golden curls, and lifted it up over her head and off.

"Well?" she prompted after a moment,

sinking onto her backside again. She didn't try to cover herself, or lower her eyes shyly.

Remarkable lass. "More lovely than sunrise, ye are," he said aloud, still smiling. "I think I'll come to ye, this time." He moved over her, tugging at her legs until she lay flat on her back beneath him.

This time her kiss was as hot and open-mouthed as his own. He kissed her until they were both out of breath and panting, then slowly moved down the slender length of her, teasing at first one breast and then the other, tracing her breastbone with his lips and meandering down to her belly button and then lower until with a dart of his tongue he tasted her.

"Good heavens!" she squeaked, nearly clobbering him with a knee. "Oh, I'm so sorry."

By way of response Ranulf slid a finger inside her, and she groaned. Mm. She was hot and wet — for him. "Sweet Christ," he murmured, moving in with his tongue again.

This time she shuddered and pulsed, coming with a sweet rush that made her cry out and his cock jump convulsively. "That . . . Oh, my," she managed, laughing breathlessly.

"My turn now, I think," he rumbled, kissing his way up her body again. He'd been more patient than a saint, for the devil's sake, and he badly wanted to bury himself in her tight depths.

At the last moment he remembered the French condom he'd dropped into his coat pocket on the chance that his plans for the day had proceeded as he wanted. With a curse he rolled off the bed, found his coat by the door, and dug the thing out.

"What's that for?" she asked, lifting up on her elbows and already looking deliciously disheveled.

"To keep ye from getting with child," he answered, slipping it on and tying off the ribbon.

"So that's how it's done. It's very pretty."

"Nae," he said, returning to the bed. "A man's cock is 'grand,' or 'handsome,' or 'proud.' It is nae pretty."

Moving over her once more, Ranulf nudged her knees apart and settled between her thighs to kiss her sweet mouth again, teasing at her breasts with his fingers. When he had her moaning in pleasure once more he canted his hips forward, entering her slowly and with as much care as he could manage. The urge to simply take her, immediately and repeatedly, pushed at him again, but he held himself back.

"Ready?" he drawled.

She nodded silently, her eyes wide and her fingers kneading into his shoulders. He told her to take a deep breath and hold it. When she did so, he pushed forward, past the thin edge of resistance, and entered her fully.

Charlotte squeezed her eyes shut, took a second shuddering breath, and looked up at him again. For a long moment he stayed where he was, kissing her until she relaxed again and swearing to himself that this was the last time he would ever cause her pain.

Finally he pulled back a little and pushed in again. "Better?"

"Yes," she returned. "I want more."

"Well, then."

Ranulf rocked inside her again, then began a slow, full pump of his hips. She felt . . . exquisite and tight around him, her soft moans driving him faster and deeper. They both might know their philosophies as much as their lives made them incompatible, but it didn't feel that way. Skin to skin, sweat intermingled, tongues tangled, they fit extraordinarily well.

She came again, pulsing around him, and finally he gave in to the urge to well and truly take her. Harder, deeper, faster, until with a surging groan he spilled into her.

Collapsing onto his back, he pulled her

over across his chest. For a long moment they lay there, limbs tangled and her breath warm on his skin. Her carefully coiffed hair was a shambles, and one by one he pulled the pins from the soft golden mass, letting it fall across his chest like sunlight. Her blistered palm lay flat over his heart, and he wondered if she could feel it beating.

He'd never believed in fairy tales, in the phenomenon of love at first sight. That was what had driven his father to drag an English bride into the Highlands. She'd wanted a title, and he'd wanted her, and disaster had ensued. But he knew for certain that Eleanor MacLawry would never have run outside at night to help battle a fire on her own family's property — much less anyone else's. And she never would have stood her ground to the point that her hands blistered.

Charlotte had done more than that. She'd helped organize the chaos of men and buckets and water, and men who couldn't possibly know who she was had listened and obeyed. She was lovely and kind, but stood her ground and spoke her mind — even to him, when no one dared do so.

Most tellingly, she'd come to his bed after he'd agreed not to run off and attack Berling. When he'd worn his proper, civilized attire and sworn to let logic and reason carry the day. Was that such a difficult thing to do? He'd been raised in a place where a man held power with both his fists and his mind. Was there a different way to proceed?

Ranulf frowned as he twined his fingers softly through her hair. He'd bedded his share of Scottish lasses. They were pretty, and enthusiastic, and otherwise forgettable. The woman presently in his arms was anything but forgettable. Were the two of them so incompatible, after all? What would he have to give up, but punching a deserving scoundrel or two? Evidently, since he'd gone to the bother of having sketches made and collecting evidence, he'd already decided that he was willing to utilize legal means to stop Berling. Whether he removed Donald Gerdens or the law did, the results would be the same — with one crucial difference. Charlotte Hanover.

"Are you asleep?" she whispered, curving a lazy circle now over his heart with her forefinger.

"Nae. I'm gathering strength for another go."

"Mm."

Just the way she said that went a fair way to making him hard again. "I'm thinking we spent a long afternoon at the museum and stood for quite a long time ogling those naked Greek statues ye like so much."

She chuckled, the sound reverberating into his chest. "I think I prefer the Scottish version, actually."

He damn well hoped so, because he had no intention of parting from this English lass. What had begun as a mild curiosity had altered and deepened. In fact, he meant to keep hold of her until he could put a ring on her finger and tell all the world that Charlotte Hanover belonged to him. Forever.

Charlotte rested her head on one elbow to watch Ranulf pad naked and magnificent to the bedchamber door. Pulling it open, he leaned into the hallway. "Owen!" he bellowed. "Sandwiches!"

"Very regal," she commented, as he returned to his big bed and settled back against the headboard.

"I'm hungry."

That was no surprise, considering his exertions. And she was rather famished, herself. "Are we dining in the museum's tea room, then?" she asked, shifting a little to run a finger along his ribs. Touching a man's skin — his skin — was indescribably arousing.

"Aye. And I assume we're sipping tea from dainty cups and nibbling at wee sandwiches with the crusts trimmed off."

"Yes, we are. And then I think we'll take a leisurely stroll among the sarcophagi and mummies before you return me home.' "

He slid down the bed until their faces were even. "I like the British Museum. What other sights around London could ye show me, *leannan*?"

"What does that mean? *Leannan*?"

Shrugging one shoulder, he captured her right hand and brought it up to examine it carefully. "Ye know, Debny has some horse liniment that would likely do ye."

She grimaced. "I do not want to smell like horse liniment."

One by one he kissed her fingertips. The sensation, the gesture, made her shiver. "We've been slathering it on fer years. Bumps, scrapes, sprains — it cures everything, according to Debny."

"I prefer to suffer, thank you very much." Charlotte flexed her hand. "You aren't going to tell me what *leannan* means, then? I can ask Winnie, you know."

"Ye're a persistent lass, Charlotte." He tugged her over his chest again, wrapping his strong arms around her. "I suppose the best translation would be 'dear friend,' " he drawled.

That sounded very nice. What it didn't sound like was a term someone would use to describe a partner in a one-time union resulting from simple mutual attraction. Of course, at this moment there was nothing at all simple about how she felt. Or how he felt against her. Indeed, the only simple fact was that she didn't want this to be the one and only time she shared his bed.

"What's this, then?" she asked, tapping her nose and trying to distract herself from unhelpful thoughts.

He tilted his head to look down at her face. "Ye've a yen to learn Scottish, then, do ye?"

"It's a pretty language."

Before either of them could question if she had more on her mind or not — something she certainly couldn't even answer to her own satisfaction — his door rattled. "M'laird," Owen's voice came, "I've yer sandwiches."

"Leave 'em on the floor."

"Fergus already ate one of 'em on the way up here."

"Oh, fer Saint Andrew's sake," Ranulf muttered, and slid out from beneath her again. Striding to the door, he pulled a blanket from the back of a chair and knotted it around his hips. Unlocking the door, he stepped into the opening. "Ye keeping the maid occupied?" he asked, taking the tray of food from the footman's hands.

"She's been as tight as a nun, m'lord, looking at us like we all smell rotted."

Charlotte abruptly wondered if she wasn't asking too much of Simms. The maid had been in her employ for the last seven years, since she'd turned eighteen, and in all that time she didn't think she'd ever done a single thing for which she'd needed to enlist Simms's discretion.

"I hope you're not frightening her," she said, gathering the disheveled sheets around her and standing.

"Nae," the footman protested, craning his neck to see her around Ranulf's shoulders. "We're gentle as lambs, we are."

Ranulf shifted, blocking Owen's view again. "That'll do. Go away."

"I can't stay much longer," Charlotte put in.

His broad shoulders rose and fell. "Have the maid come up here in ten minutes," he amended, "and the barouche brought round in thirty."

"Aye, m'laird. Are ye certain y—"

Closing the door, Ranulf locked it again and faced her, the tray of sandwiches in one hand. For a moment his gaze took her in from head to toe, pausing at her breasts and her face. "Come over to the table," he said, pulling a second chair over to his small writing table. "Ye may as well eat someaught before ye go."

Stifling an urge to send a regretful look back at the bed, Charlotte hefted the trailing sheets and followed him. "We've accepted an invitation to the Duke and Duchess of Esmond's soiree tomorrow night," she said, sitting. "Will you be attending?"

Almost immediately she regretted asking, because he'd been forcibly removed from the last grand ball he'd attended, and for good reason. Odds were that he wouldn't have received an invitation to the next one — or to any others this Season. She should have been thankful that he wouldn't have another easy opportunity to brawl in public, but at this moment she mostly wished she had another chance to dance with him.

He wolfed down a sandwich and started on a second while she nibbled at hers. Yes, she felt famished, but a lady did not stuff food in her mouth as if she were worried that someone else meant to take it from her.

"Myles was invited," he said, between bites. "I'll go along as his guest."

"Oh. That's good, then."

He eyed her. "Ye've nothing to worry over, Charlotte. As long as ye dunnae give Berling a dance while I'm there."

Warmth swept through her all over again. Was he jealous? He certainly didn't sound like a man who'd scratched an itch, so to speak, and was now continuing on his merry way. On the other hand, she well remembered what had happened the last time he and Berling had met over her dance card.

"I would hope, Ranulf, that if you and Lord Berling did meet again, you would decide not to hit him, simply because you're an intelligent, articulate, thoughtful man who has no need to resort to the basest method of . . . anything."

Ranulf chewed and swallowed. "And I say again, dunnae give Berling a dance, and ye'll nae have anything to worry over."

If her miniature tirade hadn't wiped the easy amusement from his face, perhaps she had made some progress with him. Deciding this was worth risking his ire, she held out her right hand. "An agreement, then. I won't dance with him, and you won't punch him."

Wiping his hand off on the blanket girding his waist, Ranulf reached across the table and with obvious care gripped her fingers. "Aye. An agreement."

Charlotte smiled at that; she couldn't help herself. Because if he could decide on some restraint, of serving his mind rather than his pride, then perhaps they weren't as entirely incompatible as she'd thought. And perhaps they could arrange to see more sights in London they would never actually visit before he went back to Scotland to marry a lady who wasn't a Sasannach.

She shook off that thought. He wasn't with some Highlands lass at the moment, and she'd never spent as enjoyable a day as this. "You still have my hand, sir," she pointed out, her grin deepening.

"Do I, now?" Without warning he tugged her over the top of the table and kissed her. The remaining sandwiches and the tray bounced to the floor.

She settled onto his lap, wriggling her hips as she felt him hardening beneath her thighs. Male anatomy truly was a wondrous thing. No wonder young ladies were supposed to remain ignorant of it until marriage; knowing the delights of sex would, in her opinion anyway, alter the way a woman looked at every potential beau. She, at least, would certainly insist on first seeing a prospective husband naked.

A polite knock sounded at the door. "I'll send yer Simms away, shall I?" he murmured, slipping his hand into the folds of the sheets she wore and flicking a fingernail across her nipple.

She jumped, desire spearing through her all over again. Oh, she wanted to send everyone away, to spend every remaining moment in the ecstasy of his embrace. But her maid waited just outside, along with her reputation and her family and Society. With a last, lingering kiss she pushed away from him and stood. "You should put your clothes back on, too, so you can see me home."

Narrowing one eye, Ranulf climbed to his feet. "As ye will, then, Charlotte."

While she walked to the door, he collected his boots and trousers, along with his shirt, coat, cravat, and waistcoat. When he stopped in front of her, Charlotte looked up into his deep blue gaze.

"*Sròin,*" he murmured.

"Beg pardon?"

With a faint smile he leaned down and kissed the tip of her nose. "*Sròin,*" he repeated, and pulled open the door with his free hand. "I'll be in the room across the hallway if ye should have need of me." Ignoring the stiff, wide-eyed Simms, he left his bedchamber.

Charlotte took a deep breath. "Simms, come help me dress."

"Yes, my lady."

Dropping the sheets to the floor, Charlotte went to find some of her things. *"Sròin,"* she said experimentally, touching her nose.

Somewhere in the past fortnight her life had become interesting, unexpected, and even exciting. She knew precisely whom to thank for that, and with all her heart she hoped it would continue. Whatever it was she and Ranulf had — a mutual attraction, a sense of incompatibility that had, at least on her part, begun to weaken — she looked forward to discovering what came next. And she wondered if, and hoped that, Ranulf felt the same way.

"Aren't ye going to ask me about Lachlan?" Arran asked, as he and Rowena and Jane sat in the Hanover House garden.

She shook her head. "No. I've given him a chance to miss me, or to come after me. If he hasn't done either, well, I want nothing more to do with him." It sounded like something she should say, anyway, and beside her Jane was emphatically nodding her head.

Her brother didn't look nearly as convinced. "A month ago ye swore to me that ye loved him and meant to marry him. And so ye've been saying, since ye could talk."

"I was a little bairn — baby — and I was wrong."

"I'm glad yer heart can mend so quickly then, Winnie," he returned, "though ye should know that Lachlan volunteered at least twice to ride down to London and help Ran fetch ye back."

Rowena shrugged. "Two English lads have already proposed to me, you know. After three or four dances. Lachlan's had eighteen years."

With a nod her brother reached out to pull a petal from a rose and roll the delicate white thing in his fingers. "If ye can forget him so easily, it makes me wonder how much of yer heart he truly had in the first place."

She held his gaze. "No more than I had of his heart."

Rowena had lately begun to realize that making Lachlan MacTier jealous — when he remained hundreds of miles away surrounded by pretty, fawning lasses all fluttering their eyelashes and admiring his property and not telling him he was an idiot — was a hopeless proposition. It cut her deeply that he hadn't bothered to so much as send her a letter.

After last night, though, she'd begun to think that perhaps something more pressing was afoot. She could hardly believe that her oldest brother, always so concerned with the rest of the family's safety and the entire clan's well-being and happiness, might have found a lass who kept his attention for longer than a day. But something had convinced him to purchase a house in London. And something had sent him out sightseeing, unexpected as that was. And she was fairly certain it wasn't anything she'd done. And the fact that the lass was a propriety-minded English lady of all things . . . She didn't have any idea what to make of that.

All the same, it felt important that she at least discover the truth. And that, after everything he'd done for her since her earliest memory, she do whatever she could to determine whether his heart was truly involved, and if the woman he'd perhaps selected was the right one to become a part of Clan MacLawry, to become the Marchioness of Glengask, and to make Ranulf finally and forever happy.

A few minutes later Rowena heard a carriage clatter up the front drive and stop. She pushed to her feet. "Ran and Charlotte are back, I think."

The three of them made their way in through the back of the house, until Arran caught her arm and slowed her down. "Is Ran courting Lady Charlotte?" he asked, keeping his voice low.

"I'm not certain," she answered truthfully. "I mean to find out, though."

He nodded. "That's why I'm here, as well. He sent me a letter about buying that house. I couldnae figure out why in God's name he would do such a thing. What I *did* see was the way he kept mentioning a lass called Charlotte."

"*That*'s why you came to London?"

"Aye."

Oh, dear. Rowena took a quick breath. She loved all her brothers, and she well knew that her second-oldest brother was the most logical of the lot of them. Ranulf listened to Arran's advice more than he did to anyone else's. And she couldn't imagine that Arran would ever suggest that Ranulf bring an Englishwoman back to Scotland.

She jabbed a finger into his chest. "You just keep your opinions to yourself, Arran."

He lifted an eyebrow. "My opinions aboot what?"

"About everything. You don't know what's going on here."

"And ye do?"

"Not yet. But at least I mean to figure it out before I step in the middle of it. This isn't about who they are or where they're from. It's about how they feel about each other. I like her, and I don't care that she's English. And you're not permitted to give Ranulf your opinion until you exchange more than half a dozen words with her."

For a long moment he looked at her. "So says the lass who tries to woo her man by leaving the country and swearing never to return."

She drew herself up as tall as she could, which was still only to Arran's shoulder. "Perhaps I came because I wanted to know what — who — else was out there. And as it turns out, Lachlan MacTier isn't the only man in the world." She crossed her arms over her chest. "So what do you think of that?"

"I think I'll keep yer advice in mind, Winnie, and hold on to my opinion where both ye and Ran are concerned. I'll nae promise more than that."

That was something, anyway. "Good. Because Ran's intentions don't concern us."

"Everything Ranulf does concerns us. All of us. The clan and the family. And while I mind yer advice, ye'd best remember what I've said, as well."

He might keep his opinions to himself for the moment, but he wouldn't do so forever.

Which meant that she needed to figure out what was going on between Ranulf and Charlotte before he did. Because he would weigh whatever Ran wanted against how it benefited the clan — and with the Mac-Lawrys, the clan always came first.

CHAPTER ELEVEN

Ranulf heaved another stack of charred lumber into the back of the wagon. As he did so a barouche full of young ladies passed by — the second time they'd done so. While he would have preferred to offer them a two-fingered salute, he was being gentlemanly today. Instead he sketched a jaunty bow.

"I feel like a damned animal in a menagerie," Owen muttered from beside him as the footman emptied a shovel into the wagon's bed.

"Ye think those lasses were ogling you, do ye?" Debny put in with a snort.

Clapping his heavy work gloves together, Ranulf returned to the stable ruins for another load. His white shirt was torn and filthy, but according to Ginger an aristocrat did not appear bare-chested in public in London. He *had* untucked the thing, and decided if it fell off on its own he would bloody well call it providence and leave it that way.

"They do have men ye can hire to haul away rubbish such as this, ye know," Owen pointed out, helping to stack another set of ruined, warped boards.

"Less gabbing, more cleaning," Ranulf grunted, heaving the mass onto his shoulder and making his way back to the wagon.

Yes, he might have hired men to tear down the remains of his stable and haul it away. In truth, though, since he'd been in London the most exercise he'd managed had been in bed with Charlotte yesterday. At home, at Glengask, there was always some task or other that needed doing, from helping to clear a new field to cleaning out irrigation ditches to helping a cotter replace a roof or helping to shear the fat Highland sheep — the only kind he would tolerate on his land.

Here, today, the ache and flex of his muscles made him feel as if he were accomplishing something, whether he might have hired someone else to do it or not. Rolling his shoulders, he returned for a stack of roof shingles.

"Where's Lord Arran off to, if I might ask?" Owen said, dragging a blanket covered with singed and melted tack away.

"He went to find some of his army

friends," Ranulf answered. "Fergus'll keep an eye on him."

He hadn't quite believed Arran, actually, when his brother had announced that he meant to spend the morning visiting. It seemed an odd choice after he'd ridden all the way down from Glengask to perform some sort of rescue. Then again, perhaps his brother had realized that a rescue wasn't necessary.

After all, Rowena hadn't repeated her oath not to return to Scotland — not in his hearing, anyway. And owning a house in London made sense, if it gave him more of a presence in standing against his unhappy fellow Scots. Whether or not they would admit to being Scots at all.

With him and most of the staff working at it, they should have the old stable cleared away sometime tomorrow. And then he would hire someone to build him a new one. The Duke of Greaves had offered use of his stable for as long as necessary, but Ranulf didn't like owing a favor to a man he didn't know.

None of this would prevent Berling from stopping by and burning down a new stable, or even the house, of course. He did have a few thoughts on that subject, however. Charlotte had asked him not to fight Donald Gerdens at tonight's soiree. She hadn't said anything, however, about afterward. And he'd found on a few previous occasions that a direct confrontation together with a concise explanation and demonstration of consequences could cool many a man's ire. After all, most men were cruel only when they thought they could get away with it.

Charlotte. The moment he conjured her in his thoughts, which he seemed to be doing almost constantly today, she refused to depart again. God knew the trail would have been easier if he'd set himself after some bonny Scottish lass who understood how troubles were dealt with in the Highlands and had no difficulty with that fact. Someone who knew how a laird was expected to lead a clan and wouldn't even think to disagree with his methods.

But it wasn't a Scottish lass who'd caught him up in her skirts and made him half mad with wanting her. It was Charlotte Hanover, and if he couldn't turn away from her, she would twist more than his heart. That would certainly be simpler, to leave London immediately and go home to marry the first lass he set eyes on.

What if Charlotte didn't wish to live at Glengask? After what he'd experienced with his own mother, he certainly wouldn't —

couldn't — force her into that kind of life. Other clan lairds lived far from the Highlands. One or two had never even set foot there. They went about making that so-called barren land they owned as profitable as they could, setting sheep to graze it and hiring thugs to burn out the few cotters remaining on their ancestral soil.

That wasn't him. The MacLawrys had risen to power because of the strength and loyalty of the clan. And now the clan would remain safe and prosperous because of the strength of the MacLawrys.

So he knew where he stood, but then he always had. He wasn't the complication. Yes, Charlotte had proved herself brave, and yes, he knew her to be kind and thoughtful. And he supposed if he'd been his father he would simply marry her, drag her off to Scotland, and let the future fall where it would.

But clearly he wasn't his father, because it wasn't enough that Charlotte pleased his heart, made him happy, filled every other thought with a healthy lust to be with her. He wanted her to be happy in return. And that was where the difficulty lay.

"M'laird?"

Ranulf started. "Aye?"

"I thought ye'd turned to stone there, fer a moment." Owen sent him a concerned look. "I called ye thrice."

"And I decided to answer ye the third time," Ranulf retorted. "Now were ye just calling me fer amusement, or did ye have a point?"

"I had a point," the old soldier said, straightening his shoulders. "Lady Winnie's just arriving."

Ranulf turned around. Sure enough, a closed coach was stopped at the front of the house, and Rowena, closely followed by Una, stepped down to the drive. Peter Gilling, perched up front beside the liveried coachman, hopped down, as well. Rowena said something to the driver, and with a nod he sent the team back into the street. Only then did Ranulf notice that the vehicle bore the Hanover coat of arms on its doors.

"Sweet Saint Andrew, it looks even worse by daylight," his sister said, lifting her skirts to carefully pick her way through the rubble.

"I'll have a new one up before ye know it," Ranulf returned, pulling off a glove to scratch Una behind the ears.

She nodded, glancing at him then away again. So far as he remembered, they'd parted on good terms both after the dinner and fire, and then yesterday when he'd returned Charlotte home. Whatever was unsettling her, he didn't think he'd done it.

He stepped over a pile of wood, shedding his other glove and dropping them both onto a barrel. "Fancy a sit in my garden?" he asked, offering her an arm.

"I am not holding on to you," she commented, wrinkling her nose. "You're filthy."

"Then I suppose ye don't want me kissing yer cheek, either." With a grin he motioned her to precede him up the short path to the walled-in garden.

"This is pretty. Did I tell you that?"

"Aye."

"Oh. Well, it is."

"Thank ye."

She wandered about for a minute, then took a seat in one of the wrought-iron chairs beneath the big elm tree in the center of the flowery plantings. Ranulf dragged the other chair closer and sat down facing her.

"Now that we're finished with the pleasantries," he drawled, "what's amiss?"

"Amiss? Nothing's amiss. Why would you say that?" she returned, fiddling with her skirt.

"Because ye're here, fer one thing. And because ye can't seem to look me in the eye. Last time ye did that, it was because ye'd decided to freshen my bed with lavender, and dumped an entire bottle of scent into the middle of the mattress."

Rowena laughed. "It smelled very pretty, after three days with the windows open."

"And I still cannae abide lavender. So what brings ye here, Rowena? I thought ye'd be shopping, or having a coze with yer new friends."

She folded her hands in her lap. "You're my brother. Do I need an excuse to come see you?"

"Nae. But if ye had one, what would it be?"

Abruptly Una seemed to need a sound belly rub, because Rowena sank down in the grass to give her one. A prickle of uneasiness stole through Ranulf's skin. His sister was thirteen years his junior. And in her entire life she'd never hesitated to talk to him about anything. Whatever this was, it couldn't be anything pleasant.

"The Hanovers are very nice, aren't they?" she finally offered, her gaze still on the happily wriggling hound.

Was that it? Did she wish to live with them permanently? His heart clenched, but he took a short breath to cover it. "Aye, they are."

"I'm glad Lady Hanover and Jane kept in touch with me for all those years. It was nothing they were obligated to do."

Yes, they'd been so friendly that she'd felt

315

comfortable fleeing her home to come stay with them. But they were also Charlotte's family, and so he wasn't going to say anything ill about them. "Why wouldn't they wish to correspond with ye, Rowena? Ye're a bonny lass."

"I didn't know anything about Charlotte's fiancé being killed in a stupid duel. I didn't even know she'd been engaged. That was very sad, wasn't it?"

"Aye." Though he doubted he'd ever find himself weeping tears over James Appleton's demise.

She glanced up at him, then down again. "Did you like the museum yesterday?"

"I liked it well enough."

"I didn't think Charlotte would speak to you again, after that fight at the Evanstone soiree. But since you went sightseeing together, I suppose she's forgiven you."

Ranulf frowned. "Berling tried to push at me, and I shoved back harder. There's nothing I need to be forgiven for."

"But you are friends, aren't you?"

"What?" Ranulf didn't know what the devil was afoot, but he didn't like it. "Berling and I will ne'er be friends, Rowena. He nearly killed Bear, in case ye've forgotten, and I'll wager he set this fire, too."

"No, no, no. I didn't mean Lord Berling.

I meant Charlotte. You're friends with Charlotte, aren't you?"

Well, that made more sense. "I suppose so," he agreed, trying not to put too much emotion into the words.

"I think she likes talking to you. Several times she's said that you have a unique way of looking at things."

Abruptly it dawned on Ranulf what his sister was about. "Are ye matchmaking, Rowena?" he asked.

Finally she abandoned Una and scooted over to take his hands in her slender ones. "I think you already like her. Otherwise you wouldn't bother even talking to her."

"Wouldnae that make me rude?"

She tilted her head. "There's polite, and there's nice, Ran. You're being nice to her."

"She called me a devil," he reminded his sister, wondering whether it was amusement or terror he was feeling. If Rowena, so concerned with her Season and with whether Lachlan MacTier would come to his senses that she could barely see straight, had noticed a connection between him and Charlotte, others must have noticed, as well. *Damnation.* This business with Charlotte was complicated enough without everyone else putting in their pennies.

"Only because you were throwing punches

willy-nilly. She's accustomed to gentle gentlemen. She told me that 'civilization' has the word 'civil' in it for a reason, and that we'd all be better people for learning that calling someone a name doesn't deserve a bloodying as a response, or we're all no better than animals."

Well, wasn't that interesting? "So she called me an animal?"

Rowena flushed. "Nae! No, I mean. We had that conversation directly after the ball, when we were all angry with you." She squeezed his hands. "Just this morning she told me that you seemed to be a very fine, honorable gentleman."

That answered that. "Ye *are* matchmaking, Rowena MacLawry." He twisted his hands so that he gripped her palms in turn. "What makes ye think that a man who's willing to throw punches — and worse — to protect his own is in any way compatible with a lass who thinks no blow ever struck is justified?"

He hoped she would have an answer. If she'd arrived there with miraculous answers to all of his concerns, he would have been willing to believe her. Because so far, he wasn't having much luck seeking them on his own.

"It's simple, Ran," she returned. "If ye

love her, ye need to learn to be more . . ."

"Civilized?" he supplied.

"English," she countered, then swallowed. "But don't —"

" 'English.' " He repeated slowly, the taste of the word uncomfortable on his tongue, mostly because he was saying it without the usual wash of contempt. "How so?"

"I . . ."

She trailed off, then retrieved her hands and stood. Clearly she was as surprised by his response as he was. But if he couldn't figure out precisely what it was that Charlotte wanted, and more importantly, how to go about achieving it, he'd already lost.

"First of all, then, no more kilts."

"My kilts dunnae punch people."

Rowena's mouth twitched. "No, but it makes you seem more antagonistic. It's as though you've called everyone out, and you're only waiting to see who steps forward first."

There were occasions when he *had* to wear a kilt — when he stood at weddings, at formal clan meetings, funerals, all the sundry duties the chief of the clan had to his name. But none of those took place in London. "At home *not* wearing a kilt is antagonistic. But I think I can manage to wear naught but trousers in London."

His sister nodded, then furrowed her brow. "I didn't think ye'd even agree to that," she confessed, her surprise showing in the return of her Highlands accent. He'd missed hearing it, but now didn't seem to be the time to comment. "Give me a minute to think of the rest," she continued.

"Why don't ye come in and have luncheon with me?" he suggested. "Arran's off seeing friends, and I've missed chatting with ye."

"If you weren't so dirty, I would hug you, Ran."

He grinned, feeling lighter than he had since he'd parted with Charlotte yesterday. In all his imaginings he would never have considered that the person who could best help him win Charlotte Hanover would be his bairn of a sister. "Well, I'll go change my shirt and we'll see to that, then."

The tall man with the thin scar across the bridge of his nose sent a sideways glance at Arran MacLawry. "I imagine I can get us into Boodles this close to luncheon," he said, directing his chestnut gelding around a slow-moving rag and bone man. "But White's won't have a table for an hour."

London was more crowded than it had been the last time he'd passed through, but Arran noted that only peripherally as he

held in his quick-footed black Thorough-
bred, Duffy. His last visit hadn't been during the middle of the Season, of course,
which could explain the difference, but he
preferred places where he could better see
his surroundings. "I know it's an inconve-
nience," he returned, "but there's someone
I need to take a look at, and I have it on
good authority that he's at White's."

His companion sighed. "I suppose that's
why you called it a favor."

"Aye. And I'll owe you a large one after
this, Will."

"Am I permitted to ask who it is you're
looking for?" William Crane, Viscount
Fordham, asked, keeping his gaze and
presumably his attention on the crowded
street.

Will was likely to figure it out on his own
soon enough, anyway. "The Earl of Berling."

"Ah. Does this have anything to do with
the beating your brother handed him last
week?" Fordham asked, not sounding the
least bit surprised.

"Not entirely. But if we should coinciden-
tally come across him at White's, and as I
dunnae think he knows who I am, if ye
could call me John Reynolds, say, I would
appreciate it."

Will coughed. "Wasn't that the name of

321

the captain you wagered a hundred quid over whether you could shoot his hat off his head?"

Arran sent his friend a mock frown. "I *did* shoot his hat off his head."

"Along with half his ear."

"He moved."

They reached the plain-looking front door of the club, and a stable boy ran up to collect their horses. As Fordham had warned, White's was packed to the gills, and the best the head footman could offer them was a pair of seats and a bottle of cognac in the library.

"If I need to introduce you," the viscount asked quietly, "are you certain you want to be Scottish?"

"Nae. Say I'm yer cousin from York."

"You don't sound like you're from York."

"I will. Take us by way of the dining room, if you please."

Shaking his head again, the viscount surreptitiously handed five pounds to a second footman, who immediately left them on their own. "I don't see your friend," he said after a moment, as they made their way through the obstacle-laden dining room.

"Keep looking. I heard he was here." It had cost him twenty quid to root out the information, actually, on top of the favor he now owed William Crane. "And introduce me to as few people as possible. I don't want them realizing I'm not who I say."

"You're not titled, Ar— John. No one cares who you are or what you're doing here, so long as you don't cause trouble."

That was the way he preferred it. He knew London — and the English — better than either of his brothers or his sister, but there were things — alliances, friendship, animosities — that he needed to view and decipher for himself. And at the top of the list of things he needed to see with his own eyes was Donald Gerdens, Lord Berling.

"There he is," Will said, on the tail of his thought. "Blue coat, eating pheasant, bruised jaw. On the left."

"I see him."

Berling didn't look all that formidable, with his delicately held fork and the hanging weightiness on his face. But danger didn't always come from straight ahead, and it didn't take physical strength to light a fire. Arran kept a blank expression on his face as he walked up behind Will.

"Lord Berling, isn't it?" Fordham said, utilizing all of his considerable charm. "Fordham. I know we haven't been formally introduced, but since last week I've been wanting to shake your hand."

The earl inclined his head, wiping off his fingers and shaking hands with the viscount. "It's good to meet another man of conviction," he said with a brief smile, then gestured at the two men seated with him. "Fordham, Charles Calder and Arnold Haws. Gentlemen . . ."

"Will Crane, Lord Fordham," Will supplied with a smile. "Pleased to meet you." He gestured at Arran. "This is my cousin, Mr. John Reynolds, down from York."

Ranulf had warned him that Berling seemed to have allied himself with the Campbells, so he wasn't surprised to see them sitting there together. Steeling himself, Arran also shook hands with the three men. If he'd been the sort of fellow who preferred a knife, he might have ended Berling and his cronies right there. But for some reason Ranulf had been set on gathering proof, which evidently meant they were going to attempt something legal. Either that, or blackmail.

"Glengask's had his share of trouble since that fight," he noted, stifling his brogue. "His stable burned down two nights ago."

"Did it?" Berling's eye twitched, and he reached for his glass of wine. "How unfortunate."

"I would love to know who to thank for

that," Will took up, chuckling.

"I wouldn't, necessarily," the earl returned. "Glengask doesn't respond well to threats — much less direct violence. I'm in no mood to get my nose broken again because some Englishman or other doesn't like Highlanders and I'm easy to blame."

Well, that was a surprise. Or a very clever statement. Arran touched Will's shoulder. "I think that's our table ready," he commented. "Again, pleased to meet you, Berling. Gentlemen."

Once they were out of earshot, Will slowed his retreat to the library. "What do you make of that?"

"I'm not certain. But I do mean to find out."

Whether or not Berling had set that fire, he'd certainly done damage to the MacLawrys before, and as far as Arran was concerned, he needed to be dealt with. If he wasn't the one burning buildings next to where his brother and sister were dining, though, someone else was. And that someone needed to be found. Which meant Ranulf needed to know what Arran had been up to today.

That wouldn't go over well. The idea of anyone else taking risks on Ranulf's part had never sat well with his brother. In fact, the only thing he was likely to be angrier about was when Arran advised him to leave the English lass alone before he got himself forced into a marriage he couldn't possibly want. And to think, he might have stayed at Glengask. *Damnation.*

"Charlotte, may I borrow your pearl ear-bobs?" Jane asked, hurrying into her sister's bedchamber.

"Certainly. They're in the jewelry box."

Seated at her dressing table, Charlotte glanced at her sister in the mirror's reflection. While Janie had always seemed young — and after all, seven years separated them — since yesterday the difference had become even more marked. Janie had her dreams about beaux and breaking hearts, but she'd experienced none of the reality of it.

When James died, Charlotte felt that she'd abruptly and without reason been denied her dream of a happy life. Until yesterday she hadn't actually known what a man, a marriage, meant. And the knowledge was rather . . . thrilling. Invigorating. Arousing.

"Oh, Char, you look so lovely," her sister exclaimed, walking up for a closer look. "Are those onyx?" Jane touched a finger to the black ribbon threaded through black beads and braided into her blond hair.

"They are. It was Simms's idea."

Jane caught the maid's arm. "Say you'll show Maggie how to do that, Simms."

"Of course, Lady Jane."

Once her sister had pranced out of the room again, Charlotte turned her head to look at the lady's maid. "Thank you again," she said quietly. "I know yesterday was nothing you could possibly wish to find yourself entangled with."

Simms curtsied. "I only hope no harm comes of it, my lady."

"So do I." And the fact that she'd thought of almost nothing but deep blue eyes and strong, warm arms and the gloriousness of that fit, hard body inside hers, couldn't possibly bode well.

Their mutual attraction may have been dealt with to *his* satisfaction, but she wanted more. She wanted more sex with him, she wanted to fall asleep in his arms, and wake up to see him beside her. If he'd been anyone but who he was, she would call him perfect.

"That should do it," Simms said finally, stepping back to admire the tumble of hair shot through with black, sparkling beads.

"You've outdone yourself," Charlotte returned, standing.

"I wanted something to complement that magnificent gown." A brief smile dimpling her cheeks, Simms busied herself with straightening up the dressing table.

Not even to herself could Charlotte pretend that she hadn't dressed tonight with Ranulf in mind. The deep red gown with the delicate black lace over the bodice and dripping from the sleeves, the black beads sewn into the skirt — she had no idea why she'd ever had it made in the first place. But now, tonight, it seemed a perfect match to the way she felt inside.

The family was already gathering in the foyer when she left her bedchamber, and she steeled herself for more questions about who might have caught her eye, and did she know she stood a risk of putting the debutantes to shame. Well, tonight she felt like that woman. And it was nice — very nice — to simply be a wicked, wanton woman for a few minutes before she had to become Charlotte the older sister well on the shelf once more.

"Charlotte, do you have a moment?" her father said, emerging from his office just as she passed by it.

"Of course, Papa." She followed him back inside, and he quietly closed the door behind them. "Has Jane begun writing bad poetry about some man again?" she asked with a grin.

"No, nothing as dire as that." He faced her. "Lord Glengask."

For a brief, horrified moment she thought Simms might have told. But her father wasn't swearing, and her mother wasn't even present, much less weeping over her older daughter's ruination, so Charlotte pasted a frown on her face. "What about him?"

"The two of you went driving yesterday."

She nodded, her mind racing ahead of the conversation, seeking for answers he hadn't yet asked — but likely would. "He wanted to see some of the sights."

"I thought he detested London."

"I told him he was wrong to claim hatred of something he'd never bothered to experience." That happened to be the truth, at least. The idea of lying to her dear, patient father made her feel ill; there were some things she couldn't tell him, but as much as possible she intended to be honest.

"And has his opinion altered?"

"He did say several complimentary things, but I believe it's still too early to tell."

"I see." He drummed his fingers on the back of a chair. "Is he courting you?"

Her breath caught. "Really, Papa. I'm

English. You know what he thinks of us. And I told him that brawling with people was the basest resort of petty minds." Abruptly it occurred to her that insulting Ranulf to her father was not the wisest way to endear one to the other — if such a thing was required. But jumping to his defense would make her father suspicious, and rightly so.

"Good."

That made her frown deepen. "What's good?"

"That he isn't courting you." The earl took a slow breath. "It's one thing to have his sister lodging here. She's young and charming and not political. He, on the other hand, has enemies caustic enough to burn down his stable. And there are rumors that his grandfather was a Jacobite. There's even talk that *he's* a Jacobite, given the way he keeps to the Highlands with an army of fighting men around him."

She couldn't disagree with any of it. "I don't know about his politics," she said slowly, her heart beginning to ache as though someone had squeezed it, "but I think you know how I feel about anyone with a penchant for mindless violence."

Walking forward, her father kissed her on the forehead. "That, I do. And though I'm sorry you have a very good reason for your squeamishness, at this moment I'm rather relieved you feel this way. Because if I know one thing, it's that being in the Marquis of Glengask's company is dangerous."

Charlotte wouldn't say she felt relieved about anything, no matter how safe or perilous her predicament. It was likely a good thing that her father had reminded her of the negative parts of a relationship with Ranulf MacLawry, because on her own she might have decided to overlook what seemed to be a few brawls. But it was much, much worse than that. He was, quite simply, a man at war. And if she fell for him, and he was hurt or . . . killed, she didn't think she would be able to stand it. Not again. Not after what she'd discovered in his arms.

It might have been different if he'd wished for a different sort of life, but she'd never seen any evidence that he wanted anything other than what he had. Well, she wanted something else for him. And she wanted him to at least acknowledge that another way existed, for heaven's sake. Luckily for her, though, she'd learned long ago that wishes were as plentiful as clouds, and as impossible to grasp.

She followed her father out to the foyer, and Winnie grasped her arm as they all headed out to the waiting carriage. "You look so lovely," the younger girl said with a grin.

"As do you." Charlotte indicated the emerald-colored silk gown Ranulf's sister wore. "You didn't acquire this here, did you? I don't recall seeing it before."

"No, this is the gown Ranulf bought me for my birthday. Of course he thought I would be wearing it to my own party, and not to a London grand ball." She swished the skirt, grinning excitedly. "I'm sure that having both my brothers in attendance tonight will make them more civilized, since they won't feel so outnumbered. Though practically the only thing that could make Ran fight is a threat to his loved ones."

"He punched Lord Berling for claiming a place on Charlotte's dance card," Jane pointed out as she settled back into the coach.

"No, he punched the earl because Berling shot my brother, Bear. Munro. Then the scoundrel fled to London to pretend to be civilized. I know I was furious about the fight, but I've been thinking about it, and I believe that Ran just reminded Berling that actions have consequences."

"It was still an appalling show of violence, my dear," Charlotte's mother said from the opposite seat of the coach. "I know you love your brother, but thank goodness you were well clear of that mess. And I'm also pleased that you told him how ungentlemanly his actions were, Winnie. It wouldn't have had the same seriousness to it, coming from other than family."

"My brother's a good man, my lady," Winnie said stoutly. "And he learns from his mistakes. You'll see."

Charlotte just wished everyone would stop talking about Ranulf, both his faults and his manliness, and give her a blasted minute or two to think. She'd chastised him more strongly than his own sister had. Yes, he'd vanished for a week, but not because he wished to hide. He'd reappeared with a house and a civilized, amusing dinner. It had been charming. *He* had been charming.

According to her father, the fire that had ended the evening had been Ranulf's fault for having enemies. At the time she'd been more concerned with the disaster than what had caused it, though she supposed now that if he hadn't hit Berling, the fire might not have happened. But then what came next might not have happened, either.

"What if both your brothers wear kilts tonight?" Jane asked from the other side of Charlotte.

Winnie shrugged. "I don't think they will.

This isn't a clan gathering, and I do believe Ranulf's trying to fit in."

"I certainly hope so," Lady Hest said under her breath.

For the very briefest of moments, despite what both she and Winnie had told him, Charlotte hoped he *would* wear his kilt. Because she'd never seen a more magnificent sight in her entire life — except, of course, for when she'd seen him naked.

CHAPTER TWELVE

"A man hesitates to accept responsibility for starting a fire and ye think that makes him innocent of it?" Ranulf slammed a fist against the wall of the coach, rocking the entire vehicle.

"I only said he didnae have the look of a man pleased to have acted against an enemy," Arran returned, pulling at the sleeve of his dark brown coat as if he hoped it would come off at the shoulder.

"Of course he didnae, firstly because ye confronted him about it, and secondly because the man's a yellow-bellied coward."

"I dunnae —"

"Damn it, Arran, do I truly have to remind ye nae to go anywhere that'll see ye outnumbered? Charles Calder is the bloody Campbell's grandson!"

"I can take care of myself, as ye well know, Ran. And if ye thought it more important to go mooning after some proper Sasannach lass, someone else had to take a look at Berling."

Ranulf glared at his brother across the coach's seat. "I'm nae mooning after anyone," he stated flatly. "And tomorrow ye can hie yerself back to Glengask."

"Nae."

" 'Nae'?" Ranulf repeated, lifting an eyebrow. "I wasnae asking."

"And I'm nae leaving ye here to watch over Rowena while the wolves circle the lot of ye. Especially when yer mind's on someaught else."

That was twice Arran had accused him of distraction. What did his younger brother think he'd seen? Whatever his own intentions toward Charlotte, he wasn't yet willing to discuss them. And certainly not with someone who'd just arrived the previous day.

"My mind's precisely where it needs to be, Arran. As always." He folded his arms across his chest. "But have *ye* considered what'll happen tonight when all the duke's guests see ye introduced as a MacLawry?"

Arran gave a grim smile. "I reckon we might be in for a bit of a row."

Damnation. "Nae, that willnae happen. Rowena wants a proper Season. And I dunnae want us seen as animals. Tonight we're gentlemen."

Rowena wasn't the only one who wanted a fight-free soiree. The fact that he could attribute the request to her, though, certainly made things easier on him. His sister had given him some surprisingly sound advice, actually, and he intended to make good use of her counsel. He merely didn't wish to explain to Arran why he was acting as he was.

"*Gentlemen.* Until she came here, Rowena thought we *were* gentlemen. And we'd nae have to worry over being outnumbered and burned out if ye'd brought her home to Glengask as ye said ye would. Do ye mean to stay in London all Season, now?"

Ranulf sent his brother a level look. Time was, no one would have spoken to him like that. Charlotte had done so, and everything had changed. Arran didn't know anything of that, though. Had *he* changed, then? Was it something that others could perceive? If so, he needed to stop. Immediately. A perception of weakness might as well be a death sentence in his world.

"I'll stay in London as long as I deem it necessary. If ye want to stay as well, then do so. But if ye think I mean to allow ye to continue stirring up trouble because ye dunnae like the way I'm dealing with things, ye'd be dead wrong. This is a different world, Arran, and we need to learn how to navigate it. Nae for Rowena, but for Glengask's future. And we willnae be accomplishing anything by countering each other's moves. Are we clear?"

His brother nodded. "Aye. That's all I wanted t'hear."

"And I want to hear that ye willnae be brawling tonight. For any reason."

"Then ye have my word." Arran sat back, flicking aside the carriage's curtain to look out at the deepening twilight. "Then we're not discussing the Sasannach lass?"

"We are nae."

He couldn't order Arran to close his eyes to what he saw; after all, he frequently made good use of his brother's keen observations. If Arran wanted to draw his own conclusions where Ranulf and Charlotte were concerned, no one could stop him. What Ranulf *could* do, though, was keep him from discussing it. And from offering an opinion Ranulf didn't particularly want to hear.

"And Berling?" Arran asked after a moment.

"I may not agree with ye, but I'm nae a fool. If ye think there's a chance someone else is involved, I'll pay attention. But fer God's sake, next time tell me before ye slip off to confront someone."

Finally Arran's smile touched his light blue eyes. "I can do that."

Once they'd retrieved Myles from Wilkie House, it was only another five minutes until they reached the tail end of the crowd of carriages surrounding Mason House. As they made their way inside, the noise of the street was replaced by the din of hundreds of voices trying to be clever. If anything, the party seemed more crowded than the Evanstone soiree. Perhaps the guests were hoping they would see another fight. That might well be, but neither he nor Arran would be involved with it. Through it all he listened for one voice, one honey-sweet note of sanity in all the chaos.

"Are we allowed to dance?" his brother muttered.

Ranulf damned well hoped so, since the only reason he'd bothered to put on his best clothes had been to claim a waltz with Charlotte. "Aye. But ye're nae to step on anyone's toes," he returned in the same tone. "Literally or figuratively."

"Berling's here," his uncle noted under his breath.

"Just give him a smile, *bràthair,*" Ranulf instructed his brother. "Let him come to his own conclusions."

"I'm grinning. Not at all sarcastically."

"Ye'd best nae be."

He understood that Berling was dangerous. He'd disliked the man and his arrogant, self-serving manner even before the torching of the schools and the wounding of Bear. From that moment on, dislike had become hatred.

Given all that, tonight the earl at most felt like a nuisance. A distraction. Ranulf kept his gaze moving, identifying each guest who crossed his path as someone he'd met or someone he hadn't. After that, he dismissed them from his thoughts. None of them was the one he was after.

Then he caught sight of her, and time simply . . . stopped. Close by the double row of windows Charlotte tilted her head, a smile touching her mouth as she handed her dance card to the round fellow, Henning. She looked almost like a Thomas Lawrence painting, so exquisite she was. But no portrait could capture the scent of her, the taste of her, or the way simply seeing her sent warmth searing beneath his skin.

She'd worn red and black, rich and bold and striking against her fair skin and golden hair. He tried not to read anything into the fact that she'd also garbed herself in two of the three colors of the MacLawry tartan, but in seeking every strand that connected her to him, he couldn't help himself. His fingers curled, wanting to tangle into the soft folds of her skirt and pull her up against him.

"This way," he said, otherwise not bothering to see if his brother and uncle followed him as he strode forward.

When he was halfway across the room she stilled, then turned to look at him. It might be witchcraft, or it might not. He didn't care any longer. All he knew was that he wanted her. Immediately.

Before he could reach her, Rowena moved in front of him, blocking his path. "Good evening, *bràthair,*" she said, dipping a curtsy.

With some difficulty Ranulf forced his attention down to his sister, his reason for being in London in the first place. "Ye wore yer birthday gown," he drawled, taking her hand.

Sometime when he'd lost sight of his sister, when he'd been distracted by tracking her down and by being annoyed that she'd left home without permission, Rowena had stopped being a wee sprite in pigtails who always asked for dresses covered with lace and frills and ribbons. She'd grown up, and in looking at her instead of seeing her, he'd nearly missed it.

"What is it?" she asked, furrowing her brow.

"Ye look very like our mother," he murmured.

She smiled, sudden tears shining in her eyes. "Do I?"

He studied her face for a moment. "Aye. Only prettier, *piuthar.*"

"That you are," Myles put in, kissing her on the cheek.

Lord Hest stepped in and offered his hand. Whatever else the earl was, whatever his character, at this moment he was simply another obstacle between Ranulf and Charlotte. "I do think that tonight I'm escorting the four loveliest ladies in London," the older man announced.

"I'd have to agree with ye," Ranulf said, shaking the earl's hand. His future father-in-law, whether Hest would approve of the notion or not.

"Oh, Jonathan," the countess said with a blush, cuffing her husband lightly on the shoulder.

There. That had to be enough in the way of pleasantries. Pausing his breath, Ranulf slipped around his sister — to find his brother chatting with Charlotte. After Arran's comments about the Sasannach lass,

342

Ranulf didn't like what he saw. At all.

"Arran," he said, moving in, "go write yer name on Rowena's card." What good was it being the patriarch of his clan if he couldn't order others to leave his most precious thing — his obsession — alone?

His brother sent him an unreadable look and strolled over to join Rowena and Jane. Once Arran walked away, Ranulf ceased paying attention to him. "Hello, Charlotte," he said, reaching out to take her hand and bring it to his lips. It wasn't enough, and he just barely kept himself from pulling her into his arms.

"Ranulf," she greeted him, her hazel eyes sparkling brown in the chandelier light.

"I think I may have made a mistake," he continued, lowering his voice and moving in more closely on the pretext of taking her dance card.

"What sort of mistake?" She sent him a suspicious look, her smile dropping.

"My attraction to ye doesn't seem to have eased at all. And in that dress ye look more delicious than the apple that tempted Adam."

Charlotte cleared her throat. "I believe that to be a mutual difficulty, then. Despite my better judgment."

"Aye, that's the rub, dunnae ye think? But

tonight my better judgment can go hang itself. I want ye, Charlotte."

"I think you should write your name down beside that dance," she said a little unsteadily, indicating the second waltz of the evening. "And I want you, too," she continued in a whisper, her changeable eyes meeting his in that way few other people ever dared.

In that moment he vowed to himself that whatever man she wanted, he would be. It would likely cost him, but if Charlotte was the prize, he would pay the price. Pushing against the ridiculous urge to burst into song or something equally unmanly, he scrawled his name where she indicated. "Take me sightseeing again, *leannan.*"

Her lips parted in a soft smile, and he caught himself leaning down toward her. Propriety was a damned nuisance. But it was what she felt comfortable with, and so he would be patient. Handing her card back, he brushed his fingers against her red, elbow-length gloves.

"How are yer hands?" he asked, annoyed that he hadn't asked her that immediately. In his defense her appearance had dazzled him, but she'd gotten those blisters on his behalf.

"Much better. In another day or two I

daresay no one would ever know I had blisters."

"I would know."

"Ah, there you are, dear Lady Charlotte," a dry voice came from behind him. "Tell me you haven't given away every dance."

Thankfully for the sake of his resolve, it wasn't Berling. But that didn't actually leave him feeling any better. A tall, fair-haired fellow of about Bear's age stood there, an easy smile on his face and his body clothed in a well-made dark blue coat that might or might not have had padded shoulders.

"I believe I have a free dance or two remaining, Lord Stephen," Charlotte replied, then gestured at Ranulf. "Lord Glengask, may I present Lord Stephen Hammond? Lord Stephen, the Marquis of Glengask."

"You're the Highlands fellow," Hammond commented.

"Aye. I am."

When Hammond offered his hand, Ranulf shook it. That was what gentlemen did. But he didn't like it, any more than he liked the way Charlotte smiled at the new arrival. The other men with whom she generally danced weren't much in the way of rivals. This was different. And now that he thought about it, Miss Florence had mentioned something about a Lord Stephen Hammond who'd said she looked like an orange. That didn't leave him more disposed toward liking the pretty fellow at all.

Back home he would have flat-out asked if this Hammond had done as rumored. And then he would have added some character to his face. It was still tempting; Ranulf could claim to be defending Miss Florence's honor, while he could at the same time remove Lord Stephen from where he currently stood smiling too prettily at Charlotte. *His* Charlotte — whether he could announce that to all and sundry or not.

"Charlotte, that trouncing you gave me in croquet last year still stings, you know," Lord Stephen went on with a grin as he took her card and penciled in his name. "I want a rematch."

"I'm willing to oblige you," Charlotte returned, "if you don't fear further humiliation."

Hammond returned her dance card. "Life is a risk. And I believe he who hesitates is lost." He sketched a bow. "I must go beg a dance from your lovely sister, now. I'll claim you later."

Still grinning, Charlotte watched Stephen make his way over to Jane. She, of course, was already surrounded by eager young men. When Charlotte returned her attention to Ranulf, though, he didn't look nearly as amused.

"Who is Lord Stephen Hammond?" he asked, glancing from her to her dance card.

"He's the second son of the Duke and Duchess of Esmond. This is their soiree." She made the statement as matter-of-factly as possible, hoping Ranulf wasn't about to begin punching people again. Yes, she liked the idea that he might be jealous. No, she didn't want him to act on it.

She saw him take a breath. "Then I suppose he's allowed to ask a dance of the bonniest lass in the room," he said.

Oh, thank goodness. Just when she thought she had him figured out, he surprised her again. "You exaggerate, but thank you for saying so."

"The only thing I ever exaggerate aboot is the size of the fish I nearly caught. Ye're Aphrodite, *leannan.* Ye take my breath away."

That was very nice of him to say. In fact, she would have been quite content to just stand and listen to the sound of his voice for the rest of the evening. For the rest of her life, really. But then she noticed her father looking at the two of them, his expression less than pleased. "You have to go talk to someone else," she whispered regretfully. "People will begin to think you're courting me."

"Ah. And what if I am?" he returned.

Before she could decipher the explosion of . . . everything that rattled her insides at his words, he gave her a jaunty grin and strolled over to disrupt the crowd around his sister. *Did he mean it?* He couldn't possibly, with what he clearly believed about the unsuitability of English ladies to the Highlands. So was he merely teasing her? And if they were so wrong for each other, why did those few words make her feel so . . . excited?

"I don't suppose ye have a jig left fer a poor stranger, do ye?" Ranulf's brother said, appearing on her other side.

"No jigs, but I do have a country dance," she returned, looking up into his pale blue eyes, very different from both Ranulf's and Winnie's.

"I reckon that'll do, unless Ran chases me off again." He wrote his name beside the next dance as the orchestra played the last few notes of a quadrille. "Why do ye think he'd do such a thing, my lady?"

Perhaps Arran MacLawry wasn't quite as good-humored and easygoing as she'd thought. Ranulf had said the middle brother was the clever one. "You would have to ask him," she said, then put a smile back on her face. "It was good of you to come down to London. I think your brother feels more comfortable having you here."

Arran inclined his head. "I think my brother keeps his own counsel, but it's kind of ye to say it, anyway." With a glance in Ranulf's direction, he moved off toward the refreshment table.

Before she could ponder what any of that meant, several of her friends arrived to chat about the crush around them and to compliment her dress and her hair. Elizabeth Martin had come out the same year that she had, and Margaret Cooper the year after. Both of them were married, Elizabeth with three children, and Margaret with a boy and a girl. At times she'd envied them for choosing husbands who didn't see being laughed at as a murderworthy offense, for finding the lives they'd wanted and managing to hang on to them where she hadn't.

Now, though, as she looked from Mr. Martin with his self-important preening and Lord Roger Cooper with his too tight waistband to the magnificent Lord Glengask laughing at something his sister said, she wondered for the first time if things didn't happen for a reason. Yes, she would have been perfectly content with James Appleton, and she would have lived a happy and perfectly predictable life.

Immediately that question pushed into the front of her mind again. Why had Ranulf jested about courting her? Or if for some reason he wasn't teasing, did she want a life with him when it would entail danger and violence and threats both from her own kind and from his fellow Scots? Charlotte shook herself. Everything she knew about him, both through her own observations and in conversations with Winnie, said he wasn't serious. Therefore she didn't need to decide. She didn't need to choose between him and what was fast becoming a dull, predictable, and yet supremely safe life.

When Lord Berling appeared from the card room and made his way toward her, she wasn't surprised, but a tangle of uneasiness curled down her spine. Would he push at her to try to antagonize Ranulf? Or would his mere presence beside her be enough to make the marquis break his word and attack?

"Lady Charlotte," the earl said, inclining his head. "Mrs. Martin, Lady Roger."

"My lord," she returned with a curtsy, as her friends swiftly made their excuses and backed away. No doubt they'd at least heard about the incident at the Evanstone soiree, and wanted no part of an encore performance.

"I never got the chance for our dance at the last soiree," he drawled, "and I wondered if we might give it another try."

Her mouth was getting tired from the number of forced smiles she'd already used this evening. It was much simpler to be pleasant when she didn't know any better, she realized. "I'm afraid my dance card is full tonight, Lord Berling. Thank you so much for the kind thought, though."

Moving as quickly as a snake, the earl snatched the dance card from her gloved fingers. "You're mistaken, Lady Charlotte," he said, looking down at the thing. "You have several dances available."

Oh, dear. She'd made Ranulf a bargain: no dancing with Berling in exchange for him not brawling with the earl. If the cad wrote his name down — or if Ranulf saw the exchange now — she didn't want to know what might happen. Taking a breath, she offered Berling a genuine frown. "Is this how a gentleman reacts when faced with a lady who doesn't wish to dance with him? I was attempting to be polite."

"You've danced with me before, my lady.

We've even waltzed a time or two."

"Yes, we have. And there are other parties where we didn't dance at all. I believe you to be looking for trouble, and I want no part of it."

The earl moved a step closer to her. "And yet I see here that Glengask has a waltz with you. And the other one has a dance, too, whoever he is."

Charlotte held her ground, praying that Ranulf and his brother both were otherwise occupied. "His sister is our family's guest. Do I owe you some additional explanation?"

"No. But a dance would still be nice, to demonstrate that we're all friends here."

"No, my lord. My card, if you please." She didn't hold out her hand; that would make it too obvious to everyone looking that she'd made a request and he hadn't answered it.

"You haven't developed a tendre for the Scottish devil, have you? He isn't at all civilized."

"I don't think it's my behavior being called into question, Berling," Ranulf's low brogue came, as he moved in from one side. "The lady asked fer her dance card back."

Berling's face went as pale as Charlotte felt. "And if I refuse?"

Ranulf pulled a blank dance card from his pocket. "Then ye can wander aboot carrying that wee bit of paper like a fool, and she'll use this one," he replied coolly.

"Bah. You dog; pick it up off the floor." With that Berling dropped her dance card to the ground and walked away.

"Good thing I'm not as stiff-arsed as he is," Ranulf mused, squatting down and retrieving the card. Pocketing the blank one, he dusted hers off and handed it back to her.

She looked up, studying his lean face for any sign of the anger she expected. What she saw was a perfectly level expression that should have reassured her, but didn't. "You kept your word," she murmured.

His gaze lowered briefly to her mouth. "As did ye." Ranulf offered his arm. "Let me show ye to yer dance partner."

Arran moved in from the other direction. "No need. I'm her partner."

It actually shook her a little that both men had been so near and yet neither of them had struck. If Berling had moved a touch closer to her, or if she had been an ounce less firm . . . But nothing had happened, and all was well.

Before Arran took her arm, Ranulf leaned in and whispered something to his brother. Then with a nod at her, he went to collect his partner for the country dance. Arran offered his arm, and together they took their place on the dance floor. Once the music began he bowed and she curtsied, and they joined hands to step in a wide circle around their fellows.

"What did Ranulf say to you?" she muttered as they parted and then moved up opposite sides of the line.

"If he'd wanted ye to hear, he wouldnae have whispered it," he said, stepping back up the center with her again.

Stubborn Scotsmen. "Lord Berling called you 'that other fellow,' " she commented, deciding to try again. "Have you never met?"

They did another set of steps and turns, facing each other, before they joined hands again. "I met him today at luncheon, actually."

"What?" She stifled her overloud comment with a cough. "Then why —"

"I might've given him a different name," Arran returned with a cynical grin.

The MacLawry men didn't seem to be timid about much of anything, Charlotte decided, looking for Ranulf and catching sight of him walking up the second line of dancers, a pretty redheaded lady holding his hand. Thank goodness he was making an effort to fit in, to become acquainted with his peers. And whether English or Scottish, or Welsh or Irish, the aristocrats here were his peers.

At the same time, though, as she caught a glimpse of the redhead's face when she smiled at him — good heavens, was that Madeline Davies? — for a brief, selfish moment she wished other ladies didn't look at him in the same voracious way, as if they all wanted to take him on sightseeing tours of London.

Perhaps her wish wasn't so selfish really. If ladies didn't view him so . . . lustfully, then perhaps their husbands and beaux would look at him as a potential friend or an ally rather than as an uncivilized rival.

"Ye aren't going to ask me why I gave Berling another man's name, then?" Arran said as he circled around her. "I thought ye'd be more curious, considering ye ask aboot everything else."

Charlotte shook herself. "I'm extremely curious," she replied. "I have noticed, however, that you're even worse at answering questions than your brother is."

He gave a short laugh. "I mean to take that as a compliment. And this is likely a conversation best had at another time and in a different setting, anyway."

Annoying as it all was, she had to agree

with his assessment. In a way it was odd that she *was* so interested in all the subterfuge and machinations; a few weeks ago she wouldn't have wanted to hear that one man seemed to be baiting another into any sort of confrontation. But she knew things, now. She knew that Lord Berling had done some things for which he likely should have been arrested.

She didn't like that he'd walked up to her and tried to use her to start a fight — twice now. The first time it had worked, though he couldn't have been pleased with the outcome. Only arrogance could convince him to try the same approach again and expect a different outcome — and yet there *had* been a different result. Ranulf hadn't risen to the bait. In fact, he'd taken steps to avoid fighting. And that was a very good thing.

When the dance finally ended she half expected Ranulf to appear and suggest they go out to the balcony for some fresh air. The yearning to kiss him again, to hear his low voice saying things meant only for her, left her shaky and feeling exceedingly wicked.

She looked about for him, but before she could spot his tall, broad figure, Jane appeared. "Hello, my dear. What are —"

"This way," her sister hissed, and half dragged her through a hallway, around a corner, and into the dark, empty library beyond.

"Janie, what —"

Jane put a hand over her mouth. "Shh. Come here," she mouthed, and led the way to the window.

Alarmed, Charlotte followed. The room overlooked the front of the garden, and while the curtains were open, the window was not. Jane squeezed one eye closed and very slowly pushed the glass open an inch or so.

"— humiliated me twice," Berling's low, angry voice came. "Who the devil does he think he is, anyway?"

"The Campbell says he's dangerous."

"In the Highlands, yes. He's the king of his own little army of cotters and drovers and fishermen. But we aren't in the Highlands, are we? Where's his army now?"

"Aye," a third voice agreed. "You called him a dog, and he just stood there. Picked up the card you threw down, as well."

"I tell you, he's afraid of us," Berling insisted, excitement raising the pitch of his voice. "And not just us. Unless that fire was accidental, Glengask has more enemies than most people have friends."

"I thought that was you, set the fire," a fourth voice murmured.

"Only if you can prove it, George."

"That other big fellow he's brought here is his brother. Arran MacLawry. I heard it from Hest."

"You know he took in two dozen Campbell cotters when we pushed 'em off Glen Helen. Makes 'em think they don't have to jump when we say so."

The fourth voice gave a low laugh. "His father was the same damned way. Didnae do the Seann Monadh much good, did it?"

"That's no laughing matter," Berling retorted. "Both my uncles vanished after that."

"Ye think I dunnae know that, Donald?"

"The Campbell said old MacLawry made a pact with the devil and had 'em dragged below to join him."

That prompted the sound of spitting, followed by speculations about what had happened to the two Gerdenses. Charlotte exchanged a glance with Jane, pressed wide-eyed against the wall. They should go before someone noticed the window open and came looking to see who might be listening to their conversation. She had a dance with Francis Henning starting any moment. And yet these men were talking about Ranulf.

And if she learned something that could help him . . .

But then it might also send him after these men. And it would be on her head. When had all this become so complicated? At eighteen, love had been simple and straightforward.

Charlotte took a sharp breath, putting a hand to her heart. *Love?* Was it love that twisted her insides and made her think that dropping a vase or two out the window and onto someone's head would be a good idea? Love that made her hate the men below just for speaking their minds, because they spoke against Ranulf? Her Ranulf?

What a stupid female she was. He wanted a lover for London; he'd made that perfectly clear, and she'd agreed. A mutual physical attraction. But, oh, it was so much more than that. For her, anyway. Of course, they would never suit, and nothing would come of this . . . infatuation of hers, but for goodness' sake. Her own silly fault or not, she loved him. And her heart would shatter into a hundred million pieces the day he bid her good-bye.

It was all wrong, wrong, wrong. And even knowing that, she leaned closer to the window so she wouldn't miss a word. Anything that could harm Ranulf needed to be stopped. At once.

"I'm not going toe-to-toe with him," the second voice was saying.

"I already did. If I confront him again tonight, everyone will see me as the antagonist, and we'll gain nothing."

"I'll do it," the fourth voice drawled. "Havenae had MacLawry blood on my hands for a good three years, now. It's an itch needs scratching."

"Just keep in mind that you have to make him look like the aggressor, or it's for nothing."

"Ye don't have to remind me of that, cousin."

The music for the quadrille began, drowning out any remaining conversation. Very carefully Charlotte pulled the window closed, then sagged against the back of a chair. "Good heavens," she whispered. "How did you know about this, Janie?"

Her sister had a hand to her chest and looked pale as moonlight. "I was leaving the dance floor and heard someone say they needed a quiet place to discuss Lord Glengask, and Lord Berling suggested the garden by the front wall." She took a ragged breath. "My goodness. They were talking about hurting people. And worse than that."

Charlotte straightened, sweeping forward

to embrace her sister. "You were so brave," she said feelingly.

"But what are we going to do?"

"We need to tell Ranulf."

She had no idea what would come of it, and with the way her heart was pounding she felt just as likely to kiss him as to rail at him for . . . for being who he was. But he did need to know. At once.

"Come on," she said, grabbing Janie's hand and hurrying to the door. Every action had consequences, and she was about to set some very large actions into motion.

And yet.

And yet all she could think about was how safe and content and happy she'd felt in Ranulf's arms. She couldn't lose him. She wouldn't lose him. Not on someone else's terms. Not when she'd just discovered what she had.

CHAPTER THIRTEEN

"Where is she?" Ranulf demanded, grabbing a fistful of Arran's lapel.

"I told ye, she and her sister ran off somewhere," his brother grunted. Tellingly, though, he didn't fight Ranulf's grip. Evidently Arran had realized how very close to violence he was.

"And I told you to keep her close," Ranulf returned, enunciating every word. In a crowd this big Charlotte could be anywhere, with anyone, and he couldn't see any sign of Berling or his cronies, either. Yes, he was angry, but it wasn't just that. He was worried. Extremely worried.

"Either pitch me off the balcony or let me help ye find her, then." Arran lifted his hands in a placating gesture.

Exhaling with a growl, Ranulf released his brother. "I'll look fer her," he snapped. "Ye keep both yer eyes on Rowena, if ye can manage that."

"Aye. I can. I will."

The music for the quadrille began as he stalked back into the ballroom, Arran on his heels. People moved to the dance floor and others to neighboring sitting rooms or the card rooms or the refreshment tables — faces he didn't know, blue bloods who served no purpose at the moment but to keep him from finding Charlotte.

Where the devil was she? He'd seen her dance card. He knew she'd agreed to dance the quadrille with the round man, Henning. Ranulf strode across the edge of the dance floor, unmindful of the stir he was causing. When he finally set eyes on Henning standing to one side and looking bewildered, his heart dropped. Charlotte wouldn't leave a dance partner standing. It wasn't polite.

He drew a deep breath to bellow her name, whatever the damned consequences — and then caught sight of her. Her sister in tow, she hurried into the ballroom through the hallway door. *Thank God.* Relief flooded through him, heady and welcome, and Ranulf moved forward. She was not going to dance with anyone until he'd touched her and made certain she was well.

A lean, dark figure stepped in front of him, blocking his view of Charlotte. Ranulf started around the man, only to find his path blocked again. "The Marquis of Glengask, as I live and breathe."

With a scowl Ranulf wrenched his attention to the man now standing directly in front of him. Tall, though not as tall as himself, with reddish-brown hair that partly hid a faint scar running from just beneath his ear and down to the right side of his mouth. A tickle of familiarity pricked the hairs at the back of his neck, but he couldn't quite place the face.

"Have we met?" he asked, still moving forward.

The fellow kept pace, backing up to remain in front of him. "Not directly."

"Then ye'll have to excuse me. I'm meeting someone."

Ranulf started to step around the man, only to find his route cut off yet again. Now it was clearly intentional, which as far as he was concerned, removed the need for him to be polite.

"Get oot of my way, *amadan.*"

The shorter man favored him with a polite smile. "I doon't think I will."

"So ye want me to knock ye on yer arse in front of all these bonny lasses," he returned, speaking loudly enough that those directly around him could hear.

"I jest want a word with ye, friend."

A nice, quick punch to the gut as he moved in, and no one would likely notice anything but him helping the fellow to the floor as he spewed sick over his own boots. Ranulf stepped in, coiling his fist.

"Lord Glengask," Charlotte's breathless voice came. "There you are! Your uncle's been taken quite ill, I'm afraid. Please come with us at once."

Ranulf straightened his fingers. No punching. That was Charlotte's one rule. "Excuse me," he repeated forcefully, fixing the lean fellow with the direct gaze that caused most men a sudden need to examine their own shoes.

Inclining his head, the scarred fellow stepped aside, then abruptly caught Ranulf's elbow as he pushed by. "That sister of yers is a bonny lass," he murmured, "with an especially fine mouth. I know just where I'd have her put it."

Ranulf stopped in his tracks. In the next heartbeat, before he'd even registered the action, he had both fists wrapped into the man's lapel and lifted him off his feet. Black fury blasted through him like thunder. No one — *no one* — threatened Rowena.

A soft hand in a red glove touched his sleeve. "You're being baited," Charlotte breathed.

If she'd spoken in any other voice, yelled or pushed or pulled at him, he likely wouldn't have noticed. Of course he was being baited. That didn't matter. The words had still been said. Words that couldn't be unsaid, or forgiven, but only paid for in blood.

"Your uncle needs you," she persisted in a louder voice, her hand squeezing his arm.

Her hand with the blisters she'd gotten trying to save his stable. Every muscle tight and fighting, gut versus mind, he took a step sideways and set the man down. "Excuse me," he said for the third and final time, even though he felt like he'd been ruptured and was bleeding inside. "Ye seemed to be stepping on my foot."

Taking Charlotte's hand, he placed it around his arm and walked away. Behind him the scarred man laughed. Ranulf rolled his shoulders and kept going. This was what it took to keep Charlotte in his life. He would eat a hundred insults and smile at their foul words in exchange for a kiss and a smile from her. As she kept telling him, they were just words.

"I need to talk to you," she said tightly, sending him a sideways glance. "And for heaven's sake, you need to use your mind and not your muscles."

"I prefer to use them in tandem," he returned.

"Is that what you were just doing?"

"If my mind hadnae been involved, ye would know it. Now hold a bit. We have to find Myles first. I assume he's well?"

"I have no idea. It was the first excuse I could think of." Another glance. "I'm sorry I snapped at you just then. Are *you* well?"

"I'm a gentleman," he returned, trying to sound mild when fury still bit at him with tiger's teeth. "I'm always well."

"Ranulf."

"In a minute. There's Myles."

His uncle stood talking with the Duke of Esmond and his oh, so charming son, Lord Stephen Hammond. *Bloody wonderful.* Well, Charlotte had chosen the game, so he would play along with it.

"Myles, let's find ye a chair," he said, reluctantly releasing Charlotte to grasp his uncle's elbow. "Ye shouldnae be walking aboot if ye're still feeling light-headed."

Lord Swansley frowned, then put an abrupt hand to his temple. "Perhaps I will sit for a minute," he said. "If you'll pardon me, Your Grace, Stephen."

"Certainly, Swansley. The duchess is expecting a dance, anyway."

Four strong now, they went upstairs and

found a sitting room. As he pushed open the door a young lady lurched to her feet, an older man yanking his hand from beneath her skirt and then trying to cover his bulging nether regions with a pillow. Ranulf barely had time to raise an eyebrow before they fled. As much as he wanted Charlotte, he had little sympathy for the couple — a man should have more consideration for his lady than to lead her to a place where they could be discovered.

"What's going on?" Myles said, once they were alone. "Why am I light-headed?"

"That's my fault," Charlotte admitted. "I needed to speak to Ranulf in private, and you were my excuse."

"I was busy having a disagreement with a fellow," Ranulf added tightly, "before I remembered that I'm a gentleman."

Jane paced back and forth behind the couch as they spoke. Ranulf hadn't given her much thought earlier, but now that he looked, she seemed supremely uneasy. Charlotte appeared much calmer, but then she didn't unsettle easily. In the dimmer light of half a dozen candles, far from the hundred lights in the dramatic chandeliers, she looked even more stunning.

"What happened, *leannan*?" he asked, leaning a hip against the arm of the couch.

At the Gaelic word Myles sent him a quick, surprised look, but he ignored it.

She told him. It wasn't difficult to guess that the participants with Berling had been Charles Calder and Arnold Haws — as far as he could tell, the three of them were nearly inseparable. The fourth man stumped him for a moment, until Charlotte noted that the mystery man and the fellow he'd nearly flattened in the ballroom had the same laugh.

"I think Lord Berling called him cousin," Jane put in.

"George," Charlotte said a heartbeat later. "Someone said George."

Now it made sense. "George Gerdens-Dailey," Ranulf said slowly. *Damnation.*

Myles began swearing under his breath. Ranulf felt much the same, but he was abruptly more concerned with deciphering how Dailey's arrival in London would affect his family and those he loved. The woman he loved, who was frowning at him.

"Who is George Gerdens-Dailey?" Charlotte asked, her scowl deepening. "I mean, I know he's a Gerdens, but clearly there's something more going on here."

She needed to know. Even if in telling her, he would have to confess the one thing she could never forgive, the one thing that might cost him . . . everything. Her. Straightening, he held out his hand to her. When she twined her fingers with his, it took every ounce of will he possessed not to kiss her right then. "Stay here," he said to his uncle, indicating Jane. "We'll be back in a moment."

He led her through a side door and into what looked like a spare dressing room. Only after he'd brought in a candle and latched both doors did he release her hand. No one would be surprising them in here.

"I'm rather alarmed," Charlotte said, watching him pace back and forth. The candlelight flickered when he stirred the air with his passing. "Who is this man?"

Finally Ranulf stopped to face her again. God, she looked like a wicked angel, golden hair and black and scarlet gown. "Ye lectured me a while ago aboot how violence only leads to more of the same, how it has no reason and the only way to stop it is to not begin it in the first place."

To his surprise, she smiled. "You were listening."

"I've listened to every word ye've ever spoken, Charlotte. Every breath, every sigh means the world to me." Ranulf shook himself. "I don't mean to use sweet words to sway ye, but it's the truth." And it might well be the last time she would ever stand for him even speaking to her.

"Tell me," she said quietly.

"One more thing first." Ranulf closed the distance between them, put his palm across the nape of her neck, and took her soft, sweet mouth with his.

Her gloved hands swept up around his shoulders, and she leaned along his body. The unhesitating trust she showed was utterly arousing. He sank into the moment, savoring every heartbeat of time spent with her in his arms. To think it might end because he felt the need to be honest with her . . . Well, all the more fool, he. But he would rather face the consequences now than later.

In a sense, though, the perfect harmony between them now only made what would likely happen at the end of this conversation worse. Savoring a last kiss, he set her upright again. "Enough delays, then," he drawled, half to himself.

She would have kept her hands around his shoulders, but he pulled away. He didn't want to see the disappointed expression on her face when he'd finished with what he needed to say, but to have her pull away from him as well was more than he cared to put in front of himself.

"I told ye how my father died," he began, making himself stand still. "Half the clan called it an accident, while the other half knew it was murder. I may only have been fifteen, but I knew what it was. And I knew who'd done it. The Earl of Berling and his brothers, Harry and Wallace."

"Not *this* Lord Berling," she said, indicating somewhere vaguely outside the dressing room.

"Nae. His father. I'd seen 'em arguing with Seann Monadh — my father — trying to bully him into turning a good twenty acres of cotters' fields into sheep grazing. He called 'em shortsighted, selfish fools who'd regret turning on their own people, and sent them away. Two days later he was dead."

He could discuss it matter-of-factly now, but at the time he'd felt all the wind knocked from his lungs, and it had stayed that way for months. He hadn't been able to catch his breath, to think, and the mourning, lost clan had all looked to him for answers and leadership. His mother had been inconsolable, but over *her* loss, *her* burden. As if she'd been the only one to feel pain from Robert MacLawry's death.

"I'm so sorry, Ranulf," Charlotte breathed, but didn't attempt to approach

372

him again. She knew that part of the tale, and she knew that wasn't what he'd dragged her off to tell her.

"After the funeral I took my father's old muzzle-loading hunting rifle and a shovel, and went to find the Gerdenses. Berling was already gone back to London — a cowardice shared by his son. The other two were at home, though, at Sholbray Manor, cozy in their parlor and drinking, talking aboot how Seann Monadh had fought and squirmed while they held his head under the water of his own loch, how he'd shat himself when he died. I crouched beneath the window and listened to all of it."

Charlotte's face paled, but she held her ground and her silence. And he'd thought her likely to shatter in a stiff breeze. She might look delicate as fine china, but she had damned steel in her spine.

"There were at least two dozen Gerdenses and their men and women and servants in the house, so I crept away and found a place down close to where they penned their sheep to wait. I waited fer two days until Harry and Wallace showed themselves, just the two of them. And I shot them, and killed them, and buried them where no one would ever find them. And then I returned home and tried to be the man my clan needed me to be." He looked down at his hands, then met her gaze again. "George Gerdens-Dailey is Harry Gerdens's son."

Silence, so profound he could hear the orchestra tuning one floor and half the house away, hear her soft, shallow breathing. Eye-for-an-eye violence may have been older than the Bible, but that wouldn't make it any more acceptable to her.

"Were . . . were the bodies ever found?"

"Nae. I wanted them gone, with no one able to weep over a tombstone or lay a thistle on a grave." And awful as it had been, he would still have done it again.

She took another breath. "If you hadn't killed them, what would have happened?"

"A clan war, most likely."

"But that didn't happen?"

"The MacLawrys figured the Gerdenses were involved in my father's death. When the two brothers vanished, it made everyone a mite . . . uneasy. Up in the Highlands when the fog and the mist roll in, it's easy to believe in witches and curses and the like. Folk began to say that justice had been done by some unknown hand. That was all I required. It was all anyone required."

Ranulf sank back against a dresser. "I ken that ye would have brought in the local beadle and had the Gerdenses arrested and dragged before a magistrate. But it would have been an English judge, and English law, and the only one to hear a confession from the killers was old MacLawry's eldest son, who might well have murdered the marquis himself to take the title. The Gerdenses would've gone free, and the accusations on both sides would have made things worse."

He couldn't know that for certain, of course, but he'd seen how legal claims, before and since, were handled in the Highlands. And justice generally had more to do with maintaining peace and keeping one family from standing too tall — especially a family that wanted naught to do with English rule. Independence, strength, and defiance were not encouraged. Ever.

"Why did you tell me this?"

Ranulf shrugged. "Firstly, ye asked me who George Gerdens-Dailey was, and that's who he is. Secondly, if I hadnae told ye, nothing between us from here on would ever be completely honest." He started to reach for her hand, then stopped himself. "I've never told a soul what I just told ye, Charlotte. Arran suspects I had a hand in the disappearances, and so does Myles, I'll wager, but I've never admitted it to them. And I never will. None of what happened is

Arran's burden to bear, especially if he should inherit the title. It's my burden."

He looked at her intently, as if he expected her to pronounce sentence on him. Charlotte, though, stayed where she was. What was she supposed to say? How was she supposed to react? Ranulf MacLawry had just confessed to killing, murdering, two men. She should be more than shocked and unsettled. She should be appalled and sickened. She should flee the room and run straight to the Old Bailey to swear out a statement against him and have him arrested.

And she knew she would do no such thing. Not only because he'd trusted her in telling her any of this, but because in the deepest part of her heart, she couldn't blame him for what he'd done. It was everything she'd railed against for the past four years, a man resorting to violence simply because it was the quickest, easiest way to solve a problem, to regain damaged male pride and erase embarrassment. Except that in this instance, in his shoes, she was fairly certain she would have done the same thing. Or she would very much have wanted to do so.

"What are ye thinking, Charlotte?" he asked.

An unbidden tear ran down her cheek, and she wiped it away. The things he'd been through, all while leading people who relied on him. She could scarcely imagine it.

Ranulf swore. "And now I've hurt ye for no damned good reason," he growled. "Let me take ye back to yer sister. I'll —"

"You asked me what I'm thinking," she interrupted, ignoring a second tear. "Do you have any intention of letting me answer you?"

"I thought the tears answered it well enough."

"Well, you'd be wrong." She fought the stupid quavering of her voice. "What I think is that as a fifteen-year-old boy, you did what you had to do, and I'm so, so sorry that you've had to carry this burden all by yourself for so long. No one should have to do that."

He stared at her. "Then . . ."

Clearly he wouldn't believe her words alone. Charlotte stepped forward and tangled her fingers into his dark, lanky hair, pulling his face down to hers. "I said, I understand," she whispered, and kissed him.

Ranulf lifted her into the air so that their faces were level. Tongues tangled until she couldn't tell where she ended and he began. They were at a grand ball, for heaven's sake, with two hundred guests just beyond the flimsily latched doors of the dressing closet. Her sister and his uncle sat only feet away.

None of it mattered. All she wanted in the world was Ranulf. Everything else just faded away. What he'd told her — he no longer had to shoulder it by himself. Yes, his shoulders were broad, but she could be strong, too. For him, she could be.

He sat her down on the dressing table, pulling up her red skirt to step between her knees and continue kissing her. It wasn't enough, though. Now that she knew what it was like to be with him, she craved him, constantly and badly. And they were not leaving this room until she'd had him.

"Touch me, Ran," she murmured, taking his hands and placing them on her bared knees.

Shifting his kisses to her throat, he slowly and lightly ran his fingertips up her thighs, under the rumpled material of her skirt, until he curled his forefinger up inside her. She jumped, clenching her fingers into his hips and pressing against his hand. How something so . . . simple could feel so exquisite, she had no idea, but he made it so.

"Unbutton me," he rumbled, taking her right hand in his free one and moving it to the front of his trousers.

She undid the top button of his trousers, panting as he teased at her again with his fingers. *Oh, goodness.* Charlotte moaned, hooking her hands into his waistband and pulling him closer.

"Christ, Charlotte." Shoving her hands out of the way, he finished undoing his buttons and shoved his trousers down to his thighs. His impressive member sprang free, hard and jutting.

"What do you call this in Gaelic?" she asked, running her finger along the length of him.

"Ye want a lesson now?" he asked, his gaze on her fingers.

She curled around him, stroking gently. "Tell me."

"In English, it's a cock. In Gaelic, a *ball-bearta.*" Lifting his gaze to her eyes, he reached up to cup one breast through her silk gown. *"Bruinne,"* he murmured, then slid his hand beneath the lace to pinch her nipple. "*Sine.* Do ye wish to continue quizzing me, *leannan*?"

With a chuckle that sounded breathless to her own ears, Charlotte shook her head. "Show me, instead."

Ranulf put his hands around her thighs and drew her forward until with a satisfying slide he entered her. Trying to stifle the pleased moaning sounds she couldn't help making, Charlotte buried her face against his shoulder. The hard muscle with its velvet-soft skin sank hot into her again and again until she couldn't breathe, couldn't think, couldn't do anything but hold on to him and try not to shriek with pleasure as she came around him.

With a low groan he started to pull away from her. She knew why. She knew what it meant. And she wrapped her ankles around his hips, folding her shaking hands into his lapels at the same time. "No," she said, looking up at him.

"Charlotte." He grunted, then pushed deep into her again, shuddering.

It was about trust, and the way she felt more alive, more . . . necessary when she was in his company. It was about showing him that she meant it when she said she would share his burdens. But how did anyone put that into words? This was the best she could manage.

He leaned his forehead against hers. "Ye shouldnae have done that, *leannan,*" he murmured. "Ye make me wish I lived a safer, saner life."

That sounded like he was about to walk away and leave her behind. After he'd teased her about courting her, after he'd told her his darkest secret. Did he not want her in his life, or did he think her incapable of sharing it with him?

Was she, though? Capable? Could she live in a world where fathers were murdered and killers vanished and the wrong word said to the wrong person could at best mean a fight, and at worst mean a war? It was maddening, wanting to be with him so badly and not knowing if she had the courage to remain. Or even if he wanted her to.

"We should get back," she said slowly, lifting her head to gaze at him again.

He brushed a finger across her cheek and kissed her, this time so gently it made her heart ache. "With George Gerdens-Dailey here, lass, everything's more complicated."

She nodded, steeling herself for what she needed to say next. "I think he might be the one who shot your brother."

Ranulf's expression cooled to ice. "What makes ye say that?"

Oh, dear. She wouldn't have told him, but he'd shared so much with her. "No bloodshed, Ranulf. Please. Not because of anything I tell you."

He backed away, tugging her skirt down roughly and then refastening his trousers. "Ye want a bargain, do ye?"

"I said I understood what you did when

your father died," she said, hopping down from the dressing table and straightening her skirts. "That doesn't mean I want to be the reason you murder someone."

Abruptly he approached her again, seizing her hands in his. "If I prove to ye that I can be a peaceable man, Charlotte, if I find a way to stay away from these troubles and keep them away from my family, could ye . . ." He trailed off. "I love ye, ye know," he finally said, his voice low. "Ye drive me mad, but I love ye."

Her heart stopped, so quiet she could hear it whispering to her, sighing in surprised happiness. It wasn't just her. Whatever either — both — of them had intended when this began, he felt it, too. Relief, joy, a hundred things galloped through her as her heart began drumming again. Future be damned. At this moment Ranulf loved her. It was enough for now. It would have been enough for forever, if she had any faith at all in happy endings.

"He said he hadn't had MacLawry blood on his hands in nearly three years, and that he had an itch for more." Charlotte took a ragged breath, afraid if she stopped she would lose her nerve again. "I love you, too, Ranulf. And you drive me mad, as well."

CHAPTER FOURTEEN

The conundrum seemed something more fit for Tantalus or Solomon, Ranulf decided as he escorted Charlotte back to her sister.

While he would always consider Berling a party to his brother's shooting, he now knew who'd actually fired the shot. A man whose father he'd taken away in retaliation for losing his own. The Gerdenses had struck first, of course, but the deed had been done.

For Gerdens-Dailey to shoot Bear, who'd been eight when the Gerdens brothers had vanished, and now to turn his gaze on Rowena, who'd only been two — Ranulf wouldn't have been inclined to excuse that, regardless. And now the stable fire, which — if what Arran had surmised was true and Berling hadn't set it — looked very much like George Gerdens-Dailey's handiwork.

If he took his revenge as he wanted to, though, he would be proving to both Charlotte and himself that he *was* a savage, a man who'd be a fool to bring any kind of proper wife into his life — much less one who couldn't abide the idea of fighting over words or deeds. And he wanted her in his life, as much to prove that he could head a clan in an intelligent, progressive way as because she comforted and settled and inspired him with merely a smile.

"We were beginning to worry," Jane said when they stepped through the sitting room door. "You were gone for quite a while."

"I had a great deal of explaining to do," Ranulf said, avoiding his uncle's gaze.

"Are we leaving the party, then? I've already missed two dances, and I need to make my apologies to, oh, everyone." Young Jane scowled.

"We're staying," he decided. "Ye're feeling much improved, Uncle."

"I'm feeling much improved, suddenly," Myles repeated.

Ranulf took Charlotte's right hand, and Jane's left. "If ye cross paths with any of those men ye overheard, ye'll have to pretend to know nothing of their conversation. Can ye do that, lasses?"

"Yes," Charlotte said without hesitation, squeezing his fingers.

"I think so," Jane seconded, not sounding

384

nearly as certain. "I'm just glad my card is full so none of them can ask me to dance. That would be terrifying."

"Well, they won't, so you needn't worry," Charlotte put in, releasing his hand and instead putting an arm around her sister. "And none of them but Berling have ever so much as given me a glance, so I have no concerns at all."

Together the four of them returned to the ballroom, and Ranulf had to watch Charlotte apologize to Henning for missing their quadrille and offer the round man the very next dance. He didn't want to share her, even with her friends.

"You called her *leannan*," his uncle muttered under his breath as they came to a stop at one side of the room.

"I know what I called her. It wasnae an accident. She has my heart." And his mind, and his soul. Saying it aloud was easier than he expected, though he imagined making the same statement to Arran would be a much stickier conversation. Time to stop dissembling, though — it felt like he was dishonoring Charlotte by doing so.

"Do you mean to marry her?"

"Nae unless I can be sure my life won't bring her hurt and heartache."

"Ranulf, that —"

"I know. It sounds like an impossibility." He forced what he hoped was a jaunty smile. "I do like a challenge, ye know."

Rowena was dancing a quadrille with Arran, which had at least served to keep his younger brother and sister out of trouble. As for Berling and his cowardly friends and his troublesome cousin, they were nowhere to be seen. Perhaps they'd decided to leave and plot another tactic when insulting his family to his face hadn't worked.

He could only hope that they would continue to target him, alone, while he decided on a way to deal with them that would satisfy Charlotte, his family, his clan, and his God. He paused. Evidently he'd altered the order of his loyalties without even realizing it. The new order might not be entirely Scottish, but it satisfied his heart.

"What the devil happened?" Arran demanded the moment the dance ended and he and Rowena managed to navigate through the crowd to where Ranulf and Myles stood. Evidently his uncle had decided to serve as his bodyguard tonight. While it likely wouldn't alter anything, he did appreciate the gesture.

"Naught I care to discuss here," he said aloud. "Keep yer eyes and yer wits about ye. And the MacLawrys — none of us —

are to begin, finish, or middle any altercations tonight. Is that clear?"

"I thought we already had this particular conversation," Arran retorted.

"We did. Things have changed."

Arran glared at him. "What things?"

Ranulf took a deep breath. "George Gerdens-Dailey is here tonight. I just wanted ye to know, so ye'd not be surprised if ye set eyes on him."

"George . . . Damnation. I thought he kept to Aberdeen."

"Evidently not."

Ranulf recognized the look on his brother's face. "Yer word," he said, forcing Arran to meet his gaze. If his brother went after one of Berling's cronies, Ranulf would have to support him. And that would ruin everything before he'd barely begun.

"Aye," Arran grated. "My word. No trouble. I only hope to hell ye know what you're aboot, Ran."

Sending a glance at Charlotte prancing about the room with a mollified-looking Henning, Ranulf nodded. "I do," he returned. He was keeping his word, in exchange for a lass. That was what he was doing. Trying to justify it any other way was just a useless complication.

Rowena was dancing now with a light-haired lad far too young and pretty for Ranulf's peace of mind. His sister hadn't so much as mentioned Lachlan MacTier in days — a far cry from a few weeks ago, when she could barely speak a sentence without uttering his name. If he hadn't been so consumed with Charlotte, he would be concerned. After all, if he married an Englishwoman, they would — could — return to Glengask. If Rowena married a Sasannach, he'd likely never see her but at Christmas and if he came down to London again for the Season. That was unacceptable.

"I don't mean to pry, lad," Myles said after a moment. "But —"

"Aye, ye do mean to pry, Uncle," Ranulf cut in. "I need ye to introduce me to a few likely . . . friends. English ones."

"Why?"

So he could prove to a stubborn lass that he was civilized. "Because I clearly cannae trust my own kind here. How better to learn the lay of the land than by making the acquaintance of its people?"

"That sounds very reasonable."

"I am very reasonable. Or I'm trying to be."

His uncle clearly remained skeptical, but as long as the viscount did as he was asked,

Ranulf could tolerate Myles's doubts. God knew he had them, himself. The quadrille seemed to last forever, but when it finally ended he watched Henning return Charlotte to her parents, then moved in as the pretty lad likewise relinquished his sister.

"Introduce me, why don't ye, Rowena?" he suggested smoothly.

She blushed. "Lord Glengask, this is Mr. Harold Myers, Viscount Chaffing's brother. Harold, my brother, the Marquis of Glengask."

From her expression she expected him to run the delicate fellow off with a boot to his arse. But Charlotte and her family were right there, so Ranulf smiled and offered his hand. "I'm glad to see my sister making the acquaintance of proper young men," he said.

"Thank you, my lord."

Perhaps this was how the English conducted themselves; a smile and handshake on the outside, and bored disdain on the inside. Was that all it was? He needed to learn to be a better liar? It seemed . . . wrong, unworthy, but Charlotte was smiling. She wasn't a liar, but then she was also one of the few truly good-hearted people he'd ever met. It was the sour ones who lied, then. The ones who were rotted on the inside and trying to keep their decay a secret.

Well, he didn't think he was that far gone, but neither was he as pure as Charlotte. All of which had the effect of making this business of not speaking his mind, of not taking the action his heart told him to, that much more difficult. But he would do it. He would learn to do it, for Charlotte.

"That was very nice of you, Ran," his sister said, looking at him like he'd sprouted wings from his forehead.

He inclined his head. "Who are ye dancing the waltz with?" he asked, keeping his tone light and unconcerned.

"Sir Robert Mason," she returned, practically bouncing on her toes. "He's a war hero."

"Did he tell ye that himself, then, *piuthar*?" Arran put in as he joined them again.

"He did not. Jane's friend Susan told me. And he has a limp."

Arran laughed. "Tom MacNamara has a limp, too, but he got his from drinking too much and trying to milk a bull."

Rowena slapped Arran's arm. "Sir Robert did nothing so foolish."

"Well, I wouldnae admit to that, either. It's a tale everyone else tells."

"Never mind that." What Ranulf wanted

to say was that Sir Robert Mason had likely never attempted to milk anything in his entire soft life, but that definitely wouldn't help anything.

"I happen to know Sir Robert," Myles put in. "He's a very pleasant fellow."

That sounded somewhat like damning with faint praise, but again he kept his thoughts to himself. Keeping his own counsel, at least, was something to which he was accustomed. Even so, when the orchestra struck up the fanfare for the waltz, he was more than ready for a moment to have Charlotte in his arms once more.

Stepping forward, he offered his arm. "I believe this is my dance, *leannan,*" he drawled, using the word intentionally and catching the stunned look Arran sent him. Even Rowena looked surprised, and she'd tried a bit of matchmaking on his behalf.

She wrapped her hand around his sleeve, and he walked her out to the dance floor. Stunning as she was, a handful of other men turned to watch her pass. *Let them look;* he was the one who'd been inside her thirty minutes earlier. She belonged to him, whether he could yell it to the sky yet or not.

"Tell me something," she said, as he placed a hand on her waist and stepped into the swirling, twirling waltz with her.

"Aye?"

"You've called me *leannan* twice tonight in front of your family, and Arran, especially, nearly had an apoplexy. What does it mean, truly?"

He smiled. Of course she would notice his family's openmouthed reaction. "Love," he returned. "Lover, sweetheart — all of those things."

"You might have told me that before."

"I didnae want to scare ye away, lass."

Charlotte grinned back at him. "Words don't frighten me."

She had the right of that. "What aboot a blizzard so harsh the snow falls sideways?" he asked. "Would that frighten ye?"

"That depends," she replied "Am I inside by a fire or at least wrapped in a warm coat, or am I standing in the middle of the snow in nothing but my night rail?"

"A roaring fire in a fireplace tall enough fer a man to stand upright in. And a warm blanket and mulled ale, besides."

"Then no, that wouldn't frighten me."

"I might've waxed a bit poetic there," he conceded. "Those storms can last for days, lass, with a cold that digs into yer bones and willnae let go. And the Highlands is a great, empty land with more red deer than people. There are only a few grand houses close by Glengask, families of clan chieftains and the like."

She didn't look the least bit hesitant. "Tell me more."

"The village of An Soadh is on my land, down the hill at the foot of the falls, with Mahldoen up higher in the hills at the other end. Handfuls of cotters' houses lie scattered here and there, by planted fields or farther up on the lake for the fishermen, and drovers and herders tend the cattle. And that's it. There are nae parades of carriages driving aboot, nae grand theaters or museums until ye drive all the way to Perth or Aberdeen — which we only do two or three times during a year."

As closely as he studied her sweet face, all he could make out was interest, and a fondness that made his heart thud inside his chest. "I'm still not frightened," she said.

"Then the only thing that frightens ye aboot my life is me."

Charlotte shook her head. "I'm not afraid of you. I'm afraid for you."

"Ye dunnae have to be. I told ye, I'm a changed man."

"Your sister certainly seems to think so," she noted, grinning. "I think she was prepared to be in love with Mr. Harold Myers, until you approved of him. I imagine that now she will very soon find him to be terribly dull — which he is."

"One can only hope," he said dryly. But he had to concede her point; his first instinct had been to bloody the boy's nose, but this would be much more effective, and his sister couldn't blame any of it on his actions.

"The first . . ." She trailed off, her hazel eyes widening as she caught sight of something behind him. The color left her cheeks. "Ranulf."

A hand tapped his shoulder. "Glengask, may I cut in?"

He turned to look, and anger slammed into his spine. Charles Calder, the Campbell's grandson, stood there, his expression arrogant but his eyes speaking of much less certainty. "Nae," he said, as coolly as he could manage.

"That's hardly polite."

No, he didn't imagine it was. And he was equally sure that an English gentleman would give up his claim to his dance partner the moment he was asked. "Go away, Calder. Ye've nae claim here."

"And you don't belong here at all."

"It's all right, Ran," Charlotte murmured. "I don't mind."

He did. He minded a great deal. And if he

held out any longer, everyone would know. Charlotte would know he couldn't even manage this small bit of civility. Clenching his jaw, he released her and stepped back.

With a grin, Calder moved in and took his place, swirling away with Charlotte in his arms. Rather than watch, Ranulf turned his back and left the dance floor. Every curse word he could think of and in several different languages caught in his throat, fighting him to roar free. *No.* He wouldn't allow it. He was a bloody gentleman.

Charlotte's parents, Lord and Lady Hest, stood talking with a small group of their friends. Hc didn't know whether they were oblivious to their older daughter's dance partner, or if the change made no difference to them. But now that he was far enough away that no one else was likely to notice him staring, he found her red-clothed form on the dance floor and didn't take his eyes off her. And he continued repeating to himself that nothing would come of this, and that it would be worth it.

Charlotte kept her gaze on the thin-faced man with one hand clasping hers, and the other on her waist. Light brown hair, forgettable brown eyes, and a broad, flat chin that gave him a permanent stubborn expression. She knew she'd seen him before, though as small as the English aristocracy was, she didn't think they'd ever exchanged a single word.

And as they turned lightly about the dance floor, she began to wonder if they ever would have a conversation. Or perhaps he hadn't planned anything beyond attempting to take the dance over from Ranulf. Perhaps he'd expected a brawl, and he was now at a complete loss. She rather liked that idea. And silence was much easier, anyway. Heaven knew she had quite enough to think about as it was.

Foremost in her thoughts, of course, as he had been almost from the moment they'd met, was Ranulf MacLawry. Even without looking she knew he stood at the fringes of the room, watching. Probably looking for a reason to step in and begin punching people. Well, she would not be providing him with the excuse. She wanted him to prove to her, to her father, to himself, that he could make his life, rule his clan, without resorting to fighting and feuds and bloodshed and death.

"How do you know Glengask?" Charles Calder asked, nearly making her jump.

"I don't even know you, sir," she returned with a slight, cool smile. She wasn't about to give him information without gaining anything in return. After all, they might not have met, but she'd heard his voice quite clearly an hour or so ago.

"Well, then. Charles Calder, at your service." He gave a smile that was undoubtedly meant to be charming.

"Mr. Calder."

"And I know that you're Lady Charlotte Hanover. Now that that's been taken care of, how do you know Lord Glengask?" he repeated.

"His mother and my mother were friends." There. True and innocent sounding, all at the same time.

"Your family has an unblemished reputation, Lady Charlotte," he returned mildly, his expression except for his eyes becoming one of kindly concern. "And that's why I think you should know that every one of the MacLawrys is trouble. He most of all."

It took all her effort to keep her expression mildly curious. "Goodness, that sounds dire," she commented. "What makes you say such a thing to a complete stranger, Mr. Calder?"

"Because it's important. The MacLawrys might claim blue blood for some favor an ancestor did for a king three or four hundred years ago, but these days they're little better than animals. They don't deserve their land or their title, and they damned well don't belong among the good people of Mayfair."

Charlotte wanted to hit him. The very thought stunned her, but she was fairly certain no mere set of sharply crafted words could adequately describe how very angry he was making her. How dare he insult Ranulf? By association he'd insulted her, as well, but that didn't matter. The deep slight to Ranulf, however, did. "If you have proof of any of this, why did you approach me? Why not my father, or the courts, or the Regent?" *Ha.* She was not as gullible or naïve as he clearly seemed to think her.

"Because it's you I see him hanging about, my lady. You're always on his arm, and it's you he watches from across the room. You therefore seem more in need of a warning than anyone else." He offered her a slight frown. "For your own good, you should stay well away from him and his kin."

By now she expected the warning, but Charlotte was still somewhat surprised he had the nerve to deliver it. "Well," she returned, deepening her careful smile, "I shall certainly keep what you've said in mind. Considering that I'm much better acquainted with the MacLawry family than I am with you, however, you'll have to forgive me if I attribute most of what you say to some sort of jealousy or a private vendetta."

His grip on her hand tightened, then relaxed again. "That would be a mistake. You don't want to be caught up in this. Blood's spilled over it before, and I imagine it will again."

She narrowed her eyes. "And now threats. To me."

His sympathetic expression faltered. "My lady, I think you mis—"

"I don't think I've misinterpreted anything, Mr. Calder. You're either trying to frighten me, or to convince me to tell Lord Glengask about this conversation in order to incite him to action. I won't call you a coward, sir, but I will ask that you henceforth keep your opinions to yourself."

The forgettable brown eyes stared holes straight through her. "You're about to step onto dangerous ground, Lady Charlotte," he muttered. "Perhaps you should speak to your family before you continue. They may not agree with your conclusions."

No, they likely wouldn't. And neither did she wish to see them put in danger simply because she had an overwhelming desire to tell Charles Calder to go to the devil. She lifted her chin. "Before you begin declaring English families with unblemished reputations to be your enemy, you might consider the ramifications of your actions. We don't like to be threatened."

She put every ounce of regal affront she possessed into the comment, and had the satisfaction of seeing him blink. If Ranulf required proof that words could carry more weight than blows, this was a prime example. As the waltz came to an end, she pulled free and backed away.

Before she could turn away and make her escape, though, Calder stepped forward and took her hand again, bowing over it. "You, my lady, are a bitch and a shrew," he murmured, "dried up, on the shelf, and so desperate for a man you're willing to become a Highlander's whore." He straightened, releasing her fingers. "And I dare you to tell him I said that."

For a moment she couldn't even move. No one — *no one* — had ever spoken to her like that. She felt almost as if she had been physically slapped and thrown to the ground and stepped on. Finally, before anyone could wonder why she stood alone in the middle of the dance floor, she forced herself to turn and walk back toward her parents.

Was this a challenge to her philosophy, or the means by which Ranulf would fail to live up to it? He would kill Calder for saying that to her. At the least, the ensuing brawl would utterly ruin his reputation in London. And where her father was concerned.

"Ye look pale as a banshee," he said, walking up and offering his arm.

She took it gratefully. "He's quite an awful man."

"Aye. That he is." They walked a few feet in silence. "Are ye not going to tell me what he said, then?"

Charlotte shook her head. "No. It was just words."

Ranulf stopped, bringing her up short beside him. "What was just words?" he asked crisply.

She would have to tell him something, if only for his own safety. And if she concealed the truth, it didn't mean that Ranulf had kept his word to her about being civilized. It only made her a liar and a coward. "He said you and your family were trouble, and that I would be wise to keep my distance from you."

"Ah. And that's why ye look ready to faint, *leannan*?"

"I'm not ready to faint," she retorted. "He called me some names. I believe I'll survive."

Ranulf pulled her closer. "What names?"

401

he enunciated very clearly.

She met his fierce, burning gaze. "You gave me your word."

He continued glaring at her. "Aye, that I did. So tell me what he said to ye, Charlotte."

If she told him, she *knew* he would go straight for Calder's throat. And if she didn't, he might very well attack anyway. "He said I was a bitch and a shrew, old and so desperate for a man that I became your whore." The words tasted strange and filthy on her tongue, and she hoped never to have cause to speak them again.

Ranulf closed his eyes for the space of half a dozen heartbeats. She kept her grip on his arm, even though she knew that if he went for Calder she would never be able to stop him. It felt like minutes, but could only have been a matter of seconds before vivid blue caught her gaze again.

"Just words," he muttered, and moved forward again. "I think it's time for us to leave."

"We can't, Ran," his sister pleaded as they reached the rest of the group. "I've promised every dance to someone."

"So have I," Jane added. She'd danced the waltz with Arran MacLawry, Charlotte realized belatedly.

"Is something amiss, Glengask?" Lord Hest asked, his expression cautious. From what he'd said about Ranulf, he no doubt expected trouble.

A muscle in Ranulf's lean jaw clenched. "Nae. Just a feeling."

"Then you're free to go, of course. I think we'll stay."

For a long moment Ranulf stood silent. "Come along then, Rowena, Arran."

He reached for his sister's hand, but she took a step backward. "I'm not going, Ranulf."

"Then who do ye expect to keep an eye on ye, Rowena?" he returned flatly.

"No one. For heaven's sake, *bràthair*, this is a grand ball. Nothing is going to happen to me here. And I'm eighteen. I'm not a little girl with pigtails."

Ranulf hesitated. It was the first time in their acquaintance that Charlotte had ever seen him indecisive about anything. The effect was oddly heartbreaking. Finally he nodded. "Arran and I will go, then. Unless ye've other plans, Arran."

"Nae. I'll go with ye," Arran replied, looking rather stunned to be asked.

"Good." He sent a glance at his uncle, who nodded, evidently realizing his duty. Then he looked at her, a stiff smile touching his mouth and fleeing again. "I'll call on ye tomorrow."

With that he and his brother left the ballroom. Immediately the room seemed smaller, the light dimmer, the music cheap and amateurish. And as much as she tried to deny it, her heart felt dimmer, too.

Of course she was being silly; she'd spent weeks attempting to convince him to see her point of view. Insisting that it was wrong to answer words — especially words that only insulted a man's or a woman's pride — with bloodshed. So now that he'd listened, she had no right to feel like a fairy princess whose one true love had just walked away from the battlefield rather than staying to defend her honor.

After all, she knew why he'd left; he'd done it so no one else would have any reason to threaten or insult her or Rowena or Janie. It had been the wise, mature decision. Neither had he been weak in conceding to his sister's demand to stay. He'd only been attempting to avoid causing a scene, as any proper gentleman would do.

And so she did not, absolutely did not, feel disappointed.

CHAPTER FIFTEEN

Ranulf had read somewhere about insects that devoured their victims from the inside, leaving perfect, empty shells in their wake. And he wondered whether fury could do the same thing to a man, eating his heart and organs alive, consuming them with heat and flame, leaving naught but a hollow wretch behind.

Part of him wished that, if emptiness was the end result, his anger would hurry up and get it over with. Because the raw hate he'd been fighting during a night of pacing and drinking and punching half a dozen holes in his bedchamber wall showed no sign of easing.

All he wanted to do was strike out — at Calder and at Gerdens-Dailey and at Berling — and permanently remove the threat those men represented to his loved ones. And that was the one thing he could not do. Not if he wanted to keep Charlotte

Hanover in his life.

Arran leaned around the breakfast room door frame. "There ye are," he said, but didn't move into the room. Instead his light blue eyes found Owen and one of the new footmen they'd hired. "My brother and I need a moment," he said.

"Aye, Lord Arran."

Once Owen had dragged the other servant out of the room, Arran stepped inside and shut the door behind him. Silently he poured himself a cup of tea, chose a hard-boiled egg and some ham slices from the sideboard, and took the seat at the foot of the table opposite Ranulf.

"Ye've a note from Myles," he said, sliding the folded paper down the table.

After he took another drink from the whisky at his elbow and emptied the accompanying bottle of the stuff to refill his glass, Ranulf picked the note up and unfolded it. "I'll be going to luncheon at White's," he said, refolding the note and pocketing it. Evidently Myles had found an Englishman or two for him to befriend. Lovely. Now he would have to find a way to be polite, when all he wanted to do was smash things into wee pieces.

His brother nodded. "I thought I might see if Winnie and the Hanover lasses care to go for a picnic luncheon," he said, his tone still low and flat and careful.

"Ye do that, then." Ranulf took another drink.

They sat in silence for a few minutes, before Arran cleared his throat. "I thought ye might've still been to bed this morning," he said, "so I knocked on yer door. I think ye might have some wood beetles in yer walls. Ye've a bit of damage."

If he'd been in a better mood, the care with which Arran was speaking would have been amusing. "I noticed that," he returned.

"If ye need any assistance getting rid of these insects, I hope ye keep in mind that I'm here, and I'm more than ready to help."

That couldn't be allowed. Not only could Arran be hurt — or worse — but any Mac-Lawry doing violence could cost him Charlotte. "Nae. The world's full of insects, and they'll eat what they will."

"So ye mean to let 'em pull down yer house, just because that's what they do?"

It was a fairly apt metaphor, Ranulf decided. "What I mean to do," he said, standing, "is go to White's for luncheon. And ye'll be having yer picnic. If ye don't mind, tell Charlotte I won't be able to come by today, after all."

He wanted to. He could scarcely think of

anything or anyone else. But he knew that seeing her before he'd found a way to wrestle his rage into something he could control would be exceedingly unwise. Because when he so much as imagined her golden hair and wise hazel eyes, all he wanted to do was go find the man who'd insulted her and force him to apologize. To make certain none of his so-called countrymen could ever hurt her or Rowena or anyone else in his family ever again.

"I'll tell her that," Arran said, clearly not reading his brother's thoughts. "Are ye certain there's not someaught ye'd care to tell me?"

Ranulf kept walking. "Aye. Stay oot of trouble."

His brother couldn't possibly be satisfied with that response. Ranulf wasn't happy with it, either, but there wasn't a thing to be done about it. Yes, he could pursue the burning of his stable legally, but all he and Arran had been able to determine was that Berling had quite possibly not done it. As for the insults to Rowena and Charlotte, ungentlemanly or not he didn't think it illegal. And unless he had overwhelming evidence of a heinous crime, trying to bring legal action would only make him look weak. Weaker.

When he returned to his bedchamber, Ginger was attempting to hang a painting over one of the holes in the wall. Several of them were already covered, in fact, with an ill-fitting mismatch of paintings, a picture cut from a catalog, plates of delicate china, and what looked like a tea cozy.

"I think that's more pointing them oot than covering them up, Ginger," he commented, and the valet jumped.

"I'll have Owen hire someone to make repairs," the valet said, setting the painting on the floor. "Such poor craftsmanship. There's no excuse, my lord."

Ranulf thought there was an excellent excuse; it was either the wall or Charles Calder and George Gerdens-Dailey's faces. "Thank ye," he said aloud. "Now find me someaught to wear to White's, will ye?"

"White's? Yes, my lord. Of course. With pleasure."

This was what he did, Ranulf supposed. He tried to put aside a handful of hurtful words and ignored the fact that they could signify the start of something much more dangerous. He went to stuffy luncheons and made stuffy, proper acquaintances and called them friends and pretended to like wee cucumber sandwiches with the crusts cut off.

As he dressed, Fergus rose from his place before the fire and butted Ranulf's hand with his nose, demanding scratches. Absently Ranulf complied. The poor fellow was indispensable in the Highlands, both for protection and for chasing down rabbits and deer. Here, though, he was mostly a curiosity, unusual for his size and fearsome appearance, but of no use at soirees and Society's proper gatherings.

He was rather the same, now that he thought about it. In the Highlands decisiveness and a firm hand kept those dependent on him fed and safe and thriving where most others brought uncaring greed and shortsightedness that forced their own people into the cities or the Lowlands or across the sea to America. In London, though, everything he knew was wrong, everything he was skilled at was inappropriate, and others played the game better than he did.

A logical, sane man would likely leave Town and return to where the world was right side up. But today he wasn't a sane man. Today he was a man in love. Giving Fergus's rough fur another ruffle, he finished dressing and went downstairs to collect Stirling.

Debny had saddled his own horse, as well.

Rather than spending time arguing, Ranulf swung up on the big bay and headed toward Pall Mall. However tired and angry he happened to be, in a very few minutes he was going to have to be charming and personable. He meant to be the sort of man to whom Lord Hest would be happy to hand over his daughter, whether he could barely tolerate himself or not.

"Come back for me in an hour or so," he told his groom once they'd reached the unassuming front door of the club.

"And if ye leave before that?" Debny asked, catching Stirling's reins.

"I'll hire a hack."

"M'laird, I am nae going to see ye without an ally."

Ranulf took a breath. "I'll keep Myles with me," he said.

The groom nodded. "That'll do, then."

"I damned well hope so," he muttered, and walked up to the door. Now his own servants felt comfortable dictating to him.

The door opened as he reached it, and a liveried doorman stepped forward, blocking the entrance. "Are you expected, sir?" he asked politely.

So now he had to explain himself and his business to servants and strangers. "Lord Swansley's expecting me," he ground out, attempting a mild expression and fairly certain he wasn't succeeding. "The Marquis of Glengask."

The doorman stepped aside. "Welcome, my lord," he said, gesturing to a passing footman. "Franklin will show you to your table."

Well, that was more like it. Myles and two other men sat close to the middle of the room, and all three men stood as he approached. Inwardly swearing, Ranulf inclined his head as he recognized one of his lunch companions.

"Lord Stephen Hammond, aye?" he said, shaking his uncle's hand and taking the one open chair at the table.

"Yes," the Duke of Esmond's second son replied, and indicated the stocky, brown-haired man seated opposite Ranulf. "And this is my good friend Simon Beasley. Simon, Lord Glengask."

"Lord Swansley tells us you have a large holding in Scotland," Beasley commented.

"Aye." Ranulf had no desire to elaborate. "How do ye know my uncle, Mr. Beasley?"

"Our families are neighbors," the stout man returned with an easy smile. "Our family patriarch is the Marquis of Dunford, but I'm several cousins away from him."

"Simon and I attended Oxford together,"

Lord Stephen put in. "Both of our families have pedigrees dating all the way back to the second Henry."

"There's a club of sorts at Oxford," Simon added, his grin deepening. "A gathering for descendants of England's original earls."

That seemed singularly uninteresting, but Ranulf nodded. The Sasannach talked so much, they probably had knowledge of all sorts of useless, inane information.

"How far back does your title go?" Lord Stephen asked, as a waiter came by and took their luncheon orders.

"I dunnae track back to a Henry," Ranulf drawled, catching his uncle's warning look.

"Ah. How recent is it, then?" Simon signaled a footman for a bottle of wine.

Bah. Wine might as well be water. "A mite older than that. My ancestors were Vikings and Celts. The first jarl of Glengask was, according to legend, a great bear of a man called Laurec. He took to wife a wild Celtic lass who painted her face blue and danced naked in the moonlight."

"Ranulf," Uncle Myles rumbled.

"Well, it's an old legend," he conceded. "Quite possibly exaggerated."

The other two men exchanged a glance. Hm. Evidently stories about Vikings and naked, blue-faced lasses were too scandalous for polite Society. He wasn't even certain why he'd told the story, except that he'd been drinking for the past ten hours and perhaps it was finally beginning to blunt the edge of his anger and frustration.

"It's a fascinating tale," Lord Stephen commented. "With roots so deep in the Highlands, Glengask, what are you doing in London?"

"That's right," Beasley seconded. "I've never seen you here before."

Ranulf shrugged. "This is where the parties are."

Myles laughed, though he didn't sound terribly amused. "His sister, my niece, turned eighteen a few weeks ago. She wanted her London Season."

The conversation stopped for a few moments as waiters brought their meals. He'd requested roast venison, but the mess he received was nearly drowned in a gravy so thick and salty he might well have been eating beef. Or even chicken.

"So when your sister's had her Season you'll be returning to the Highlands, I presume?"

He glanced over at Lord Stephen. "Aye. More than likely."

"Are those Highland lasses as bonny as they say?" Beasley asked, chuckling.

"And as wild?" the other one added.

"There are some bonny lasses. And some wild ones. Just the same as there are here, I would imagine."

"I would imagine a marquis, a descendant of a Viking and a blue-faced Celt," Lord Stephen said over his glass of wine, "would have his choice of the prettiest and best-bred Highland ladies. Women of a similar breeding and with similar . . . expectations."

This was beginning to sound insulting, though it wasn't the words as much as it was the tone. He glanced over at Myles, and was surprised to see the intent look his uncle sent him before the viscount returned to his pheasant. Was he missing something? With these reduced expectations, he should be able to manage. Being tired and half drunk certainly wasn't helping, though.

Or perhaps Myles was merely warning him not to tell any more Viking stories. Ranulf frowned inwardly. If this was the path of his life now, he was going to have to at least pretend to be content, if not happy. *She* would be that part of his new life, and that would make him happy.

"Did you know Charlotte Hanover was once engaged?" Lord Stephen commented smoothly.

Now Ranulf was interested. "Aye. James

Appleton died in a duel, she said."

"He did." Stephen nodded. "A damned tragedy, all over a bit of clumsiness. Appleton would eventually have made her a viscountess, with a lovely old house on Charles Street that's perfect for hosting soirees. And they would have spent the rest of the year in Trowbridge, just outside of Bath."

"Since they weren't married," Beasley took up, "she couldn't wear full mourning, and she had to be out of black in six weeks. But we all knew, and we let her be."

"I'm certain she was grateful," Ranulf said, realizing his jaw was clenching. He forced himself to relax.

"She was quite a prize to pass by, too — the daughter of an earl with a dowry that was impressive to start with." Stephen did some calculations on his fingers. "Now, seven years later, it's probably more than double what she was worth at eighteen, just as compensation for her being five-and-twenty."

Ranulf took a swallow of weak wine. "I would wager the two of ye are making a point of some kind," he drawled.

"Just that you have your women and we have ours, and no one likes a poacher." Lord Stephen angled his glass of wine in Ranulf's direction, toasting him. "Especially when a man is a visitor. It's rather like being asked in for dinner and then stealing the silverware."

Now it made sense. He wasn't the point of conflict; Charlotte was. That surprised him, though now that he considered it, it likely shouldn't have. "I have a house here in London," he said, then realized that he sounded submissive and apologetic. He might be attempting tolerance, but he damned well wasn't anyone's whipping boy. "And even if I didnae," he continued deliberately, "if a lass doesnae have a ring on her finger, she's fair game."

Beasley's left eye twitched. "We'll just call everything fair game, then."

Ranulf fiddled with the knife beside his plate. "Ye live in a soft land, lads. Before ye declare the start of someaught, keep in mind that I came here fer polite conversation and a good meal. I can leave that same way, with ye knowing that once I depart London, I'm nae likely to return anytime soon. Or ye can begin someaught that may not end the way ye like."

With a laugh that didn't sound at all genuine, Lord Stephen sat back in his chair. "We're merely conversing here, Glengask. There's no need for threats."

"I agree," Ranulf drawled. "So stop making them."

Myles leaned in to empty the wine bottle into his glass. "I heard that Sullivan Waring is sending five horses down to Tattersall's next week. The rumor is they may go for as much as three hundred pounds apiece."

"That's ridiculous." Beasley snorted. "Not even Waring's horses are worth that much."

Lord Stephen continued gazing at Ranulf, who coolly looked right back at him. If the fellow thought a good stare would frighten him off, well, Ranulf had overestimated the Sasannach. And his expectations had been fairly low to begin with. Finally the duke's son turned his eyes to Simon Beasley. "I think it's safe to say that we all know where we stand here, and that perhaps we began today on the wrong note."

"Well said," Myles agreed. "May I suggest we begin again?"

"I dunnae quite see the point." Ranulf set his utensils down, giving up on the gravy-drowned monstrosity on his plate. "Ye spoke what ye meant — more or less. Anything now, polite as ye may word it, would be a lie."

"But we all lie to each other, Glengask. I told Simon his new coat could well begin a new fashion, for example, when truly I think it hideous and the color of vomit."

Beasley brushed at his front. "I say, Stephen."

"Oh, for God's sake, Simon, it's lime green."

If these two men had been suspicious and hostile, Ranulf could have tolerated it. He would even have respected it, to a degree. But as he listened to the two men debating the merits or lack thereof of a lime-green coat, he realized that every smile he ever gave them, every quip he laughed at, would be a lie. These men and he would never be friends. They came from different worlds, and other than a shared fascination with Charlotte they had absolutely nothing in common.

Because he had a great deal invested in this experiment, he stayed through the end of the meal and even made an effort at nonsensical small talk. It was exhausting, and he'd nearly decided that he preferred anger to boredom when the Englishmen climbed to their feet.

Lord Stephen offered his hand. "I assume you mean to continue your pursuit of Lady Charlotte Hanover, then?"

"I dunnae think that's any of yer business, Hammond."

The duke's son lowered his hand again.

"That's good to know as well, Glengask."

"Aye. I thought we should be clear."

Ranulf walked outside with his uncle. Even London air felt welcome after that, and he took a deep breath. "So were they meant to be friends, or did ye have someaught else in yer head?" he asked, as the Swansley coach circled around to meet them.

"You accused me once — and rightly so — of being too trusting. I try not to make the same mistake more than once. And those two make me . . . suspicious."

"Aye. My skin's still crawling," Ranulf agreed. "Anything particular ye care to share?"

Myles shook his head. "No." As they climbed into the coach, he sat forward. "I did want you to be aware that that sentiment exists among some of my fellows. But for God's sake don't judge every peer by the behavior of those two men. There are good people here, and I would be proud to introduce you to some of them."

The viscount's voice shook a little. Was he worried that he would once again be judged by the company he'd elected to keep? Or did he truly want Ranulf to find friendships in London? Either way, it was touching.

"Give me a day or two to get the bad taste

oot of my mouth," he returned, "and I'll be happy to meet yer actual friends."

And skeptical as he was about the whole thing, he had one very good reason to give London and Londoners another go — Charlotte liked it here, and he would not make the mistake his father had in keeping an English lass locked away in the Highlands when her heart lay elsewhere. Especially when his heart lay squarely with her.

Charlotte leaned closer over the map she'd found of the Highlands. Tracing out the latitude and longitude, she referred to the book of property holdings she'd liberated from her father's office and marked out the approximate boundaries of Glengask. Even with the small scale of the map, Ranulf's property was impressive and immense, dwarfing most English estates. It crossed the river Dee at two points, and was cluttered with vast, shallow valleys and craggy hills and gorges and windswept grass and farmlands.

For a long moment she sat looking at it, lost in imaginings of riding alongside the wild river and walking through high-walled canyons where trees found sanctuary from the cold and winds. And always beside her was Ranulf, showing her the beauty of the

Highlands and making her love his land nearly as much as she loved him.

Blinking, she returned to the property book. She wasn't there to measure the wealth of Glengask. Running her finger down the endless lists, she found the name Gerdens, and carefully marked out that property, then did the same with Campbell and Dailey and Calder.

Then she sat back. While Glengask was by far the largest estate — which made sense as the MacLawrys were the only ones to refuse to sell off any of their land — it was definitely surrounded by the others. From what she could tell he had a few allies at the fringes, like the MacTiers and the Orlins and the Lenoxes, but farther out in almost every direction lay someone who'd either threatened a MacLawry, or actually wounded or killed one.

"My goodness," she breathed. Why hadn't she realized it before? Ranulf wasn't imagining enemies or puffing out his chest because he enjoyed being notorious or because he felt his pride was being dented. Now that she knew him better, knew how precious his family and his people were to him, she could see quite clearly that he had spent years making himself the largest, most frightening devil in the Highlands — a man no other man would dare to cross.

And she was telling him to be civilized, to settle his disputes with words. What would be more likely to stop one man from trying to kill another? A sternly worded warning, or the well-founded belief that if a fellow acted, he would be the next one put beneath the sod? These men had grown up in the wildest, most dangerous place in the kingdom. Even if some of them now lived in more civilized places, their ancestors, fathers, grandfathers, had passed down the traditions of hatred for fellow clans and fear of change. And most definitely they all feared a man who refused to bow to anyone — up to and including the current Prince Regent.

He'd already refused to react thrice when he'd been challenged — by Berling, Gerdens-Dailey, and once by Calder. As much as she wanted to, she couldn't convince herself that Clan MacLawry had been made safer by his actions. Or rather, his lack of action.

And he'd done it for her, because she was enlightened — or squeamish, or had once been hurt because a man had more pride than brains and she'd then decided that any show of force or violence was useless and barbaric. But she didn't live in the Highlands, and she'd never been pressed by her fellows to alter who she was or how she chose to live.

She'd lost James to a senseless, stupid, utterly avoidable act of violence that he'd brought upon himself. He'd never had much of a sense of humor — at least not about his own foibles. Even five years after his death, she remembered the red-blotchy flush of his cheeks, the way he'd practically dared anyone to laugh at him for something as . . . innocent as tripping. And then someone *had* laughed, and nothing would serve but that he reclaim his honor and his pride by walking forty paces and shooting a pistol.

Ranulf MacLawry was not James Appleton. She doubted the two would have tolerated each other, much less have been capable of being friends. But where James had been obsessively self-concerned and frivolous, Ranulf seemed to be anything but that. And whatever else he might be, Ranulf was not foolish.

Charlotte stood up from the library's table and walked to the window. One man had died senselessly, and by her advising a second, even more extraordinary man to be . . . civilized, she might well be dooming him to the same fate. And that — and that would be more than she could bear.

Arran had said that Ranulf was going to have luncheon at White's today. He'd also muttered something about his brother going mad and deciding he needed Sasannach friends, but all she'd heard was that he was attempting to be civilized.

Now, though, she abruptly wasn't so certain that was a wise idea. He'd led his clan for better than fifteen years now, and had found ways to provide his people with improved education, better houses, higher income, and an ongoing independence from England and the pressures from their neighbors to break the clan apart.

She clenched her fingers into the windowsill. More than anything else right now she wanted to see him, to apologize for trying to force him to follow her philosophy when she hadn't understood his. And she wanted to kiss him, and to feel his warm, solid body against hers.

He lived a dangerous life. And even knowing that, she could not imagine anywhere she'd rather be than at his side. If she hadn't destroyed him. She left the window and walked out of the library. "Winnie?" she called.

A footman stepped out of the dining room. "I believe you'll find Lady Rowena in your sister's bedchamber, my lady," he said.

"Thank you, Thomas."

She found Janie and Winnie lying on their stomachs across the bed, both of them perusing the new *Ackermann's Repository* and giggling. They looked so young, so carefree, so naïve — it was nearly impossible to believe that once, not so long ago, she'd been the exact same way. And for far longer than she cared to acknowledge.

Her sister looked up. "Char, can you see me in one of these bonnets?"

Charlotte walked forward, tilting her head to look. "I think it's a monstrosity," she returned, putting on a smile. "Good heavens."

Both girls laughed. "I told you she would hate it," Winnie exclaimed, the slight brogue she couldn't quite disguise making her even more charming than she likely realized.

"Winnie, I wondered if you'd like to visit your brothers at Gilden House," Charlotte said quickly, wishing she could just grab Rowena by the hand and drag her out the door. "I'd be happy to escort you."

"She just saw Arran," Janie returned, wrinkling her nose. "And Lord Glengask was in such a foul mood last night."

Rowena, though, slid off the bed. "I was just thinking there was something I forgot

426

to tell Arran."

"Do you want me to come?" Jane didn't sound even a little enthusiastic, and Charlotte had to smile at her sister.

"Oh, no," Winnie said, taking Charlotte's arm and pulling her to the door. "We won't be long. Thank you for going with me, Charlotte. I think Mitchell's still worried that Ran will sack her for helping me flee Glengask, and she's trying to stay out of sight until he forgets." She clucked her tongue, and a large gray dog squirmed out from beneath the bed. "Come along, Una. You can visit Fergus. I know you miss him."

Charlotte asked for the coach to be brought around, and in ten minutes they were on their way to Gilden House. She had no idea how she would say it, but she knew she needed to apologize, and to tell Ranulf that he needed to stop listening to her when it came to managing his fellow Highlanders — and quickly, before something terrible and irreversible happened.

"You like him, don't you?"

She jumped, looking across at Winnie. "Beg pardon?"

"Ran. I told him that if he would just stop bellowing and ordering people about, you would see that he wasn't a complete devil."

"I never thought he was a devil," Charlotte returned, surprised. "You told him to behave?"

"He's very witty, you know, and he loves all of us to distraction. But he's so accustomed to being in Scotland, and he doesn't know how Englishmen behave."

"But there aren't just Englishmen here."

"You're talking about that awful Lord Berling. He may not be an Englishman, but he's definitely not a Highlander."

"It's not just Berling, Rowena. And your brother is the way he is for very good reason." She drew a breath. "I only wish I'd realized that earlier."

Rowena leaned forward and seized her hand. "You didn't turn him away, did you?"

"No. Of course not."

"Oh, thank goodness. Because he's quite smitten with you. No one else ever talks back to him, you know. Except for me. And even I always end up doing as he says — except for coming here. And I know he wants me to marry Lachlan MacTier, and I thought I wanted that, too, but now that I've been here I think maybe Lachlan might not be the right man. He thinks I'm just a wee bairn, you know, and there are men here who definitely know I'm a young lady. Some very handsome men."

Oh, dear. She would have to tell Ranulf

about this, too, then. But there were other things that he had to know first. She wanted him to know that she didn't love him in spite of his so-called devilish ways, but because of them. Because as much as he wanted to keep his family and friends safe, she wanted the same for him.

CHAPTER SIXTEEN

Arran stared at him. "What do ye mean, ye want to sit down with the Campbell?" he asked, his face going alarmingly pale.

"We've been feuding fer better than a hundred years," Ranulf returned. "I think it's time we had a chat."

"Ye'll never make it into his castle alive. And if ye did, ye damned well wouldnae make it oot again."

"So ye'd rather we go on as we are? They take one of ours every so often, and we shoot one of theirs in return?"

Standing, Arran paced the sitting room. "Ye've lost yer damned mind!" he finally burst out. "Ye know how we survive. We stand strong, and they leave us be because they're afraid of what we could do to them if they dared strike."

Ranulf sipped at his coffee, willing the pain in his skull to ease. While he would admit to being tired and having an aching head, he didn't think he'd lost his mind. Not yet. "We're likely to gain more ground with the Campbell than we are with the Gerdenses. To talk with them, I'd have to deal with Berling."

"Ye dunnae need to talk to anyone," his brother insisted. "If ye go to them, they'll see it as weakness. Except fer the school fires and an offer to purchase land, they've all let us be fer fifteen years. And that's because of ye, Ran."

"They've let us be except fer Munro being shot by Gerdens-Dailey, and the matter of my stable fire." He blew out his breath. "I want my family to be safe," he finally said. "I want to be able to bring a wife to Glengask and nae have to worry every time she goes outside to pick wildflowers."

"Well, the only way ye'll make peace with the Campbells is if ye burn out yer cotters and villages and lose enough people that they can call themselves better than we are. And ye'd likely have to sell off a third of Glengask for sheep grazing just so they'll believe ye."

"There has to b—"

"And ye'll nee'r make peace with the Gerdenses, so ye'd only be weaker by half and facing one fewer set of killers — unless the Campbell decided seeing ye on yer belly meant he could grind the lot of us beneath his heel."

Arran generally made a great deal of sense, and Ranulf couldn't find fault in any of his reasoning this time, either. "Then what do ye suggest I do?"

"I suggest ye stop letting those *amadan* insult ye, for one thing, and that ye start thinking again with yer brain and not yer cock. The stronger ye are, the more likely they are to leave us be. And that's what'll make us safe."

"And if I cannae go aboot thrashing people fer no good reason?"

"Then think of a good reason, Ranulf. Fer God's sake. Ye've never thrown a punch for any but a damned good reason before now, anyway." His brother slammed his fist into the back of a chair. "If she has ye gelded now, we'll all be dead by winter."

Ranulf shot to his feet. "Enough!"

"Why? Ye cannae hit me, or yer lass will frown at ye." Arran jabbed a finger in his direction. "And the minute the Campbells or the Gerdenses or anyone else realize that, we're all done for."

He knew Arran was correct, and he knew he was being foolish to let a lass dictate how he conducted his business. After all, he'd lived this life. She hadn't. "I want her in my life, Arran. I want her to be happy, and I want her to be safe."

Arran looked at him. "I dunnae think ye can have all three, Ran. Two of them, perhaps. But not all three."

"And I think ye're wrong."

The sitting room door opened, and Rowena pranced into the room. Immediately the whole house felt lighter, more like home. The unexpected sight of his sister made him smile; Rowena never seemed to have both feet on the ground at the same time. "What are ye doing here, *piuthar*?" he asked, planting a kiss on her cheek.

"Can't a sister visit her brothers?" she returned with a grin. "Arran, take me for a walk."

"I'll go with ye," Ranulf said, heading for the door.

"No you won't. I left you a present in your office. When we get back you can tell me if you like it." Grabbing Arran's hand, she half dragged him into the hallway.

Ignoring for the moment the fact that no one was supposed to set foot in his office without his permission, Ranulf watched them down the stairs into the foyer and out the front door. He could hear Una and Fergus in the morning room chasing each other and likely breaking things. "Owen," he called down to his footman-cum-butler, "settle down the dogs, will ye?"

"Aye, m'laird." With an oath the stout Scotsman charged into the morning room, where odds were he'd cause more damage than the two dogs combined.

If Bear were here it would be almost perfect. Crossing the hallway, he pushed open his office door.

"Hello," Charlotte said, standing in front of his tall window.

Her sunshine hair glowed like spun gold. His heart stuttered, then sped to twice its normal speed. Now only Bear's absence from London kept this moment from absolute perfection. Wordlessly he crossed the room, not stopping until he had her wrapped in his arms. Leaning down, he kissed her sweet, upturned mouth.

"Hello," he murmured back, kissing her again. Oddly, all the anger and frustration that had been biting at him simply fled, as if they couldn't withstand the sunlight of her smile. Perhaps she had a bit of witch in her, after all.

"Arran said you weren't coming by today." Charlotte brushed hair from his eyes. "But I wanted to see you."

"I'm nae complaining aboot that." He took her hand, twining her long, elegant fingers with his broad, callused ones. "Come with me to the sitting room."

She leaned against his shoulder, the intimacy and trust she showed astonishing him all over again. To protect her, he would do anything. No price was too great to pay. He would find a way, because being without her was simply unacceptable. Unimaginable. Intolerable.

Yowling and barking and crashing echoed up from the morning room as they crossed the hallway. "Are ye dead, Owen?" he called.

"Nearly, m'laird. Not quite."

"Ye and yer ghost stay clear of the sitting room."

"Aye, m'laird!"

Charlotte covered her mouth with her hand, laughing silently as he closed the door behind them. He grinned at her. "Now, what brings ye here, *leannan*?"

"First, kiss me again."

"Ye'll get nae argument from me." Cupping her cheeks, he kissed her in a tongue-tangling rush that left him breathless. "Are ye certain all ye want is a kiss?"

"Oh, I want more than that," she breathed, her arms loose around his shoulders as she gazed up at his face. "Tell me how you say 'handsome.'"

"*Brèaghe.*"

"You're very *brèaghe,* Ranulf MacLawry."

"And I find ye *àlainn,*" he returned, kissing her softly. "Ye're a fine, bonny lass, Charlotte Hanover. And now tell me why ye needed to see me."

She took a heavy breath, plucking at his cravat. If she, of all people, was hesitant to tell him something, it couldn't be good. A chill settled into his heart. Had she decided that he wasn't what she wanted? That his way of life was too dangerous for her, even if he meant to change it? The worst part of it was that he already knew it was true — no sane woman less than desperate for a title could possibly wish to risk marriage to the chief of Clan MacLawry.

"Just tell me," he whispered, "for Saint Andrew's sake."

The briefest of smiles touched her mouth. "I plotted out Glengask on a map," she said, her gaze still fixed on his chest. "It's enormous."

He hadn't expected that. "Aye?" This damned well wasn't about greed, so what was she getting at?

"I also plotted out your neighbors' lands. You're surrounded by rival clans."

Ah. This was about the lack of safety he could promise her, then. So be it. "What say ye finish yer tale in a bit, Charlotte?"

"I —"

He captured her mouth with his. With every ounce of his being he wanted her in his life, for the rest of his life. But with that same conviction he knew that no matter what he did, he couldn't keep her as safe as she would be in London, as safe as she would be with someone like Lord Stephen Hammond. But by God he wasn't going to let her go without loving her one more time.

"Ran, you n—"

Pulling loose the ribbons at the back of her pretty brown and yellow gown, he yanked the dress down her shoulders and took her right breast into his mouth, sucking and flicking the nipple with his tongue. He caressed the other one with his free hand, squeezing and tugging until she gasped and arched her back against him.

Freeing her arms from the muslin, he pulled her gown down around her hips and let it fall to the floor. Then he took her mouth again, freeing his hands to unbutton his trousers and throw off his coat. The rest of his clothes could wait. He wanted her, needed her, now. Nothing else mattered.

Lifting her in his arms, he laid her on the narrow couch and climbed over her, thrilling when she reached up to grab his shoulders and pull him closer for another kiss.

Before she could regain her sanity he nudged her knees apart and pushed himself inside her, fast and deep. *Mine,* he thought fiercely. For these few moments she belonged to him, as utterly as he belonged to her.

She came immediately, shivering around him, making him even harder, drawing him in deeper. Keeping his gaze locked on her face, he entered her again and again and again, until he couldn't hold back any longer and spilled himself inside her.

Breathing hard, he lowered his head against her shoulder. That was all he could do. He couldn't lock her away any more than he could lock the world away. All he could do was love her, and let her go. Even if it killed him.

"Ran," she whispered, drawing her fingers through his hair, "I think I was wrong."

He kept his eyes closed, trying to steady his breathing. She'd come to say it, and he'd let her do so. "Tell me," he forced out.

"You're not from London," she said quietly, idly playing with his hair in a way that brought warm shivers of pleasure down his spine.

"Aye. I'm aware of that."

"What you do, the way you live, it's the way that works for you. It's how you keep everyone safe."

"But I dunnae keep everyone safe," he countered, ordering himself to muster some damned courage and lifting up on his arms to meet her exquisite hazel gaze.

"No one can keep everyone safe. But you do a . . . a damned fine job of it." She grimaced. "Three men tried to bait you into a fight last night. And I think the second two tried it only because you didn't make the first one back down."

Something odd seemed to be happening. Ranulf reluctantly pulled out of her and climbed to his feet, fastening his trousers and then offering her a hand to help her sit up. He collected his dark gray coat off the floor and gave it to her. It was far too big for her, nearly swallowing her when she put her arms through the sleeves, but seeing her covered up did help his brain to function a bit better. Straightening his shirt, he sat on the couch beside her.

"So. Are ye saying I —"

"I'm saying you should have bashed George Gerdens-Dailey. Or Berling. Or Calder. Or at the least made certain they all knew you could have done so."

For a long moment he sat beside her, just looking at her. With her legs curled beneath her bare arse and her hands just showing beneath his pushed-up sleeves, she looked terribly demure and terribly arousing all at the same time.

"I thought a brawl was the first resort only of inferior minds," he drawled.

"I was wrong."

"Can ye say that again? I didnae quite make it oot."

"Awful man," she muttered, slipping beneath his arm and tucking herself up against his side. "Here, two Englishmen fighting over some idiotic matter of pride or honor *is* ridiculous. For you, when you punch Lord Berling in the nose you aren't doing it because . . . well, because you're big and strong and you can. You're doing it to warn him and his to keep their distance, because it's an alternative to having to kill one of them."

"Ye almost make me sound reasonable, Charlotte."

"You are almost reasonable." Leaning up, she kissed his jaw.

"Deaths still happen, lass," he made himself say. "And the dearer someone is to me, the more likely they are to be hurt." He sighed. "And I'm nae certain that a brawl or two would ever change that."

"I'm willing to —"

"M'laird!" Owen shouted, pounding frantically on the closed sitting room door. "Trouble!"

Ranulf was at the door in two strides. "What trouble?" he demanded, yanking it open.

"One of the new stable boys was oot walking Stirling, and he saw Laird Arran and Lady Winnie surrounded by a group of men. I —"

"Get dressed," he ordered over his shoulder, dread freezing his heart, and went pounding down the stairs. Fergus and Una were yowling at the front door, and with a curse he flung it open. He didn't need to ask where his brother and sister were; the dogs would find them. This was what happened when he relaxed, when he took a moment to fall in love — even when he knew nothing could come of it.

Charlotte dove for her gown and yanked it on, taking only a moment to knot the ribbons at the back closed. Stepping into her shoes, she ran for the door, her heart beating so fast she thought it might explode from her chest. If anything happened to his siblings, Ranulf would never forgive himself. But if something happened to him, she wouldn't survive.

She reached the front door as Owen came hurrying out from the servants' hall, a huge gun in his hands. "Where were they?" she asked, falling in with him.

"Ye should stay inside the house, m'lady," he wheezed, turning up the street. The groom, Debny, was several yards ahead of them. Ranulf and the dogs had evidently outstripped all of them.

Charlotte ignored the warning; this wasn't about her. And her presence could possibly prevent whatever might be about to happen. Or she hoped it would. If the situation called for it, at this moment she found herself more than willing to punch someone. The MacLawrys were her clan, after all.

Just inside the borders of a small park tucked behind a square of lovely old houses, she saw them. No one was on the ground and no one was bleeding, though she had no idea why — or whether that bit of good fortune would continue. Seven men stood around the two MacLawrys, clearly keeping them from either advancing or retreating.

Ranulf ahead of her slowed to a walk, the dogs keeping pace on either side of him. Their hackles were raised, and she could hear the low, snarling growls even from thirty feet away. "Was there someaught ye wanted, Berling?" the marquis called out in a booming voice that held more danger in it than either of the dogs' growls.

The earl was there, she noticed, and so were George Gerdens-Dailey and that awful Charles Calder. *Oh, no.* Were they armed? She knew that Ranulf was not, because he'd been half naked just a few minutes ago.

"We thought we might get a few things settled," Berling returned, glancing from the marquis to the donkey-sized dogs and back again.

"At least three of 'em have pistols, Ran," his brother called. Arran had one arm around Winnie, putting himself between her and Gerdens-Dailey. The black-haired beauty looked truly frightened, and given how carefully her three brothers had protected her for her entire life, Charlotte wasn't surprised.

Stopping a few feet away from the group, Ranulf stood with his hands at his sides, his stance looking as relaxed as if he were chatting at a soiree — or even more relaxed than that. She knew him well enough to see the tension in his straight shoulders, but she doubted any but his own would know it.

"What is it ye want to settle, then?" he asked smoothly.

"I owe you a broken nose, at the least," Berling returned, a slight, nasty smile on his face. "That's a start."

"I'm right here, Berling. My sister and

brother have naught to do with yer ugly face."

"You expect me to do something with those beasts standing there? I wouldn't call that a fair fight, Glengask."

Ranulf actually laughed. The sound raised the hairs on the back of Charlotte's neck. "So ye want a *fair* fight now, do ye? Ye're a damned *cladhaire,* Donald Gerdens."

The earl slid a look at the man standing beside him. "Cousin?"

"He called ye a coward," Gerdens-Dailey translated. "And I'd have to agree with that."

"What?"

"When ye bring six men with ye and go after a man's sister, that makes ye a coward."

Berling's face reddened. "Then why are you here, George?" he snapped.

The earl's cousin pulled a pistol from his pocket and aimed it at Arran. "Because I'm inclined to make an innocent man disappear. Unless Glengask would care to explain some things to me and take the ball himself."

Charlotte gasped, putting a hand to her chest. Ranulf flinched a heartbeat later, and she realized he hadn't known she was there behind him. Beside her Owen lifted the blunderbuss. Terrible things were about to happen. Terrible, irreversible things. Taking a shaking breath, she held out her hands. "Rowena, come over here," she called in her most soothing voice.

"Nae," Winnie sobbed, clinging to her brother.

"Rowena, do as Charlotte says," Ranulf echoed. "I'll nae have one of these *amadan* shooting ye by accident."

Crying, the girl fled the corner of the park. Charlotte wrapped her arms around Winnie, angling them so that while she could see what transpired, Rowena wouldn't be able to do so.

"Now," Ranulf said, taking a slow step closer to the armed Gerdens-Dailey. "What do ye want explained, George?"

The earl's cousin kept his weapon and gaze aimed at Arran. "I've a suspicion ye know what happened to my father, Glengask. And I'd like to know what possessed ye to take him from me two days after ye lost yer own."

"I didnae *lose* my father," Ranulf retorted, emotion touching his voice for the first time. "Yer *athair* and yer *athair*" — and he pointed at Berling — "and yer uncle Wallace murdered him."

"The way I heard it," Gerdens-Dailey returned, " 'twas the Campbells' doing."

Now Charles Calder frowned. "Never. Pigheaded as the MacLawrys are, the Campbell would never agree to killing Seann Monadh. They were friends, once."

Ranulf took another step forward, the dogs still keeping pace with him. "It wasnae the Campbells. After we found my father, I tracked riders back to Sholbray Manor."

"That's nae —"

"And I hid in the rain beneath the drawing room window and I heard yer father and Wallace boasting about how they and Berling murdered my father. I heard them say it, and I saw their faces." Anger clipped his voice. Charlotte could hear it clearly, just as she could hear the truth in his words. She kept her attention on him; if, when, he moved, she would drag Rowena to safety because that was what he would be worried about. Just as she was terrified for him now.

"That's not the end of the story, though, is it?" Gerdens-Dailey said, turning his head to look at Ranulf.

"That's all I mean to say in front of these cowards. If ye want more, ye'll put that away and stand where we can speak, two men together."

"Ha," Berling bit out. "If you think any of —"

"Shut yer mouth, Donald," his cousin

446

interrupted, and pocketed his pistol.

"Arran, call the dogs," Ranulf ordered.

His face white and tense, Arran did as he said. Slowly, clearly reluctant and their tails down, the dogs left Ranulf's side and slunk over to stand beside his brother. While Charlotte held her breath, Ranulf and George Gerdens-Dailey approached each other, stopping beside an old, leaning elm tree.

"What are they doing?" Winnie whispered, twisting her head to look.

"They're talking." She had no idea whether it was the wisest course of action or not — despite the fact, or because of the fact, that this was precisely what she'd urged him to do.

"But they hate each other."

Charlotte nodded. "Very likely. But I think they also have a great deal in common."

"When they surrounded us, I thought . . . I thought they were going to murder Arran. And then — I don't know what they would have done to me."

Hugging the younger lady, Charlotte kept her gaze on the two men. "All you need to remember is that you and Arran and Ranulf are all well. With all of us here, nothing's going to happen now."

"But what about tomorrow? What if they

go to the Lansfield ball tomorrow?" She shuddered. "What if one of them asks me to dance?"

"You will tell them no," she returned, wishing mightily that she could hear what the two men were saying.

She understood why Gerdens-Dailey wanted to know for once and certain what had happened to his father, just as Ranulf had wanted to know. But if Ranulf confessed to two murders, especially to the son of one of his victims, he could well find himself in prison. Even hanged, if the English courts could be influenced to rid the Highlands of its most stubborn, troublesome resident.

After what felt like hours, but couldn't have been more than twenty minutes, Gerdens-Dailey gave a stiff nod and turned away. "We're finished here," he stated.

Berling scowled. "But —"

The earl's cousin strode forward and grabbed the earl by the throat. "We two need to have a talk, ourselves," he growled, "about why yer father lied to me." He shoved, and Berling stumbled backward, nearly falling to the street.

"I don't —"

"Glengask, ye'd best be there, or I'll come looking fer ye," Gerdens-Dailey interrupted his cousin again.

"I'll be there. But not because ye'll come looking fer me."

With a nod, George Gerdens-Dailey led the way to a standing group of horses. In less than a minute they'd ridden around a corner and out of sight. Only then did Charlotte begin breathing again, her knees feeling wobbly.

"Dogs, off. Come," Ranulf said, slapping his thigh. Immediately the hounds' tails went up, and they romped over to him again.

Arran followed a few steps behind. "Where is it ye're supposed to be, precisely?" he asked, then pulled his older brother into a hard embrace. "And thank ye. That was aboot to get unpleasant."

Ranulf hugged him back, then caught up Rowena. "All's well, *piuthar*. Dunnae fret."

"Charlotte said everything would be fine."

Looking over his sister's head, Ranulf gave her a slow, delicious smile that warmed her to her toes. Then he took his sister's hand, offered her his arm, and turned back for the house. "Owen. Put that damned blunderbuss away, will ye?"

"What the devil happened?" the footman demanded, lowering his weapon.

"I'd like to know that, too, Ranulf," Arran commented. "Where are ye to meet that man? If it's a duel, I'll tie ye to a damned chair."

"It's nae a duel," Ranulf retorted, tightening his arm to bring Charlotte closer against his side. "I told him that I'd show him where his father's buried."

"Ran," Charlotte whispered.

He shrugged. "It's time fer it, *leannan.* All the wrong George Gerdens-Dailey did us is because the old Lord Berling told him 'twas the Campbells killed my father, and that the MacLawrys went after the Gerdenses fer the hell of it." Deep blue eyes met hers. "Peace, all done with a few words. Imagine that."

She grinned. "And after I told you that bashing was acceptable."

"I will keep that in mind, lass."

CHAPTER SEVENTEEN

Owen looked Ranulf up and down as he descended the stairs to the foyer. "I thought ye just settled things down. Are ye certain ye want to stir them up again?"

Adjusting his silver-plated sporran edged in rabbit fur, Ranulf lifted an eyebrow. "Ginger nearly fainted," he commented. "But as I happen to be a Scot, I mean to dress like one."

"And I cannae have my brother making me look like a Sasannach fop," Arran took up from the landing. Like Ranulf, he'd donned a dark jacket, though Arran's was gray rather than his brother's black. And both men had donned kilts bearing the Mac-Lawry tartan of black and gray and red.

"Ye bring a tear to my old eyes," Owen stated. "Right proper Highland princes, ye are."

"Don't let the English hear ye saying that, or we're likely to begin another war," Ranulf noted dryly.

Tonight he felt . . . exhilarated, as if a weight he'd been carrying for a decade had been lifted. It had, in a sense; they weren't friendly, by any means, but at least Gerdens-Dailey had agreed that they were even. A death for a death. Horrific, perhaps, but it was what their kind was accustomed to. And unless Berling could somehow convince his cousin that it had indeed been the Campbells who'd murdered Seann Monadh, the Gerdenses would keep their distance.

With the Gerdenses' influence, the Campbells might, as well. At the least the old Campbell had been surprisingly . . . uninterested in stirring up old rivalries. As Charles Calder had said, though, the Campbell and Robert MacLawry had once been friends. That left the Daileys, but he much preferred the idea of facing one problem rather than three.

"Ye're smiling, ye know," Arran pointed out as they climbed into the coach. "I do hope ye're aware that neither of us was invited to the grand dinner at the Lansfields' tonight."

"Aye, but we *were* invited to the dance afterward. I'll consider that progress."

"So we're still trying to be civilized and make the Sasannach like us? We're the pet monkeys?"

Ranulf frowned. "I broke Berling's nose at the first grand ball of the Season. I nearly choked Gerdens-Dailey at the second. So when I'm invited to the third, I consider it progress."

His brother grimaced. "Well, when ye put it that way."

"That's how I choose to put it."

When Arran kept gazing at him, Ranulf settled in to look out the window at the dark London streets. Was it dangerous that for the first time in years he felt . . . optimistic about the future? That he thought he could be the gentleman he'd promised Charlotte he would be?

"Charlotte Hanover," Arran said into the silence.

"Aye? What aboot her?"

"Are ye going to marry her?"

"I'm thinking I will." He turned to face Arran again. "Why? Do ye have an objection?"

His brother shrugged. "She's a proper Englishwoman who a very short time ago thought ye were a savage and a devil, if I recall. Are ye not that man any longer?"

Ranulf settled deeper into the corner. "Maybe it's that she's not quite as stiff as ye think," he returned.

"I hope ye're —"

"Enough, Arran," he broke in. "We're going to a proper soiree, we're going to behave, and I'll figure out the rest, if ye dunnae mind."

"Fine."

"Fine."

Well, wasn't that splendid. The sense of euphoria that had filled him all day flattened. He was still a Highlander, the leader of his clan, and she was still an English lady accustomed to soft winters and warm summers. And whatever she might have said about understanding his use of "bashing," as she called it, she couldn't possibly feel easy about it.

"Ran, I didnae mean —"

"Ye've helped me quite enough, Arran. I only hope when ye find the woman ye love, she'll be perfect and ye'll ne'er have a complaint or worry aboot her. And vice versa."

"That sounds a wee bit dull, actually."

"Aye. And dunnae ye forget that."

Arran blew out his breath. "I wasnae trying to talk ye oot of anything. I'm only . . . I worry that she'll be —"

"She's nae Eleanor," Ranulf commented, finally understanding. "She's nae after a title, and damn the consequences. I want her to be happy. Not just . . . by my side."

His brother looked out the window for a long moment, much as he had earlier. "Then I think she's rather bonny. And I think ye look happy when ye're together. Just . . . Be certain, Ran. Please. Fer both yer sakes."

Ranulf had informed Charlotte ahead of time that he would be in full Highlander regalia, giving her the opportunity to scowl or argue with him before he appeared in public. But she hadn't done either, which at the time he'd taken as a good sign. Now he couldn't help wondering if she was just . . . humoring him — and whether he actually embarrassed her. How could he be certain, as Arran suggested? The answer wasn't in his mind, but in hers. And he couldn't know it, until she told him. If she told him.

That was a glum thought. When the coach stopped in the street outside Lansfield House he nearly changed his mind about going in. But he'd made his bed, so he might as well wear a kilt in it. Or something like that.

"Lord Glengask and Lord Arran Mac-Lawry," the butler intoned, as they stepped into the ballroom. He could hear the swarm of whispers beginning at the front of the room and swelling to the back. Whatever the damned fuss over a man showing off his knees, he might as well enjoy it — or at least become accustomed to it.

Now that he considered it, there was another possible solution; he could remain in London. The idea of not seeing Glengask except for the occasional holiday made him ill to his stomach, but he supposed he could do it if by staying in England he could have Charlotte.

Almost as soon as he conjured that idea, though, he discarded it again. Whatever the MacLawry family crest said, it wasn't *any* MacLawry whose presence at Glengask signaled to his people that all was well and they were safe and protected; it was the marquis, the clan chief, who needed to be there. And that, for better or worse, was he.

A swirl of gold caught his eye, and he looked up as Charlotte and her family strolled into the ballroom. She'd chosen to wear a gold silk with an overlay of black lace and beads that made her look both elegant and eminently desirable. He let out a slow breath as he took her in from head to toe and back again. Magnificent.

"Are we going to stand here all night, or —"

Without waiting for his brother to finish, he set off toward his sister and the Hanovers. Tradition said he would have to ask Lord Hest for his daughter's hand, and he likely should have asked by now. And he knew precisely why he hadn't. Firstly, the earl would refuse him, and secondly, he still hadn't been able to convince himself that taking her to Scotland wasn't utterly selfish.

She smiled as she caught sight of him, and he had to work not to speed his steps. Glorious, she was. All the men who'd looked at her and passed her by, out of courtesy or because they wanted a new debutante or because they only saw her as the betrothed of a dead man — they were all fools.

"Good evening," he said, inclining his head as he reached the group.

"Glengask," her father intoned, sending both him and Arran a sour look. "Why do you insist on making a stir?"

"I'm nae making a stir," he returned, straightening his shoulders. "I'm being the Marquis of Glengask."

His sister leaned up and kissed him on the cheek. "I think you look *brèagha,* Ran," she whispered. "You and Arran, both."

"My thanks, *piuthar.*"

Charlotte held out her hand, and he lowered his head to kiss her knuckles. "I think you look *brèagha* as well," she said with a smile.

"Ye nearly have a proper brogue," he returned. "Tell me there will be a waltz tonight."

"There will be two. Which would you like?" She produced her dance card from her reticule.

"Both."

"Ranulf."

He narrowed his eyes. "Have I mentioned that the Sasannach are too stiff-spined?"

With a chuckle, she handed him the dance card and a pencil. "Yes, I believe you have." When he chose the second waltz of the evening, she took a step closer. "Have you heard anything more from Berling or Gerdens-Dailey?"

"Nae. In fact, Debny had word that George left London for Sholbray Manor. I'm to meet him there at the end of the month, but he may have decided to go out looking on his own. I told him the approximate location of the grave."

"That was a very brave thing you did," she said, her changeable hazel gaze meeting his.

"Brave? Nae. I will agree that it was the correct thing to do. And I'll also say that Gerdens-Dailey surprised me a bit. I actually thought he'd be more likely to answer me with a knife to the gizzard."

Her fair skin paled. *Bloody hell.* She'd paid him a compliment, and he'd replied once again like a barbarian. Of course he was a barbarian, according to most people. There were times he liked the title. Whether she truly wished to be known as the devil's wife, though, he had no idea. But he was going to have to ask her. Very soon. Because the only thing worse than having her refuse him would be speculating endlessly over how she would break his heart.

"Charlotte," he murmured, gripping her fingers. "I need to ask ye a question."

Charlotte's breath caught in her chest. Would he do it? Would he finally ask her? She smiled up at him, wishing no one else were around so she could kiss him until neither of them could breathe. "I'm listening."

A hand slid around her other arm. "Charlotte, people are beginning to stare," her mother said, favoring Ranulf with an uneasy smile. "And look who's here — Lord Stephen Hammond."

Ranulf released her hand as if he hadn't noticed how long he'd been holding it. She liked that, that he liked touching her. Heaven knew she craved touching him, even if it was just a brush of fingers or her mouth against his. "Ranulf," she murmured.

459

"I'll find us a private moment or two," he returned in the same tone.

"Ah, Lady Charlotte," Lord Stephen said, walking up and taking her hand. "Please tell me you haven't given away both waltzes tonight."

She fixed a smile as she faced the light-haired duke's son. In the past he'd been generally polite, if somewhat . . . patronizing. But over the past year or so his treatment of her had changed. In fact, until he'd appeared at the Esmond soiree and been so pleasant to her, he'd been just as likely to make jokes — ones she was no doubt meant to hear — about spinsterhood and poor shots.

"I —"

He took the dance card from her hand before she could finish. "Ah, I see you haven't. The first waltz must be mine, then."

Charlotte cleared her throat, very aware of Ranulf standing like a granite mountain directly behind her. "My apologies, my lord, but I've promised that waltz to Lord Arran MacLawry." It wasn't perfect, but Arran was standing close by, and he was firmly in the category of ally.

"Nonsense," Stephen insisted, and she noticed that his good friend Simon Beasley had appeared, as well. "Simon," he went on, penciling in his name and then handing her card over to Mr. Beasley, "which do you want — the first quadrille, or the last country dance?"

"Lord Stephen, I don't intend to do much dancing, tonight," she tried again. "Please give that back to me."

Stephen laughed. "You don't want everyone thinking you've fallen for a Highlander, do you? Once he's gone, and I've been assured he will be gone soon, likely never to return, you'll have no hope at all of netting a husband. Who in his right mind wants to think he's lapping up after a Scot? Especially when you're already, well, on the back of the shelf."

A hand darted out from past her shoulder, retrieved her dance card, and smoothly handed it to her. "Feel free to cross those off," Ranulf drawled. "Ye were more polite than I would've been."

Her sudden alarm became relief. He evidently *had* found a way to use his brain rather than his muscles — though both were exceedingly fine, and even more dear to her. "Thank you, my lord," she said, doing precisely as he suggested.

"You're making a mistake, my dear," Simon Beasley commented, leering at her. Good heavens, he was drunk. And that meant Stephen more than likely was, as well. "If we wished it, we could see that you never have a partner for a dance ever again."

"That hardly seems likely, gentlemen," her father put in, his jaw tight but his expression uneasy. If anyone disliked a scene more than she did, it was the Earl of Hest. "I suggest you go somewhere and recover yourselves."

"And I suggest you —"

"Why is it," Ranulf interrupted, just the sound of his voice shutting the duke's son up, "that when ye have some difficulty with a man, ye instead go to insult the people standing close to him instead of saying what ye mean?" He moved up to stand beside Charlotte.

Stephen snorted. "Because a fool is a fool, and has no idea how very poorly he shows, even if you try to make that *burningly* obvious to him. Those standing around him, though, should know better." He narrowed his eyes, gazing at Charlotte again. "You'll be lucky if you don't have to pay someone to —"

Ranulf's hand shot out again. This time it was coiled into a fist, and it struck Lord Stephen Hammond flush on the jaw. Stephen staggered backward, flailing his arms. In the next moment Simon Beasley leaped forward and threw a punch at Ranulf's head. Then three more men charged in, all swinging at the marquis.

They weren't drunk, she realized in the horrified second after she deciphered what Hammond had meant. He'd been the one to set fire to Ranulf's stable. Since that hadn't stopped the marquis, they'd done this. And now they'd merely been waiting for Ranulf to strike first. And then they would no doubt beat him half to death and claim they were only attempting to subdue the devil. "Stop it!" she shrieked, batting at Beasley with her reticule.

Arran MacLawry appeared and dove into the melee — so at least Ranulf wasn't alone. Everyone else . . . could all go to the devil. They stood well out of the way, pretending to be appalled and at the same time jockeying for a better view and making wagers on the outcome.

From somewhere else the gray-haired Viscount Swansley arrived, swearing, and dragged someone off Ranulf. Was it truly to be the MacLawrys against the rest of Mayfair? Why? For heaven's sake, Ranulf had made every effort to fit in. They wouldn't let him. And if it was because of her, because some stupid aristocrat didn't like that a Scotsman might win over an Englishwoman when none of them had done so . . .

"Gentlemen!" she yelled, smacking someone else with her small, beaded bag and wishing it were a great deal more substantial. "Cease this at once!"

"Charlotte, move away!" her mother cried, darting forward to pull at her sleeve. "For heaven's sake!"

Tears wet her cheeks, though she didn't know when she'd begun crying. She caught a glimpse of Ranulf, his face bloody. "Stop!" she shouted again, then got knocked backward by someone's elbow.

Cursing, her father pulled her to her feet, then waded into the fight. For an awful moment she wasn't certain who he was assisting, until Simon Beasley staggered by her and then stumbled to the floor with the help of her father's boot.

"Enough!" the mild-mannered Lord Hest bellowed. Finally, evidently spurred by the sight of her well-respected father attempting to stop the fight all by himself, footmen and guests and their host, John Lansfield, the Marquis of Ferth, moved in to begin pulling men off each other.

Already she could hear Lord Stephen's friends blaming the fracas on the Marquis of Glengask. "Barbarian" and "devil" and "damned Scot" echoed around her. That could not be allowed to stand.

Gathering her skirt in her hands, she marched up to where her father and Lord Swansley each had Stephen Hammond by an arm. "You are no gentleman, sir," she said sharply, "and I am ashamed that I ever called you a friend."

He sneered through a bloody lip. "Talk to that big devil," he retorted. "He —"

Charlotte slapped him. It stung her hand, but she didn't care. "All Lord Glengask did was step forward when you misbehaved. Shame on you!"

Stephen Hammond glared at her, but didn't say anything further. Hopefully he'd realized that arguing with her would only make him look more like the bully he was. Squaring her shoulders, she turned her back on him, delivering the most direct cut and show of her contempt that she could.

Janie stared at her, wide-eyed, then turned her back on Lord Stephen, as well. Their mother followed suit a moment later, then Winnie and another half-dozen women — most of whom were either near her supposedly advanced age of spinsterhood or were not considered the Season's beauties and had undoubtedly been told precisely that by Stephen — gave him their stiff, disapproving spines. *Ha.* She hoped it stung him.

The rest of the men had climbed to their feet. Now she finally took a good look at Ranulf, and couldn't help her gasp. One coat sleeve was torn off, the other ripped, while his shirt was half untucked and spattered with bright red blood. Even one knee was cut, though his kilt looked intact. Thank goodness for that.

In addition to the ruin of his clothes, his lip was cut, his nose bloody, and one eye squinted. As she watched, he took the loose tail of his shirt and wiped it across his face. His brother didn't look much better, but Simon Beasley and his awful friends all looked to have fared even worse.

She walked forward, lifting a hand to his face and then at the last minute remembering herself and lowering it again. "Are you hurt?" she asked, though it seemed an utterly ridiculous question.

He shook his head, his expression grim. "Nae. I'm so sorry, lass. I couldnae . . . I couldnae just stand and listen to that *amadan*'s drivel."

"I know. It's —"

"Gentlemen," Lord Ferth announced, wiping his hands together as if he'd touched something distasteful, "you are no longer welcome here. I will not have this barbarism in my house." He glanced at Charlotte.

"It does not matter who instigated this. I will not tolerate it."

Grumbling something that sounded very unpleasant, Arran took his uncle by the shoulder and motioned at his brother. "Let's be oot of this damned place, Ran."

Ranulf nodded, his gaze still on Charlotte, as if he were trying to memorize her features. As if he never expected to see her again. Her heart stopped in her chest, leaving her hollow and cold. *No.*

That stupid, stubborn man. He closed his eyes for a moment, then swung around to follow his brother and uncle off the dance floor. Of course he would do the noble thing and leave, because he thought he'd failed her. Because he thought he'd done the one thing she would never forgive — stepping into a fight for no other reason than pride.

He was wrong.

Charlotte took a breath, then strode forward. Her mother grabbed for her, but she easily evaded the countess's fingers. Catching up to the lean, hard mountain of a man, she put her hand on his shoulder and pulled.

Ranulf stopped and turned around. "What are ye doing, lass?" he muttered, surprise crossing his features.

What *was* she doing? What could she say

here, in front of everyone, that would convince him she didn't blame him for what had just happened, that he'd stood as a gentleman and then acted as one? That it wasn't the same thing James Appleton had done and that she'd condemned for so long?

The answer, clearly, was nothing. There was nothing she could say that he would think was anything but her being kind.

And so Charlotte wrapped both hands into the front of his torn shirt, lifted up on her toes, and kissed him full on the mouth.

He held absolutely still, clearly astonished. Then his mouth molded against hers, and his strong arms swept around her waist, crushing her to him. She didn't know if anyone gasped or fainted or anything else. All she knew was that he kissed her back.

After a brief, forever moment he lifted his head a little, gazing down at her. His dark blue eyes blazed. "Ye've ruined yerself."

"I know."

His mouth curved in a slow smile. "I do love ye, Charlotte," he murmured. "Ye are so dear to me I dunnae think I could bear to be without ye."

"And I do love you, Ranulf," she whispered back. *"Leannan."*

"Then for God's sake say ye'll marry me, lass," he returned, his voice carrying and unsteady at the edges.

She nodded, tears running down her cheeks once more. But this time they were tears of joy. "I will marry you. I want to marry you. I want to live with you at Glengask. I'm not afraid. I never was."

With a roar he firmed his grip on her waist and lifted her into the air, circling with her in his arms. "I love ye, Charlotte!" he yelled, laughing.

Charlotte grinned down at him. "I love you!" Her wild Scot. Her Highlander. Her Ranulf.

ABOUT THE AUTHOR

A native and current resident of Southern California, **Suzanne Enoch** loves movies almost as much as she loves books, with a special place in her heart for anything Star Wars. She has written more than thirty Regency novels and historical romances, which are regularly found on the *New York Times* bestseller list. When she is not busily working on her next book, Suzanne likes to contemplate interesting phenomena, like how the three guppies in her aquarium became 161 guppies in five months.